QUEEN'S FLIGHT

By the same author

Reap the Whirlwind

QUEEN'S FLIGHT

Tamara Lee

Hodder & Stoughton

Copyright © 1997 by Tamara Lee

First published in Great Britain in 1997
by Hodder and Stoughton
A division of Hodder Headline PLC

The right of Tamara Lee to be identified as the Author
of the Work has been asserted by her in accordance with the
Copyright, Designs and Patents Act 1988.

10 9 8 7 6 5 4 3 2 1

A CIP catalogue record for this title is available
from the British Library

Lee, Tamara
Queen's Flight
1. English fiction – 20th century
I. Title
823.9'14 [F]

ISBN 0 340 67247 1

Typeset by Hewer Text Composition Services, Edinburgh
Printed and bound in Great Britain by
Clays Ltd, St Ives plc

Hodder and Stoughton
A division of Hodder Headline PLC
338 Euston Road
London NW1 3BH

For Oliver

'Tis all a Chequer-board of Nights and Days
Where Destiny with Men for Pieces plays;
Hither and thither Moves, and Mates, and Slays,
And One by One, back in the Closet lays.

The Rubaiyat of Omar Khayyam

PART ONE

1

Gabriella Castlemaine was suddenly awake. Everything seemed peaceful enough. Yet something had snatched her to consciousness.

She kicked off the heavy linen sheet, twisted her waist length blonde hair into a knot and lay still. Perhaps Nicholas had cried out?

She leaned over the basinette which stood next to the big double bed, but in the flickering light of the nursery lamp she could see her baby was asleep, snuffling quietly against his clenched fists, his tiny mouth moving as though at the breast. The surge of relief was tinged with apprehension. Nothing was wrong with Nick, so why had she woken so violently?

Since the beginning of the Rodney King trial two months ago, California was a cauldron which threatened to spew its frustrated anger over the leafy suburbs and luxury estates of the wealthy. The four white policemen, who'd beaten the black motorist senseless in the glare of their car headlights, had started something to which only justice in the courts could put an end. If that justice failed, then how long would it be before the ghetto reached out to the manicured lawns and white stucco of the beach-front homes?

With a cluck of impatience, she dragged her thoughts back to the present. I won't get any sleep at this rate. Something's wrong – and until I know what it is, I won't be able to rest, she thought crossly. Maybe it's just the heat, but surely that wouldn't make me leap out of sleep

3

like that. She shook her head. It had to be something else.

Climbing restlessly out of bed, she padded out to the balcony. It was three o'clock in the morning and it was as if she was the only person awake in the world.

'What the fuck do you think you're playing at, Vic?'

The angry words fired up to her from downstairs.

'Jesus Christ, don't you have anything between those dumb ears of yours?'

A heated exchange followed and Gabriella breathed a sigh of relief. Now she understood what had woken her. It was Greg and his brother playing poker – arguing as usual, getting heated over the turn of a card – so there was no cause for alarm. Yet she was angry at having been woken. Surely there was no need to get quite so irate – it was only a game after all.

Gabriella leaned on the cool white parapet and looked at the patch of light thrown from the ground-floor windows onto the garden. The sound of the men below reminded her of Hereford and the noisy exchanges in the officer's mess after a gruelling mission; and as she stood on the balcony in California, she wondered why she suddenly missed home and those familiar surroundings.

With a shake of her head, she decided she might as well go back to bed. If Greg and his friends were playing cards, then it could be dawn before her husband crept upstairs. She didn't like his gambling, but he was never short of money, or worried by debts, and the family import-export business was strong on the stock exchange and still growing. The Castlemaine family had proved that the American Dream was still attainable. Now she and Greg were living that dream to the full. That was how they'd been able to afford this house, as well as the apartment in New York, the yacht and the private plane.

'For fuck's sake! Bring the son-of-a-bitch to me and I'll deal with it. But this is the last time, Vic. The last time.'

Her footsteps faltered at the unmistakable anger in Greg's voice. There was a cruelty in it she'd never heard before – a violence that made her flesh crawl. 'What on earth's going on down there?' she muttered. It sounded far more serious than a game of cards.

She leaned over the balustrade as Greg's voice was joined in a garbled crescendo by two others.

They'll wake the baby in a minute, she thought crossly. What the hell's happening? Jamming her feet into slippers, and throwing a robe over her nakedness, she headed for the door. Enough was enough.

The landing was a long one, and by the time she'd reached the stairs she was blazing. Greg's temper might be roused, and he would be furious if she disturbed him, but how dare he make such a row in the middle of the night with a five-week-old baby asleep upstairs. Did he have no sense?

She reached the bend in the stairs and looked down the graceful curve to the rotunda that served as an entrance hall. After the gloom in the bedroom she was almost blinded by the light of the vast chandelier that hung from the stained glass cupola. It enhanced the brilliant white of the walls, and made the chessboard floor stark. Blinking rapidly, she was about to hurry on when a sound froze her to the stairs.

It was quite distinctive that sound and it made her stomach curl. It was a man's deep, choking sobs, and a voice broken and pleading through tears. The desperation in it was chilling.

Gabriella sank into the shadows.

The hall was suddenly plunged into darkness, and she caught her breath as the doors of the drawing room were flung open and a stream of light again flooded the black and white marble squares. Although her pulse raced and her heart hammered, she couldn't tear her gaze from the unfolding scene below.

A man who looked familiar stumbled out of the room. He fell with a smack against the unyielding floor, then scrambled to his knees, arms raised in submission as the shadow of someone else darkened his face.

'Leo?' she breathed as she finally recognised him. What's he doing here? He should be in New York.

Her immediate reaction was to cry out, to call his name and put a stop to his fear, but intuition stopped her. Leo was a native New Yorker, with fists like hams and a body honed to a muscled bulk. He was not a man to succumb easily to fear – and he was not alone.

She rapidly dismissed the idea of intruders. Greg and his brother had been in the room with him, she'd heard their voices only minutes before. Gabriella melted further into the shadows as dark thoughts pursued one another. Perhaps they were dead, killed by the unseen assassin whose shadow fell across the hall. Were she and the baby next?

She had to call the police – get help.

Yet, as she tried to move, tried to quench the fear, she realised she was trapped in the glare of the lights below. If she made a sound they would realise she was there – and she knew in that instant that she was not supposed to witness this.

Mesmerised, she watched the long shadow move over the cowering man and darken the far wall. Now she could see who it was that threatened Leo – and the knowledge filled her with dread. The man standing in the glare of light was no stranger – no mysterious intruder – but someone all too familiar. And yet not. She had never seen her husband like this before.

She stifled the urge to call out, for she knew she was as powerless as Nicholas against such malignancy.

'I trusted you, Leo,' purred Greg, as he leaned down and caressed the man's face with his index finger. Although his American accent was soft and cultured, it had a sharp, dangerous edge to it. 'Don't I pay enough? Is that it, Leo?'

'I won't do it again, boss.' Leo's words, with their Brooklyn slur, tumbled one over the other as he knelt in front of Gregory Castlemaine the Third. 'But they was leaning on me. I had to do something or they would have taken my kid.' His hands reached out to paw the hem of his persecutor's trousers.

Gregory stepped back, a curl of distaste on his lips as he regarded the fawning Leo. He selected a Gauloise from a silver cigarette case, tapped it, then put it in his mouth.

Gabriella's astounded gaze was on Gregory's eyes. They never wavered from the face of the man at his feet – not even when Vic stepped forward to light his cigarette. There was a cruelty in his hooded eyes, lean face and arrogant chin. It matched the arctic spark of the diamond stud he wore in his left ear. The brutish set of his shoulders beneath that Armani jacket was a force of unspent violence – an anger – which emanated from him and made him deadly. From the top of his sleek black hair to the point of his hand-made shoes he was a power house of imperious authority. Her husband was suddenly a stranger.

In that instant of intelligence, she was reminded of Mount Rushmore and the granite, unwavering solidity of those carved figures. If she could have reached out and touched him, she knew his skin would have been cold – but at the same time she was aware of being in the presence of a reptile. A large, venomous cobra poised to strike. And all she could do was watch.

'So, Leo. You like the white powder? You like using it instead of selling it? You take your orders from what you shove up your nose, and not from me.' Greg shook his head slowly as if in sorrow. 'Why, Leo? Addicts are our customers – not our employees.'

Gabriella could see no pity in Greg's ebony eyes. No softening in the curve of his mouth as he watched Leo squirm.

'I'm sorry boss. It won't happen again. Give me another chance, boss. I'll kick the habit. I swear. On my kid's life.' Leo shuffled on his knees towards Greg's polished shoes as if he was about to kiss them.

Greg reached down, twisted his fingers in the cloth of Leo's coat, and hauled him to his feet. The movement was over almost before it had begun.

Gabriella winced.

7

The two men were nose to nose. Gregory Castlemaine, thirty-five, lithe, dark and deceptively strong, was unquestionably in charge. Although Leo Spinoza was taller and broader than Greg, he now appeared much smaller.

Greg blew a stream of cigarette smoke into Leo's eyes, making the man wince and splutter. 'You don't steal from me, Leo.'

'I'll pay you back. Give me another chance.'

Slowly, and with great deliberation, Greg brushed the smouldering tip of his cigarette across the flesh beneath Leo's eyes.

Leo screamed, his body jerking in pain.

Gregory kept his gaze on the other man's face whilst maintaining the stranglehold on Leo's collar. 'How will you replace two million dollars worth of coke, Leo?'

Gabriella tasted bile in her throat, and she rammed her knuckles against her mouth. She wanted to look away, to close her eyes, but a horrified fascination kept her riveted to the scene below.

Vic stepped from behind his brother and took his cigarette. It was replaced by the cold glint of steel. The click of the blade's release sliced through Leo's screams, cutting them off instantly as he realised what was about to happen.

'You've broken the rules, Leo. You've got to pay.'

The flash of metal caught the light as Gregory slit Leo's nostrils. When he released his hold on Leo's jacket, the man fell to the floor.

Gabriella was trembling as she tried to deal with what she'd witnessed. This can't be happening, she thought desperately. This is a nightmare.

Yet Leo's screams were real enough. The ripe smell of burning flesh and newly spilled blood sickening enough. The sadistic cruelty of Gregory Castlemaine was undeniable. But still she couldn't look away. That was the most frightening part – she was as transfixed as Leo.

She watched Greg reach out and saw Vic, the brother-in-law

she'd always thought of as a friendly buffoon, give him a gun. There was the click of the safety catch as Greg's fingers played over it.

Dear God, NO! The scream was locked in her head – frozen in her throat – silent. Would this ever end?

Leo looked up. One hand shielded his tortured face, the other was stretched out in supplication as he pleaded for mercy. Beneath the blood, Gabriella could see that his face was grey, his eyes bulbous with fear. He scrabbled on his knees, edging away from the two brothers.

Gregory and Victor Castlemaine gazed down at him. With each step measured and ruthlessly purposeful, Gregory followed the crawling man across the hallway.

'You want to give up the white powder, Leo? Let me help you.' His voice was a caress.

Leo had reached the curve of the far wall, his back pressed to cold white marble. There was nowhere to go, nowhere to run, nowhere to hide. Fear screamed in his eyes as he watched the man tower over him. Terror was in every pore, every movement as he begged for mercy.

The dull plop of the silenced gun stilled him, and a rose of blood blossomed where his left eye should have been.

Gabriella flinched as the bullet struck. Horror washed over her as Leo slumped – and there was the taste of copper in her mouth as the smear of scarlet traced his descent to the floor.

Leo had given up his habit. Permanently.

Greg touched the limp body with his shoe, then turned away with a grimace of revulsion. 'Get rid of him, Victor.'

The words were clipped and Gabriella felt the force of them.

'Make sure you dispose of him properly. I don't want him found. Then clear out his New York apartment and silence his wife. It's a nuisance, but you'll also have to find another minder for Gabriella.' He jabbed Victor's barrel chest. 'This time little brother, find somebody who won't steal from us.'

Vic looked uncertainly at Greg, then was swept up in his embrace, restoring his confidence. He slapped his brother's back and began to pull away.

Greg snaked an arm around his neck and held him closer. They were face to face, inches apart, and Gabriella could almost smell Vic's fear.

'Don't bring scum to my home again. Deal with it yourself. Dad would disapprove of tonight's work. It's unprofessional.'

Home? How could such a word be used for this killing field? Gabriella closed her eyes in an attempt to block out the images. If only I had the courage to stand up and show myself – to face Greg and tell him that I know what kind of man he really is. But as she looked again at the hall and the men on the black and white marble, a cold reality stifled the defiance. Silence was her only weapon – it could also be her deliverance.

Greg pinched Vic's cheek, and Gabriella realised it was no friendly gesture, by the grimace and angry flush in Vic's face.

'You're constantly reminding us all that you're in charge, Greg, so I thought you'd want to deal with Leo yourself,' he said sourly as he rubbed his cheek and glared balefully at his elder brother.

'So I am, Vic. But never do this again. I don't want Gabriella knowing our business yet. Let her enjoy our son for a while – then, if the time is right, we'll see.' He released the grip on Vic's neck and stepped away.

Vic smiled warily. 'Gabriella will know something's up when Leo doesn't show. What then?'

Gabriella held her breath as a spiny finger traced her back.

Greg laughed and lit another cigarette. 'She's my wife, Vic. What difference does it make if her chauffeur leaves? He was only a servant.' He shrugged. 'Don't worry, Vic. She's got other things to think about. Like shopping.'

Gabriella heard their soft laughter and felt nauseous. At their feet a blossoming pool of blood crowned the body on the floor. They showed no remorse, no feeling at all for poor Leo. This was evidently not the first time they had killed.

'When will you tell her, Greg? She'll have to know eventually. You'll be company president, soon.'

Greg ruffled his brother's mop of curly hair, smoothed the rumpled jacket over the pot belly and straightened his tie. Vic's untidiness was an irritant to his older brother, but now he laughed as though he hadn't a care.

'All in good time, Vic. Her ignorance won't last for ever. We can't have the future cartel boss ignorant of his heritage, now can we?'

It was as if an icy hand clutched Gabriella's heart, and it took all her willpower to remain silent as Victor sniggered and reached for the phone.

It was at that moment another figure emerged from the drawing room – another witness to the brutality of Leo's murder – one whose silence and demeanour meant that he too was a part of this madness.

Gabriella stared at his face, so recognisable to thousands of Americans, and knew the corruption was deep rooted and unassailable. She'd seen too much already – but this man's presence underlined the danger she was in, and emphasised the influence and power of Greg Castlemaine – her knowledge had signed her death warrant.

I have to get away from here, she thought as other men arrived and began to obliterate all trace of Leo and the murder. Have to get back to Nick before they see me. Yet she remained on the stairs, paralysed with fear.

It was the sound of whimpering from the bedroom that finally galvanised her into action. One sound, one rustle and the men cleaning the hall would hear her. Hardly daring to breathe, she inched along the passage towards the restless mewling of the baby.

As she finally closed the bedroom door behind her, the

first strangled sob erupted and she leaned against the oak to steady herself. Clutching the door handle, she gave into the horror. How could I have been so naïve – so stupid? I should have guessed. The clues were there, only I was too in love to notice. Too blinded by his wonderful voice and dark, dark eyes, too swept away by his charm. Jesus Christ. What do I do now?

The knot in her stomach clenched into a fist and she just made it to the *en suite* bathroom. Retching, heaving, cold sweat beading her forehead, she was soon empty of everything but fear.

Splashing cold water onto her face, she shook herself out of her stupor and avoided the mirrored wall above the basin. She didn't want to see the horror of the past few minutes reflected in her eyes, or the guilt that was surely etched beneath the tanned mask of her face.

'And I am guilty,' she muttered. 'As guilty as the three men downstairs. I might not have pulled the trigger, but my God, I didn't do anything to stop them.'

The restless whine of the baby snapped her to her senses and she went back to the bedroom. Bending over the crib, she caressed the softness of his cheek. How beautiful those long black lashes were against the dewy skin.

She picked him up. He was hungry and needed a clean nappy, but she had to hold him. Had to feel his comforting weight in her arms before she could go on. Nick was real. Nick was the only thing that mattered. And nobody must be allowed to harm him.

She changed him, put a fresh cotton nightdress on him and held him to her breast. The tug on her nipple was reassuring, the tiny fist pressed against the fullness of her breast gave her strength. But she didn't feel twenty-six and all grown up. At this moment she felt as small and as vulnerable as Nick – and what she needed most was her mother's embrace and the windswept flatlands of Norfolk.

It had been three years since she'd left England for California and the chance to earn enough to start her own business, but it felt longer. She understood the way of things in Norfolk, knew the rules. California and this great white mausoleum of a house was a stage setting, a glossy veneer hastily drawn over the violence of its reality. Like Gregory Castlemaine the Third, it had its dark side. A dark side she'd been forced to witness tonight. A dark side which had brought her marriage swiftly to an end and her life in jeopardy.

Gabriella shivered and held the baby closer. She remembered how Greg made love to her, his long, slender body moving over her, his hands running through her hair, his face buried in its luxuriant thickness. He'd said it reminded him of spun gold, and he'd called her his Rapunzel. How she'd loved the touch of his hands, the feel of his mouth. That now seemed a lifetime ago, for she had seen behind the mask and knew him for what he really was. Evil.

Would he kill her as easily if he discovered the extent of her knowledge? Take her baby and mould him to his own image? The answer was irrefutable, inevitable.

There's only one thing I can do, she thought. And that is to run. Take Nick and get as far from Greg as possible. But it can't be done in a rush,

She thought of the senator who'd watched from the shadows. If he knew of her involvement, he would be swift to silence her. He had the means and the backing of the law enforcement agencies. The Castlemaine corruption was far-reaching and unassailable.

I'll have to wait for the right moment, scheme, prepare and be ready to move at an instant's notice. I can trust no one – but escape is my only option.

A sound outside her bedroom door made her stiffen, her arms instinctively drawing the sleepy baby closer. Someone was coming.

She hurriedly put Nick in his crib and climbed into bed. 'If he touches me I'll kill him,' she hissed as she curled on her side and pulled the sheet over her face.

The whisper of the door sweeping across the thick carpet told her he was in the room. The image of that striking cobra was crystal in her mind, and she went cold at the thought of his hands on her.

'Gabby? Are you awake, honey?'

Gabriella squeezed her eyes shut. She had to appear relaxed, had to fool him into thinking she was asleep. But her pulse raced and she could feel the tension build. Breathe deeply, evenly, she admonished silently. Don't screw up your eyes. Breathe dammit. In, one two three. Out, one two three. Relax, relax.

'Gabby? Honey?' Greg's soft, insistent endearments dripped like warm honey in her ear as he leaned over her.

Gabriella concentrated on her breathing.

He moved away with a cluck of annoyance, and she heard the rustle of his silk tie as he loosened it, the slither of his shirt as it was placed on the chair, the zipper of his trousers rasp as he stripped to his underwear. Then the soft thud of his shoes as he kicked them off.

Breathe in. Breathe out.

The mattress tilted as he climbed in beside her. The sheet lifted, exposing her naked shoulder, then was replaced.

Breathe. Relax.

'Gabby? I need you, baby,' he whispered, his face close, his breath on her cheek.

Breathe in, breathe out.

He began to move against her, his penis hard against her buttocks, his hands cupping her breasts.

Gabriella tensed as she fought to control the conflicting emotions of loathing and fear. Not that. No. I won't let him do this. It was a silent defiance, never given life – for the baby lay snuffling in his cot mere inches away.

His hands became more urgent – squeezing, kneading, hurting. His lean body pressed close to her back as he thrust himself between her legs, searching, jabbing, painful.

I can't pretend any longer. There's no way he'll believe I'm asleep after this.

He was inside her now, rasping the dry softness with every stroke. Nicholas had taken a long, painful time to be born and although it was five weeks, she was still tender.

'Greg, you're hurting me. Stop it.'

'I can't, Gabby. Not now.' His voice was breathy, his eyes closed in exquisite pleasure as he pushed her face into the pillows and thrust deeper.

Gabriella wanted to pull away. Wanted to scream and bite and kick until his weight was off her and his intrusion banished. She wanted to tell him what she'd seen and tear away his bloodstained hands from her breasts – the breasts that Nick suckled. Yet she knew she couldn't. The thought of the baby lying so close to the bed kept her mouth closed and her rage harnessed. But something deep within her had died.

She felt the tears prick her eyelids as Greg shuddered and held her tightly in the waning of his climax. But they weren't the tears of self-pity, they were the tears of vengeful hatred. His lust had been fired not by love, but by the adrenalin charge of murder. How many more times would she have to prostitute herself to this charade? How much longer would it be before she had a plan firmly fixed in her mind – a way out – an escape? How quickly love could turn to hate.

Now all she'd felt for him was gone. Washed away in a sea of blood on a chessboard floor. All passion spent, all tenderness crushed beneath the weight of that assassination. There was nothing left. Only Nicholas.

15

2

T he night was over.
    Greg had fallen asleep immediately after their coupling
– she could think of no other word for what had passed between
them. Now he lay with his back to her, softly snoring into
the pillow. Gabriclla moved to the furthest edge of the bed,
watching the sky, waiting for dawn, dreading the new day.

The events of the past few hours remained sharp. As did
the black and white of that marble floor. The pieces were in
place for a deadly game, and now she too had become an
unwilling part of it. If she let the panic surface, she would
begin to scream. Like a riptide, it would tear through her
and she would be powerless to stop it. So she lay there and
struggled to contain it.

Think of Nicholas, she demanded silently. Think of escape.
Think of anything but what happened.

Had her love been so blind that she'd deliberately ignored
the uneasy thoughts which had come during her ten months
of marriage? Money was power, but where had that money
come from? Why did Greg disappear for weeks at a time, and
who were the men who came to the New York apartment
after dark, who fell silent when she entered the room?
Besotted and stupid, she'd closed her eyes and enjoyed
the luxuries and the parties, the travelling and shopping,
the sights and sounds of a life far removed from the one
in England. Life was fun, she was young and in love with
the 'All American Boy'. Just because Greg's family was

seriously rich and powerful, didn't neccessarily mean they were corrupt.

Nevertheless, she admitted coldly, I saw the truth tonight. Now I've put my son in mortal danger. Idiot. Utter bloody fool!

Too anxious to sleep, she leaned over the crib. Lifting the sleeping baby, she tip-toed out onto the balcony. She could no longer stay in the same room as Greg.

How can he sleep, knowing what he's done? she thought as she looked back at him. Men like Gregory were a breed apart. A species distanced from the rest of humanity by their lack of soul. She'd met others like him on the army base in Hereford. Men with eyes that were haunted despite their smiles. Men who could kill, then come home to their wives as if nothing had happened.

Gabriella shuddered. Her father had been such a man. Perhaps that was why she'd been drawn to Gregory Castlemaine.

She sat in one of the white cane chairs and looked out at the ocean, her thoughts going out to the child in her arms as she rocked back and forth. It didn't matter that he couldn't hear or understand – it gave her comfort.

Your grandpa was a brave soldier, Nick. A brigadier with a chest covered in medals. He would have known what to do. He wouldn't let anyone hurt you.

Nick's hand curled around her finger. It was as if he was trying to reassure her.

I loved him very much and he was good to me, fair and loyal – but he would have preferred a son. Someone just like you. She felt the tears threaten and swallowed them. Too many tears had been shed tonight. They couldn't change things or bring Dad back.

Like all little girls, Gabriella had adored her father, looked up to him and used him as her role model. He'd been a man of little compromise, and calculating determination, who expected obedience and loyalty from his family as well as his men in the regiment. Perhaps that's why I chose someone just like him to marry, she mused.

She watched the sleepy baby. He was so tiny. How on earth was she going to protect him from the Castlemaines and their influential conspirator? From Greg's father, who'd never disguised his disapproval of the marriage? The man frightened her, with his silent, closed face and strange amber eyes. She remembered how his mouth became a cruel line beneath the long patrician nose when they'd first been introduced. The only thing colder than his expression was the blink of the diamond on his finger.

Gabriella shuddered and pushed away the image of the old man in the wheelchair. To think of Nicholas in his power was too much to bear – and Greg was just like him. Why hadn't she seen that before?

She contemplated her past and her future with bitterness. Marriage to Gregory Castlemaine had taken away her freedom, just as her father had. She'd had no choices as a child and she had none now. Her life was ruled by the man she lived with. And as she thought back, she realised how isolated her existence was. The minute he'd put that wedding ring on her finger she'd become his property.

And it had all started with such promise. Liana, an American exchange student at university, had offered her the chance to earn enough to build her own health studio back in England. She had persuaded the manager of the health club to by-pass the need for a green card, but she'd omitted to tell Gabriella the place was owned by a drug baron. And she must have known – she'd worked there during the college vacations since fresher year.

Gabriella sighed. All that training, all those years at university wasted. Marriage to Greg had put a stop to any thoughts of a career. A working wife didn't fit the image he portrayed to the outside world. She blinked rapidly and stared out at the ocean. Now what have I got? Who can I turn to? Not Liana – she never forgave me for marrying the boss. How was I to know she was besotted with Greg and had her own plans for him? And the other girls? She shook her head. They couldn't be trusted – not when Nick's future was at stake.

She looked down at him. It's you and me, Nick, and I promise on my life you won't be harmed. If it should come to that, then so be it. She shivered, despite the warmth of the sun. If I run from Greg I might never see Mum again. Am I strong enough to resist the temptation to pick up the telephone and call her – or try to see her? Can I really be so cold-blooded as to ignore her, when she's so frail and riddled with arthritis? What if she dies – she's almost seventy – how will I cope with the guilt then?

A steely determination clarified her thoughts. If she was to protect her mother and her baby, then she would have to disappear – become as anonymous as possible. Take on a new identity, a new life, a new history. The influence of the Castlemaines was widespread, and she would have to spend the rest of her life out of its reach. Have to learn to outwit them. Never trusting anyone not to betray her.

Her restless mind taunted. If only she hadn't listened to Liana and gone to San Franciso. If only the Castlemaines hadn't owned the gymnasium. If only she hadn't agreed to take over for Liana on that fateful day Greg had decided to visit his investment. If only. The world was full of people whose dreams had been shattered by those two words. She was just another casualty.

Gabriella watched the ocean lap against the sand. It was very beautiful here, but she could never escape the memories. Could never go into that hall again without seeing Leo's tortured face – or see the marble floor without thinking of what had lain there.

'Gabby? What's the matter, hon? You feeling OK?'

Gabriella's pulse thudded at the sound of his voice. She needed more time. Needed to be alone with her thoughts before she had to face him. But he was here – touching her arm, bending close, his voice soft and concerned. She shook her head, her gaze averted. Closing her eyes, she leaned into the cushions, every nerve stretched, every breath agony.

'Just tired.' The words felt alien on her tongue and sounded distant and strange.

He didn't appear to notice. 'You should ease up, hon. All that exercise can't be good for you so soon after the baby. I know! Let's have a picnic here on the balcony and forget the gym this morning. The ocean looks great and it's not too warm yet.'

Gabriella felt his touch on her arm, his breath on her cheek and wanted him gone. She somehow smothered the urge to snatch her arm away. The thought of having to sit opposite him and force food between her lips made her nauseous. Yet she must acquiesce. He must not guess her loss of innocence, or suspect it wasn't tiredness which had sapped her energy.

'If you want, Greg. But I'm not very hungry.'

'You must eat to build up your strength, honey. You have Nicholas to think about now.'

He paused, and she felt the brush of his arm against hers as he touched the baby. Then he was lifting her hair from her shoulders and kissing her neck.

Gabriella froze as the butterfly kisses searched for the pulse in her neck. His touch was venom, his lips leaving an impression on her skin that made her feel unclean.

'I don't like to see you looking so tired. Where's my beautiful Rapunzel? Why the sadness in your eyes. Aren't you happy?'

This was dangerous territory. She would have to look at him. Have to reassure. Have to lie.

She opened her eyes, and shielding them from the rising sun with her hand, she attempted to meet his gaze. Greg was squatting next to her, looking at her with eyes that reminded her of a doleful puppy. Anxious to please, desperate for recognition, he was the clean-cut American prototype. Was it only yesterday that she would have kissed that mobile mouth and put her arms around his neck to reassure and give comfort? She drew on all her energy and smiled.

'A picnic is a wonderful idea. We could have those lovely cinnamon rolls your mother sent us.'

His face was immediately transformed as his eyes shone and he shouted in delight. 'OK! That's more like it, babe. I'll see to it. You sit there and rest.'

Gabriella watched as he turned back into the room and threw a robe over his silk boxer shorts. It was as if she'd dreamed the whole nightmare scenario of the previous night. This Greg was loving, boyish, energetic and easy to like.

She wrapped her robe more tightly over her tender breasts. It was almost time to feed Nick again. Strange how her body still functioned. Strange how everyday things didn't change, even though her world was shattered. Her thoughts were dragged back to Greg who was now dressed and standing in the doorway.

'I've told Rosita to fix breakfast. There's a couple of faxes to send out, and I've a call to make to New York. Back as soon as I can, hon.' He blew her a kiss, then left.

Gabriella lifted her hand to acknowledge his kiss, closed her eyes and felt like crying. He could be so wonderful. Why, oh why, did there have to be the other side of him? Perhaps he could change? Perhaps, if she could influence him and show him how wrong his life was, he would leave the family business and return with her to England?

The idea was stillborn. He would never change. It was too late and he had too much to lose. Gregory Castlemaine was a seasoned killer. He could never be anything else.

Nick began to grumble, and pleased she had something else to occupy her mind, she took him back into the bedroom. After making him comfortable, she fed him, laid him back in the crib and watched him chase the early morning shadows with his fingers. She could have stayed there all morning, but Greg would be back soon and she wanted to be showered and dressed so there would be no repetition of last night.

22

She went into the bathroom, and as she let the robe fall to the floor, it was as if she was shedding the skin of her life with Greg. Her reflection showed the independent, resourceful Gabriella she had once been – and motherhood had given her the edge of a ferocious courage. From that moment on, she knew that escape was possible.

Turning on the shower until the water jetted hot needles, she made her plans. She would have to build up her fitness programme slowly. Having a baby had sapped her stamina, and she couldn't afford to overdo things. The last three months of her pregnancy had slowed her down, and although she'd swum regularly and watched her diet, she knew that a pulled muscle or overstretched tendon would only hamper her escape. Pinning up her hair, she stepped beneath the stinging heat of the shower and began to scrub away the feeling of contamination. She had to be strong in mind as well as body if she was to succeed. It was no good reliving the nightmare. She had to push it away – break free, once and for all.

Gabriella was back on the balcony, showered, refreshed and dressed in a swimsuit and sarong, before Greg returned. She felt positive, and more able to cope with the situation than she had done an hour before. After breakfast she would swim as many laps as she could in the pool. Then work out for half an hour in the gym Greg had had built in the basement. They weren't due to leave California for another six weeks, so there was plenty of time to take things slowly.

'I need to talk to you, Gabriella. It's important.' Greg folded the linen napkin into its ring, then put it on the table amongst the debris of their almost silent breakfast.

Gabriella had forced down a little of the cinnamon roll and orange juice, now they were drinking hot, fresh cappuccino. Her hand shook as she lifted the cup to her mouth. He wasn't going to confess, was he? Not already. It was too soon and she didn't want to hear, wanted no part of it.

23

She stayed silent, the cup hiding her mouth as she pretended to drink.

'I have to go to New York. Dad's health is worse. It's time for me to take over the presidency of the business.' Greg was studying his manicure, seemingly unconcerned for the reality behind the careful words.

How many more lies will you tell? She shivered, despite the rising heat of the sun. 'I don't feel strong enough to travel yet. When were you planning to leave?' She put down her cup and dabbed her mouth with the napkin. If he insisted upon her accompanying him, then escape would be almost impossible. There were too many eyes and ears in New York. Too many family members who would recognise her and give her away if she tried to hide in the city.

Greg opened the silver cigarette case she'd given him on his last birthday. He tapped the Gauloise on the lid, put it in his mouth and lit it. Each movement was slow and methodical – mirroring the ones he'd made the night before. When his dark eyes meandered away from the horizon and rested on her, she felt the coolness of his scrutiny. He appeared to be carved from marble, unapproachable, distant, full in charge of her destiny. '*We're* going the day after tomorrow.'

Gabriella heard the emphasis on the 'we' and her confidence tumbled. 'I have a hospital checkup next week.'

'There are very good doctors in New York.' His gaze was still unwavering, penetrating.

Gabriella held a tight rein on the rising panic and forced herself to meet those eyes. 'But Dr Weinberg's been with me for the last two months. He was there when Nicholas was born. I feel safe with him. I don't like the man in New York.'

Don't overdo it, she admonished silently. Keep calm, logical, put my side reasonably. And stop wringing the table napkin. He'll realise you're lying.

She waited for his answer.

Greg flicked ash. 'Mom and Dad want to see their grandson. He's the heir to the family fortune, and one day he'll be president of the company.' His voice was soft, and fluid – and it ran over her like iced water.

'I'm only asking for another couple of weeks, Greg. Surely they can wait until then? You wouldn't want me to get ill in New York, would you? And Nicholas is thriving here in the sunshine and fresh air. Think of the heat and the dirt in New York. That can't be good for a baby.'

Had she gone too far – pushed too hard? Her nails dug into the palm of her hand as she maintained a steady gaze.

The cigarette was placed carefully in the ashtray, his scrutiny intense. 'It's out of the question. Your place is with me.'

He leaned forward, catching his fingers in her hair, pulling her closer. His eyes darkened as he watched the light dance and spark in its rich tresses before returning to her face.

Gabriella was transfixed. Speech impossible.

'Maybe I'm being selfish,' he said thoughtfully. 'Maybe you should stay. But only until the doctor says you're OK to travel. Then you can come home to New York. I'll talk to him.'

Her heart thudded, and she lowered her eyes to mask the relief.

His fingers stopped running through her hair and caught her chin, lifting it, turning her face towards him. 'Why is it so important to stay?' he fired at her. 'Why the disappointment?'

She could hear the menace underlying the words, feel the strength in his grip. Her mind raced.

'I'm disappointed because I love it here. New York's so big and dirty. The people have no manners and everything's done in a rush. I like the pace here, the sun and the fresh air. Nick is thriving and I wanted to be fully fit before we went back. I thought we were here for the summer.'

She smiled back at him, her duplicity making her feel cheap. 'I wanted to be well for you, Greg. To be as I was when we first married. But I'm not ready yet. Can you understand what I'm trying to say, my love?' She almost choked on the endearment.

Greg pulled her close. After a long, searching kiss, he released her, leaned back in his chair and smiled. 'Gee, I'll never understand women,' he said. 'First they want one thing, then another.' He gave a good humoured shrug. 'OK. You can have two more weeks. Then you've got to come home.'

Gabriella heard the authoritative order in the last sentence, but she'd been given the time she needed. She poured another glass of juice and drank it down. She wanted to be rid of the feel of his mouth, to hide the glitter of triumph she knew was in her eyes.

'I think Mom would appreciate a vacation in California,' Greg said casually. 'I'll send for her. Then she can spend some quality time with her grandson.'

Gabriella froze as her triumph shredded. Was he suspicious? Surely not? Maybe he was just keeping tabs on her, which she wouldn't have noticed before. Suddenly everything appeared more threatening, with secret meaning behind every gesture and word.

She tried to remain calm, to keep the edge of panic out of her voice. 'I'm sure she'd love it. Why don't you telephone her? Then we can begin to make plans for her stay. I'll have the maid prepare the guest apartment.'

Greg stared at her, doubt in his eyes. Then he stubbed out his cigarette, mashing it into the glass ashtray before he stood.

Her gaze was drawn to that dead cigarette. She remembered the burning flesh, the agony in Leo's voice as he pleaded for mercy that was not given.

'What's the matter? Gabby? Gabby?'

She tore her attention from the ashtray. 'Nothing. Just daydreaming.'

'Don't you want Mom here in California?'

She gave a shaky laugh. 'Of course I do. Don't be silly. Go and phone her.' She focused on him and held steady, but fear constricted her throat and she wondered if he could read it in her face.

His dark brows shadowed his eyes, drawing a hard line

above the long nose. Then, without a word, he strode into the bedroom.

Gabriella's breath was released in a rush as she stared towards the sea. Yet she didn't see the ocean, or notice the gulls scavenging in the seaweed, her mind was working too fast. If his mother came, how to escape? It would be difficult enough with Vic hanging around, but 'Mommy' was a whole different ball game.

She listened to Greg's side of the conversation. It was rapid, but the essence was clear enough – he was ordering his mother to come.

'She'll be here at the end of next week. Friday,' said Greg as he stepped through the open French windows. 'With Dad so ill, she doesn't think it's right to leave him.'

'Sounds serious,' replied Gabriella with studied concern. Her mind was making rapid calculations.

He shrugged. 'It's to be expected. Poor Mom. She's too good. Dad takes advantage of her.'

There was a rebirth of hope. Thank God for that, Gabriella thought. If sainted Mom wasn't coming until the end of next week, then she had ten days.

3

G reg sat in the shade of an umbrella and watched as Gabriella swam in the pool. Those lovely long legs propelled her with speed, and her hair floated behind her. She looked like a mermaid. But something was wrong. Something cold and distant that puzzled him. She appeared to be as strong and healthy as always, no sign of the tiredness she complained of when he wanted to make love to her. So why had she insisted upon staying?

What game are you playing Gabriella? What's going on in that pretty head?

He ran a finger down the length of his nose. It was a good idea to bring Mom to California. Gabriella was up to something, but as yet, he had no idea what. She hadn't seemed at all interested in his forthcoming promotion, or asked her usual catalogue of questions. She'd just accepted his explanations – and that made him uneasy.

His finger stopped at the bridge of his nose, his eyes narrowing as he regarded his wife. Had she seen something the other night? Or overheard the quarrel?

Greg sat motionless, watching her plough up and down the length of the pool. Why was she swimming as though she was training for the Olympics? She'd spent an hour in the gym this morning, and last night and the morning before. Surely it was too much too soon?

His mind ticked methodically over the past two days. With cold efficiency he recalled the way she'd avoided his gaze. The almost imperceptible flinch when he'd touched her. Barely noticed then, but now sharply in focus as he conjured up the last hours he'd spent with her. There had been an alertness in her too, as though she was waiting for something. An aura of tension that spoke in the way she moved and held her head.

Something was going on behind those green eyes which meant trouble. He'd been around it for too many years to be fooled, hadn't survived this long in the drugs business without recognising the signs. Too many men had found to their cost that Greg Castlemaine might appear to be a wealthy magnate who ran his corporate enterprises with the utmost respectability, but behind that façade was a mind as sharp as a stiletto, and the influence in the underworld to silence all who stood in his way.

Well, let Gabriella plot and scheme. Let her stay in California where she thinks she's safe. I'll know every move she makes. But just to be sure, I'll speak to Victor and Mom. They mustn't let her out of their sight until she's back in New York. Give her enough rope, though, just to see what she'll do with it, he decided. Shame I won't be around, could be interesting. But I have to know that her loyalties are with me. There's too much at stake.

Taking out his sunglasses, he polished the lenses and put them on. Defeat lay heavy in his chest and his shoulders slumped. He was saddened that he couldn't trust his beautiful wife. She had become a stranger, even though he knew every inch of that wonderful body.

In that fleeting moment he wished his life had been different. Would it always be like this, he wondered. But he knew the answer even before the question had fully taken shape. Of course it would. The responsibilities of the family business had a heavy price tag. One he'd been glad to pay – until now.

He lit a cigarette, watched the smoke drift into the warm breeze, then shook off the regrets. He hadn't come this far to allow some bitch to ruin it all. Let Gabriella do what she felt she had to, then he would see. She was his wife, the mother of his son. Surely that meant something to her?

Didn't it?

He hoped so. He didn't want to lose her.

And Nicholas, what of him? The safest way would be to take him to New York, but that would alert Gabriella to his suspicions and he didn't want that. If she was plotting something, then the kid would have to stay with her. Besides, she was breast feeding and he didn't want the problem of finding a nanny.

He gripped the wrought-iron arms of the chair. If she did anything to deprive him of his son he would kill her. Then he relaxed. She would never dare. But just in case, he would change a few house rules.

He looked at the gold Rolex and saw there was little time before his flight. His head buzzed and the sun beat down with an intensity that matched his anger. He must stay in control. One false move on his part and she could put them all in danger. Slowly, slowly. Ice cool. It was the only way. A lifetime's experience had taught him that.

Greg reached out and picked up the sheet-sized towel that lay over the sun lounger. Easing from the chair and smoothing the creases in his jacket, he stepped to the edge of the pool.

'Enough, Gabriella. You're making me tired just watching you.' He held out the towel as she reached the end of a lap. His gaze was deliberately impenetrable behind the sunglasses, his face immobile as he waited.

Gabriella smeared back her hair, rubbed water from her face and blinked up at him.

Was that wariness deep in those eyes? Was there distrust, or fear peeking out beneath those lashes that dripped water like diamonds? He couldn't be sure. The look had been so fleeting, he'd been unable to capture it. A coldness settled round his heart and despite the heat, he was chilled.

As she emerged like Aphrodite from the water, he placed the towel over her shoulders and kept his hand on the back of her neck. He kissed her mouth, the pressure of his hand drawing her close. She tasted of sunshine and chlorine and her mouth moved under his in a way that made him want her. But something was different. Something not quite right. She was so tense.

Before he released her mouth he opened his eyes and was shocked to find her staring back at him. There in all its nakedness was her fear.

He tightened his grip on her neck and disregarding his expensive suit, pulled her to him. 'What have I done to make you look at me that way?'

He felt her tense and try to push away, but his grip was steel, his voice a whip in the silence of the pool area. 'I'm speaking to you Gabriella. The least you can do is answer me.'

Gabriella closed her eyes and he could feel the tattoo of her heart against his chest. She was afraid of him. He hadn't been mistaken. It was in every breath she took, every flutter of her eyelashes, every hunted sweep of her gaze.

'I'm afraid for our future, Greg. You're going on to bigger and more important things, and I fear for Nicholas.'

A brave speech. One that told him she knew more than she was letting on. 'It is my inheritance, what I've been groomed for since I was barely able to walk. Why do your eyes accuse, when I am only trying my best for you and Nick?'

Maintaining his grip on her neck, he took off his glasses and flung them towards the chair, then slid his other hand around her waist. Her skin was cold, slicked with water, her stance defensive.

Gabriella tried again to break away. 'I'm not afraid of you, Greg, only the life we'll lead once you take over the presidency. We'll spend our lives moving around the world – and there'll always be the threat of kidnapping. He'll be a prime target. What kind of future is that for our son?'

He didn't relax his hold. She was lying. But how to prove it?

She looked up at him then, eyes wide and shining with

unshed tears, face devoid of make-up, hair plastered to her finely sculpted head. At that moment she was utterly beautiful, heartbreakingly open.

Perhaps she was telling the truth after all. Perhaps this was her way of telling him that she understood his commitment to the family empire. Perhaps she was merely afraid of the future, afraid for her son, afraid of her husband's good fortune. Perhaps this was what motherhood did to women. He desperately wanted it to be so, for he loved her.

He kissed her forehead, her eyelids, her cheeks, her nose, her mouth. Then relaxed his grip and held her gently against his ruined suit.

'I'm sorry, baby. But there's no going back. I promise you though, that both of you will always be safe with me for as long as I live. Trust me.'

He cupped her face with his hands and lifted her chin so he could look into her eyes. His words had chased away the fear, but a coolness remained. His grip tightened. There was a sudden fear in him and he was angry at his weakness.

'But if you should betray me, I'll never forgive you. Once you are a part of me it's for ever. You cannot walk away. Do you understand? For life. For ever.'

He covered her face with kisses, and, with a sense of profound relief, felt her begin to respond. Everything was going to be all right. He'd been mistaken, that was all. Too used to the scum that plotted behind his back. Too accustomed to looking over his shoulder. This was his wife. His lovely, innocent Gabriella. She would never betray him.

Forgetting the time, forgetting where he was, he slipped the strap of her bikini off her shoulder. Her heavy breast filled the palm of his hand and he caressed the brown nipple until it became erect. Then he bent his head and ran his tongue over and around it until Gabriella gasped.

Encouraged, he feverishly pulled off the flimsy suit until she was naked, her lovely body unmarred by her pregnancy, her flesh tanned golden and glistening with water. He could see

33

her limbs trembling, her hands fluttering over her nakedness as she stepped away from him and threw hasty glances around the deserted sun terrace and he was reminded of an unbroken colt.

'No one can see us, baby. There's nothing to fear. Come here and let me love you.' His voice was thick with arousal.

'I don't want to, Greg. It's so . . . open here.'

He took her hands and kissed her fingers. 'No one will disturb us. I need you Gabby. Need to show you how much I love you.'

Her eyes were downcast, her demeanour modest – and it turned him on. This was a different Gabby to the one who often made the first move and entered into love-making with enthusiasm and imagination – this Gabriella was a challenge. His need became compelling, and he led her back to the lounger, sat down and pulled her close, his hands encircling her tight buttocks. She was still tense, still unresponsive and it aroused him to the point of almost losing control.

Running his tongue over her belly, he dipped into the sweet chalice of her navel, tasting the chlorine and sweat, feeling his need for her ache deep within him. His hands stroked her back, revelling in the silkiness of her skin, the delicious roundness of her firm backside.

He felt her try to push him away, heard her moan. It acted as an aphrodisiac. Things had gone too far to call a halt. He had to have her.

His teeth and tongue nipped and lapped over her as he maintained his grip with one hand and stripped off his jacket and ripped away his shirt and tie with the other. Then he pulled her closer until his face was buried in the gold wiry hair between her legs.

He felt her tense, and heard the gasp.

Encouraged, he flicked his tongue over that golden mound, searching for a way to the hidden trigger that would make Gabriella tremble, not with fear, but with passion. Then, having found it, coaxed the tiny nub to swollen desire with his tongue, sucked the heady saltiness of her body, lapped at the soft flesh until she began to move against his face and her hands pressed his head even closer.

With a growl of victory he pulled her down onto the lounger. Kicking off his shoes, he got rid of the trousers and shorts that hampered him. He wanted to take her, needed to feel her legs around his waist, ached to have those tight, secret muscles enfold him.

But he knew how to hold on. Knew how to wait until Gabriella was on the brink of climax, before giving her what they both wanted.

He kissed the soles of her feet, sucked each pink tipped toe, then ran his tongue over the smooth tan of her legs. The soft, silky flesh of her inner thigh quivered as he parted her legs. The gold mound of hair was now dark and wet and he buried his face in its muskiness. Tongue flicking, teeth gently nipping, he brought her close to the point of climax, then stopped. Moving quickly, he knelt over her, his hands pinning her wrists to the pillow, his knees holding her legs apart. Then slowly, slowly he entered her. Holding back his excitement, he inched forward, feeling her tighten around him, experiencing shock waves of desire at the very root of his erection before partially withdrawing.

Gabriella moaned and thrashed her head from side to side.

Greg smiled. His first conquest had been on his thirteenth birthday, the women he'd had since then had taught him well. He could be patient when he needed to be – could put aside his own desire when he knew the outcome would be so much more satisfying if they peaked simultaneously.

The sun beat on his back, Gabriella moved beneath him and he entered her again. Deeper this time, holding himself there for a moment, his arousal heightened by the throbbing, velvet wetness of her before slowly retreating. But he didn't withdraw completely. This time he teased her, finding the tiny trigger with his finger, playing with it until it brought her gasping to a point where he knew there was no return. Then he plunged into her and gave himself up to the exquisite torment.

Her legs wrapped themselves around his waist, urging him on. Her hips lifted in time with his plunges, the muscles surrounding him drawing him deeper and deeper as her hands flexed and clawed within his grip on her wrists.

He closed his eyes and lifted his face to the sun, the pleasure of her making his mind swirl, bringing flashing stars before his closed eyelids.

There was no pretence in the way she accepted his body. No masking of her feelings as they raced towards that spiral of erotic climax. No doubt that she loved him. None at all.

Greg felt his seed rush into her. Felt his breath caught in his lungs, his head spin with the pleasure. Spent, he released his grip on her hands and rolled off her.

They lay for a moment and waited for their breathing to return to normal. The sun shone down from the clear blue sky, the water lapped on the edges of the pool and all was right with his world.

Finally, he lifted himself up onto one elbow and looked down at Gabriella. Her eyes were closed and her mouth was slightly open. He could see by the rise and fall of her chest that her breathing was still ragged, and there was a pulse beating in her neck which he found very endearing.

He kissed that pulse and murmured in her ear. 'Come back with me to New York, Gabby.'

Gabriella lay in the sun, completely spent, utterly defeated. Greg's love-making had taken her by surprise and her body had betrayed her. Despite everything she'd witnessed, she could still be aroused by the touch of his hands, his mouth. Was still capable of giving herself to him.

And the realisation sickened her.

Those hands which were capable of such violence, had been the same as those which had caressed and coaxed her to a shuddering climax. That mouth which had looked so cruel the other night, was the same as the one which had teased and provoked her to lose all control. It was as if she could still feel the imprint of his hands and lips on her flesh and she wished she could wipe them away. Wished she could curl up like a baby and shut him out of her life. Yet all she could do was reach for her sarong and cover her nakedness.

His murmured words brought her sharply back to the present, and once again she recalled those black and white squares in the hall. She reluctantly turned her head and, squinting in the bright light that danced on the water, she opened her eyes.

Greg was lying beside her, his melting gaze drawing her dangerously back from the edges of her resolve. To be strong and determined in her thoughts was all very well, but soon she would have to put thought into action. Until then he must not suspect. Her performance just now had been faultless. She'd even managed to fool herself.

Shaking her head in reply to Greg's softly spoken question, she leaned forward and tasted her body's own betrayal as she kissed his lips. Then, as casually as possible, she lay back and watched him. If she was to complete the charade, then she would have to appear as relaxed and contented as she had before.

'You promised I could stay. And anyway, it will do your mum good to have a holiday. She doesn't get much chance to relax in New York.'

He rolled away from her, and she sensed his impatience in the staccato way he stripped off his watch and plunged into the pool.

Gabriella watched through half-closed lids as he struck out and swam two lengths. Her mind was racing. There had been an alertness about him, a defensive, closed look in his eyes as he'd listened to her reply. Perhaps she'd been too insistent. Perhaps New York wasn't so bad after all. It would be more difficult to get away there, but it was obvious Greg really didn't want her to stay in California. And she was afraid that if she was too adamant, he might realise she knew more than she should. She'd already said too much.

Greg swam to the side of the pool and rested his arms on the terracotta tiles. His hair glistened darkly in the sun, his tanned skin looked warm, but his thoughts were unreadable in the shadow of those hooded lids.

Gabriella pretended to be dozing, but her knuckles whitened in the folds of the sarong. It had become a lifeline, a barrier between her and the man who could arouse such conflicting, powerful emotions.

'OK. You and Mom stay here. I'll be too busy to give you much attention anyway,' he said nonchalantly.

That reply was too easy. Too careless. Even after our love-making, does he see something in my eyes that gives me away?

Gabriella watched him for a moment as he turned back to the water and swam another length. She felt suddenly vulnerable, lying there almost naked. She could feel the shame of what she'd done heat her face and although the pool was completely sheltered, she had the uneasy feeling they had been watched.

With a quick glance at the surrounding wall of shrubbery, she decided she was imagining things. It was her own shame that was making her feel guilty. The servants were forbidden in this part of the garden, and Vic knew he must never interrupt Greg when he was with her.

She leaned back into the soft cushions of the lounger and watched as he hauled himself out of the pool. When would it be safe to leave? When could she escape into the house and plunge beneath the boiling, cleansing water of the shower? Too soon and he would wonder why. Too late and he might want her again.

The thought of him touching her again made her cold, so she sat up and pulled on her bikini pants, her gaze darting across the distance between them, wary and uncertain of what would come next.

He stood for a moment with his face lifted to the sun, then shook his head so the water drops caught the light as they flicked off his hair. With skin the colour and texture of caramel silk, and the muscle definition clearly marked in his lean torso, he looked beautiful. Yet Gabriella was aware of the deadly core behind that beauty.

To mask her inner thoughts, she looked away as he bent to pick up his watch, wrapped a towel around his hips and turned towards the house. She wanted him to go. Needed to be alone.

But he suddenly stopped and looked at her over his shoulder.

'Get dressed and come with me to the airport. Nicholas can stay here with the maid.'

It wasn't a request. It was an order. And she could do nothing else but obey.

Greg paced the floor of the drawing room, repeatedly glancing at the hands of the clock. Showered and dressed, his bags packed and ready in the trunk of the Cadillac, he was impatient to leave. Orders had been carried out and telephone calls completed, everything was done. He'd already missed one flight, he didn't want to miss another.

Lighting a cigarette, he stopped pacing and looked down at the magnificent chess set he'd bought two months ago at an auction in Milan. He'd wanted it the moment he'd seen it in the catalogue and although the price had been higher than he'd expected, it was worth it.

Sculpted from marble and enhanced with gold, the pieces stood six inches high and represented the ancient Gods of Greece and Rome. The Roman pawns were black eagles, the castles Roman pillars. Jupiter and Juno ruled over Mercury, Neptune, Mars and Pluto. The white pawns were griffins, the castles Greek columns, the king and queen Zeus and Hera.

Hermes, Poseidon, Ares and Hades ruled the Greek side of the board.

He picked up Jupiter and held it to the light, feeling pride in ownership, awe at the sculptor's skill.

'Magnificent. What skills the man had to make such beauty.'

Replacing the black king, he looked carefully at the board. A game was in progress, had been for several days, and the only person capable of giving him a run for his money was Gabriella. It had been a surprise to find she had such a talent, but her father had been a good teacher, and she was a cunning player. They had spent long evenings and many weeks over a game, and his ego had taken a knock when Gabby had proved to be a wily adversary.

'I have the advantage this time, Gabby. But you're a foxy lady – I'll have to be careful. What move do you propose next, I wonder?'

He regretted having to put this game on hold – New York and his father were more important – but he enjoyed the analytical reasoning behind each gambit, the studied care necessary before making a sacrifice or exchange. Chess mirrored his life, therefore he understood its vagaries.

The musical chime of the French ormolu clock interrupted his thoughts and he looked at the time in exasperation. What the hell was Gabriella doing up there? If she didn't show soon, he would have to go without her.

Yet that was not part of his plan. He wanted to see her eyes as he kissed her goodbye. Wanted her to get the message that she belonged to him. That her life and everything she did reflected on him and therefore was a part of him.

There was only one more thing to do before they left. Something that only he could order. Where the hell was Vic? He'd rung through to the guest house over half an hour ago. He hated lateness in other people. He was a firm believer in always being on time and didn't see why others couldn't feel the same. It was a question of orderliness, neatness and a sense of pride.

The sound of footsteps in the hall stopped him pacing and he looked towards the door.

Vic came hurrying into the room, a bustle and fumble of a man who was attempting to straighten his tie and button his jacket all at the same time. His hair looked as though it hadn't seen a brush for days and his shirt was rumpled, the buttons straining over his paunch.

'Vic, you're a mess. Don't you have any pride? This jacket looks as if you've slept in it, your shoes are unpolished, your trousers need pressing and your hair . . .' Greg didn't go on. There was nothing more he could say about his younger brother's appearance that he hadn't already said a thousand times before.

Vic hung his head and shrugged as Greg straightened his tie and brushed lint from the jacket lapels.

'One fussy dresser in the family's enough. Besides, it's too hot to wear a suit and tie.'

'This is an expensive suit, Vic, utterly wasted on you. You can't be a bum all your life.' Greg stepped back a pace and scrutinised his brother's appearance.

Victor kept his gaze on the floor. 'I don't care a shit what you think. Who wants to look at me anyhow? You're the big shot around here – not me.' He swept an arm towards the antique furniture and priceless paintings. 'I hate all this crap – why can't I live the way I want?'

Greg was stung by Vic's words. 'If it wasn't for all this "crap" as you call it, there'd wouldn't be any fancy apartments in Chicago and New York, no fancy schools for your kids – or fancy cars and fast women. Is that what you really want?'

'I didn't mean . . .'

'What? You've had all the advantages, Vic – the same as me – and what have you done with them – nothing! You're a slob, and it's time you grew up and got responsible for your behaviour.' He grasped his brother's arms and shook him.

'I know and I ought to be grateful. But . . .'

'Do you want to end up drinking yourself stupid under the

table in some flea-bitten bar in the Bronx? Would life be more appealing if you had no responsibilities, no family, no ties? It can be arranged, Vic. Just say the word.'

'You know I don't want that, but it isn't easy to be a Castlemaine. You're a hard-assed taskmaster, Greg – like Dad – and sometimes I just want out.'

'Dad gave us his lifetime's work, it's fed us, educated us, opened doors in some of the highest placed, most secret organisations. We owe him some loyalty and respect, Vic and now it's payback time.'

Greg's hands were shrugged off as his brother stepped away.

'It's not loyalty to Dad, it's loyalty to your ambition. I never wanted the same things as you – we're different people. As far as I'm concerned the whole deal's a load of bullshit.'

Greg watched his younger brother pace – a ridiculous figure in an ill-fitting suit, but his brother nonetheless. He was shocked. He'd never realised Vic felt so strongly about anything. Least of all the wealth and position he'd been born into.

'All I want is a quiet life. A life where I can damn well wear what I want, go where I please and eat when and where I want. You already have what you want, and soon you'll be president of the company. You don't need me any more.'

'But you're my brother, the only person I can trust. You are as much a part of this as I am – and in far too deep to just walk away.'

'No. I can't, can I?'

The words were almost spat into his face and Greg narrowed his eyes as he looked at Vic. He hadn't realised how much hatred there was in the man. He'd been too busy empire-building to notice. He would have to be careful. He couldn't run the risk of Vic selling out – he knew too much.

'I love you, little brother, despite your fondness for junk food and sloppy dressing.' He patted the roll of fat where Vic's waist used to be and smiled. 'We are family, brothers, it's important to me that you're happy. We shouldn't let other things come between us.'

'Then you must respect me as a man, Greg. I'm not the hired hand around here, not the country hick to be laughed at.'

'I understand that, and I'm sorry if your feelings have been hurt. Of course I respect you. I always have. But as my brother I want you to look good. You're young, you shouldn't be so overweight and out of condition. I only want what's best for you. I've always looked out for you and your wife and family, haven't I? Always been around when you've had problems?'

Vic looked penitent enough as he struggled with the knot in his tie, but Greg could still feel his hostility.

'Yea. I just get pissed when you ball me out about my clothes. I feel like a dummy in this get-up.' He gave a long sigh. 'What d'you want anyway? Jake said it was urgent.'

Greg put an arm over his brother's sturdy shoulders.

'I have a problem, and you are the only one I can trust to take care of it.' He caught the surprise in Vic's expression. The hostility had been replaced by inquisitiveness. He nodded grimly. 'I need you to watch Gabriella. She seems hell bent on staying here. It can't be another man, hasn't had a chance to meet one. And anyway, who would want a woman who was carrying another man's child?'

Greg had spoken with deliberate carelessness, but the words hurt and deep down he wondered if he was falsely accusing his wife – but he had to be sure – had to be certain of her loyalty before he took Dad's place.

Victor stayed silent, his gaze watchful, his expression puzzled beneath the heavy brows and untidy hair.

Greg kept his hand on Victor's shoulder as they paced the floor. 'I want her watched day and night. Nicholas can't be left on his own with her except at night when the alarms are set in the house. Understand?'

Victor nodded, his eyes betraying the questions which were unspoken.

Greg was thankful for his silence. He had no real answers

for his brother, merely a gut feeling that all was not well. He'd trusted that feeling before and it hadn't let him down.

'She thinks Mom's coming next week, but I've changed plans. Her doctor's appointment is in three days' time, not next week, but don't tell her until it's absolutely necessary. I don't want Gabriella suspecting anything. But I want her to have just enough freedom, so that if she is up to something, she'll get careless.'

Greg saw that Vic understood and lit a cigarette. He took the smoke deep into his lungs and felt its effects in his head. He'd needed that. Facing his reflection in the Venetian mirror, he smoothed his tie and brushed the lapels of his jacket. Turning back to Victor, he twirled the ring on his finger and watched the diamond flash in the sunlight, his face deliberately masked of all emotion. He couldn't let his brother see how much this was hurting.

'I've increased the security arrangements, and I want you to make sure the alarms are tested every couple of hours. I don't want any visitors. Tape and log all telephone calls. And be extra careful when she keeps her doctor's appointment. Drive her yourself that day and stay with her. Don't let her take the baby out of the house any other time.' He paused for effect. 'Understand, Vic. No other time.'

Vic nodded. 'Don't worry. She goes nowhere without me.' He looked at Greg, then began to chew on one of his nails. 'But what if there is another guy, or what if she tries to run off with the kid? What then?'

Greg's arm slithered around Vic's neck and held him in a vice. 'Then you bring him straight to New York. If the bitch betrays me in any way, then she's of no use. Understand my meaning?'

He held his brother's chin with his wrist, forcing his head up until he had nowhere to look but into Greg's face.

'Don't foul up on this one, Vic. Or I'll have your eyes.' His gaze was unswerving, his voice cold and threatening. He felt his brother swallow, then saw him nod.

44

Good. It was understood. Now he could go to New York with an easier mind. Things would be taken care of here.

Gabriella's bare feet made no sound as she softly padded off the balcony. Her heart was thudding and she could feel cold droplets of perspiration run down her cleavage. It was as she'd expected, they'd forgotten the open window behind the curtains in the living room, and every word they'd spoken had drifted up to her. If she did what she was planning, then her life, and that of her baby's hung in the balance. Her survival meant as little as Leo's.

Whatever the outcome, Nicholas would survive – yet the knowledge gave her little comfort. Survive for what? To become like his father and grandfather before him? That was not what she wanted for the child who lay gurgling and cooing in the cot. That was not the inheritance she would freely choose for her innocent baby, and if it meant sacrificing her own life, then so be it. It was worth a try. Worth everything to get him away from this hateful house, and the men downstairs.

The thought of what she was about to do wiped away the last shred of love she'd ever had for Gregory Castlemaine. Her body would never betray her again.

To try and bring some harmony back into her thoughts, she picked up her son and buried her face in the warm sweetness of his neck. His tiny hands clutched at her face and she kissed each perfect finger. He was all she had, and although it would put her in mortal danger, the Castlemaine family was not going to have him.

4

'I'll always love you, always take care of you.' Gabriella whispered as she hugged Nicholas. 'And God help both of us,' she muttered. With a last, lingering kiss, breathing in the smell of him, reacquainting herself with every tiny feature, each delicious finger and toe, she laid him in the cot and covered him with a sheet.

The rosary hung from the canopy over the cot and she eyed the slender silver crucifix thoughtfully. Brought up a Catholic, her religion had once played an important role in her life. Could it help her now? How could God forgive her for the part she'd unwillingly played in that terrible scene? Her guilt of omission, of closing her eyes to the truth, was as profound as Greg's. She'd known that things weren't all they seemed, but she'd allowed herself to be drawn in – to be dazzled by the life style, the sheer opulence of her surroundings and was blinkered by her love for him.

Gabriella turned from the cot and stared out of the window. She felt an unfamiliar yearning to go to Mass again, to smell the incense and to light a candle. There would be peace in the familiar surroundings of the high altar and stations of the cross.

'But I can't even do that,' she murmured. 'There isn't a priest I'd trust within a thousand miles of here.' Greg was a respected and generous supporter of the church both here in California and New York. She had once seen a cheque Greg had signed over to Father Dotti in Queens, and the amount had astounded her. Yet when she'd questioned him, he'd merely looked at her with those dark eyes and told her it would help ease a lot of pain in the ghettos.

She'd thought then that she'd understood his reasons. Greg's grandfather had come from the slums of Chicago, it would be logical for him to do such a thing. Now, with hindsight, another picture was emerging. How much loyalty had been bought with those generous donations? Just how high and how wide did his influence stretch, and to what depths was the church prepared to sink?

Gabriella shook her head as the thoughts crystalised. She would probably never know the extent of Greg's influence, but after the events of the past two days she could give an educated guess that several highly placed Catholic priests were in his confidence: his eyes and ears on the streets, and in the board-rooms, their presbyteries perfect sanctuaries for those outside the law.

As she returned to the crib and sat down, she grew thoughtful, and the more she mulled it over, the more certain she became that the priests turned a blind eye. They knew there was blood on that money. Knew it had come from a source where shady dealings and violence lay deep beneath the veneer of respectability that was Gregory Castlemaine. But they took it anyway.

'Gabriella, what the hell are you doing?' Greg's shout came from the hall below. 'We're going to be late!'

She flinched at the sound of his voice and looked quickly towards the bedroom door. She didn't want him to come up to the room. Didn't want him near the baby. Stabbing bare feet into sandals, she grabbed her handbag, and after a lingering kiss on Nick's cheek, she turned and headed for the door.

A sense of foreboding stilled her, and she realised she had almost made a fatal error. The game of chess that had begun on that marble floor was still in progress, and she had almost made a move without reading the situation clearly. What if this was a ruse to get her away from Nick? What if, when she returned, she found the baby gone, whisked away by one of Greg's security guards?

'Gabriella, get your ass down here – now!' Greg's voice rasped in the silence and echoed along the landing as his tread became a metronome on the marble staircase.

Gabriella raced to the cot. Picking up the baby, she wrapped him in a cotton blanket. 'If he refuses to take you, then I won't go either,' she whispered fiercely against the soft, downy cheek of the sleeping infant. 'To hell with him.'

'I'm coming,' she called. With Nick tucked securely in her arms she left the room and headed for the stairs. At each step she expected to see him waiting for her and she steeled herself for the confrontation.

Tension had reached its zenith by the time she had rounded the curve in the staircase, and when she looked down onto the great hall, she saw Greg and Vic waiting for her.

The late afternoon sunlight drifted down in hazy beams of muted yellow, blue and green from the stained-glass cupola, casting the brothers into surreal shadow in that stark, white setting. Each man was dressed in black, and as if they had been placed there by a hidden scene-setter, were standing on a marble square of the same colour, their faces lifted towards her, their hair gleaming ebony in the rainbow of colour. The black king and his knight, were poised for their next move.

Gabriella's nerve faltered, then she lifted her chin in defiance and took a firmer grip of Nick. An outward show of confidence and savoir-faire had to be maintained if she was to succeed in outwitting them.

'I told you to leave Nicholas. The maid will look after him.' Greg stepped away from the black square of marble, his expression grim.

Gabriella paused on the bottom step as her stomach executed a slow roll and her heart clamoured. She was finding it difficult to breathe, but with the weight of her son in her arms to give her courage, she could face his angry glare and hold it.

'I thought that as you weren't going to see him for two weeks, you'd like us both to come with you.'

Greg returned her stare, his expression inscrutable. Then he gave a slow, enigmatic smile.

Gabriella waited. She had noticed that the smile hadn't been reflected in his eyes.

They stood in silent combat.

Just as her nerve threatened to fail, he grabbed her arm and pulled her down the last step. 'Next time, do as you're told,' he hissed, as he made a pretence of kissing her cheek.

Gabriella felt the steel of his grip and the strike of his words, but she was jubilant at having won the skirmish. Each victory, however small, was one step closer to freedom. She had to remember that, had to gain strength from it so she could carry out her intentions.

Vic stood to one side as they left the house and approached the Cadillac. He held the door open for them, his expression as inscrutable as his brother's.

Gabriella hoped to see a gleam of decency in those once friendly, laughing eyes; but his gaze slid away and came to rest somewhere beyond her shoulder.

Yes, you bastard, she thought coldly. I know your orders. But you don't have the guts to look me in the eye, do you?

Gabriella stepped into the limousine. Vic had played a clever game so far, and she had been fooled by his performance. He wasn't a buffoon, an untidy, friendly uncle with whom she'd trusted her baby. He was evil, cast from the same mould as his brother.

Greg slid in beside her and made himself comfortable on the red leather upholstery. Vic shut the door, got behind the wheel and turned the ignition. There was an echoing engine throb from the ever present security vehicle, then tyres crunched gravel as they drove in convoy down the long drive towards the heavy iron gates.

Gabriella felt the chill of the air conditioning but knew it was impossible to open the window to allow the warmth of the sun into the car. Vic had the controls on a panel between the front seats and security demanded the doors and windows remained locked on all journeys. So she wrapped the blanket more securely around the baby – he was dressed only in a nappy and a cotton vest because of the heat. Satisfied he wouldn't catch a chill, she turned her attention to the passing scenery.

What she saw made her spirits tumble. Greg's orders had already been implemented. There were two guards on the gate, instead of one, and a dog handler now patrolled the perimeter walls with a fierce looking Doberman. Each man carried a night stick and revolver on his leather belt.

In the wing mirror, she noticed the dark figures which moved like shadows in the bushes as the car made its way down the long driveway. Until now she hadn't taken much interest in the security arrangements, and the anonymous men who melted into the background had been rarely seen and always silent. She squirrelled away the information. She might need it later.

'I've arranged for extra security while I'm away,' Greg surprised her by saying. 'I thought about what you said, and decided to make sure you and Nick are safe.'

It was as if he'd read her mind and Gabriella kept her eyes focused on the view from the car window. Lying bastard, she thought.

There was silence in the car as they left the coast and headed for the city, and for that she was grateful. She didn't feel like small talk, and was relieved that Greg was engrossed in the contents of his briefcase.

Nick was asleep in her arms, and it gave her a chance to put her thoughts in order. So many questions remained unanswered. So many lies told, that she wondered if her husband knew what truth was any more. Perhaps, and this was the most chilling thing about Greg, perhaps he believed his lies to be the truth. Could no longer distinguish between fact and fiction.

As Vic swung the powerful car in and out of the usual chaotic traffic, she looked down from the third tier of the six lane highway which flowed into Los Angeles. It reminded her of Spaghetti Junction, though on a much grander scale. Like everything in America, it was bigger, better and more brash. Where else, but in California, could you look down from a motorway and see acres of neon and palm trees?

As she looked at those smog-diseased palms, she was reminded of other heavy, green fronds that dipped towards the warm sea and white coral beaches of the Maldives. She and Gred had spent their honeymoon cruising in the Indian Ocean.

Sitting beside her husband in the frosty atmosphere of the car, the sharp images of their wedding day came back to her. It had been hot then, but neither of them had seemed to notice as they took their vows on the lawn of the Castlemaines' New Jersey mansion. She'd been so happy, so in love and excited about the new life she was about to live, that she hadn't seen the storm clouds. She hadn't taken much notice of the large, incongruous gathering of elderly men who'd arrived in limousines with tinted windows. They'd been introduced to her as business colleagues who had come to pay their respects. Now she suspected that they were in fact members of the drugs cartel.

She could see herself so clearly, it was as if it were hours, not months that had passed since that day. Mum had been flown over for the wedding, and despite the crippling arthritis, had been determined to walk without her sticks to the altar with her – but she'd known what an effort it was for her to put weight on her frail limbs.

There was the full white gown encrusted with seed pearls and crystals and Greg, darkly handsome in his morning suit, waiting for her at the altar. His voice was deep, coloured by the American twang as he repeated the vows, his kiss warm and full of promise as he'd swept her up in his arms and carried her back down the aisle of garlanded marble statues to the wedding breakfast. Each scene was clear and colourful as it rolled through her memory, but the knowledge that it had all been a sham made her bitter.

Greg shut his briefcase with a snap and brought her sharply back to the present, putting an end to her daydream, just as the events of the other night had put an end to her marriage.

'You're miles away, honey, what are you thinking about?'

'Our wedding. The palm trees reminded me.'

Greg snorted as he turned the pages of the *Financial Times* and reached for the mobile phone. 'You have a son now, you must look forward, not back.'

Gabriella looked down at the sleeping baby. 'Yes. I'll do that,' she said softly.

Greg rustled the paper impatiently, cutting off any further conversation by making a series of short, sharp telephone calls.

Gabriella leaned back into the upholstery and looked at the sky. The sun was setting behind the Hollywood hills, darkening the trees and bruising the blue canopy that always hung above the smog. A jumbo jet, heavy bellied and roaring, climbed above the high-rise apartment blocks towards that darkening sky. The rumble of its engine made her ache for Norfolk, for freedom and piece of mind.

If only it was me and Nick on that plane. If only we were free to fly away. If only . . . But my life must never be ruled by what might have been, she admonished silently as the cars came to a halt and Victor was joined by the two guards as he opened the door for his brother.

Greg folded his newspaper, snatched up his briefcase and got out. When she moved to follow him, he slammed the door. The click of the central locking was loud in the silence. Sliding along the seat, she pressed her hand against the cold glass of the window, the square-cut emerald in her engagement ring sparking green fire in the electric lights of the airport entrance. The panic began to build. What was going on?

Victor pressed another button on the remote control he always carried, and the window slid down a few inches.

'Stay in the car.' Greg's voice was clipped, his eyes hostile. 'Vic and I have business to discuss.'

'But . . .' Gabriella fell silent. He had already moved away and the window hissed shut again.

She slumped back into the seat. If he didn't want her with him, why had he insisted on her coming? What the hell was he up to?

As she sat there trying to understand the reason behind this latest twist in his game, her gaze flickered over the people who hurried towards the airport building. Their voices were loud and excited as they loaded trolleys with their luggage and bustled children to keep up. She envied them.

The terminal's automatic doors slid open and shut as the passengers flooded through them. How close those doors were. How few steps it would take for her to pass between them and become lost in that milling crowd. How clever of Greg to lock her in the car. To taunt her with the significance of those doors and the freedom they offered. He was playing the game with ruthless cunning.

Gabriella admitted silently that he had won this move in his opening gambit, but it didn't make much difference. She had no ticket and no money, she wasn't prepared. She would just have to be patient. But how those doors beckoned. How the distant roar of the planes made her ache for the freedom they offered.

She tore her attention from the hypnotic doors and watched the two brothers. They were in deep conversation, but too far away for her to hear what they were saying.

'It doesn't matter,' she murmured. 'I know what's between you.' She dug her nails into her palms. 'Go, Greg. Just go. Then I can begin to plan. I can't think with you around. Can't function when I know you're watching me.'

Greg nodded tersely to his brother, who pointed the remote control and opened the window. Then he was approaching, leaning into the car, his Armani aftershave crisp on the cooling summer breeze.

'You look cold, Gabby. Perhaps you've caught a chill?' He sounded concerned as he touched her face with long, supple fingers, but his eyes told another story. They were hard and questioning and his gaze slid away as she searched for some hint of the warmth that used to be there. Her heart lurched and something cold settled on her spine.

He knew.

'The air conditioning's too powerful,' she replied tersely.

He signalled to Vic who was standing some way off and the window whined down further. 'You'll be wanting to get the baby home,' he said quietly as he reached in and touched the sleeping baby's head. 'There's no need for you to see me off.'

Gabriella nodded. There was so much she wanted to say, so many things that needed to be out in the open, but the emotions were jumbled, twisted and confusing and her throat was too tight for speech.

'Look after my son, Gabriella.'

She thought she saw doubt flit through that searching gaze, but it was gone as quickly as it had come.

'Vic will look after you. Anything you want, just ask him. Mother will be here next week.'

Liar! she wanted to scream. I know your plans. I know your bloody mother's not coming and I only have three days. As for good old Victor, he'll give me something all right – a plot in the nearest cemetery if I'm not careful.

But she swallowed the bitter words and forced herself to smile. 'Don't you worry about us. We'll be fine, and I'll make sure your mum has a holiday to remember,' she added with a touch of spice and tilted her face towards him for his kiss.

He bent his head towards her. Stopped. Cupped her chin and looked into her eyes. 'Goodbye's too final, Gabby. Let's just say so long.'

It took all her willpower to look into his face. The grip of his fingers on her chin had tightened almost imperceptibly, the warning in his eyes direct as he kissed her. She felt trapped by those eyes. Trapped by his mouth. Trapped by his hands on her face. The message was clear. As clear as if he'd put it in words.

He released her, then smiled, drawing his lips back over his perfect teeth before turning away. Yet, as she watched this performance, Gabriella thought the smile more lupine than human, the baring of teeth – a snarl of warning to the prey of his readiness to strike.

Gregory Castlemaine stopped in front of the airport doors and glanced back at her. The robotic sheets of glass slid open and shut behind him. Open and shut. As if giving her a last glimpse of freedom, before snatching it away.

As they closed behind him for the last time, the sun dropped below the hills and Hollywood was plunged into night. Gabriella shivered. She never wanted to see him again.

'Mind your head, I have to close the window.'

Gabriella tore her attention from that retreating figure and looked at her brother-in-law. His expression was set, his eyes unreadable in the shadows. What was he thinking? Has he already planned where to dump my body? She studied him as he climbed back into the limousine. Vic didn't look like an assassin, neither did Greg, but Vic didn't possess the same powerful aura of his brother. But if one looked closely enough, she decided, there, in the line of his mouth, the curve of his nose, was the same predatory sharpness. The same cruelty. He was just as dangerous and she mustn't allow his more approachable veneer to fool her.

'The baby's getting cold. Would you turn off the air conditioning?'

Vic nodded, pressed a button on the console, and Gabriella felt the warmth flood the car. Yet she remained chilled. The glare of her husband's eyes was still with her.

She looked up and met Vic's gaze in the mirror as he pressed another button and the glass partition closed between them.

Gabriella understood the message in that simple action. She was his prisoner.

As she hugged Nick close and endured the long drive back to the house, she noticed how Victor constantly glanced in that mirror – it was as if he was reaffirming his control.

The heavy double gates swung open and the cars swept up the long driveway. Headlights pierced the darkness, making the surrounding trees and shrubs look alien and one-dimensional as they loomed over the gravel. The house, built on two floors, glowed white in the darkness, and shafts of light shone from the downstairs windows. To her fevered imagination it appeared to be watching her, waiting to see what she would do next. Had it only been a few days ago that she'd loved it? Now it represented something far more sinister.

It sprawled leisurely across the manicured lawns, its twin balconies trailing greenery over the stark white pillars that ran the length of the house. Graceful palms shuffled their fronds against its walls, and in the distance, she could see the moon-touched water and the small white ripples of the ocean. It looked so peaceful – so idyllic – but the cold whiteness of those stuccoed walls and the harsh yellow light from those windows held no comfort. This was not a home. This was a prison.

The convoy drew up outside the front door, but Vic remained seated, watching her in the mirror as he released the central locking.

Gabriella stepped out and looked up at the imposing entrance with its studded oak door and cathedral arch of stone, the baby whining and restless in her arms. It would take a tremendous effort of will to walk up those steps and go back into the house – but there was no alternative.

The slap of her sandals echoed on the marble floor as the heavy door clicked shut behind her.

She looked down. The squares of ebony and ivory were stark in the electric light. The ornate staircase silent and majestic. The house seemed poised, waiting for her to make her first move.

57

With Nick held tightly in her arms she looked at that chessboard floor. At that moment she saw herself as the white queen, alone in the black king's territory and, with the house surrounded and his men on alert, she realised he had already set up the strongest position on the board. In chess terms, it was called the Sicilian defence.

5

Delta Airlines, Flight 101, landed at JFK in New York and taxied towards the terminal which blazed with lights. The plane docked and the usual scramble of passengers began. It was 10.00 p.m. eastern time, and Greg corrected his watch.

He ignored the questioning glance of his bodyguard and sat in his first-class seat and waited. For the first time in his life he was reluctant to see his father, or stay in the Manhattan apartment he and Gabriella had moved into after their wedding. Without her it would seem empty. And what could he say to Dad about his suspicions – if he dared say anything at all?

He stared out of the window. It would be a betrayal of the old man's trust if he stayed silent, he admitted regretfully, but to confess his shame and lay it bare before his father was not something he relished. The problem had been nagging him for the past two days, but he was no nearer resolving the puzzle, and as they'd approached New York, he'd become more uneasy.

He sighed, and without really focusing, watched the straggling line of passengers elbow their way along the aisle. If Gabriella was up to something, then talking to Dad about it wouldn't help. The old man would simply say I told you so, and demand he got rid of her.

And he didn't want that. Not yet. He wanted to give her the freedom of choice. The chance to prove her loyalty. If she broke her promises to him, then he would be the one to punish her, not Dad. She was his wife, his property. Therefore, his right to deal with the situation.

Although the flight had been swift, the events of the past few days had left him tired and out of sorts. Now he looked forward to a long hot shower and clean clothes. Yet he knew that all the time Gabriella was in California, he wouldn't rest. Couldn't dismiss the thought she was plotting behind his back.

There had been a coldness behind that façade of uncharacteristic English reserve, a wariness which had never been there before. Especially when she'd said goodbye at the airport. Her eyes didn't tell the same story as her mouth and her body language was hostile. She must have seen something the other night. It was the only possible explanation. Gabriella wasn't stupid – far from it – and if she had witnessed Leo's murder, then she would question other things. And that made her dangerous.

'Mr Castlemaine? The other passengers have deplaned, sir. Is there a problem?'

Greg was snatched from his musings and looked up in surprise at the soft voice of the stewardess. 'Thank you. There's no problem.' He gave the girl one of his most dazzling smiles and picked up his jacket and briefcase. He was used to women's admiration, was proud of his appearance and liked their company – as long as they knew their place and allowed him to make the first move.

She was quite a looker. Tall, slim and neat in her uniform, her blonde hair coiled into a bun at the nape of her neck. Her skin gleamed with health, her smile was wide and her teeth a miracle of dentistry. He read the invitation in her eyes and felt the lingering touch of her hands, just a little too familiar, as she helped him on with his jacket.

At any other time I might have taken you up on the offer, he thought. Could have done with a good screw, but Dad's waiting and I don't dare be late.

'Have a nice day,' he murmured as he headed for the door. He didn't miss the disappointment flit across her wavering smile. Maybe next trip, he thought. A fast, anonymous fuck could be had any time. There are plenty like you in New York. He'd put her out of his mind even before he'd left the plane.

The bodyguard followed closely as he made his way through baggage claim without lingering, and out onto the concourse.

The black leather briefcase was his only luggage, but Greg had not let it out of his sight since leaving California. The contents would be explosive in the wrong hands, could shatter the very foundations of Wall Street, and rock the pretentious bastards off their fat asses.

He indulged in a pleasant thought, his lips twitching in amusement. If they knew the truth behind the market fiasco a few months back, then they might not remain so smug. I've got them by the balls.

'Welcome back to the Big Apple, Mr Castlemaine.'

Recognising his father's driver, he gave a brief nod, dispatched his bodyguard to the following car, and climbed into the Mercedes. It was chilly in New York after the heat of California, and his lightweight suit didn't give him much protection. 'Turn the heater on, Max.'

As the warmth flooded the car and they weaved in and out of the snarl of traffic, he began finally, to relax. I'll have to put the problem of Gabriella to the back of my mind, he decided. There's a lot to be done before I take over from Dad. I mustn't allow her to cloud my judgement. Time will tell if I've been mistaken about her, and I hope I have – for everyone's sake.

'How's Dad, Max?' The driver had been his father's valet for years and the two old men had forged a strong friendship.

'He ain't so good, Mr Greg. Stays in the apartment all the time now. The others gather like vultures. It's a good thing you've come home. He needs you.'

Greg fell silent and stared out of the window. Dad had been a distant figure during his childhood, but a force to reckon with. He had expected his sons to do well at school and college and to remember at all times that wealth had its own responsibilities. As soon as Greg was mature enough to understand, Dad had begun to reveal the secrets behind the family fortune, and groom him towards the time when he, Greg, would head the family dynasty. A law degree at Harvard, and three years at business school had added polish to that earlier education, now his father needed him and it was payback time.

Gabriella was looking down the barrel of a gun. It was close to her face and she could see the smear of grease that lay within the darkness of that metal hollow. The barrel loomed closer and she heard the click of the safety catch.

'Goodbye is too final. Look after my son.'

She awoke, startled, the nightmare still clear in her mind – Greg's voice still echoing in the room as though he'd really been there. Yet he was thousands of miles away. He couldn't hurt her. Couldn't take Nick.

Despite the heat, she felt chilled. Her skin tingled with it and she could feel the short hairs prickle on the nape of her neck. What she was about to do was dangerous. But she had to do it, had to escape – or the nightmares would become reality.

As she lay there in the darkness, she listened to the night sounds. It had been two days since Greg had left for New York, and the house seemed so still. Yet that stillness was a charade bought by wealth. Behind the closed doors were servants, and in the grounds the claustrophobic presence of the men on patrol. Greg's eyes and ears, his spies.

She had been aware of being watched as she walked around the gardens, or took her swim in the pool. One of the guards even stood on the steps leading down to the ocean and watched her paddle. Yet she hadn't spent those hours idly, even though she kept to her usual routine of gym and swim, meals and naps.

As she ploughed from one end of the pool to the other, or

lay supine on a lounger in the sun, her mind was ticking over. She'd been allowed out, but Vic always drove her. The day before, she'd tested him by going to Rodeo Drive. Even then, he'd entered the exclusive boutique behind her and had waited, staring at some spot in the distance as she leafed through silk lingerie. She had hoped to telephone her mother in England and arrange for money to be deposited somewhere in a false name, but Victor was always there – always two feet behind her – always watching.

As the dream fragmented and lost its power, she found it easier to think more clearly. She was still no closer to a solution, a plan for the escape.

'Money's the biggest problem,' she muttered. Greg was generous with cash and credit cards and she'd not had to worry about it since her marriage, but the harsh reality was – she had nothing of her own. 'I have to have cash. That American Express and the other gold cards will be stopped the minute I run, so I daren't count on them.'

Restlessness drove her from the bed and she paced the floor. 'At least they don't know about the passport,' she muttered. She had checked it every day since Greg had left the house, but it wouldn't hurt to check again. There could be no slip-ups, no risking an inquisitive maid or probing Victor.

Pulling it from its hiding place, she held it for a moment. It was a ten-year passport, with two years still to run, and although she was now an American citizen, she had kept up dual nationality. Her reasons for doing so had never really been clear – perhaps it gave her a sense of identity – perhaps it was her one defiance, one strike for a vestige of the independence she had once held so precious. Whatever it was, she was more than thankful she'd done it. It was her ticket to freedom.

She returned it to its hiding place in the bottom of a large handbag. Nick's birth certificate folded between the pages.

'You forgot the passport, didn't you, Greg?' she whispered into the darkness. 'Old army habits die hard. Daddy was a firm believer in keeping an ace up the sleeve. He taught me well. You'd be amazed at what I carry around.' She gave a chuckle of victory and hid the handbag under a jumble of shoes and old sweaters. It would be safe there for the night. Tomorrow she would keep it with her.

A sense of peace calmed her as she sat next to the cot, and in those moments, a plan began to form, and she examined it closely. It was simple, dangerous – but exciting. She checked her watch. It was three o'clock in the morning – the deadest hour – the perfect time to make her move.

'Use what Dad taught me,' she whispered. 'Think of this as a game of chess against Greg. Think like a Castlemaine, and stay one move ahead – then you'll succeed,' she whispered. 'But first . . .'

Slipping on her dressing gown, she checked the baby and opened the bedroom door. Her pulse raced as she listened for footsteps. All was quiet, but that didn't mean she wasn't being observed. She would have to be very careful.

The short flight of stairs at the far end of the landing led her down to the kitchen. Padding across the flagstones in the gloom, she reached the door that led into the hall and almost lost her courage as the full realisation of what she was doing made her hesitate. If caught now she could give a reasonable explanation of her night foray into the kitchen. A few more steps and there would be no plausible reason for her to be where she was. The consequences of her actions tonight could be the end of everything.

Her mouth dried as the adrenalin surged. The double doors to Greg's drawing room were enticingly close across the marble floor. This would be her first gamble – the first real test of her courage – and she was not about to fail it.

It was very early in the morning when the telephone rang beside the kingsize bed in the Manhattan apartment. Greg snatched it up, instantly alert. There was only one person who had access to this line. And that meant trouble.

'What's happened?'

'She's been in the safe.' Vic's voice was clear, despite the distance between them.

Greg felt a stab of regret that was swiftly replaced by anger. 'How do you know?'

'Jake was patrolling outside and saw her go into the living room. It was after three in the morning and he wondered what she was up to, so he came and got me.'

'Get on with it, Vic. How do you know she'd been in the fucking safe?'

'I was coming to that, dammit, listen.'

'Watch your mouth. Remember who you're talking to.'

'Sorry.'

He didn't sound very apologetic, but Greg let it go. The tale was taking too long already.

'I told Jake to stay where he was and watch. I hid in the dining room.'

Greg hissed and gripped the receiver against his temple. If Vic didn't get on with it, he'd explode.

'She was in there for a long time, then suddenly she opened the door and went upstairs through the kitchen. I checked later and she was having a shower.'

'Victor! How do you know she opened the safe?'

His brother seemed unfazed. It was almost as if he was enjoying himself. Even had the temerity to snigger and it made Greg catch his breath to harness his irritation.

'The only way for me to know that someone had been in the safe, apart from the alarm, which I'd had switched off by the way, was to leave something in there that would incriminate. I collected dust from the maid's vacuum cleaner, and sprinkled it over the shelves. When I checked it at midnight, it was still there. But after Gabriella had been in the room, the dust had gone. Polished away. I knew it would be, you see. She'd used her nightgown as a duster, and it was filthy,' he ended triumphantly.

If he was seeking praise, he was to be disappointed. Greg sank his chin to his chest and closed his eyes. This was confirmation of his worst fears, what he'd dreaded hearing. There was no going back now. Gabriella must be allowed to do whatever she was planning.

There have to be no misunderstandings when I confront her, he thought. No excuses for her behaviour when she faces me for the last time.

The sound of Vic's voice coming down the line sharpened his thoughts. I have to be clear headed. Have to dismiss the regret for what she's doing to me. He pinched the bridge of his nose and brought his wandering thoughts into line.

'Remember what we discussed at the airport the other day? See it's done.'

'You think she's planning to hightail it out of here, don't you?'

'That's none of your business, Victor,' snapped Greg as his patience finally reached breaking point. 'This is between me and my wife. Just do as we agreed. I won't risk losing my son.'

'She'll make a scene. You know what women are like, all that screaming and tears. I don't know if I can handle that in the middle of . . .'

'You will handle it, Vic. Because if you don't, you'll spend the rest of your life without a tongue. Understand me?' He didn't raise his voice, didn't need to. Vic had witnessed Gregory Castlemaine's brand of justice too many times to doubt the validity of that threat.

'OK, Greg. I understand. What do you want me to do about the security arrangements here once I've gone?'

'Have Jake call me later today. Just concentrate on Nicholas. I'll see to everything else.' He hesitated for a moment, then added. 'Don't foul up on this, Vic. I'm counting on you.'

'Sure thing, Greg. What are brothers for?'

Greg put down the receiver and slumped back on the pillows. He was too angry to sleep. Too roused by Gabriella's betrayal to relax. She would pay for this.

* * *

Dust in a vacuum-sealed safe didn't make sense, but the absence of money and her most valuable suite of diamonds and emeralds did. Greg had blocked her gambit – had known her next move and forestalled her.

Gabriella shifted uneasily in the nursing chair. Her pulse still raced after her foray into the drawing room, but with hindsight, she realised why it had been so easy. Somewhere, in the shadows, behind a curtain or partially closed door, they had watched her, waited to see what she would do, then reported back. It had been careless and stupid to wipe away her fingerprints, but she'd panicked. Her actions tonight had confirmed any suspicions Greg might have had – and it meant that for the next few hours, she and the baby were in great danger.

Her freshly washed hair was cool on her shoulders and back, but it did nothing to diminish the fever of her anxiety. It no longer mattered about the safe, there were far more important things to think about. With only a few hours to go, she and Nick would be on their way to the hospital and their chance of freedom. She was playing against the odds, against so many variations of possibilities that it made her head spin. Today's journey was the only chance she had of making her break. Vic would undoubtedly follow her right to the door of the doctor's office, but somehow she had to distract him. Had to get him to leave her alone with Nick for just long enough for her to escape. Then she would have to run. Run as she'd never done before. Then away – and out of California.

'It all sounds feasible, lying here. Simple and straight-forward. But reality will be far more difficult,' she muttered. 'What if they change their minds? What if, after they reported back to Greg tonight, they have orders to snatch Nick? Who would hear me scream, who would come to help? This damn place is just too well guarded and isolated.'

This latest turn of thought disturbed her, but she knew there was nothing she could do about it, but watch and wait.

If Greg was as cunning as she thought, then he would allow her to make the journey into LA, allow her to think things were running smoothly and lull her into carelessness before he pounced. She would have to be on her guard from now on. Take nothing for granted – suspect everyone.

Restless energy forced her out of the chair, and she began to pace. Everything was ready. The trip to the hospital meant she could take only the usual bag for Nick. Luckily, babies needed nappies, changes of clothing, wipes and a host of other paraphernalia, even for the shortest of journeys, so the bag was a large one and wouldn't arouse suspicion.

Sliding back the panelled door of the wardrobe, she dragged the hold-all from the shelf and checked what she'd already packed. There wasn't much room left, she realised. She would have to run in the clothes she wore that day. A couple of thin t-shirts, underwear, leggings and a silk shift dress would be all she could take. But there was still her oversized handbag. She could fill that with smaller things. Things she could pawn.

As she approached the dressing table, her reflection was thrown back at her and she turned away from the pale face and shadowed eyes. Yet she had seen too much – it reminded her of how vulnerable she was.

The jewellery Greg had given her over the past few months had been depleted since she'd last looked at it. There were only the few pieces she wore almost daily and which Greg had seemingly overlooked. There were her diamond earrings she'd worn to the airport, her gold bracelets and chain, pearl studs, a gold locket and the square cut emerald engagement ring. Several inexpensive silver rings and a collection of gold ear studs made up the rest.

Gabriella picked up each piece and let the light play over it, remembering the occasion he'd brought it for her. They weren't as valuable as the diamond-and-emerald choker, bracelet and earrings he'd removed from the safe, but worth enough to buy her a plane ticket, or hire a car.

'I'll have to sell them,' she muttered. 'But I won't be

sorry.' She looked at the small collection with contempt. Apart from the gold locket which had been her mother's, the jewellery represented a part of her life that was over. She could never wear it again without wondering how many lives it had destroyed.

Wrapping each piece in a screw of tissue, she dropped them into the sponge bag she always carried when travelling with Nick, then zipped it up and put it in one of the pockets of her handbag. Her fingers slipped over the neat slit in the lining and she felt the solidity of the passport, still safe in its hiding place.

She looked at her watch. It would be daylight soon. Vic still hadn't told her what time the appointment was, in fact, he hadn't told her anything. Yet there was nothing else she could do but wait for the day to unfold, for there could be no turning back, no change of heart. She was set on this course and would see it through. Nick had to be taken to safety and she knew now, that she had the strength and courage to do it.

Sunrise finally came and she began the routine of her day. Things had to appear natural and normal, but her nerves were frayed, and insistent, painful fingers of a headache pressed on the tendons in the back of her neck. Nick seemed to have caught her mood and was fractious, and his continuous crying was driving her nuts. It didn't matter what she did, he would not be comforted, but it was too dangerous to leave him unattended, and she kept him with her throughout the morning despite the interference of the maid who went off to her apartment in a bustle of disapproval.

Vic seemed to be everywhere as she moved around the house that morning. A shadow behind a swiftly closed door. A distant figure against the shrubbery which surrounded the pool. He never approached her, never spoke. It was as if they were strangers. The tension in the house was tangible.

Gabriella bided her time, waited for the moment she knew

Vic must collect the guards' reports from the gatehouse, then hurried back to the drawing room. Her own surveillance over the last few days had made it clear she would have little time – but then she didn't really need much for what she was about to do.

The living room was white, Greg's favourite decor. It was a beautiful room, with high ceilings and gilded furniture. A formal room which was a showcase for Greg's antique collection, not a place to bring a child or feel comfortable. The chairs were too delicate, the china too fragile, the pictures and mirrors too valuable. The sumptuous carpet deadened the sound of her footfalls as she laid Nick on a Louis XIV couch and circled the room.

Greg had a penchant for the trappings of wealth, but now she could put them to better use. It wouldn't do to be greedy, but it could be weeks before she found someone willing to part with cash for these undocumented antiques. Without the bill of sale, it would be impossible to get what they were really worth, but it had to be better than nothing. She and Nick would have to eat, to find shelter, and be able to move on at a moment's notice – and for that, she needed more than the $300 in her purse.

She made her choice from the smaller gold photograph frames which stood on the marble and gilt occasional tables, then added three pieces of exquisite porcelain from the display cabinet. Several antique pill and snuff boxes and a pair of miniatures were swiftly tucked into the roll of nappies she had placed into her shoulder-bag for just that purpose. A tweak here, an adjustment there, and at a glance, no one would notice the missing pieces.

Her gaze fell on the magnificent chess set. She regarded the board and the state of play in this latest game with her husband. As usual, Greg had the upper hand, but he hadn't thought it out properly, and had laid himself open to her capture of his bishop. That was his problem – over confident and inclined to make emotional decisions when it came to the nitty gritty of the end game. Dad had taught her well, but then he'd been an expert in military strategy.

Moving the pieces back to their original squares, she regarded them for a moment, then picked up the white queen and the white king and placed them in her bag. 'This is one game you won't win, Gregory Castlemaine,' she muttered bitterly. 'Not while I can draw breath.'

She turned once more to the ancient Gods of Greece and Rome. 'Sorry Jupiter, this time you lose.'

Taking the intricately carved black king, she placed him in the time honoured position of defeat – on his back in the middle of the board. Then brought the white griffins forward into the Sicilian Defence. Greg would have no doubt about her intentions – but she would be long gone before he saw this chessboard again.

The handbag now dragged on her shoulder with the weight of her booty. The house was still quiet, but the thud of her pulse was so loud in her ears she was certain it could be heard. Yet no one challenged her as she carried Nick across the hall and climbed the stairs to her room.

With her gaze flitting repeatedly to the clock on the bedside table, she switched on the television and began to dress. The silence in the house was beginning to get to her.

The muffled burr of the internal telephone interrupted her thoughts. Maybe it was Mum? But how to get a message across that couldn't be deciphered by those listening downstairs.

Her spirits sank as Victor's voice shattered her hopes.

'We leave for the hospital in five minutes.'

'I'll be down when I'm ready.'

He cut the connection before she'd finished the sentence.

Gabriella glanced at her watch. It looked as if they meant her to keep the appointment.

As she reached to switch off the television an announcement held her attention. The Eurasian reporter was standing outside the now famous suburban court house. The woman looked immaculate as always, but there was a tension

71

and a suppressed excitement in her as she spoke to the camera.

Gabriella turned up the volume.

'The jury's out and expected to reach a verdict within the hour. It has been two months since America has been focused on the four white policemen accused of beating Rodney King.'

Gabriella sank onto the bed, her attention fixed on the screen.

'Mr King is a convicted felon, but the incriminating videotape evidence must surely bring these four men to justice. Los Angeles is strangely quiet this afternoon. It's as if the city is holding its breath.'

Connie Chung looked straight into the camera, her dark eyes serious. 'The Rodney King affair has forced the resignation of the city's Police Chief, Daryl Gates, and there are reports coming in of large groups of blacks and hispanics congregating in Watts. Extra troops have been ordered to patrol the area around the court house, and the National Guard is on stand-by.'

Gabriella looked at the jostling, moody crowd behind the reporter and shivered. Even through the miles of cable she could feel the tension in those angry, dark faces; and read the fear in the reporter's eyes. The cauldron was about to boil over.

She checked on the time again. She'd kept Vic waiting just long enough, it was time to leave. The hospital was out towards Beverley Hills and the journey would take almost an hour if the San Diego Freeway hadn't already snarled with traffic. Hopefully, Vic wouldn't be watching television or listening to the radio. If he decided it was too dangerous to leave the house for the city, or if Greg telephoned from New York, then all her plans were for nothing.

'The last thing I need is a riot,' she muttered as she switched off the TV. 'I've got enough problems already.'

With the baby firmly buckled into a carrying sling, she

picked up her bags and took a deep, energising breath. It was out of her hands. Whatever happened next was up to fate, but there could be no turning back. Her adrenalin was pumping. She was ready.

Vic was waiting beside the limousine, but didn't offer to help as she struggled with the baby and the bags. She was grateful for that rudeness, he would have been suspicious of their weight, and his manner, and the lack of an escort car, meant he'd not heard about the brewing trouble.

His glance slithered away as he closed her door and climbed in behind the steering wheel.

What's going through his mind? Can he see in my face, my eyes, that I'm poised for flight? Gabriella quickly tamped down on the flutter of nerves. He didn't need evidence for that – he already knew – was alert and ready to pounce at her first move.

She looked out of the window as the wheels crunched over the gravel drive. Her heart was thudding to the rhythm of the tyres as they drove through the great iron gates for the last time, and out onto the road.

She didn't look back, for she had no regrets. Now it was up to her.

6

The San Diego freeway was jammed with late afternoon traffic, and she was startled out of her thoughts by Victor leaning on the horn and swearing. It hadn't helped ease the traffic snarl though, she noticed as he slapped the steering wheel in frustration.

Yet her mind wasn't on the traffic. She was keyed up for the sound of the mobile telephone. Greg could call at any minute and tell Victor to turn back. Victor could switch on the radio and hear the news. So many things could go wrong – and she was powerless to do anything about it.

As they inched towards the city, she became aware of Victor's fleeting glances in the rear-view mirror. Those glances were sly, yet she thought she also recognised a gleam of excitement, of cunning – and it made her shiver. It was as if he knew. As if he was waiting for her to make her move.

She had never felt so trapped. So alone.

Vic was beginning to sweat, despite the air conditioning. The flight was due in less than three hours and if he didn't get off this fucking freeway, he would never make it.

He glanced at his watch, then back to the traffic. They hadn't even reached the stretch of highway which led to LA International yet. They'd only just crossed Carson and by the look of things, it would be one frigging hold up after another.

'Move that bitching rust heap outa' here, asshole!' He

leaned on the horn, the release of his anger coarsening his speech and making him feel little better. It didn't move the traffic any faster either, merely caused a babel of car horns and obscene jestures.

His temper was never far from the surface and now it swelled inside him, making his head ache and his skin fevered. It was at times like these he wished he'd learned to master his emotions with Greg's icy control. But that dormant beast grew and fought to be released and he had to succumb, or he would go crazy.

He drummed his fingers on the steering wheel, glanced in the mirror and saw Gabriella calmly sitting in the back seat.

'Bitch,' he muttered. If it wasn't for her, I'd be in Chicago. A smile twitched the corners of his mouth as he lit a cigarette. She'd soon learn not to mess with the Castlemaines. 'See how cool you are when me and the kid fly outta here,' he muttered through the smoke.

His temper churned and his body heat made his collar tight and his suit a straitjacket. Slamming his fist against the horn he let rip a string of obscenities. But the traffic refused to budge and he began to feel like one of the flies he and Greg used to catch in jars when they were boys. Angry, buzzing and trapped as they'd hit the glass walls.

He ran a finger round his collar, and loosened the hated tie. With a belligerent glance at the driver in the car alongside him, he revved the engine and crept slowly forward.

If I ball this one up there'll be another fucking argument with Greg and I've had enough of his attitude. He might be Dad's favourite, Mom's golden boy, but he'd be nothing without me. Who else would do his dirty work?

As those heated thoughts hurtled through his mind, he pushed away the thrill of fear which threaded its way up his back. Greg was the only man who really frightened him. He could be so cold. So ruthless. Sometimes, it was as if he wasn't human, and Vic knew that Greg, brother or not, was capable of killing him if he screwed up again.

He took another quick glance in the mirror. She was watching him with those cool, untroubled eyes. Arrogant English bitch. I'd like to slit her throat, right here in the back of the car, then run with the kid. Why not just turn off at the next exit, find somewhere quiet, do the business, dump her and run? It would be so easy. So much quicker than all this dumb play acting Greg had ordered. And what was it all for? To prove Greg's superiority in the game of cat and mouse they were playing? To show how clever, how cunning he could be? She knew she'd given the game away. Knew they were watching her. Why not just get it over and done with?

Yet the thought of what Gregory would do to him if he changed the plans poured ice on the heated thoughts. So he screamed abuse at the other drivers and pummelled the horn. He just wanted out. Out of this fucking city. Out of this fucking car. Home to his fucking wife. For a good fuck, he added with a grin at his own wit. He liked that word, it could be spat with such feeling.

Vic saw a gap in the traffic and swiftly changed lanes. A few more minutes and they'd be out of this hell-hole, through Watts and up towards Hollywood. As he drove along the down ramp his temper waned. Harbour Freeway was clear of traffic. It shouldn't take long now.

He lit another cigarette from the stub of the last, but his attention was taken off the road by a persistent tapping on the glass partition.

'What's she want now?' he grumbled. He pressed a button and the glass slid down a few inches. Her face was close. So close he could see the beads of perspiration on her top lip and a tantalising glimpse of lace at her cleavage.

Bastard, Greg, he thought. Always was lucky with women. I'd like to run my tongue down those breasts and give her high-class pussy a poke she'd never forget. A frisson of pleasure tingled in his crotch. Perhaps he'd do just that before he killed her?

The thought sharpened the thrill and he had to squeeze

his knees together. But he kept his gaze on the road and his expression bland as he spoke to her. 'Yeah? What's your problem?'

'Where are we going Vic? Haven't you heard the news?'

He had no idea what she was talking about, his mind was elsewhere. If he glanced over his shoulder, he could just make out the curve of her tits, and the hard nub of her nipples thrusting against her t-shirt. He'd seen her naked. Watched as Greg screwed the hell out of her by the pool the other day. She might give the impression she was colder than a witch's tit, but she'd shown then that she was hot stuff. He'd been aroused by what he'd seen and had had to jerk off, but catching a hint of what she had to offer was proving exciting. It was more erotic, more forbidden when it was under wraps, and he was imagining what it would be like to strip her.

'There's going to be trouble in Watts, Vic. Turn the car around and get back on the San Diego Freeway.'

Who does she think she is, ordering me around? I'm not a servant, a dumb-assed piss boy to be told what to do. No one did that, except Dad and Greg.

'You wanna walk?' His voice was gravelled with lust and resentment as he swerved towards the side of the road and slammed on the brakes.

An angry blast of car horns and the screech of rubber on tarmac came from all sides, but he took no notice.

She didn't meet his gaze in the mirror. 'No. But Vic, it isn't safe to go this way.'

'If you don't wanna walk, then let me decide what to do,' he said coldly as he shut her behind the glass barrier.

He could see her mouthing at him, but he took no notice.

'Stupid bitch doesn't know what she's talking about. Watts is the fast way and I'm in a hurry,' he muttered as he slammed the car into drive and hit the accelerator.

Gabriella slumped. It was pointless trying to make him see reason and she'd almost blown it by getting into a panic. If he was heading for the airport, then she would have to be ready for anything. She closed her eyes and willed her racing pulse to steady.

The streets of downtown LA seemed unnaturally quiet. A few youths stood on the street corners, their eyes enviously following the car as it raced past, but they didn't seem about to riot, even though she could feel the tension and hatred in those smouldering looks. Dismembered cars lay like rusty, broken toys against the sidewalks. Junk food litter lay in the gutters and flapped under the wheels of the Cadillac as they passed the rows of dilapidated houses and poor shop fronts.

She heard the roar of an engine close behind her and quickly looked over her shoulder. A beaten up Chevy was hanging on their tail, livid in bright orange and purple livery. She caught an impression of the occupants behind the swinging mascots that hung above the dash. Dark faces, pointing fingers, open mouths. Even through the closed windows of the limousine she could hear the deafening rap music and feel the hate pouring from those abusive lips.

Looking back at Vic, she saw him glance in the rear-view mirror and felt the car pick up speed. He too must have felt the danger.

The twelve-mile stretch of Harbour Freeway seemed endless as they were pursued, but the Chevy didn't have the power to catch them, and once Victor had reached the boundaries of LA itself, the youths stopped and headed back to their neighbourhood.

City Hall finally loomed in the distance and she could see the mass of the LA Community Hospital which lay off to the right of Olympic Boulevard. Gabriella took a series of deep breaths. The plans hadn't been changed. This was it.

Victor swung the limousine into a parking bay and killed the engine.

Gabriella met and held his glance in the mirror and in that

moment they recognised and accepted the parts they would each have to play in the coming minutes.

It was Gabriella who was first to look away. She had read the contempt in his eyes, seen the twist of sadistic anticipation to his mouth. The knowledge didn't change her plans. It sharpened her perception. She was ready.

With the straps of her bag over her shoulder, she checked the harness on the sling, grasped the hold-all and stepped out of the car.

Victor was waiting for her. He slammed the door, pressed the central locking button on the remote control, then took her firmly by the arm.

Gabriella pulled away. 'Don't manhandle me. I'm quite capable of walking without your assistance.' She spoke loudly and clearly, each word dropping like iced crystals into the heat of the late afternoon, the very British accent making people turn to look at them.

She saw the flit of uncertainty in his eyes and whilst he hesitated, she moved away and began walking towards the hospital entrance.

They both heard the buzz of the car phone.

She was aware of Victor's hesitancy, the slowing of his footsteps beside her. Saw him glance towards the car, then back, his expression anxious.

She took a firmer grip on the baby. 'Hadn't you better answer that?' she snapped. 'It might be my husband with more orders.'

The deliberate sarcasm was to unbalance his confidence, and she felt a surge of hope as he hesitated, his gaze darting back and forth between her and the insistent buzz of the phone. He was torn between his need to answer it and his orders to stay with her.

He reached for her, but she twisted sharply aside and turned towards the doors that were now so close. 'I'll be on the third floor. You'd better not keep Greg waiting. He wouldn't like it,' she threw back at him.

Each step she took was a heartbeat. Every inch of that paved walkway a mile. She focused on the doors. But they seemed to remain out of reach.

'Shit!' he spat as he clenched his fists in an agony of frustration. 'I told Greg this wouldn't friggin' work.' The bitch had him on a string and there were too many people around if she caused a scene. He would lose sight of her in a minute, but if he didn't answer the phone, the shit would really hit the fan.

He watched her approach the doors and knew he was in danger of losing her as well as incurring his brother's wrath.

'Jesus H Christ! What do I do?'

He cursed his carelessness, jabbed the remote control and flung open the car door. He should have taken the frigging phone with him. Greg had told him to always carry it, but his mind had been on screwing the ice queen and now he was in deep shit.

The telephone sat in the hollow between the seats, a red light blinking like an angry eye as it buzzed for attention. The sound of it shredded the already frayed edges of his temper, making his fingers clumsy. He threw a glance over his shoulder.

Gabriella was now almost at the doors. A few more steps and she would be out of sight.

Snatching up the phone, Victor slammed the door and began to run. Locking the car didn't matter. If he lost the bitch now, he would have no need for it. Or for anything else. The persistent buzz spurred him on as he wrestled to answer it.

'What?' he gasped as he lumbered out of the car park. He was closer to her now, but if she went through those doors he didn't stand a cat in hell's chance of catching her.

'Victor! What are you playing at? Where's Nicholas, and why didn't you have Jake along as escort?' Greg's voice was sharp on the other end of the line.

'We're at the hospital. Everything's fine. I didn't need Jake,' gasped Victor. He tried to sound casual, but it wasn't easy to talk and run at the same time when you were overweight, and even he could hear the panic in his voice.

'Get them out of there, Victor. Now. The cops got off, and there's going to be real trouble. I've altered the arrangements with the doctor – he isn't part of the trap any more, so he won't be expecting you. Bring them back to New York. Both of them.'

Vic had almost reached the doors. He could still see the tan and yellow stripes of Gabriella's shirt as she weaved through the main entrance hall.

'OK,' was all he could manage before he disconnected the line to his brother. His breathing was jagged, his shirt clung damply to his back and his collar was strangling him. Riot? Cops? He had no idea what Greg was talking about, but if he didn't catch the bitch his balls would be in the grinder.

The telephone was stubbornly refusing to fit into his pocket, so he looked away to deal with it. When he looked up again, the striped blouse and long blonde hair had disappeared.

He began to run towards his last sighting of her. Had she taken the elevator to the third floor, or was she still somewhere here in the crowded foyer?

His feverish gaze swept over the shifting wheelchairs and trolleys, hobbling, bandaged patients and white coated interns. The fear was bitter. He couldn't lose her. His life depended upon it.

As the door slid open, Gabriella felt the adrenalin surge. Her footsteps quickened and her heart seemed lodged in her throat. A glance over her shoulder confirmed that Vic was lumbering across the car park.

He was close, but not close enough if she moved quickly.

'Hold on, darling. This could be rough,' she murmured to Nick. She weaved through the people in the foyer, her stride long and purposeful as she searched for a door, a way out – a staircase.

'The lifts are too obvious,' she muttered as she pressed the button to call one. Turning swiftly away, she headed for the east wing. If she could find Accident and Emergency, she stood a chance. It was always chaotic.

Another glance over her shoulder. Vic was standing in the middle of the foyer. He hadn't seen her. Yet.

She began to run, holding Nick close, trying not to jolt him. There had to be somewhere she could hide in this labyrinth of corridors and walkways.

All too soon her breath was jagged and her muscles burned under the weight of the hold-all. Still she ran. Up flights of stairs and down back corridors. Along hallways that seemed to have no end. Past startled patients and nurses who called out to her.

Nick was screaming, and the sound of it ricocheted off the walls and resounded in her head. Yet she couldn't stop – couldn't risk the possibility of being caught.

'Where the hell am I?' she gasped as she stopped for breath in a dimly lit corridor.

She hitched Nick closer. His angry cries pierced her eardrums, and her head was beginning to throb, but it didn't matter. Nothing mattered but their freedom. She turned away from what appeared to be the kitchens, and crashed through a series of swing doors.

'Hey, lady. What you doin' here? This is for hospital staff.' A fat porter loomed out of one of the doorways and barred her flight.

'Sorry – got lost,' she gasped before dodging away. She pushed through heavy rubber doors and headed in another direction. The long corridor stretched before her. A line of doors on either side were closed and silent. Do I dare try one? Is there a way out through there?

'Don't be daft,' she hissed. 'You're on the fifth bloody floor. What you planning to do, abseil, hang-glide?' The panic rose as she headed for the stairs and she bit her lip. I look suspicious enough – talking to myself is a one-way ticket to the funny farm.

The bank of lifts lined an entire wall, and as she crossed the polished floor, one of them opened.

Victor.

Their eyes met and Gabriella knew what fear really was. She could feel it in his hate-filled eyes, taste it in her mouth, hear it in the drumbeat of her heart.

He elbowed his way out of the lift, but Gabriella was already running. Vic was fat. Vic was out of condition. Vic was as frightened as she. Surely she had a chance to outrun him, outwit him?

Down the stairs three at a time. Feet slipping, sliding on the smooth stone – fingers gripping the baby, bag slamming against her thigh. Breath caught, hot, dry and aching in her throat. Faster, Gabby. Run like you've never run before.

Vic's heavy footsteps pounded behind her. She could hear the rasp of his breath, the wheeze of his lungs. He was too close, too close.

The last step loomed and she was back in the foyer. There was no time to look behind her, no time for breath, or time to rest. Vic was on the flight above and descending fast.

She headed for the lifts. The door was open. Maybe she could reach it before it closed.

Her feet barely touched the floor as she raced towards that slowly disappearing chance of escape. Nearer and nearer she came, faster and faster the doors came to closing.

'Stop! Wait!' She yelled over Nick's screams, ramming her foot in the gap.

There was a rumble of discontent, but she ignored it. Her attention was focused on the opening, on the sound of the footsteps behind her.

Gabriella stumbled in and turned to face the concourse. He was at the bottom of the stairs. He was looking around. Then he was heading for the lift. Nick's cries had given them away.

The doors closed with a sigh and the lift began to move. The flight up was swift and she wondered what to do next. Victor was on the ground floor, but he too could catch a lift. She had to find some way out of this place. But how?

She jabbed the fifteenth-floor button and waited. At least she was getting a chance to catch her breath. She would need it for the stairs again if Vic caught up with her.

The doors slid open and she looked up and down the long corridor. Empty. The bank of lifts was silent, the yellow buttons tracing their passage through the central artery of the great building. The nearest one was on the twelfth floor. Was Victor in it?

The hold-all dragged on her arm. The straps of the bag and sling dug into her shoulders making her neck muscles scream. Yet she had to ignore the pain – had to find a way out. And soon. Vic must have phoned for help. The place could be crawling with Greg's men within minutes.

She looked around her, and realised she was hopelessly lost. There were no signs anywhere and the silence was ominous. Trying the door handles, she peered through windows. Everything seemed to be locked up, the staff gone for the day. Then a handle dropped and a door opened. Gabriella felt a surge of hope. There was a fire exit on the other side of the room.

Weaving round the desks and silent computers, she yanked on the heavy iron bar. The heat from the late afternoon sun bounced off the white washed walls and concrete, hitting her with such force she gasped.

But she had finally discovered a way out of the hospital.

Dropping the hold-all and clasping her hands beneath Nick's bottom, she leaned against the hot wall and tried to soothe him.

His screams quietened to sobs as her breathing returned to normal, but she could see he was very distressed, and there was no time to do anything about it. She too was uncomfortable, her shirt and t-shirt clung to her, her sweater strangled her neck and her hair trailed over her face in damp tendrils. She felt no jubilation – there were many miles to go before she would be home and safe.

Nick whimpered and squirmed and she wished she had time to give him a drink, but he would have to wait. As she took stock of her position, she realised she was on a balcony terrace at the back of the hospital. It was a peaceful, sunny place, high above the city, but if she stayed, it could become a trap.

There was a shallow flight of steps leading away from the terrace, and she picked up her hold-all, tucked Nick more firmly against her and headed for it. It led to another terrace, then another as it snaked its way down the side of the building. Heights were her one phobia, and she gripped the banister that was the only protection between her and the streets below as she began the long descent. She couldn't look down, for the building seemed to be swaying and the sight of those distant, tiny figures below made her head spin.

Her calf muscles ached, her arms felt leaden and the headache had taken over, but now she could see a road, and behind that road she recognised Wiltshire Boulevard and the Hollywood Freeway. There would be taxis on Wiltshire.

With her fear of heights firmly blocked, she hurtled down the smooth white steps, not stopping until she reached the tarmac. Nick was squirming against her, his demanding cries jarring her nerves. As she paused to catch her breath, she stroked back the hair which lay in damp curls on his head, and wiped away his tears with the edge of her shirt. It would have to do. Her only priority was to get as far from the hospital as possible. Vic could still be here. Still watching. Waiting. She had to stay focused.

With a quick glance behind her, she made her way to Wiltshire Boulevard. The wide, beautiful altar to Mammon stretched to the left and right of her, the great towers of steel and glass almost touching the sky. Famous department stores and hotels lined the street in both direction and she could almost smell the wealth above the exhaust fumes. She'd shopped here in I. Magnin's on the corner of Kingsley, and had eaten in the rooftop restaurants of some of the hotels. But she'd never been here alone before – and for a moment she was confused.

Which way to go? And why weren't there any taxis? In New York you took your life in your hands to cross a street, the yellow cabs were so numerous. But here – nothing.

Then she remembered. California didn't have cruising cabs with ticking meters. Here, you had to order one by phone from the lobby of a hotel or restaurant. This wasn't New York or London, there was no such thing as a taxi rank.

Gabriella was suddenly aware of how conspicuous she must look, standing there on the corner of the street with the child strapped to her chest, weighed down with luggage. She had to get under cover. Victor must have alerted the others by now.

Walking past the first three hotels, she entered the fourth, crossed the lobby and headed for the car rental desk.

Compared to that lot, I must look a strange sight, she thought grimly as she hurried past the elegantly groomed women who were taking tea in the foyer. What with the bags and the baby, and the sweaty clothes, I must appear demented. She found humour in the situation and grinned. Good thing I'm past caring.

'I want to hire a car,' she said quietly to the platinum blonde, Monroe clone behind the counter.

Wide blue eyes looked at her through fake black lashes and Gabriella noticed the twitch of a delicately plucked eyebrow, before the wide customary smile showed the girl's perfect white teeth.

'When would you like the vehicle, ma'am? I have very few available for today.'

Gabriella dropped the hold-all and reached under Nick to get to her handbag. 'I want a car in the next fifteen minutes. I don't care what make it is, just get me one. Here's my passport and driver's licence.'

It's a good thing the Americans are used to people being

pushy, she thought dryly. A receptionist in London would have told me to shove it.

She was close to hysteria, and the blonde's slow, methodical trawl through the passport and driving licence with her long, red fingernails made her skin crawl. She wanted to tell her to hurry up. To get on with it for Christ's sake. Every moment was a moment nearer to Victor finding her. Couldn't she see she was in a hurry?

Resisting the urge to look behind her each time the revolving doors hissed over the carpet, she stared at a point on the wall just over the receptionist's shoulder. She could see the lobby in the ornate mirror and could keep watch that way.

'How long would you like the rental for, ma'am? We do a special deal if it's over a week. For the Chevrolet Chevette, which is the only one we have ready to go at this time, it would be $30 a day or $200 for the week. That would include unlimited mileage, but of course there would be insurance on top of that.' She looked up from her computer screen and stared back at Gabriella, the brilliant smile pasted over her thick make-up.

Gabriella was very aware of the disdainful scrutiny sweeping over her dishevelled appearance as she tried to decide. I have enough cash on me, but it will leave me with nothing. I'll have to use the card. Which might not be a bad thing, she reasoned. They could trace the card, know I've hired a car – but they would have no idea of where I was headed. I might even manage to get out of LA tonight.

'I'll take the week, and I want a child's car seat as well,' she said firmly as she handed over the American Express Gold card. Greg wouldn't have had time to put a block on it yet, and they never checked gold cards. I might as well use it whilst I can.

'Thank you, ma'am. If you could just fill in this form, then sign it here, here and here. I'll ring through to the lot, and have the car brought around.'

Gabriella almost snatched the forms, then began to fill in the details. Good grief, she thought. They want to know everything but your bra size. Yet, finally, it was done.

The blonde looked through the forms with agonising slowness, then ran a check on her card, her fingernails drumming a tattoo on the polished oak desk.

Gabriella stood alone as the other people swirled around her in the hushed opulence of the lobby. She could feel the perspiration trickle coldly over her ribs. I must look worse than I thought for her to run a check.

'Thank you, ma'am. Have a nice day.' The smile was switched on in full neon, then extinguished just as rapidly as she turned to her computer and the next customer.

Gabriella picked up her bags, shoved the documents in her trouser pocket and sat behind a vast potted palm where she could keep an eye on the main door. To sit was a relief, but Nick was screaming to be fed and they were both hot and sticky. It would have been nice to find the rest rooms and wash and change him, and run a brush through her hair. But she couldn't afford to miss the man with the car.

She caught the disapproving glances from the tight, surgically lifted faces of the women around her and dug into the hold-all. She had a bottle that she'd filled earlier with milk. She tested it. It was warm and Nick didn't seem to mind the taste of the rubber teat. At least it's shut him up for a bit, she thought wearily. Perhaps now I'll get a chance to catch my breath and prepare for the next hurdle.

As she sat behind the palm, she kept a wary eye on the street. Several times she drew back sharply as she thought she recognised Vic's face in the crowd.

'Mrs Castlemaine? Here are the keys to your car, ma'am.'

Gabriella was jolted from her surveillance by his voice. The speaker was a tall, slender youth with a mop of blonde hair and a tan that had turned his skin to mahogany. The car rental company's logo was stitched into the lapel of his breast pocket.

'May I help you with bags, ma'am, while you take the

baby?' He was smiling and helpful and she was relieved to see him.

'Thanks. I'm in a hurry. Where's the car?'

'Just outside, ma'am. This way.' He took the hold-all and waited for her to follow.

Gabriella kept the bottle in Nick's mouth with one hand and eased her bag on her shoulder with the other. At last, she thought. I'm on the move.

The little car, which looked so much like the Astra she'd had back in England, gleamed white in the gloom of dusk, and she'd never been so pleased to see anything in her life. Gabriella quickly strapped Nick in, then climbed behind the wheel and listened impatiently as the man explained the mechanics of driving an automatic.

'And don't forget ma'am, we drive on the right.' He grinned and gave her a ghost of a wink.

Gabriella took out her purse, found a few cents and dimes and thrust them into his waiting hand. She felt embarrassed she couldn't give him more, but he would have to be satisfied.

His smile slipped a fraction as he stepped away from the car, but Gabriella had already forgotten him.

Greg's Cadillac was cruising towards her up the Boulevard and she could see Vic behind the wheel.

7

The repetitive buzz of the telephone was driving Vic crazy. Yet he couldn't answer it. For it would as sure as hell sign his death warrant if he told his brother the truth. But if he didn't answer it soon, Greg would guess what had happened and telephone the house. Then he would really be in the crapper.

'Shit, shit, shit,' he spat as he pummelled the steering wheel. The bitch had really done for him this time. Outsmarted him – outrun him – disappeared into the chaos of LA without a fucking trace, and there was nothing he could do about it.

His body was slick with sweat and his heart pounded so alarmingly, he wondered if he was about to have a heart attack.

'I'll get you, you cunt, and when I do, you'll know pain.'

He ground his teeth as he drove along Wiltshire, off to Olympic, back to Pershing Square, then past City Hall.

'She must be here. She can't possibly get very far with the kid hanging round her neck,' he muttered as he peered right and left at the sidewalks.

The thought that she might be at the hospital still nagged. He'd been all over the frigging place, searched everywhere, but there'd been no sign.

He chewed on a cigar as the vitriol churned. What if the bitch had merely hidden, waited him out, then tricked him into believing she'd left?

Victor opened the window and spat out the cigar.

'Bitch! It's not fair. Greg expects too much.' He wanted to cut her, to slash that pretty flesh and grind his boot in her face. Then he would screw her. 'I'll teach you to cross me, Gabriella Castlemaine. You'll beg for death before I'm through with you.'

The graphic images those words conjured up didn't cool his temper; they merely gave it an edge, a focus on which to concentrate. He was willing her to come out of hiding. Willing her to show her face so he could let that inner, rumbling volcano explode and the molten lava of his fury pump into her.

And the telephone still buzzed.

It was almost dark now, but the neon lights gave that darkness an eerie glow. He finally parked outside a hotel on Wiltshire, and lit another cheroot. Nothing about this place was real. Yet the thought that this might be the last few hours he had on this earth made him sick. He didn't want to die in this place of pretend. He didn't want to die at all. Yet, it was inevitable. Greg probably wouldn't do it himself, but somebody would get the order and he'd get a bullet in the brain when he least expected it.

He puffed on the cheroot. The buzzing telephone had become a familiar background noise, and he could almost ignore it. The anger simmered, but with each drag on the cheroot, Victor could feel the drip, drip, drip, of icy calm wear away the edges of that heat.

His thoughts drifted with the smoke as he looked back over the years. Even though I'm the younger brother, I am director of the Chicago branch, with a big house in the suburbs and an apartment block in the city. As a Castlemaine, I have a great deal of power. Power, and respect, which I've earned, despite Greg. I am a wealthy man in my own right.

'Hasn't brought much happiness though, has it?' he muttered as the depression came in the ebb of the adrenalin rush. An arranged marriage to a woman I don't love, just so Dad could combine two conglomerates and make even more money. I'm treated like a servant by my brother, with no time or freedom to do what I want.

The resentment was cold. I've always tried my best for the family, but now, because of that stuck-up, English whore, I'm in deep trouble, and I don't know what to do.

Staring out of the window, eyes misted in thought, he idly watched the white rental Chevette screech round a corner and disappear down a side street.

The stench of impending doom was strong, and as he turned his attention to the telephone – to the blinking red light – he knew he would have to answer it.

Gabriella was lost. All the streets looked the same once she'd left Wiltshire and now she drove out of sheer desperation. It was dark now, but there was a curious red glow in the sky, and away from the neon of Hollywood and Wiltshire, the streets looked empty and dangerous.

'Where is everyone?' she muttered. 'And why so little traffic?'

She turned off into another street, with the vague idea that she was heading towards the airport. But it all looked so different at night and she'd never driven herself in LA before. She could be going round in circles.

Peering out of the window, she realised with a chill that she'd driven into one of the poorer parts of downtown LA. The rich department stores and gaudy tower blocks had given way to shanty houses, mean streets and ramshackle convenience stores.

Panic rose as she searched for a street sign – any sign at all to tell her where she was. But this wasn't England with its neat white name plates on every corner. This was ghetto USA where nothing was neat or ordered.

With a glance at the dashboard clock, she realised it was almost nine. She'd been on her own for more than four hours. Nick was still grizzling, she was still in LA and her nerves were shredding with every minute that passed.

'I can't stay here. I'm nowhere near the bloody airport. What the hell do I do now?' She tried another turning. There must be a freeway somewhere, if only she could find it.

The dark streets and silent pavements were beginning to close in and she switched on the radio for company. Static hissed and after twiddling the knobs, she managed to get a reasonable reception.

'The mood here is ugly and as the minutes tick by more and more arrive to swell the ranks. There has been no violence yet, but it will come.'

The reporter's voice was calm, but Gabriella could hear the angry chanting in the background.

'Kill the pigs. Kill the pigs. Kill the pigs.'

'Los Angeles is on the brink of a street war, which has been ignited by the jury's verdict of not guilty, this afternoon.' There was the sound of a microphone falling to the ground and the transmission was abruptly cut.

'The jury's out. They let them off! But they couldn't have – not with that evidence. Christ Almighty, what now?' Gabriella slowed the car as she concentrated on the news report that had been resumed.

'I can see a man lying on the street,' shouted the reporter through the static. 'He's just been dragged from his truck and beaten. His face is covered in blood. He's trying to get up. Nobody is going to help him.'

Gabriella glanced back at Nick and bit her lip.

'The situation is out of control. I'm getting out of here.' The reporter's voice was urgent, filled with fear, and the transmission was cut.

Gabriella switched off the radio and looked up. She'd almost drawn to a halt as she'd listened, but in those few moments things had changed.

She was on the intersection of Florence and Normandie. The very heart of Watts and Inglewood, and as if from nowhere, people had emerged from the shadows, crowding the sidewalks, spilling into the street. Menacing and silent they began to converge on the car.

'Oh, shit.' Her mouth dried and her hands were slick on the steering wheel.

A black Trans-Am roared past her, scattering the clusters of black youths that loitered in the middle of the road with their baseball bats and iron bars. With a blast of its horn, it swerved off the road in front of her and headed west, the tyres screaming on tarmac, black smoke pumping from the exhaust.

Nick began to cry, the sound of it loud against the throaty mutter and chant of the youths who were leading the advance. The only way out was to follow the Trans-Am. She slammed the gear up and put her foot to the floor.

The car didn't budge.

A rock came hurtling from nowhere and crashed against the passenger door, jolting the little car on its chassis, snapping the seat belt against her neck.

The screams of the baby were loud in the confined space, the sight of the looming mob beginning to fill the windscreen.

She froze.

A giant of a man stepped out of the crowd, a meat cleaver swinging from a hand that looked as if it could break her neck with the snap of a finger. His cut-off jeans showed tree trunk legs, his torn singlet, the black ripple of muscle. In his other hand was a rock the size of a baseball.

Time stopped. He swung back his arm. The rock hurtled towards her, closer, closer, until she could almost see each tiny grain that made up that lump of granite. With a metallic clang it hit the door, bounced, then ricocheted through the glass and fell on the seat beside her.

The world was full of flying shards – full of noise – full of hate. Dark faces, dark night, dark deeds. She had to get out of here.

The crash of the rock had crystalised her awareness. Of course the car wouldn't bloody move. It was a sodding automatic and she'd put it in park. Ramming it back into drive, she slammed her foot on the accelerator and raced towards the mob, then turned the wheel and spun the car into a one-hundred-and-eighty-degree turn.

Nick screamed from the back seat. The chant of the mob became howls of fury. Rocks thudded against the side of the car. Iron bars streaked like javelins, screeching against the metal and falling with a clang onto the street. A shower of stones pelted the roof and spat through the broken window to land on the floor at her feet.

Gabriella floored the accelerator again and sped off on the wrong side of the road. Fists slammed the bonnet. Bodies hurtled out of the way. It was them or her. Dustbins scattered and rolled, screams of abuse followed her ragged path and missiles skidded off the bodywork as she shot past the crowded sidewalks.

She kept going. Two blocks – three – four – five. She was doing over eighty. Red lights no longer mattered. Intersections didn't exist. Give way – no give way.

A glance in the mirror revealed the three cars giving chase. Their occupants shouting to the mob who lined the sidewalks as they roared through what had become no man's land in a war zone.

Gabriella kept her foot to the floor, oblivious to the screams of the baby in the back. If she didn't get out of here, neither of them would survive.

The needle climbed to ninety as she roared down another fifteen or twenty blocks. The mob was no longer on the streets, and only one car still pursued her.

Then she saw the railway bridge up ahead and the up-ramp onto the highway. She slammed her foot on the brake.

The car slewed left and right as the tyres tried to hold. The rubber squealed and smoked as she fought the wheel. Jamming her foot back on the accelerator, the car rocked dangerously on its springs.

But it held – stayed upright and leaped forward. She was under the bridge and up the slip road and onto the freeway. The pursuing driver obviously hadn't learned the evasive skills that were second nature to her after the course in Hereford, and she was vaguely aware of the crump as it hit the concrete pillar beneath the bridge.

'If I stay on this, then it has to head away from the troubles,' she muttered as she kept up her speed.

She realised how wrong she was as she recognised the road and headed back towards City Hall.

A grey pall of smoke hung over downtown LA. Cars burned at the side of the road, youths smashed shop windows and ran amok as the Vietnamese shop owners fired rifles from their rooftop vantage points. Flames leaped almost three hundred feet from an enormous tower block out near the airport, and she knew she would never make it out of the city that way. The world had gone mad, and she was in the very eye of that storm of hatred.

'I'll have to try and get out through Beverley Hills. Surely this insanity couldn't have reached that far?'

As she drove quickly through the streets, she could see the bright red fire trucks. The flashing neon lights of the police vehicles and the scurrying, crouched figures of the looters. When she crossed the intersection of Fairfax and Beverley Boulevards, she was caught in a traffic diversion. There was a fire next to a movie studio, and the flames were shooting up into the hazy, smoke shrouded sky and licking at the building's skeleton. The Beverley Hills fire department was dowsing the blaze and she could see the bewildered residents coming out of their homes, almost sleepwalking as they were faced with the devastation.

Gabriella's frustration grew as she waited for the traffic to syphon through the roadblock and away from the fire. When she was finally clear and on her way again, she decided to find another freeway – and head east.

*　　*　　*

Greg had realised long ago that Vic would not answer the phone, and had made contingency plans. His men were out in force. He wearily rubbed his face. A coldness settled in his gut. She had betrayed him. He could sense her departure as vividly as if he'd witnessed it.

The television screen flickered light into the darkened room. It was eleven o'clock in New York – eight in California. He stared at the screen, his fists bunched on his knees. He didn't move, couldn't summon the will to do anything. He'd always been so strong, so capable of holding back until just the right moment, and the habit could never be broken. Not even now.

Gabriella's face was in front of him. Laughing in the sunlight, drowsy with sleep, dreamy with love and desire. Each emotion etched on her face so clearly, it was almost as if she was in the room with him. His vision blurred momentarily, but was soon restored. She wasn't worth his tears. She'd betrayed him by leaving – and for that she would die.

But what about my son? I must find him, even if it takes the rest of my life. He's my flesh and blood, the heir to all I've worked for. Greg lifted his chin, and between half-closed lids, stared at the images on the television screen.

The reporter was filming from a helicopter as it hovered over Los Angeles, his voice barely audible above the clatter of the propellers.

Greg turned up the volume, his attention riveted.

'There are fires raging on both sides of Harbor, through Inglewood, and as far out as Santa Monica Freeway. Looting is rife as black and Hispanic youths rampage through the streets with any weapon they can get hold of. I can see baseball bats, guns, iron bars, lengths of timber.'

Greg's breath hissed through his teeth as he watched the unfolding scenes of violence.

'I'm over Manchester Avenue now and the scene below is reminiscent of the behaviour that put four policemen in the dock.' The reporter was shouting over the roar of the swirling blades, his face a mask of horror.

'A gang of black youths are pulling a man out of a car. They are beating him, but no one dares come to the aid of the motorist and he appears badly wounded.'

The camera panned closer and the youths lifted their fists in defiance, overturned the car and set it alight.

'Jesus H Christ. Nicholas is in the middle of all that!' Greg reached for the telephone and rang the seafront house.

It was answered immediately.

'Jake. Get all the men off the estate and have them join the others in the city. Gabriella and the boy are somewhere in the middle of the trouble. He must be found.'

'The Mayor has enforced a curfew, Mr Castlemaine. I don't know if we'll be allowed anywhere near LA tonight.'

'Fuck the curfew. Go and find them. Keep me posted.'

He slammed down the phone, then tried the car again. There was still no reply and with a snort of fury, he pressed to disconnect, then dialled the airport where he kept his private plane.

'I need a flight plan for LA immediately.'

'I'm sorry sir, all flights have been rerouted to San Francisco. LA International is closed until the civil disturbance is under control.'

'I'll take full responsibility. Even fly the darn thing myself – but I need to leave within the hour.'

'The airport is closed to all flights, sir. The fires are making it hazardous to take off and land. I'm sorry. I can't help you.'

'Look here, you son-of-a-bitch. This is Gregory Castlemaine and when I say I want to take my plane to LA, then I get my plane to LA. Understood?'

He heard the swallow before the man replied, and the higher pitch of his voice as the words spluttered in his haste to appease.

'Perhaps I can arrange for you land at Whiteman Airport. That's east of the San Fernando Valley. It's about as close as I can make it, Mr Castelmaine?'

The question hung between them as Greg gripped the receiver.

'Do it. I'll be there in twenty minutes. Have my pilot on stand-by with the engines rolling.'

Greg hung up, then redialled. Within the next ten minutes he'd pulled together a team of men to go with him. Their brief was to find Gabriella and his brother. The net was tightening. Someone somewhere would find them, and when they did, they were dead.

Vic threw the cheroot out, pressed the button and closed the window. He'd been listening to the radio reports and could see the red glow in the sky.

He gave a wry smile. 'It'll give me some cover, that's for sure. No one in their right mind would be looking for me in the middle of all this, and I need to buy myself some time before I have to face Greg.'

The telephone had stopped ringing as he'd reached to answer it. He knew Greg would never forgive him, and for that he was sorry. Although he didn't have much love for his elder brother, he respected his position and the way he could organise.

He switched on the engine and headed away from the trouble areas. If he could make it out towards the Ventura Freeway, then he could head for Frisco. What he would do then, he had little idea – just getting out of here was a start.

As he drove, he had the uneasy feeling he was being followed, yet as he checked his rear-view mirror, he realised that paranoia had begun to set in and the road behind him was clear.

'It's something I'll have to get used to if I don't go back,' he muttered. He tried to shrug off the feeling of doom, but it stayed with him. He knew too much about the cartel. Knew too many names and faces to be able to just walk away and hope to stay alive.

After driving for several hours, he stopped outside Santa Barbara at a small diner. Ordering a steak and a side dish of fries, onion rings and mushrooms, he sipped the ice cold

Coors and waited for his food. He'd done well to get so far in one night, perhaps he could rest in the motel he'd just passed and finish the journey tomorrow.

The thought sat for a while and became more pleasant as the bottle of Coors emptied. His back ached, the sweat had dried and his clothes stank. There was a grittiness in his eyes and his limbs felt heavy and sluggish.

He smiled at the waitress who dumped his plate in front of him and ordered another Coors. It would do no harm to get some sleep. Who would think of looking for him here? If Gabriella could disappear, then so could he.

After his meal and several more beers, he turned the car around and headed for the motel. Not bothering to switch on the light, or undress, he slumped across the bed and was soon asleep.

Yet his dreams were vivid and disturbing. Greg was standing over him, the English bitch beside him. They were smiling as Los Angeles burned behind them – but there was no humour in their eyes.

'You failed, Vic – and you've got to be punished.' Greg's voice was low and menacing as he flicked open the switchblade and advanced.

Victor reared up in the bed, his heart pounding. But the nightmare had only just begun – he was not alone.

8

Gabriella had reached the crossroads of the desert. Nevada lay to the east, Arizona to the south – California was several hours behind her.

The motel sprawled across the plot of tarmac in an untidy jumble of weatherbeaten cabins linked by a wooden walk-way. The trellis work which laced the fringe of the verandah was almost toothless and the wood showed through cracks in the paint. A neon sign buzzed and flickered against the purple haze of night, and only half the message was illuminated. The place looked deserted and forgotten by the side of the highway – incongruous against the modern Circle K with its brash electric glare and plate glass windows.

Gabriella was exhausted. It was time to stop. Time to fill the tank, buy coffee and feed and change the baby. She'd driven all night, and her hands ached from gripping the steering wheel, yet the fear hadn't left her. She could feel the squirm of it in the pit of her stomach, and knew the hysteria had to be controlled, for if she gave it full rein, she would be lost.

As she regarded the bright lights of the late-night store, she realised her eyes were gritty and her mouth dry. Yet these minor irritations were eclipsed by the headache. It was as if she hadn't slept for days, but she knew that when she did, she wouldn't be able to dispel the images of those dark faces, or the sounds of the animal cries of the pursuing mob she'd left behind her.

She drove into the forecourt and parked. Now she'd stopped,

she felt drained. It was as though by switching off the engine, she'd switched off the nervous energy which had kept her going. She just wanted to sleep, and the thought of crisp cotton sheets and a comfortable bed for a few hours was very tempting.

Her eyelids drooped and she sank her forehead to her hands.

'No!' she gasped as she shook herself awake. 'Not enough miles between me and Victor. Not enough hours since leaving LA.' Dragging away from the steering wheel, she tried to focus on anything that might stimulate her senses.

The neon hummed and stuttered at the motel, and the glass in the store window splintered shards of light over the black tarmac. She blinked and rubbed her face until it tingled. Then she turned to look at Nick.

He had finally stopped crying about fifty miles back, and now his head lolled on his shoulder as he slept, but his little face was swollen with tears and his hair clung to his head in damp tendrils.

Gabriella freed him from the car seat harness and held him. He was a reminder of the reason for their escape. A warning that every moment spent here on the highway was a moment lost.

'But it's so peaceful here, Nick. So beautiful. Surely it wouldn't hurt to stay just a little while?'

After the mayhem of Los Angeles, there was absolute silence on the desert highway. The mountains rose purple and blue in the distance and the sky was now a deep sepia wash above the hard-baked red earth. The car engine ticked as it cooled – marking time – distancing her from the reality that was California.

'Just a moment, Nick. That's all I need. Just . . .' Her chin drooped to her chest and she felt sleep wash over her. It was warm and dark and oh, so inviting.

With a jerk of her head, she took a firmer grip of the baby and struggled out of the car. 'Petrol. I must get more petrol. It's almost light and I'm wasting time,' she said crossly.

The act of moving away from the car brought back the nervous energy. Where it had come from, she had no idea. She was plumbing the depths of her strength and soon it would be bankrupt. With the baby in the crook of her arm, she wrestled with the petrol gun. But the harder she pulled, the more firmly it stayed put.

'You have to pay for the gas first lady.'

The voice booming into the silence made her jump. With a grunt of exasperation, she hitched Nick further up her hip and strode into the store. She'd forgotten that in some petrol stations in America, the mighty dollar had to be handed over first and the pumps were locked.

'That's the last time I use the card,' she said to Nick as she emerged some time later with a bag of groceries. 'Too nerve-racking. Thank goodness he didn't check it.'

With a slow smile of cunning, she dropped the gold card on the forecourt. Someone was bound to find it and, hopefully, use it – a move in chess called *en prise*, when the piece is exposed to capture – but is in reality a ploy to protect something more valuable.

Lying Nick on the passenger seat and dumping the shopping on the floor, she filled the petrol tank, then drove away.

About ten miles down the road, she left the highway and parked on a deserted track which threaded aimlessly through low dunes and acres of cacti. The hillocks were high enough and the road winding enough to give her perfect shelter from the highway.

It was still cool in the Mojave Desert, the sun had not yet fully risen. Yet she knew that in a few hours the sky would be bleached to stone-washed denim and the heat would become a furnace blast.

Nick was yelling again. His legs and arms waved stiffly in anger as he screwed up his face and gave full vent to his fury.

'I don't blame you, love. I know just how you feel,' she said wryly as she picked him up and changed him. The scream was there, deep down inside her, but she couldn't let it escape – she had to keep control.

Nick was soaking wet and hot with his temper. Once he was changed and comfortable, she held him to her breast. He clenched greedily onto her nipple and sucked furiously, his little fists tightly bunched against her, his eyes screwed shut in concentration.

Gabriella closed her eyes and was soothed.

As his hunger ebbed, so did his frantic sucking, and soon he was asleep. She laid him back in the chair and strapped him in. Opening the car windows to catch some of the cool air, she drank her styrene cup of coffee. Nothing had tasted so good, or given her the boost she needed as that jolt of caffeine. Breaking off two wedges of chocolate, she leaned back for a moment to savour the taste.

Her thoughts drifted for a while, but she no longer had the aching need for sleep. Somewhere, deep inside her, she'd found the energy to go on with this crazy escape.

She opened her eyes, looked out at the silent desert and back to her sleeping child. How much courage do I have? she wondered. It was an unknown quantity, but it had to be enough to get her through the rest of her journey.

Victor stared down the gun barrel.

'What the . . .? Who are you?' He scrambled up the bed until he was pressed against the peeling wallpaper. The intruder's face was in deep shadow beneath a hat, but he could see the gleam of his eyes.

'You want money? I got money,' he gabbled, scrabbling in his jacket for his billfold.

The intruder stayed silent, the only movement a sharp shake of the head.

'Here, take it. Take it all,' spluttered Victor as he threw the wallet onto the counterpane.

'Mr Castlemaine sends his regards. You got to come with me.' The southern accent was unmistakable.

Victor felt the cold trickle of perspiration down his ribs, and the warm seep of urine on his thigh. Shame and fear were uneasy bedfellows as he digested the man's words.

The figure chuckled. It wasn't a pleasant sound, merely the splintering of the silence which surrounded them in the darkness. 'You better visit the bathroom, Mr Castlemaine. You'll want to change your underwear.'

The man cradled the gun in his lap as Victor eased his trembling legs over the side of the bed. At all costs he had to appear calm. Remember who you are, and forget the humiliation, he thought desperately. If Greg had wanted me dead, then I would never have woken up at all. There's still a chance Greg has other plans for me.

Yet the thought of escape was still foremost in his immediate plans. If there was a window in the bathroom, he could make a run for it. The shame of wetting himself was nothing compared to his brother's vengeance.

'Wait in the car,' he ordered as he struggled to regain both his composure and his dignity. 'Go on. Get out.'

'Well now, Mr Castlemaine, we can't just do that little ol' thing. See, your brother told us not to let you out of our sight. So I guess we'll be stayin' awhile.'

Victor looked at the man who stood in the shadows. Was that a hint of sarcasm in his voice? He didn't know, but he was rapidly getting pissed – there'd been enough humiliation for one night. Snapping on the light, he took a long, penetrating look at his tormentor.

'I'll remember your face, you cracker cock-sucker. You think you can speak to a Castlemaine like that and get away with it?'

The southerner merely moved the toothpick from one side of his mouth to the other, his eyes gleaming with sadistic humour.

Vic snorted, walked into the bathroom and slammed the door. 'Bastard!' he yelled defiantly through the chipboard.

Splashing cold water on his face and scrubbing at the stain

on his trousers, he shot frantic glances around the room. There was only a small fanlight set high in the wall and Vic knew he was too large to get through it. His thoughts scrambled as he tried to think of another way out, but deep down he knew he would have to face the inevitable. There was no escape – and he couldn't run forever.

'It's time to go. Git on out here.'

Vic was enraged by the insult. He grabbed the handle and thrust the door open, almost colliding with the man on the other side.

'Mind your mouth, you son-of-a-bitch – or I'll shut it for you.'

It was as if he hadn't spoken. 'We got ourselves a fair way t'go, Mr Castlemaine. So if you wouldn't mind gittin' your ass in the car. Your brother don't like being kept awaitin'. The man's voice was staccato gun shots in the silence between them.

Vic grabbed his throat, thrusting his face close to his protagonist. He saw the dart of fear in that weasel face and felt the swallow in that skinny throat. He tightened his grip. The idea that he could end this bastard's life pleased him – he liked being in control.

'One more word and you're dead. Now get the fuck outa here.' Vic pushed him away. He saw his face redden and his hands loosen the collar around his neck. Good, he'd gotten the message.

Taking his time, Vic stripped and washed as best he could with the cheap motel soap, then towelled off. The damp patch on his trousers was almost dry. He scowled at his reflection in the fly-blown mirror as he tried to bring some order to his hair. That's another thing I hate about Greg, he thought viciously. Why did I have to be the one with curls like a girl? No matter how well my barber cuts it, it still manages to spring in all directions.

Realising he could delay no longer, he shrugged into his crumpled jacket and knotted his tie. At least it was clear that the redneck with the gun wasn't meant to kill him. Feeling a little more confident, he took one last look at his reflection, then left the bathroom.

The long black Lincoln had its engine running and he could see the dark silhouettes of three men. Vic climbed into the back seat, the weasel-faced redneck following closely behind, the gun highly visible.

As the wheels spun and the tarmac sped beneath them, Vic knew that whatever was planned in the next few hours, it wouldn't be pleasant.

The heat shimmered on the desert floor and the cacti were hazy against the red backdrop. Interstate 10 stretched before her in an empty ribbon of tarmac, and she had to keep sipping water to keep her awake and alert. Her eyelids were heavy, and the unmitigating boredom of the desert road was hypnotic. To keep her mind alert, and her eyes on the road, she switched on the radio.

'The riots in Los Angeles lasted until the early hours of this morning and as the sun rises over the city, it is only now that the full devastation of what happened last night can be seen.' The reporter's voice was low and serious and Gabriella could hear the weariness in it.

'The National Guard has been called out as reinforcements for the hundreds of highway patrolmen who have already been brought in from the north of California. An estimated one hundred million dollars in damage to property has been caused. Fires are still raging in all parts of the city. Business has come to a standstill and the airport is closed because of smoke billowing over the runways.'

Gabriella felt a thrill of elation. Greg wouldn't be able to get to LA, and the confusion in the city would hamper Victor's search. Maybe time wasn't running out after all.

She switched off the radio and shivered. 'It's going to be all right, it's going to work. I just need a few more hours.'

Glancing in the wing mirror she swallowed and looked

back to the road. Perhaps it was nothing, just her imagination working overtime.

She looked again, and realised it had nothing to do with her imagination – the sun glinting on metal was real enough, the closely knit pack of bikers menacing enough as they loomed ever nearer.

'Bloody hell! I don't need this.' She eased her foot down on the accelerator. 'Hang on Nick,' she muttered. 'Here we go again.'

The roar of motorbikes swelled as a score of them spread across the road behind her. Dressed in black leather, long hair flying, dark glasses and beards camouflaging their faces, they drew alongside.

'Go away,' she hissed through gritted teeth as she snatched a glance at them and took a firmer grip on the steering wheel.

The lead biker leaned across, peering into the car through the shattered passenger window. His face was pitted with acne, his belly overflowed his trousers and his filthy leather vest showed his tattoos. With a red indian war whoop, he leaned back from his handlebars and lifted the front wheel of his Harley. A series of catcalls and whistles accompanied this bravura performance as the others closed in around her.

Gabriella kept a wary eye on the powerful machines as they edged ever closer. There were Kawasakis, Hondas, Suzukis and hybrids of impossible dimension, with long handlebars and laid back seats, but it was the Harleys, with their custom paint jobs and acres of chrome which were the most impressive. Their throaty roar and their sheer power emphasised the bikers' menace.

And they were using that menace to the full. Inch by inch, she was being forced off the road, their speed matching hers, their bikes closing in until there was a hair's breadth between car and machine.

The leader of the pack slammed his front wheel back on the road, then leaned once more towards the window.

Gabriella could feel his gaze run over her, see his tongue move suggestively along his thin lips.

She took a shuddering breath, but her mouth was dry and her throat ached. 'Bugger off,' she hissed, maintaining eye contact with the road. To antagonise them would be foolish, but if she ignored them, she would end up in the ditch.

Thinking fast, she caught the ringleader's eye and jerked her thumb towards the back seat and the restless Nick.

'You're frightening the baby,' she yelled above the roar of the engines.

The leader of the pack beat a deafening tattoo on the roof, exposed his rotten teeth in a wide grin, waved and roared away. The others swarmed around her, then passed on with a cacophony of howls and war whoops.

'That just about puts the bloody lid on it,' she muttered angrily as the bikers disappeared into the distance and Nick yelled from the back seat. 'Jesus – am I having a bad day, or what?'

Gabriella stopped the car, and as she saw to the baby she became aware of how vulnerable and isolated they were. Yet, she admitted silently, she envied the bikers their freedom. She could still remember what it had felt like when Daddy had let her ride the old Norton back on the army base, could still experience the buzz she'd got from its speed, and the exhilaration of the wind on her face and an open road in front of her. Her spirits lifted and she switched on the engine. Her destination was now only a few miles away.

The journey was an uncomfortable one – carried out in stony silence – the driver concentrating on the roads, the weasel-faced redneck watching as Vic shifted uneasily in the back seat of the Lincoln.

His mind whirled with all the possibilities for the coming meeting with his brother, and he was acutely aware of the gun loosely held on the Weasel's lap. He didn't much care for guns at the best of times, but he especially didn't like them when they were aimed at him. A gun was a woman's weapon. A man used his hands to choke, a knife to slit, his strength to weaken. Yet he would never voice this opinion to Greg, for his brother liked guns.

The discomfort grew as the miles ticked away. The beer and the anxiety were beginning to take their toll, and he needed a crap – but he wouldn't give these bastards the satisfaction of knowing just how urgent the need was. The fear had turned to rage, and he could feel it churning in his bowels. Victor grimaced at his silent attempt at humour. Let the shit-eater eat shit. An ignoble memorial for a Castlemaine.

He looked out of the window as the car slowed to negotiate a turn-off, his thoughts had been so dark, that the sight of sunlight was quite startling. A surreptitious glance at the clock on the dash told him it was almost mid morning.

The car swept through the open gates of a small, but deserted airport and up to a group of hangars. Greg's Cessna was parked on the runway, but there was no sign of him.

The Lincoln passed between the open doors of a hangar, slowed and stopped. The driver released the central locking.

To Vic, the loud click was reminiscent of a bullet leaving a silenced gun barrel, and it took all his courage to haul himself out of the car and smooth the creases in his jacket. His nerves were jumping as the car door slammed behind him and the Lincoln reversed at speed from the hangar. Sunlight was abruptly extinguised as the metal doors closed with a rattle and clang. That sound was a death knell – sending renewed fear to his vitals.

As Vic's eyes grew accustomed to the gloom, he became aware that he was not alone. The stab of fear became a plunging stiletto. It was his brother.

Greg was sitting on a chair at the far end of the hangar. Above him was a naked bulb, which shone down on him, casting everything else into shade. By his side was a table, and on that table was a carafe of water, a glass, a tumbler of ice and a gun. He was dressed in an immaculate dark suit, with a white shirt and grey silk tie. His hair gleamed ebony in the light and the diamonds on his finger and in his earlobe were twin sparks of white ice.

Vic could see that Greg was at ease in this strange place, but his eyes were cold and dark beneath those hooded lids – his mouth a thin line etched beneath that long, patrician nose.

Oh, his eyes, thought Vic as his bowels loosened and his limbs trembled. They are the eyes of the devil.

'Vic. At last. I was beginning to think you'd followed my wife's example and run out on me.'

Vic felt a surge of hope. If he could convince him it was all the bitch's fault, then maybe, he stood a chance.

'I was heading for 'Frisco when those Yankee rednecks grabbed my ass. Gabriella knows people in 'Frisco, it was logical she should head that way.'

'You had orders, Victor. Gabriella and Nicholas were not to be left alone. Now they're lost in the middle of a riot. How did that happen?'

Victor's sweat was cold and pungent. 'She ran off at the hospital. I had no chance of finding her, the place is like a maze. I did my best, even went onto the streets looking for her. She just disappeared. It wasn't my fault, Greg. She got a head start when the car phone rang.' Vic realised he'd dropped himself in it and had begun to babble. He quickly pulled himself together.

Greg flicked dust from his trousers, then inspected his manicure, before turning his attention to his brother. 'You should have had the phone with you.'

The burning sensation in Victor's bowels had spread, and now there was an urgency in his bladder to increase the agony. The sweat rolled and soaked his clothes, but he had to appear calm. As calm as the man sitting in front of him.

'You're a lazy, no-good bum, Vic. You can't even carry out the simplest task without me there to hold your goddam hand. What's your excuse this time?'

Vic knew there was no way out – yet that knowledge had

an oddly calming effect. Somehow, the end, in whatever form, did not look so terrible. What kind of life would I have on the run? Greg would never forget, and his influence reached further than any place I could find to hide. The only satisfaction I can get out of all this, is the thought that Gabriella would soon find out just how unforgiving Greg can be. God rot her soul.

The remaining shred of self-preservation was summoned to bolster his final defence. If I'm to go down, he thought, then the ice queen goes with me.

'It's your wife, you should be looking for – not me. I'm your brother. I do my best. But you know I'd never betray you. Not like her.' He took a shuddering breath. There was nothing more to say.

Greg stepped forward and touched Vic's shoulder.

Vic looked up with hope, but the sight of those dead eyes was a hammer blow. He froze as the barrel of the gun pressed into his temple.

'Jesus, Greg. Don't do this. Please don't do this!' The burning rush spilled down his legs as his bowels loosened and his spine locked.

The empty, repetitive clicks of the tumblers sounded loud in the hangar. They resounded off the walls and through the canyons of Vic's mind, until he thought the whole world was encompassed in that sound.

He opened his eyes and stared at Greg in disbelief – then he began to cry. The tears ran down his face and into his mouth as he clutched at the immaculate white shirt. 'Thank you. Thank you,' he sobbed. He clung to his brother until a sharp crack of flesh upon flesh made him choke back the tears and cup his face.

'Pull yourself together, Victor. Here. Clean yourself.'

Vic took the handkerchief, his eyes downcast, ashamed of his weakness, yet still afraid of what would come next.

'That was your first lesson. And because you're my brother, you're still alive.' He stepped out of reach, his lips curled in disgust as Vic pawed his lapels. 'You'll find the second lesson harder – but it's necessary. You've proved you can't be trusted, so Jake will take over in Chicago and you will have nothing more to do with the Castlemaine empire.'

Vic was stunned. 'How will I live, Greg? You can't do this – not without Dad's say-so. I have just as much right as you to share the business.' Death almost seemed the healthier option.

'Dad is no longer in charge – I am. The restaurant in Chicago has been signed over to you and you will have an annuity of sixty thousand dollars for the first five years. By then you should be able to support yourself and your family.

Vic was numb. He couldn't believe what he was hearing. 'I don't know anything about running a restaurant. Greg. You can't be serious.'

Greg studied him coldly, then turned away. 'It's already decided.'

Vic regarded his brother's back and realised he was beaten. He hung his head, shuffled his feet and wondered what he should do next.

The scrape of Greg's shoe on the concrete made him look up, but the sight of his brother's face gave him no comfort. It was still cold and impersonal.

'Just remember to keep your mouth shut. Break that rule and I can't protect you. Now go. You stink.'

Vic turned away. One day, he thought bitterly, one day I'll get my own back.

9

G reg watched as his brother stumbled from the hangar. The smell of Vic's terror was sharp, but he felt no sympathy for him, and no remorse for what he'd been forced to do. He should never have trusted him to take care of Nicholas – should have known Victor was inept.

The ice water refreshed him, chasing away the weariness the long flight from New York had incurred, and as he drank, he pondered the character of his brother and found it wanting. Victor might have been born into wealth, but there was something of the ghetto in the man. Was this apathy, this lack of drive and ambition inherent, something he'd been born with that was a leftover from the old days when their grandparents had been scratching for a living in the slums of Chicago? If it was, then he'd escaped its influence, but Vic undoubtedly carried the silent, pernicious burden with him – and Greg acknowledged sadly that his brother would never be free of it.

The sigh came from deep within him. It was too late for regrets, LA was once more at war and somewhere in that nightmare was his son.

He watched the condensation trickle down the crystal glass and made a decision. It was time to call in favours, time to gather together the strands of the network he and the family had so carefully constructed over the past fifty years, and the best place to begin was here in LA. With that long blonde hair and cut-glass English accent, Gabriella should be easily noticed.

His expression was grim as he picked up the mobile phone and began the series of calls, yet he couldn't dismiss the twist of regret in his gut – Gabriella was the first woman he'd truly loved, and he despised his flawed judgement.

Gabriella saw Phoenix shimmering in the heat haze of the horizon. Within half an hour she was on the outskirts, and as she'd never been here before, the street map she'd bought at the Circle K proved its worth.

She found what she was looking for in a dingy parade of shops on the poorer streets of the edges of the city. Then following the map, she found a car park two blocks away. Parking the car on the seventh floor, she slipped the keys into the exhaust pipe. It would be the last time she needed them.

The sun bounced off the dusty pavements and splintered its reflection in the grubby windows of the tenement buildings as she walked down the street. There was very little breeze to alleviate the heat, and sweat beaded her forehead as the baby's weight pulled the straps of the sling, but this was secondary to the unease she felt as she walked these unfamiliar streets. They would be looking for her by now – but how much of a lead did she have?

'Get a grip,' she muttered fiercely. 'You can't chicken out now.'

The shop was squeezed in between a row of similar small outlets which shared a common characteristic – they were all brown, all dusty and neglected – but 'Al's Emporium' had steel bars and rusty wire netting criss-crossing the windows.

Gabriella tried the door, it was locked. Then, seeing the faded notice Sellotaped to the glass, she rang the bell and the door clicked open.

After the heat of the streets, the cold blast of air conditioning was a shock, but the smell of the place soon permeated her senses and she almost gagged. It was the musty, sweaty smell of old clothes, the wormy smell of mouldering books, the coppery smell of Brasso, all smothered by the sweet, exotic aroma of burning hashish.

A boar's head leered down at her from above the counter and a whole zoo of stuffed animals glared at her with glazed eyes from their corner by the window.

The man who waited silently behind the counter was middle-aged and fat. His features were porcine, his sweating torso squeezed into jeans and a chequered shirt. The pitcher's cap was pulled low on his forehead, but it couldn't hide the wisps of long, greasy hair which had been tied at his nape in a tail. Silver and turquoise glittered from the pendant at his neck, and winked at her from the belt buckle beneath his paunch.

He seemed to be relaxed, possibly stoned, but he watched her progress with a sharpness that belied this impression. They were the eyes of someone who had heard all the hard luck stories and believed none of them – the eyes of a man who had seen many things, but never achieved the dreams he'd had as a boy.

Gabriella noticed that his nails were long and stained with nicotine, but on his little finger was a diamond ring that flashed several carats. The pawn-broking business must be doing well.

'You wanna pawn somethin'?' His voice was gravelled, his accent southern.

'Yes. I have several things. Perhaps you can offer a fair price?' The question hung between them as she unfolded the silk scarf and showed him part of her collection of miniatures, frames and jewellery. The rest were hidden in the hold-all – kept back in case of emergencies.

He eyed her in silence before turning his attention to the display in the silk scarf. He gave a long, low whistle. 'Jeez, lady. You been robbin' a bank?'

Gabriella watched as he picked up each piece and examined it. She hadn't missed the spark of greed in those piggy eyes, or the way his tongue slithered over his fat red lips. If he anticipated an easy buck and a swift deal, he was in for a surprise.

He leaned back in his chair, pushing the baseball cap further down his forehead. 'Ain't worth nothin' much,' he drawled. 'Bits of glass, is all.' He smiled, exposing tobacco-stained teeth. 'But I tell you what, li'l lady.' He unrolled a wad of notes and peeled off four twenties. 'Here's eighty bucks, an' I'll take it off your hands. My good deed fer the day.' His bark of laughter was cut short by Gabriella's angry glare.

'Like hell it is,' she said coldly. 'If you can't see the value of these things then I'm doing business with the wrong man.'

She flicked a corner of the silk scarf over the miniatures. The emerald lay between them, cool and green and very lovely in its diamond setting.

A meaty hand reached over and plucked the emerald from its nest of silk. 'I ain't sayin' I won't do business with you, lady. But it ain't reasonable to expect a man t'pay more'n he can afford.'

'And how much do you think that ring's worth? In your professional opinion?' The sarcasm was obvious, but if this was how he wanted to play the game, so be it.

He eyed the emerald through the jeweller's glass, his red lips moving as though savouring the taste of something particularly sweet.

'Good quality. Antique setting,' he muttered. 'Best I seen in a long while.'

'So how much?' Gabriella felt uneasy as those nicotine stained claws loving traced the emerald.

'Too hot for me, lady.' His scrutiny shifted from the emerald to the silk scarf and its contents, back to Gabriella. 'They gotta be stolen, and that reflects on the price.'

'They're mine, but I need the money. How much?' Gabriella was getting impatient. If he didn't stop messing about and come up with a figure soon, she'd have to try somewhere else – and she didn't know if she had the stomach to go through this again.

He regarded her steadily before picking up the miniatures. 'You got the bill of sale? I don't fence stolen goods.'

His expression was cunning, the words spoken too carelessly, and Gabriella realised he knew she didn't have the receipts, knew she'd stolen the things laid out before him – knew he could get away with offering a ridiculous price. Yet her mind was working quickly. This was a poor neighbourhood, he couldn't make much out of the junk and the moose heads and old clothes, but he could afford to wear a diamond ring that was worth thousands. Fencing stolen jewellery and antiques was probably his bread and butter.

She looked him in the eye, her expression glacial. 'I don't have receipts, but I'm willing to let the emerald and the miniatures go for a fair price. How about ten thousand dollars?'

A shaft of greed lit his eyes, then was extinguished as he threw back his head and laughed. 'Jeez, lady. You sure got balls.'

Gabriella harnessed her impatience. 'Well? How about it?'

His expression grew solemn as he inspected the collection again. 'Folks round here usually wait for me to make an offer, then negotiate. You sure in a goddam hurry, lady.'

'Yes, I am. Now are we talking a deal here, or do I leave and take these with me?' Gabriella retrieved the miniatures and put them back in the silk scarf.

'I'm just a poor ol' boy scratchin' outa livin' in these here parts. I cain't afford no visits from the police.' His voice had taken on a singsong whine, but his eyes were still sharply alert.

Gabriella wasn't impressed. She could hear the false piety in that voice, could see the greed as his fingers caressed the emerald, and noticed the way he kept running his tongue over his lips. Was he tasting victory?

She snatched the ring and put it with the other things, but before she covered them completely with the scarf, she hesitated.

He smiled then, showing teeth that reminded Gabriella of an old horse she'd once owned.

'You're on the run, ain't ya? You ain't got nowhere to go 'til we do a deal. I know I'm right. I can see it in your eyes.' He laced his fingers across his belly as he cocked his head to one side. 'A thousand dollars. Take it or leave it.'

'I'm not that desperate,' she lied. The bastard was really trying it on. One miniature alone was worth twenty-five thousand dollars, she'd seen the bill of sale when Greg bought it in New York.

'Then I cain't help you.' He paused and the moment stretched. 'But if you was willin' to negotiate?'

The question hung between them in the ensuing silence.

She took his lead and began to play the same game. 'Yeah. I'm on the run, but not from the law, from my husband who's a very violent man. You know what these are really worth. You'll be able to shut up shop and retire on the profit of the ring alone. Nine thousand eight hundred dollars – and no less.'

The silk scarf lay between them, the emerald winking in the light of the lamp he'd switched on over the counter.

He licked his lips and blew his nose on a grubby handkerchief, then he shook his head. 'That's a lot of money, lady. Where d'you think I could get that kinda dough?' He folded his arms, his breath wheezing in his lungs as the sweat trickled down into his shirt collar. 'Three thousand dollars. That's my final offer.'

Gabriella felt a surge of hope, but she was careful to keep her expression noncommittal. 'Seven thousand eight hundred for the ring and you can forget the miniatures.'

'What kinda money you think I'll get for this here emerald? It's hot – and that's bad news.'

Gabriella could see the beads of perspiration on his top lip. She began to pull the silken folds over the treasures. Each corner of the scarf slowly and deliberately dropped to hide a piece at a time.

His hand clamped down on hers as she prepared to drop the final corner over the emerald. His touch was warm and damp, and utterly repellent. She wanted to snatch her hand away, but knew that if she did, she would insult him and ruin the negotiations.

'Five thousand five hundred? You won't get a better offer.' He'd drawn closer, his voice low and conspiratorial.

Gabriella could smell the chillies and onions on his breath as she regarded him solemnly. 'Make it six thousand and you've got yourself a deal on the emerald.'

She lifted her hand, leaving the last corner of the scarf open. The engagement ring winked emerald fire and she felt a pang of regret. It was so beautiful, and she would miss it on her finger – but it was a reminder of Greg, and although the stain was invisible, there was blood marring the perfection of that cool green stone.

He reached for the scarf.

Gabriella slammed her hand on top of his. 'Cash up front. It was something my father taught me.'

'Yo' Daddy was a wise man.' He shook his head and chuckled as he leafed through a wad of notes he'd somehow spirited from behind the counter.

Gabriella watched in awe as he peeled away the notes and began to stack them on the counter. To produce six thousand dollars at a moment's notice, was one hell of an achievement, and she experienced a twinge of doubt. Perhaps she should have stuck out for more? The thought was dismissed. Enough time had been wasted already, and six thousand would see her through for quite a while.

He laid the grubby notes on the counter and waited, his fingers pawing the hem of the scarf.

She gathered the corners of the scarf together and dropped it in her handbag, leaving the ring on the counter. Then she picked up the money and counted it. It was all there.

'Pleasure doing business with you,' she said quietly, pushing the ring towards him. 'Have a nice day.'

'You tell your Daddy he makes a good teacher. Must of been an Indian horse-trader in a previous life.' He giggled at his own humour and pressed the button to open the door.

Gabriella looked over her shoulder as she stepped out into the heat, but he was already engrossed in his new acquisition and didn't look back at her. The door slammed with a metallic click and she walked away.

He was right about one thing though, she mused as she headed for the city centre. Dad was a very good teacher.

It was over an hour later, and Greg was in the limousine on his way back to the beachfront house when the phone rang.

'Ben Wise, here. Your wife hired a car from a small local company, called Freedom America. It was picked up from the Hilton Hyatt on Wiltshire at approximately five o'clock yesterday evening, and paid for by credit card. The receptionist gave me a good description, so there's no mistake.'

'Thank you, Ben. There will be a cheque in the post.'

Greg broke the connection and rested back into the soft leather upholstery. I was right. A credit card and a car. She'll use that card again, and when I find out where, I'll have a starting point. The thought of having to wait made him restless – he didn't like it one bit.

The car drew to a halt and he ran up the steps into the hall. Slipping off his jacket, he walked into the drawing room. Peace at last – home. But it could never be the same, not without Gabriella and Nicholas.

The ring of the telephone broke into his gloomy thoughts. It was his contact at American Express.

'Her gold card was used at a Circle K, outside Blythe, on Interstate 10 at about four o'clock this morning. Then again at midday in Vegas. But the last transaction can be ignored, the storekeeper ran a check, gave a description and the card was withheld.'

Greg smiled as he rubbed the bridge of his nose and digested this latest information. Vegas didn't ring true anyway, she would never dare show her face there – his ownership of two casinos made her too high profile. Phoenix sounded right, though. There were a lot of roads out of Phoenix. It was the gateway to the mid west, and had an international airport.

His gaze dropped to the small table by the window and his thoughts froze. Something was different. Something out of place. It took a moment to realise what it was, and when he did, his breath hissed. The miniatures were missing.

He slowly trawled the room for further evidence of Gabriella's betrayal and soon found it. Gold picture frames, two pieces of Meissen and a silver snuff box had also disappeared.

'Bitch!' The safe hadn't been her only target that night.

Greg began to pace, then he gave a cold, humourless laugh. I have to hand it to her, the bitch was thorough. It doesn't matter about the antiques, they can be replaced, but it's the theft of my son which makes me angry. The cunt really knows how to twist the knife.

'Where are you heading, Gabriella?' he murmured. 'Home to Mommy in England? Maybe – but first you've got to get out of the States.'

He picked up the intercom. 'Have the helicopter here in five minutes, Jake. We're on our way to Phoenix.'

Pouring a stiff brandy, he swallowed it in one, slammed the glass back on the bar counter and was about to turn away when he noticed the chessboard.

'Sicilian Defence,' he whispered as he picked up the black king and replaced him. 'So you want to play chess?' The message in the symbolism had not escaped him. 'As eloquent as always, Gabriella. Clever and more devious than I've given you credit for.'

Greg surveyed the plundered ivory and ebony ranks of the ancient Gods, then looked at his watch. There was time to make one last call.

He dialled long distance, and his contact in the East End of

125

London answered almost immediately. Greg got to the point swiftly.

'I want your men to keep an eye on the airports and harbours. Do not approach her, but follow and keep watch. Tell me immediately you have her.'

'That's a lot of muscle. What kinda money we talking 'ere?'

Greg's breath was a hiss at the sound of the Cockney voice. Didn't the English think of anything else but money?

'I'll be generous on this one, Mr Smith. Have you known me to be otherwise?'

A grunt was the only reply at the other end of the line.

'Ten thousand pounds should be more than enough,' Greg said coldly into the silence.

'That'll do for the first week, then we'll 'ave to negotiate. It'll mean a lot of my blokes 'anging about when they could be doing something useful.'

Greg kept his temper in check. He and Smith had never met, all previous negotiations having been dealt with by someone else, but if he and Smith had been standing in the same room, the man from London would never have dared be so arrogant. For the moment Smith was a useful and resourceful contact and he would just have to put up with his insolence. When all this mess had been cleared up and Nick was back where he belonged, Smith would be taught a lesson in manners.

'It's agreed. Get your men working on it immediately. I'll fax you a photo and the details.' Greg had observed Smith from a distance and could picture the man at the other end of the line – a fat man with a fat, stinking cigar. He thought for a moment, then continued.

'Do you have someone you can trust to stay silent? Someone we could use to track her down if your men don't pick her up?'

'I might.' Smith's voice was wary. 'An old mucker of mine, rum sort, went to school with 'im, lived in the same council block in Bermondsey. He's expensive, but he's the best.'

Greg mentally shuddered at the thought of Smith having once been a small boy. The idea was incongruous. 'Tell me about him.'

'Name's Tyler Reed. Ex-SAS. Medical discharge 'cos of a sniper bullet in the knee. Some bloody IRA bastard by all accounts. Keeps shtum about 'is army history, but word is he's seen action in the Far East, Iran and Iraq mostly, speaks the lingo like a native. Army put him through university, got a first in middle eastern languages. So he ain't all balls and no brain.'

Greg stayed silent. Reed sounded just the sort of man he could use right now – someone who was disciplined, someone who wouldn't cock up at the first hurdle.

Smith's voice came down the line, the tone lighter and rather too familiar for Greg's liking. 'Bloke like 'im was totally wasted in the army, but 'e had nothing to stay here for. His dad died when he were fifteen, mother done a runner years before that. He runs a security firm and detective agency with one of 'is soldier buddies, bloke called Reynolds. Bit of a strange bugger, but they're a good team. You can trust them.'

'Whether I trust them or not is up to me, Smith. Tell me more about Reed.'

'Reed's the kind of man who believes in Queen and country, honesty and fair play, but 'e don't mind turning a blind eye when it comes to bending the rules to suit 'im. Bit of a maverick, really, and as tough as old boots.' Smith gave a humourless chuckle. 'He won't have nothing to do with the kind of business you and I handle though. That's a definite no-no.'

Smith's voice sounded regretful and Greg wondered if the two men had crossed swords on the issue.

'Watch your mouth. This is an open line,' he hissed. 'And my name is to stay out of any negotiations you have with Reed,' Greg rapped out. 'Get your men on the job and let me know at once if you have anything. Hire Reed as backup.'

Greg slammed down the receiver and returned his attention to the chessboard.

The queen was the most powerful player. She could move anywhere on the board, or for as many squares as she wanted – but sooner or later she would have to meet the king. Then Gabriella would learn what a dangerous game chess could be.

10

Tyler Reed gave the chrome one last rub, then tucked the duster into the back pocket of his jeans. He admired the sleek lines of the Harley Davidson XLCR, and stroked the supple leather of the broad, comfortable seat. It was hard to believe that this temptress, this black, sleek panther was the reincarnation of the rusting, forgotten pile of metal he'd found beside the railway cutting in Missouri. Machine wasn't the name that suited her now – she was Jezebel. With her he could find the freedom and the exhilaration of power and danger that he missed so much after leaving the army.

It had taken two years to bring her back to her glory. Two years and a great deal of money. The engine was now something like a performance Harley dealer's catalogue; an S & S Crank that's 1 inch over stroke, taking the displacement out to 89 cu. Twin-plug Branch heads and Dyna Coils took care of the ignition, whilst a Barnett clutch sorted out the transmission, along with a combination of Harley and Andrews gears and a cast-iron trapdoor. The oil was kept cool by a Lockhart cooler and moved around in braided steel lines. A Zell heavy duty rear motor mount held it all in the frame and took the vibrations in its stride. She was worth every penny, every hour and aching minute he'd spent in the workshop beneath his South London flat.

Tyler stood up and tried to ease the ache in his knee.

'Irish bastard,' he groaned as the pain wormed through his shattered kneecap.

He'd seen action in the Lebanon, Kuwait, Iran and Iraq, but it had been a short assignment in Belfast, and a sniper's bullet, that had finally brought him limping back to civvy street. If it hadn't been for Jezebel, he would have gone crazy.

It was the boredom which paralysed his mind. He had the agency, but he missed the months of sitting in a desert watching for terrorist activities. Missed the excitement of working undercover in the back streets of Baghdad, and the adrenalin rush of getting in and out of the worst shit holes in the world without being discovered.

'Those were the days,' he muttered. But they were far behind him now and at forty-five he knew he had few options left.

With one last look at the Harley, he switched off the light and climbed the stairs to the one-bed apartment he now called home.

He'd been away for three months, training a Sheik's body-guards, and it was good to be back on familiar territory. The young Arabs had been so fit, so energetic and enthusiastic that it made him feel old. They reminded him too well of how he had once been, for he could no longer climb mountains or spend weeks backpacking in the more remote parts of the world. Not since his knee.

I'm a prisoner, he thought gloomily as he smeared Swarfega on his hands and attacked the oil and grease. He liked to have the silence around him though – the time to think and read and tinker with Jezebel's nuts and bolts. That silence was like an old friend after his assignments with the SAS. The hours and days of waiting in desert and jungle, mountain and city had taught him the worth of patience and stealth – the value of self-dependency.

That was the reason Marion had left him. She didn't like being alone, couldn't understand why he didn't want to go to parties or away on exotic holidays when he was on leave. He'd tried to explain, she knew he was an army man when they married, but as the years passed, she had found it harder to accept his life style and had eventually found someone else.

It had been ten years since the divorce, but once in a while he thought of her and regretted her departure. She lived on a new housing estate outside Manchester with her dull, reliable husband and two small boys, but he bore her no grudge, she was happy in the life she'd chosen, yet he was sorry it hadn't worked out between them.

Tyler dried his hands and threw the kitchen paper in the bin. It was only after his enforced retirement that he'd begun to understand how frustrated she must have been for all those years. She too must have felt caged by circumstance, living in army quarters, never knowing when he would return, or where he'd been in those long weeks of absence. Not even knowing if she was a widow until he came through the door – and there had been occasions when it had come pretty close. The sniper's bullet had come too late to save their marriage, but too soon for him to tire of the danger and excitement his work had brought him.

'*Padarsagh*!' Tyler swore softly in Farsi and set about making a cup of Jasmine tea. He hated it when he let his mind drift back over his long dead marriage.

He waited for the samovar to stew the tea and brushed back the short, wiry hair over his ears. Why did he suddenly feel so old?

Catching sight of his reflection in the mirror above the sink, he turned away in disgust. He didn't like looking at the sun-creased skin that drew lines down from his nose and etched cobwebs at the corners of his dark eyes. Didn't want to acknowledge the liberal sprinkling of silver in his once dark hair. It just made him depressed and it wasn't in his nature to let things get him down. But today was different somehow. Today he felt every one of his forty-five years, and more.

Slipping off his sneakers, he poured the tea and padded into the tiny sitting room. A settee, a table and two pine chairs were the only furniture. He didn't like clutter and could see no point in spending money on gee-gaws and pot plants. They only had to be dusted and watered and life was too short. With a favourite Little Richard track on the stereo and a copy of Clavell's *Whirlwind*, he settled down for the evening. It was good to be home.

The ring of the telephone rudely interrupted his mood, and for a moment he thought about not answering it, but it persisted and he knew he had no choice. It might mean work. Since the recession, business at Reed & Reynolds Securities had been slow and there were bills to be paid. His army pension never stretched very far when the Harley needed new parts, or a rare fifties recording was on the market.

'Reed.'

'Thought you might be out with Jezebel after your trip abroad. Or were you getting laid?'

Tyler grinned. It was his partner, Bill Reynolds.

'How's it hanging, Bill? Don't you public school blokes think of anything else but sex?'

'I'm an old married man, mate. Thinking about it is all I get to do these days.'

Tyler pictured Bill's wife Elaine, and grimaced. How the hell he'd stuck with her all those years, he couldn't fathom. The kids were compensation though. Three handsome little boys who looked exactly like their father. Same mop of ginger hair, same freckles and mischievous blue eyes. Same bloody temper too.

'It isn't all sex and wild parties being single you know. At least you have the boys.'

'Don't I know it. They're worse than a platoon of squaddies.'

Tyler laughed. 'Take after you, me old son. Now, what's so urgent you have to drag me away from Little Richard?'

'I always said you had no taste in music, Tyler. Why don't you indulge in a little Gilbert and Sullivan instead of all that fifties' nonsense? It's good for the soul.'

Tyler grimaced. 'Only a black man has soul, Bill. For an Oxford wallah, you really are ignorant.' He chuckled, it was an old ritual between them and he knew neither of them would win the debate. 'Now what was it you wanted?'

'Sniffy Smith's been on the blower. He has a job for you. Missing person. I know you don't take on maritals unless it can be helped, but this one sounds fairly easy and there's a lot of money on the table.'

Tyler lit a cigarette, the only one he allowed himself in a day, and thought about his old protagonist.

Michael 'Sniffy' Smith had earned his nickname from the line of snot which permanently smeared his top lip as a kid. His constant sniffing had driven everyone crazy, but he could fight his way out of trouble and, at thirteen, lead a small pack of boys who ran a black-market trade in cigarettes on the Bermondsey council estate.

Sniffy Smith had progressed much further than any of them had expected and was now one of the most dangerous men in London. Since the Krays and Richardsons had lost their hold over the East End, Sniffy had taken over. Only no one dared call him that any more. There had been many a slit nose or rearranged torso to warn others off.

He pulled back from the memories. 'Old Sniffy, eh? What gutter did he crawl out of?'

'The same one as usual probably, but the money he's offering is ridiculous. Double our normal fee.' Bill fell silent for a moment to let the words sink in.

Tyler puffed on the cigarette. He didn't like the sound of it. If Sniffy was involved, it was trouble. 'Why can't he use one of his own hoodlums?'

'Dunno. He refused to tell me anything.' Bill's voice dropped an octave. He knew how much his partner distrusted Smith.

'Wonder what he's up to?' Tyler stubbed out the Gauloise and made a decision. 'Let him sweat for a bit. Then we'll see what he wants. But I wouldn't trust that fat scrote with a bag of jelly babies.'

'Well, it's up to you. You're the one he wants. The money

would come in useful though, the rent's due next week and we still haven't paid Dot for last month.'

'Dot's worked for no wages before, she's a diamond. I'll see what Sniffy has to say and discuss it with you before we decide. Good night Bill. Give my best to the missus.'

Bill laughed. 'I doubt she'd appreciate it, mate. Bye.'

Tyler put down the phone and turned the music up. Sour faced bitch. Bill deserved better.

He settled down again and idly scratched the crescent-shaped scar that ran from the corner of his mouth to his chin. It was a legacy from a mullah during the student riots in Iran, and it still irritated him, even after all these years. Dragging his thoughts back to the present, he wondered what Smith wanted. It just wasn't like Sniffy to seek him out. Not after the last time they'd met.

It had been four years ago, just after he and Bill had set up the agency. Work had been steady. The ferrying of valuables across country and the escorting of Middle Eastern business men during their stay in England had meant the money was good. They also advised on security for international companies who were housed in the City, and had begun to build a reputation for reliability. With their contacts in the police and civil service they had been kept busy. Then Sniffy had appeared.

It was a very different Michael Smith who came through the office door that morning. He was still short, but now he was sleek and fat, like an elephant seal. Gone was the skinny, dark haired Bermondsey bruiser with the snotty nose; now he was balding, Napoleonic and bullish. The suit was Saville Row, the rings on the chubby fingers gold, but the man still looked cheap.

Tyler had heard the gossip, knew what Sniffy had become. He wasn't impressed.

Smith glanced around the small basement office they'd leased in a back street of Brixton, wrinkled his nose at the smell of the Indian takeaway next door, then sat in the most comfortable chair before lighting a cigar.

Tyler could see the Jaguar parked outside, and the heavyweight muscle waiting on the pavement. Here was trouble, with a capital T.

'Welcome to the manor, mate. Nice to see you back.'

Tyler nodded, but remained cool in his hospitality.

Smith puffed on his cigar, filling the office with smoke. He didn't seem ill at ease with Tyler's silence.

'I got some work to put your way. We Bermondsey boys should stick together, don't you think?' He waved his cigar towards the room. 'With me behind you, you could do better than this. I got a lotta contacts. Nice little earners for a bloke like you.'

Tyler saw the gleam light the piggy eyes in that bloated, self-satisfied face and itched to throw him out. He'd never liked Sniffy. As a kid he'd been the butt of his bullying until he'd learned to fight back. After that, Sniffy had left him alone, but he was intrigued to know why the man was here, they hadn't seen each other since school.

'I got a shipment of cheap Mexican artefacts coming into Heathrow next week and as you've got the transport, I thought why not let me old mate Tyler earn a few sovs. He's just starting out, why not give 'im a break?' Smith grinned but the smile didn't reach his eyes which were steady on Tyler's face.

'How do you know about the security wagons?' Tyler's voice was low and controlled. 'Have you been spying on me?'

'Nothing happens in my manor without me hearing about it.' Smith's voice had an edge to it. 'Spying is not a word I appreciate.'

Tyler let it go. 'These "artefacts", wouldn't happen to be stuffed with anything would they?'

'Catch on quick, Tye, me old mate.' Smith touched his nose with his forefinger. 'There's a lotta dosh just waiting to be made for blokes like us. It's better than the gold rush. They're dying for what we can supply.' He laughed at his sick attempt at humour. 'I swear to God, Tyler, I can't get it shipped in and on the streets fast enough. An eye for the main chance, that's what you gotta have these days. I knew you was the right bloke to 'ave on my team.'

He sat forward in his chair, his cigar clamped between his teeth. 'So, we got a deal?'

Tyler took a deep breath, then slowly released it, his gaze fixed to the pale blue eyes that looked so eager.

'What makes you think I want to have anything to do with drugs? I run a legitimate business and want no part of it.'

Smith sat back in his chair and laced his fingers over his belly. A smirk of derision flashed across his face.

'I think you do, Tyler, me old mate. You see I run this patch and while you do business 'ere, you do business with me. With or without your consent, you'll find the packages delivered to your storage bays. Why not make it easy on yourself and come in with me. There's a lot of money to be made if you see sense.'

Tyler stood up and rounded the desk until his five feet and eleven inches towered over the five feet two inches of the seated Smith. His fists were clenched and his face grim.

'I am not your old mate, Sniffy. Never have been. And you and I were never alike. All we had in common was Bermondsey. But I left and the army taught me how to deal with scrotes like you. If I had my way, I'd flay you, and every other dealer to an inch of your life, then give you an overdose of your own poison.'

Smith squirmed out of the chair, but he still had to look up at Tyler. His face was puce and he'd almost bitten through his cigar.

'Never call me that again. You hear? No one calls me names unless they want a permanent limp.' His voice grew sarcastic as he looked down at Tyler's leg. 'But then you already know how it feels to be a cripple, don't you?'

Tyler advanced and with lightning speed, had Smith's throat in his hand and his back to the wall. 'A centimetre more pressure and you're dead, Sniffy.' He glared down into the bulbous eyes, his fingers itching to squeeze the life out of that sweating little turd.

The cigar was bitten off and fell between them onto the floor.

Smith's squirming body was merely an irritation. His beating hands and kicking feet easily ignored as Tyler held on.

'I don't want or need your kind of business and if I see you here again, I'll do the job properly. That goes for your gorillas as well.' He applied the merest tweak of pressure and Sniffy went still. Tyler could see panic in his pale blue eyes.

'One hint of trouble from you or your thugs and you'll find your nuts cut off and stuffed in that fat mouth.' Tyler's voice was soft, sibilant and menacing. 'I've been taught by the best and can inflict such pain that you'll be screaming for me to finish you off. Do we understand one another?'

Sniffy made a garbled noise and Tyler released the pressure, but he kept his hand round his neck. With a flick of his wrist he pulled the Ghurka khukri knife from the sheath on his belt and pressed the sharp tip into the flesh beneath Smith's left eye. 'Give me grief, and I'll relieve you of a vital piece of your anatomy. First the left eye, then the right. Then your balls, your dick and each of your fingers and toes.'

The point probed the eye socket. 'Feel how sharp this is, Sniffy.'

Smith whimpered and sweat beaded his bald head and ran down his ashen face. 'All right, all right. I get the message. There won't be no trouble.'

Tyler sheathed the knife and released his hold of Smith.

Smith warily touched his eye, then massaged his neck. 'Just watch yer back and stay outa my way, Tyler,' he blustered as he edged out of the office. 'No one does that to me and gets away with it. No one.'

Tyler shook off the unpleasant memory. The office had been exchanged for a better address in Coulsdon, but obviously Smith had kept tabs on him, just as he'd followed Smith's rising status in the East End. That was what worried him.

The last thing he needed was an East End hoodlum up his jacksie.

There was no air in Phoenix. The heat evaporated any moisture and smothered the smallest gust of wind. The tower blocks shimmered, their windows reflecting the white heat of the sky back to the pavements.

Gabriella walked as quickly as she could towards the bus station. The layers of clothing had become burdensome and her t-shirt stuck to her back beneath the shirt. The added weight of the bags and the baby sapped what little strength she'd managed to dredge from her reserve. Yet still she hurried – her journey was only just beginning.

There was a queue, but she'd expected that. As the seconds ticked away, she felt the drain on her energy accelerate, she needed a drink, and somewhere to sit down.

Finally it was her turn, and grasping the ticket, she headed for the line of Greyhound buses at the back of the terminal. Being on the move again was almost a relief after the prolonged, anxious wait.

The ladies' lavatory was quiet, almost deserted, the water in the taps icy.

Gabriella pulled back her hair into a tight bun, anchored it with bobby pins, then hid it with the baseball cap she'd purchased earlier. Adjusting the peak over her eyes, she donned sunglasses, then stripped off the shirt, and changed her t-shirt. She regarded her appearance solemnly in the smeared mirror – it would have to do for now.

The line of rubbish bins overflowed beneath a swarm of flies. Screwing the ticket into a tight ball, she dropped it into the congealed mess of half-eaten burgers and sticky drink cartons. It had cost her money, yet she had a head start and maybe it would keep the Castlemaine brothers off her back long enough to disappear completely.

The thought of them made her shiver. How close are they to finding me? What's Greg doing? And where is he now?

She snapped out of the mood. To think like that was dangerous, it slowed her down.

Easing the straps on her shoulder, she took a deep breath and headed for the taxi rank. Speech would be difficult from now on – her British accent would give her away and be remembered.

The driver didn't look at her as she gave him her destination, he just switched on his meter, swung the cab in a ninety-degree turn and headed away from the bus terminal.

Gabriella leaned back and closed her eyes, but her mind was working through the strategy she would have to employ over the next few hours.

No more straight lines, no more clues or careless gambits – Greg might consider himself the master of the game, but he couldn't guess at the cunning ferocity of a mother whose child was in danger, or the determination of that mother to win.

The taxi drew up and Gabriella silently handed over fifteen dollars, then added a tip. He would remember if it was large, he would remember no tip at all, but two dollars was about right.

As she headed towards the milling crowds, she experienced something that was close to excitement. Despite everything she'd been through in the past twenty-four hours, and regardless of the dangers ahead, she had to admit she was beginning to enjoy the game.

Greg looked down on Interstate 10 from the helicopter as they swooped low over the desert highway. He could see its dark shadow chase across the bare, red landscape beneath them, and the dust lifting from the desert floor as they sped towards Phoenix.

There was little traffic, and he doubted she was still on the highway. Something told him she would change tactics at Phoenix. She'd already proved to be resourceful, had made it further than he'd expected. It wouldn't have surprised him if she was working a double bluff.

It was almost three in the afternoon, but he hadn't wasted time during the journey. Messages had flowed back and forth on the two-way radio, and he'd organised a team of men to ask questions at the bus stations, train terminals and the airport. When she left Phoenix, he could bet a dime to a dollar it wouldn't be by car.

He tapped the cigarette on the lid of his silver case. Drawing the smoke deep into his lungs, he half closed his eyes and stared down at the approaching city skyline.

I know you're down there, Gabriella. You can't hide for ever.

The hostess glanced at Gabriella's ticket, avoided eye contact and waved a hand in the general area of the second-class cabin.

Gabriella found her seat and unbuckled the baby harness. It was a relief not to have the straps pulling at her shoulder. She stuffed the bag into the gap between the seats and held it tightly between her ankles. There were too many important things in that bag to risk letting it out of her sight.

Within minutes the doors were closed and she found she was holding her breath as the engines throbbed into life.

There was an empty seat between her and the man on the other side of the aisle, but she was aware of his friendly attempts to catch her attention.

The last thing I need is a talkative, curious travelling companion, she thought wearily. Americans had to be the most friendly people in the world, but it's not always a blessing. They have the knack of asking personal questions within minutes of meeting, and I'm too tired to think straight and maintain a Boston accent. Once he finds out I'm British, I'm sunk.

As the plane began to move slowly down the runway, Gabriella looked out of the window at the airport buildings and watched the small helicopter approach. Her pulse raced and her mouth dried. What if her ruse hadn't worked?

She firmly pushed away the thought. There must be hundreds of women travelling with babies through America today. Even if Greg had traced her this far, she knew the passenger lists were inviolate – and there would be no trace of Gabriella Castlemaine, only a Mrs Rachel Goldstein and her baby daughter.

She looked at Nick and smiled. He was very sweet in that pink bonnet and shawl. That was the good thing about such a young baby. They were sexless.

The progress of the plane seemed achingly slow as it executed a ponderous turn at the end of the runway.

The helicopter landed on the far side of the airfield and was lost in the distant heat haze.

With engines peaking to a roar, Gabriella's plane thrust her back into her seat and began its hectic race along the concrete.

She had been on the run for nearly twenty-four hours – now the chase would begin in earnest.

'So, what have you got for me, Wayne?' Greg was walking away from the helicopter, his hair blowing into his eyes from the wind of the propellers. The man beside him was short and squat, almost at a run to keep up with Greg's long stride.

'Without a photo, we can't be sure, Mr Castlemaine,' Wayne O'Leary shouted above the noise of Continental flight 245 as it screamed overhead. 'But a clerk at the bus station remembers an English girl buying a ticket. She had a baby with her and appears to fit Mrs Castlemaine's description. I thought you might want to talk to him?'

'Where is he?' replied Greg curtly, sweeping back his hair and tugging at his jacket. He was hot, angry and crumpled. The repercussions were already telling. The senator had been on the phone minutes before, yelling down the line, making threats, trying to distance himself from the events of the last few days. There weren't any teeth to those threats, Greg had him by the balls and he would do as he was told – but too many people were getting involved and Gabriella had a lot to answer for.

'He's waiting in the car, Mr Castlemaine.'

Greg followed the ugly little man away from the noise of the main airport, towards a long, bright red Cadillac convertible. The guy reminded him of a gnome, which was disgusting enough, but the sight of the car, bristling with chrome and cow horns, was far more repellent.

'You have no taste, Wayne. Jake, make sure I have something decent to drive in. I refuse to get into that . . . thing.'

He clasped his hands behind his back and waited for Wayne to produce his star witness.

The youth seemed reluctant to leave the car, but when he did, Greg realised he was very young – probably a student working through his college vacation. His hair was ginger and flopped over pale grey eyes, the freckles highly visible in his wan face. There was a nervous tic at the corner of the boy's mouth, and his large hands clenched and unclenched at his sides as Wayne propelled him forward.

'They don't make them handsome in Phoenix, do they Jake?'

Jake sniggered in agreement.

'This is Billy Briant, Mr Castlemaine.' Wayne stood awkwardly beside the gangling youth, his gaze not quite reaching Greg's.

Greg accepted Wayne's nervousness as par for the course, the man had always been an asshole, but he was gratified to notice that Wayne's unease had been transmitted to the boy: he was plainly terrified. He could see the Adam's apple bob in the long thin neck, and the dark stain spreading beneath the armpits of his shirt. Good. I like things that way – it makes people talk.

'Is this the woman?' His voice was deliberately smooth, his face expressionless as his gaze bore into those terrified grey eyes.

Wayne nudged the boy and hissed, 'Answer Mr Castlemaine.'

'Yes sir,' Billy Briant whispered, as he glanced at the photograph.

'I can't hear you, boy. Speak up.'

Billy looked back at Greg, his fists clenched, the muscle in his cheek jumping. 'Yes, sir,' he said as though answering a sergeant major on the parade ground. 'She bought a one-way ticket to Houston for her and the kid.'

'And what time did this bus leave?' Greg's scrutiny was close, and he noted the way those pale eyes followed every move as he lit a cigarette.

'Twenty-five after two, sir.' The boy was almost standing to attention, his gaze now focussed somewhere over Greg's shoulder.

'How can you be sure she got on the bus? Did you see her boarding?' The smoke trickled from his mouth as he waited. Confirmation of his suspicion was a positive thing, even if it did leave questions unanswered.

'No, sir. The booking desk is round the corner from where the buses leave and arrive . . . sir.' Billy swallowed and bunched his fists tightly against his thighs.

Greg nodded thoughtfully. 'So, she might not have used her ticket at all?'

'Why should she do that, sir? I mean, the ticket costs a lot of money.' Billy looked genuinely puzzled as he finally met Greg's stare.

'That's just what I would like to know, Billy. Thank you.' Greg slipped a hundred dollar bill into the boy's shirt pocket.

Turning to his men, he barked out orders. 'Take the helicopter and find that bus. If she's on it, bring her here – and keep me informed by telephone of your progress. Jake. Where's the replacement car?'

'On its way, sir. What do you want me to do about Mr O'Leary?' Jake nodded towards the little man who still hovered by the incongruous Cadillac.

'Get him to look for her car,' Greg said quietly. 'If she's

not driving it, then it must be somewhere in Phoenix. Also, she had no money and hasn't used the credit card since the service station, get Wayne to check the pawn shops, markets and known fences. Give him the list of what she stole, those miniatures are irreplaceable and I want them back.'

Greg smoked his cigarette as he waited for his car. He needed a shower and a change of clothes. The desert heat made his skin gritty, and his suit was covered in a fine shroud of dust as the helicopter took off with a clatter behind him. Yet his mind was working rapidly behind the calm exterior he showed to his men.

Gabriella wasn't on that bus, or any other bus. The quickest way out of here was by plane – and if she planned to fly anywhere but straight to London she would have to use a passport – but he had that in his safe in New York.

'Unless she's got her English one,' he breathed. His hand stopped in mid-air as he reached for the cigarette. 'I never did find it.'

He flicked ash. I was very thorough, he remembered, so she must have left it in New York. I'd better ring the apartment and have the maid look for it.

His expression was grim as he thought of Gabriella's deceit. He'd always known how she hoarded her papers, never travelling without them, hiding them, thinking he didn't suspect. He snorted in derision: 'Conniving bitch,' he said under his breath. 'As if I could be fooled.'

But you have, an answering voice jeered in his mind. You thought it endearing at the time, an English eccentricity; but you got careless.

Greg frowned and began to pace. He was certain she hadn't had it in California, so the only other way she could leave the country would be through the British Embassy. If she did go to the Consulate, it would mean several hours' delay – for both of them. He had some contacts, but it would still take time and probably involve Dad. The idea of his father knowing the mess he was in didn't sit easily.

He ground out his cigarette and looked over at the distant runways of the main airport as his thoughts wandered back to the chess board at the beach-front house.

Perhaps she was bluffing, appearing to head in one direction, but at the same time planning a different method of transport to follow another route entirely. She could be using pawns, like young Billy, to mask her real intentions.

Greg smiled. 'Smart move, Gabriella,' he muttered. 'But not smart enough.'

The black Lincoln pulled up and he gestured for Jake and two others to accompany him.

'Where to, Mr Castlemaine?'

'The airport terminal.'

Gabriella managed to get Nick to suck at a bottle of warm milk, his screams had reached fever pitch as the plane headed for the clouds, but now he had finally settled in her arms and fallen asleep, she could close her eyes and relax.

The man in the seat across the aisle had given up trying to talk to her and was now engrossed in a tractor manual. She wished him joy of it, and could think of nothing more boring.

It seemed no time at all before the no smoking light came on and she was asked to secure her seat belt. Strapping Nick, who was mercifully still sleeping, into the baby harness, she felt the familiar plunge of her stomach as the plane began its descent.

The view from the window wasn't encouraging. Great barren stretches of tan and red earth, mingled with ochre mountains and hills. Slivers of platinum gleamed from the rivers which veined the desert floor and the taupe coloured adobe houses were almost camouflaged by their surroundings.

I wonder how many flights leave here each day? Hopefully, there'll be a night flight I can catch. She didn't relish having to find somewhere to stay in this desolate frontier outpost.

Gabriella adjusted her watch to the new time zone

and waited uneasily for Continental Airlines Flight 245 to land.

Greg looked up at the television monitors as the flight information rolled across the screen. Without knowing her destination, they told him nothing.

'Jake, find out which flights left in the last two hours, then report back to me.'

The man nodded and strode away to the information desk. He returned within minutes.

'It's a lot of flights, Mr Castlemaine. One takes off every two or three minutes. Here's a list of domestics. There were no international flights out in the last two hours.'

Greg glanced morosely at the computer print-out. There had to be forty flights listed and she could be on any of them.

'You and Paul help me work the check-in desks. Between us, we should come up with something.' Greg had tried to sound confident, but he doubted if they'd get far. Since the terrorist bombings, security had been tightened like a constipated asshole.

He was proved right. At every desk he was met with the same professional smile, the same shake of the head. The anger was ice in his gut, the urge to throttle the next person who smiled at him almost impossible to contain – but he did, it would do no good to lash out, he would merely have to find another way of getting what he wanted.

I wonder how much these girls get paid, he thought idly. A few hundred bucks might put a genuine smile on their faces if they come up with the right answers.

Greg looked at his watch. Holy Shit, it's been too long since she bought that goddam coach ticket. The bitch could be anywhere by now.

He was about to head for the Continental desk when his portable telephone bleeped.

'We found the Greyhound, sir. No sign. What do you want us to do?'

'Get back here,' he ordered sharply, then disconnected. He was not having a good day and as the hours ticked by, it was getting worse.

'I think we got a lead, Mr Castlemaine.' Paul, the young bodyguard looked uncomfortable. 'The girl at Continental has only just come on duty, but she might be persuaded to let us see the passenger lists if we give her some dough. How much you want me to offer?'

'I'll handle it.' Greg brushed past him and headed for the desk. The man was a fool, didn't he realise how important this was? If the information was wanted – then it had to be paid for. Where were these guys coming from?

He gave the girl behind the Continental counter the benefit of his most persuasive, seductive smile. She was a knockout, and it was easy to fall smoothly into his routine.

'Good afternoon, ma'am. I'm anxious to find my sister, and I was wondering if you could help?'

The dark curls bounced as she shook her head and returned his smile, but there was a glint of curiosity in her wide green eyes, a message that despite her negative response, she might be persuaded to change her mind.

He turned up the heat of his smile, leaning closer, bringing an intimacy to their conversation as he reached for his billfold. 'I would of course show my gratitude for your trouble.'

'What was the information you wanted, sir?' The five hundred dollars disappeared into her jacket pocket.

The woman's a magician, Greg thought, as he told her what he wanted. She has the most amazing eyes, too. They remind me of Gabriella's. He felt a twist in his solar plexus. The bitch still had the power to wound – even now.

'I have seven women travelling alone with children on flights out of Phoenix this afternoon. The rest are families. You did say your sister was unaccompanied, didn't you?'

Greg nodded. He could see the swell of her breasts pushing at the fabric of her blouse and despite everything, he was getting an erection. Her nipples were like small buttons beneath the

147

starched white cotton and her pupils had darkened, making her eyes limpid emerald.

His voice became a caress. 'I don't expect she's used her real name either, but you could try.'

She looked up and he felt as if he was drowning in those eyes that were so like Gabriella's.

'What name would that be, sir?' She was almost purring and Greg could feel the sexual vibes radiating from her. 'Try Whitmore.' His voice was thick with arousal.

The girl checked, then shook her head. 'No Whitmore, sorry.' She looked back at him, her smile an invitation. 'How old is the child? It would show in the cost of the ticket.'

'Only a few weeks old. A little boy.' Greg's voice broke as he thought of his son. The erection deflated.

'You're in luck. There are only five infants under the age of two listed.'

Greg waited impatiently as her fingers paused above the keyboard of her computer and she tipped her head to one side.

'Of course, I'm breaking a great many rules. They could dismiss me, then who would pay for my son's education?'

Did she make her men pay for sex too? He wouldn't put it past her. He handed over another five hundred dollars.

She did the same vanishing trick, then scribbled down the details, adding flight numbers and times of departure. She pushed it across the counter. 'Is there any other service I can provide for you, sir?'

Greg scanned the list, then tucked it in his pocket. He raised her hand to his lips and caught the fragrance of Chanel No. 5, and lemon skin cream. 'Regretfully no. Perhaps another time. Have a nice day.'

He laughed softly as Jake appeared at his side. 'That one's hot to trot,' he murmured. 'But she came up with the goods. What have you got for me?'

Jake handed over the lists and Greg scanned them quickly. There were twenty two women, all heading for different destinations with their babies. Several, like LA and New York could be discounted. She was too well known there. Within minutes, he'd put out the orders to have the destination airports watched.

'What do you want me to do, Mr Castlemaine?' Jake straightened his tie and waited while Greg stroked his nose in thought.

'I want you and Paul in Florida. She could be heading for Bermuda – it's British and the closest thing to home. Keep me informed.'

Greg stared after them thoughtfully. Paul seemed eager enough, respectful enough, but he was still wet behind the ears. Good men like Jake were difficult to find these days.

He lit a cigarette, brushed crumbs from a chair and sat down in gloomy contemplation. Gabriella couldn't have picked a worse time to run out on him. His place as head of the corporation was not finalised or confirmed – and the man called George was too close to achieving what they'd set out to do for it to be put in jeopardy. If things went wrong, he could kiss that particular opportunity goodbye.

The anger churned, and the heat rose. How dare she endanger all I've worked for. He ground the cigarette into the tiled floor. There were three hours to go before his flight to New York and his meeting with Dad. It wouldn't be pleasant, and the humiliation of what he had to tell him was already acid in his belly.

I need a drink – a very large one.

Gabriella walked into the cool interior of the Albuquerque airport terminal. The cold, impersonal grey marble floors and echoing white walls and ceilings reminded her of the house in California.

After buying her ticket for the next stage of her journey, she wandered around the almost deserted shopping mall. She found what she needed in the chemist shop, then bought a large cup of fresh orange juice and a salad sandwich and headed for the ladies' rest room. It would be quiet in there and she could feed and change Nick, then see to her own needs.

Two hours were long enough for what she planned to do.

The knowledge that she'd put hundreds of miles between her and the Castlemaines, had restored her flagging energy. But she knew she couldn't afford to relax. Greg was too sharp, too cunning. He had probably already discovered she was not on the Houston bus and was closing in.

Clutching her purchases, she gave a grim smile. She wasn't beaten yet. Far from it.

11

Gabriella sat in the mother and baby section of the ladies' rest room, the door locked, a dripping tap ticking off the minutes like a metronome. Time was up.

Dipping her head into the basin, she shampooed and rinsed her hair, then used her dirty t-shirt to dry it. 'I hope this works,' she muttered. 'Because if it doesn't, I haven't got time to do anything else.'

She caught sight of her reflection and the shock stilled her. 'Bloody hell,' she muttered. 'Even Mum wouldn't recognise me.'

A loud rapping on the door made her jump.

'What you doin' in there, lady? I gotta kid to be fed here.'

'Try the next cubicle,' Gabriella shouted back, remembering just in time to disguise her accent.

'There ain't no next cubicle, lady. You ain't doing somethin' illegal in there, are you? Git your ass out here 'fore I call security.'

Gabriella bit her lip and glanced back to the mirror. There was dye streaked on her forehead and her hair was still wet, but the bloody woman wouldn't go away.

'One minute more, and I'm finished,' she called through the door.

'Yea? Well I'm stayin' put and countin'.'

'Do what you like,' muttered Gabriella. 'Just shut up and let me get on.'

The cubicle was quite large and brightly lit, and it didn't

take long to cut a fringe and use the new, darker make-up. When she'd finished, she took a long hard look in the mirror and swung her newly cropped, shoulder length, black bob. 'I like it,' she whispered, and grinned at her new reflection.

Adding black khol to her eyes, and a sweep of blood red to her lips, she nodded in satisfaction. Swiftly climbing into the silk shift dress, she zipped it up and bundled the rest of her clothes back into the hold-all. Flat shoes, and a sweater over her shoulders completed the makeover.

'Time's up. I'm calling security.'

Gabriella dropped the hank of blonde hair into a plastic bag and hid it beneath Nick's dirty nappies at the bottom of the trash can. Picking up Nick, and the bags, she unlocked the door.

''Bout time.' The woman barged in, knocking Gabriella sideways. 'Goddam Mexes. You people should have your own rest rooms.'

Gabriella could think of a dozen cutting replies, but remained silent as she eased round the woman and left the cubicle. The ignorant bitch wouldn't have understood she was being insulted, so what was the point?

The airport was still quite busy, even though it was now late afternoon, and she weaved her way to the departure lounge. Her flight would be called soon, and that was the safest place to be. But the incident in the ladies had shown her the disguise was working.

Greg's flight had just been called when the mobile phone interrupted his bitter thoughts.

'Yes?' he snapped.

'Mr Castlemaine?'

'Who is this?'

'Spiros Papandreos, sir.' The voice at the other end was young and breathless. 'I've found her. Mrs Castlemaine's in New Mexico.' The words tumbled one over the other in barely suppressed excitement.

'Let me speak to her.' At last, things were coming right.

There was silence at the other end – followed by an audible swallow. 'She's in the passenger departure lounge, sir.'

'Then get her out!' His voice cut through the low babble of the other passengers, making silence fall and eyes drift in his direction. He moved away to an isolated corner. His nerves were frayed, his patience stretched to its limit.

'I can't, sir. I haven't got a ticket.'

'Jesus wept! Of all the stupid . . .' Greg's voice dropped several wintery octaves. 'Fuck off and buy one then.' He took a breath. 'Where's she headed?'

'I don't know, sir.'

'Are you positive it's my wife – you don't seem to know much.'

The voice at the other end sounded less confident. 'Well, um . . . She looks a little different to the photograph, but I'm positive it's her. I saw her face clearly, but she . . .'

'Is it her or not?'

'Yes. But . . .'

'Keep tabs on her.' His patience snapped, the world tilted and time became grains of sand slipping through his fingers. 'Get her out of departures if you can, if not – follow her onto the plane. Ring me before you leave.'

Greg cut the connection and hurried out of the departure lounge. If it had been the reliable Jake at the other end, then he wouldn't have worried quite so much, but the young Greek was inexperienced, there were too many things that could go wrong, and the frustration of being so far away was beginning to tell.

His immediate instinct had been to fly directly to Alberquerque, but he never trusted that first, emotional reaction. Patience had always been his strength, he'd learned very early on that hasty decisions inevitably lead to trouble.

He stood on the concourse and watched the flight monitors. If she was waiting for a flight out, then it had to be domestic. Alberquerque wasn't an international airport, so it stood to reason it was wiser to wait – rather than go on a wild goose chase.

Within minutes he had the information he needed. Three flights were waiting to board in New Mexico. Oklahoma City, Dallas and Houston.

His mouth twitched in a cold smile. Houston again. Is she trying to get to Texas and an international airport – or was it just coincidence?

'Delta Airlines regrets to announce a delay on Flight 193 to Dallas–Fort Worth. Please watch the monitors for further information.'

Gabriella froze as the announcement was repeated in Spanish. It was close to the worst thing that could have happened, and there was nothing she could do but wait for her flight to be called. It was a risk – but then she'd taken so many in the past few hours – what was one more?

She looked up at the monitors. The Dallas flight was delayed by an hour, but as she looked at the ever changing lines of information, her mouth dried. A flight from Phoenix had just landed.

The departure lounge was suddenly too crowded. The Castlemaines' influence was such that any of those faces could have belonged to one of their men, and unless Greg or Vic had arrived on that flight, she had no way of knowing who could be watching her.

Cradling Nick, she found an isolated seat at the far end of the departure lounge. It was behind a pillar, and shielded by an enormous cactus plant, but it gave her a clear view of the human tide that flowed through the doors.

Lean, sunbaked men in jeans, checked shirts and stetsons strolled by, silver belt buckles glinting in the electric light, their boot heels clicking on the marble floor. Fat women in brightly coloured crimplene dresses waddled past, bedecked in silver and turquoise Indian jewellery, their voices loud and demanding as they chivvied equally fat and bejewelled husbands to get a move on. Moon-faced Hopi Indians squatted next to their bundles, settled and stoic, seemingly untroubled by the bustle around them.

Gabriella watched the faces. Do any of them look as if they're from the city? Was that man acting suspiciously – did he look as if he was searching for someone – have I seen him before?

'This is ridiculous,' she muttered. 'My nerves are shot and I'm talking to myself.'

She started as a figure appeared around the pillar.

'I'm sorry for the delay, *Señora*, but we hope to be boarding within the next ten minutes. There are changing facilities for the baby on the other side of the lounge.'

Gabriella nodded her thanks as she tried to disguise her bewilderment at the flood of Spanish. As Señora Consuela Domingo, she would have to get used to it, and thanks to school, she knew enough to get by – at a pinch.

Picking up the bags, she adjusted Nick's sling and headed for the rest room, but as she glanced towards the door of the departure lounge, her confidence tumbled and time stood still.

The young man was coming through the barrier, and for those few seconds their eyes met. Brown trapped by green. The recognition in them unmistakable. Fear became a spidery thing that crawled deep and stayed there.

She watched him approach, Nick grasped closely to her. She was amongst strangers in a strange place. An alien in alien surroundings. Who would understand the danger this man brought with him – and what could they do?

Gabriella forced herself to move until she found a seat between two large negro women. He can't force me to leave, she thought desperately. Can't drag me off kicking and screaming without causing himself a good deal of trouble. If I sit tight, then I'll be OK.

She looked up.

He was sitting in a seat opposite, his eyes steady and fixed on her face.

Gabriella stared back at him. The room began to swim and tilt. The seat yawed like a loose saddle on an unbroken horse. Her vision blurred, and darkness closed in.

Strong arms grabbed her and she forced herself back to reality. She had to keep watch on the man opposite – had to protect Nick.

'There, there, honey. You drink this. I'spect you been over doin' it, what with the baby an' all. It's only water, but it's nice and cold.' The dark face swam before her, distorted and strange, but the eyes were kind and concerned.

She felt the cold trickle of water on her lips and savoured its passage down her throat. Grasping the paper cup she drank greedily, and with every gulp she felt reason return.

'Better now, honey?'

Gabriella nodded. The noise of the departure lounge was muffled, and seemed a long way off. Yet she was still sitting here – still opposite the stranger with the steady brown eyes.

'Don't fret, honey. I had five babies, and I know how exhaustin' they can be.'

Gabriella smiled as the soft, dark hand patted her arm. The woman's voice was buzzing in her head like an angry wasp in a jam jar.

'You fixin' to meet your man? That why you travelling alone with this here young 'un?'

Gabriella could feel the heat of the young man's eyes, there was a power in that heat that was paralysing. All she could do was nod.

The United Airlines flight to Oklahoma City was called and people began to move – and that included her kindly companions.

'You take care o' yourself now, you hear? That's one fine baby girl you got there.'

'Thank you,' she whispered, then looked across at the young man.

He was still there – poised and waiting for her to make her move.

'Attention all passengers for Delta Airlines Flight 193 to Dallas. We apologise for the delay, but will be boarding in five minutes.'

Gabriella kept her attention on the man opposite. Did he know where she was heading? Did he have a ticket for the same flight? She felt very alone suddenly, isolated in a sea of empty seats.

Grabbing the bags, she walked to the far side of the lounge to a group of elderly men who were engrossed in a game of cards. That's better, she thought. People on either side, no vacant seats, a wall at my back. I can see the whole room from here.

Time moved ponderously on, each minute seemingly taking for ever as the man moved to a space further down in the row opposite.

'Delta Airlines is now boarding at gate six.'

Gabriella didn't move. She was waiting.

The man remained in his seat. He too was waiting.

Gabriella's pulse raced and her head swam. But still she sat.

The departure lounge was almost deserted now, and he had moved closer – was sitting only five seats away.

'Would passengers Consuela Domingo and Mr Papandreos please go immediately to gate six? The aircraft is about to depart.'

Gabriella was off the seat and moving fast. Her ticket was checked and she was through the double glass doors and down the long tunnel to gate six.

Was he behind her? Was that the thud of his feet on the conveyor belt, or just her heartbeat? She didn't look back as she ran – there was no time.

Greg had been pacing the concourse in Phoenix, and when his mobile rang, he snapped it on.

'Yes?'

'Spiro Papandreos.'

'Have you got her?' It was a bark.

'No, sir. You see . . .'

'Why aren't you on that plane? What the fuck are you doing in New Mexico? Playing with yourself?'

The Greek's voice held a sob of desperation. 'I've been arrested. This is the only call they would let me make.'

'What!' The explosion was followed by an arctic chill. 'Explain.'

'I bought tickets for all the flights and followed her into the departure lounge. But she saw me, knew who I was, I could see it in her eyes.'

'Mind what you say. Someone could be listening,' Greg hissed.

'Mrs Castlemaine left it until the last minute, then made a dash for the departure gate. I tried to follow, but the airport police arrested me for suspicious behaviour. They said they'd been watching me ever since I tried bribing one of the staff for flight information, and wanted an explanation for the three tickets. I said you would vouch for me, sir. I realise now I was wrong to bring you into this. I'm sorry.'

Greg felt a dread certainty wash over him. 'Where's my wife now?'

'On the plane to Dallas, sir. But I think . . .'

'You don't think, that's your problem.'

'Will you speak to the officer and vouch for me? I don't know how much more of this I can take. They've already done a body search.'

There were tears behind the words, but Greg was unmoved. 'You screwed up Papandreos – get yourself out of the mess.'

'But sir, there's something you should . . .'

Greg switched off the phone and forgot the young Greek the minute he was on the move. There was a flight leaving for Dallas in ten minutes. He would have to hurry.

*　　*　　*

Gabriella huddled in the furthest corner of the back row seat, Nick cradled to her chest. The steady drone of the plane engines was merely a backdrop to the thud of her pulse, and she closed her eyes. She felt sick, light-headed and thoroughly drained. If she didn't have something to drink she knew she would black out again.

Nick was screaming as the plane rose in the sky, but it didn't matter. They were safe. Safe all the time she was in the air – safe until she reached Dallas. Then she would have to begin all over again. Goodbye New Mexico. Good riddance.

As the Dallas flight soared above the clouds, Gabriella shivered with foreboding. The Castlemaines had marshalled their army of pawns – unknown faces, shadows melting into crowds, eyes that watched and followed. She'd been discovered and recognised – and ultimately betrayed, for now they knew where she was heading.

She was truly isolated – her moves transmitted to the opposition with no option but to finish this particular gambit.

Greg looked out at the clouds and wondered where Gabriella's plane was. She must be close to landing by now, his own flight was over midway. The whole frigging thing was coming down around his head, he'd had to cancel the flight to New York and with it, his second meeting with Dad. The old man hadn't taken the call himself, for which Greg was relieved; but Gabriella's deceit had dropped him in the shit and for that she would pay. If she screwed things up with Dad, he would personally slit her throat.

He made a concerted effort to relax, leaned back and sipped the Jack Daniels. The ice tinkled in the frosted glass like wind chimes on a summer breeze, the sound would normally have soothed him, but as he closed his eyes, he couldn't get Gabriella out of his mind. She drifted before him, taunting with her betrayal, her green eyes feline in that smooth young face.

With an angry snort he dismissed her and tossed back the remains of his whisky. The woman had made a fool of him.

What the hell was he doing, chasing her all over the country in the middle of the night? If Dad could see him now, he would have nothing but contempt for his actions.

Greg took a shuddering breath as his bruised pride lay heavy within him, and he was forced to face the truth. I still love her, admire her in a strange way for the fight and imagination she's shown to get so far.

He closed his eyes, knowing his demeanour appeared relaxed, yet acknowledging the turmoil beneath that calm exterior. If only she had come to me, talked things over before making such a disastrous move; maybe I could have persuaded her to stay. We could have worked things out between us, others managed it. I was so certain of her, so determined to have her, despite Dad's warnings. The instincts I've always relied on were wrong. I should have stopped to think.

Anger made him sit upright, his fists clenched on the arm of the seat as he glared at the layers of cloud that obliterated the state of Texas. Why the hell am I making excuses for her? She's not smart, hasn't thought things out at all. The woman's a fool to turn her back on me, even if she did witness Leo's murder – she'll spend the rest of her life looking over her shoulder – because I'll never give up until she's silenced and I have my son.

Gabriella could not stop Nick from crying. On and on he went, his fists pummelling the air, his legs kicking against her as she tried to soothe him. There was no more formula, and he spat out the diluted orange juice.

The couple in the seats beside her asked to be moved, and she couldn't blame them, the noise Nick was making was enough to raise the dead. Yet, with them gone, there was enough room for her to change the baby and enough privacy for her to breast feed him.

Peace at last. The silence and relief in the plane was almost tangible.

Gabriella stared through the window at the darkening sky,

but all she could see was the face of the stranger who'd watched and waited for her in New Mexico. He would tell Greg about her attempt at disguise, and where she was heading – and Greg could be waiting for her as she stepped off the plane. Or maybe Victor's face would be the first she'd see – just as dangerous, spiteful in his need to pay her back for what she'd done to him.

She shuddered and Nick opened his eyes and regarded her for a moment before weariness took over and his eyelids drooped.

The engines throbbed, and the minutes ticked away. How many miles to Dallas and the final moves to checkmate?

'We'll be landing in about fifteen minutes, sir. Would you like another drink?'

Greg shook his head. He wanted his mind clear for whatever happened next. He crushed out his cigarette and fastened his seat belt. Dallas sprawled beneath him in a cluster of lights.

Gabriella had changed her clothes again and hidden her hair with a scarf, and as the wheels thudded onto the tarmac, she grasped the arms of her seat and closed her eyes. Her pulse raced and the adrenalin began to pump. Almost there.

She checked the straps on the baby harness and unclipped her seat belt. There was already movement amongst the other passengers, but Gabriella had her attention fixed to the rear door. That was the nearest exit.

The plane drew up at its allocated bay, the hostess adjusted her uniform and reached for the door.

Gabriella was out of her seat. Ignoring the comments and curses of the other passengers, she pushed her way through. The door was open, the long tunnel to the arrivals lounge stretched out in front of her.

She gave Nick a hug. It was now or never.

*   *   *

Was Gabriella already on her way home, her British passport clasped in her sticky little fingers? The servants hadn't found it in any of the houses – she must think she's gotten away with it. And why had she kept up dual nationality, she hadn't needed it once she married me, thought Greg as he looked down at the lights of the airport. Yet he knew the answer. Because she was English and wished to remain so – because she was independent, devious and wilful. Because she didn't love him.

The aircraft's engines roared as it headed for the runway. The wheels thudded against the concrete as the brakes threw him forward.

Greg felt the familiar surge of adrenalin as he tasted victory. She hadn't had time to leave for England, even if she did have her passport. Her plane could only just have landed and Dallas–Fort Worth was far bigger than any airport the British Isles could offer. It was a city, rising up out of the Texas desert – it would be easy for her to get lost – easy to make a mistake.

But he'd been here before, knew where she was heading. This would be the final run. She would want terminal four, satellite E and he was right behind her.

Gabriella was lost and confused. Endless conveyor belts, endless corridors and tunnels, now three banks of lifts and signs to numerous satellites.

'You look kinda lost there, little lady. Can I help y'all?'

Gabriella looked up – and up and up. She'd never seen anyone so large, or so broad, the stetson he wore was definitely ten-gallon. Yet the relief of seeing a friendly face was immense and she gave a shaky laugh.

'I'm trying to work out which satellite shuttle I need for the international flights.'

He smiled a slow smile that creased the corners of his eyes. 'I guess it must be England you're heading for, so you need terminal four. That's satellite E – on the ground floor.'

Gabriella hesitated.

The Texan plucked the hold-all from her grip and pressed the call button on the lifts. 'Let me help you ma'am. You look all in.'

'Thank you, but you needn't . . .'

'I guess you never heard of Southern hospitality, ma'am. Cain't have you carryin' such a heavy load and I've got plenty of time to spare.'

They stepped into the lift and he looked down at her from his mountainous height. He seemed to fill the spacious lift and Gabriella, for once in her life, felt very small.

He must have read her mind. 'I guess you never been in Dallas before, ma'am. They make everything big in Texas.' He gave a booming laugh as he punched his enormous chest.

Gabriella smiled and tried to see the funny side of it, but her humour had disappeared under the debris of the last two days. She didn't want to offend him, he'd been kind – but he was too loud, too noticeable, too much of everything. If he stayed with her what were the chances of doing anything discreetly?

The lift stopped and the doors opened.

'There's a shuttle every two minutes from here. Now are you sure I cain't accompany you further? I've got the time.'

'You've been very kind, but no. I'm meeting someone and they might not appreciate seeing me with another man.'

He tipped his stetson. 'Understood. Now, y'all have a nice day, little lady – and remember Texas kindly.'

Gabriella smiled and waved as he disappeared back into the lifts. She would certainly remember Texas, but whether it would be kindly or not depended on the next few minutes.

Greg scanned the concourse. It was crowded as usual, but there was no sign of her. But she was here, he was so close he could feel her – so near he could almost smell her perfume. Her presence tantalised him, sharpening the edges of his resolve and whetting his appetite for revenge.

He switched on the mobile. 'I've arrived. Anything to report?'

'Nothing Mr Castlemaine. We checked out the flight from New Mexico, but no one came off that fitted your wife's description. Just a bunch of Mex women and their brats.'

'Keep looking. She's here somewhere, and probably in disguise.'

He decided to go up to the observation deck, there would be a better view of the concourse there. Taking the stairs two at a time, he turned from the illuminated runways and looked down. There were the British Airways counters, half a dozen of them – but no single woman with a child in the queues.

He trawled the concourse. Maybe she'd sparked up a conversation with someone – a man on his own perhaps, appearing to be travelling with him. But no. He would have recognised the tilt of her head and the way she moved, despite any disguise she may have adopted. She wasn't there.

Gabriella rounded her shoulders and kept the headscarf pulled close to her face. With a slower, less confident stride, she gave the British Airways desk a wide berth. The sight of the Union Jack was like a homecoming, but with an Air France ticket in her pocket from Alberquerque, she had no need to stop.

As she filtered through the crowds towards the customs barriers, she darted anxious glances at the faces that passed. The blood pounded in her ears as she waited for the expected hand on her shoulder, or voice at her side, and as the moments ticked by, her throat closed and her mouth went dry. Inch by inch she melted into the shuffling queue that filtered towards the customs barriers. Her gaze was fixed to the floor, her hands cradled Nick close. One cry from him and all would be lost.

Greg lit a cigarette. Nick's down there – somewhere – close. I can feel it in my gut. But where?

Then he had an idea, and it was so sharp, so vivid in its

brilliance, he knew it couldn't fail. Taking the steps at a run, he headed for the customer information desk.

'Would Gabriella Whitmore, booked on the one forty-five flight to London, Heathrow, please come to the British Airways Information counter. This is an emergency announcement for Gabriella Whitmore.'

Greg smiled at the dark haired English girl and pressed a couple of hundred dollars into her hand. 'Thank you. It will be a wonderful surprise for my wife.'

He walked away and waited next to a newspaper stand and pretended to read the *Washington Post*. Gabriella must have booked on that flight. It was the only one to England for the next three hours.

The sense of her presence was even stronger. If she was playing the sort of game she'd been pursuing up until now, she would leave it until the last minute. She would have to come to the desk to find out what was wrong.

I have her.

Gabriella heard the message and knew he was here. The rapid thud of her pulse was almost deafening and she swayed against the woman standing next to her.

The customs officer eyed her curiously, scanned her passport, stamped it, and finally she was through into the departure area. The flight had already been called and she hurried down the corridor to the docking bay.

As the engines fired up and the wheels began to turn, she held her breath. The jumbo jet raced along the runway and she closed her eyes. The first game was over.

The minutes ticked by and the information monitors clicked monotonously. The BA flight had been called, the departure gate closed, the plane taking off.

Greg scanned the crowds for that tall, distinctive blonde, his frustration mounting. Then he crumpled the newspaper, his mood murderous. He'd stood there like an idiot for more than half an hour with no sign of her. The senator had refused to use his FBI contacts to man the customs barriers and now she'd slipped through and was gone.

He didn't like losing – never had – but he knew when the game was over. Knew when the time had come to lay down his king and concede defeat, however much he might resent it. He headed for the bar and watched the planes take off and land. She was out there somewhere and one day soon he would find her.

Then the game could begin again.

New York sweltered in the early heat wave as Greg slammed the door of his apartment on the outside world. The open-plan penthouse looked out over Central Park, but for once he was too distracted to admire the view. The bitch hadn't gotten away with it. Somehow, somewhere, he would find her, and when he did, he would take great pleasure in punishing her. It would be a slow death, he promised himself, one which would have her screaming for forgiveness at having caused him such inconvenience.

Greg stepped into the main reception area and scowled. The air conditioning was purring contentedly and the heavy curtains were drawn against the sun, making the room forest cool. Yet his mood was too bleak to take the usual pleasure in the scattered Chinese rugs of delicate green and white, the curtains of the palest eau de nile, or the white leather couches and small marble and gilt tables. Even the two exquisite Degas paintings on the white walls failed to rouse his spirits, and the collection of dark green foliage plants which filled a niche from floor to ceiling in one corner of the lounge area, merely served as a reminder of Gabriella, who'd helped plan the decor.

He cast his eye over the rare jade lion that stood three feet high to one side of the Italian marble fireplace. That too was a reminder – it had been part of his wedding present to his young, beautiful bride. It was as though her presence was still here – mocking him.

He tried shaking off the depression by dragging his thoughts elsewhere. He needed a shower and sleep, but first, he had to contact Smith in London, and make sure the odious little Cockney was carrying out his orders. If Gabriella had managed to slip past Smith's men, then Tyler Reed would come in handy. At least he'd be dealing with a professional if Smith's recommendation was anything to go by.

'Where you been, boy? I've been waiting.'

A chill dowsed Greg's thoughts as the familiar gravelled voice drifted into the hallway. He gripped the bunch of keys until they dug into the flesh of his palm. Dad was an unwelcome intrusion, but the man's presence demanded respect.

'Hi, Dad. I didn't realise we had an appointment.' His words were oiled with just enough meekness to appease, but his gaze remained low to mask his deep-seated panic.

The old man showed no emotion, but the yellow eyes were sharply intelligent as they scanned Greg's face. When the silence became stretched and Greg forced himself to meet those eyes, he wondered how profoundly his father could read his mind. Cancer might have ravaged his body, the steroids bloating his face and once virile, energetic frame, but his brain was still alive and as sharp as ever.

Greg felt vulnerable, and as it was an alien emotion, it was difficult to contain it, so he turned away and stared out through the curtains at the great sprawling park beneath the apartment block. He was playing for time, yet he knew his father wouldn't leave until he was satisfied Greg was hiding nothing from him.

How much does he know? he wondered. Most of it probably. Victor would have found it impossible to keep his mouth shut, and the scandal of Gabriella's departure had already sent a shiver up George – giving him a lever to extricate himself. I'll have to be careful, one false move and I could lose everything.

'How's Mom?'

'I'm not here to discuss your Mother's health,' the old

man rasped. 'I'm here to find out what the hell's going on. Sit down.'

Greg poured a glass of iced water and obeyed, but the tension in the room was almost unbearable.

'What's all this about your wife?' The yellow eyes were direct and piercing.

Greg's pulse quickened and he shrugged, not trusting himself to speak. He took a sip of the water which helped quench the tiredness, but it was not enough to sharpen his wits – his body felt heavy, his mind floating in molasses. Let the old man tell him what he knew, then it would be easier to circumnavigate the truth.

'Cat got your tongue, boy? Answer me, goddam it.' The voice was harsher now, the pitch higher as he struggled forward in his wheelchair.

Greg withered beneath the old man's scrutiny, but he held on to the possibility that his father didn't have the full version of events. 'Gabriella's having a vacation in England. End of story.'

Gregory Castlemaine senior clucked his tongue and gripped the arms of the chair as he thrust his face towards Greg. 'That's a goddam lie, boy, and you know it! She's left you and hightailed it back to Mom. Why else did you give chase all over the goddam States?'

Greg forced himself to meet those lupine eyes. 'OK, so she's left me. It was Nick I was concerned about. She had no right to take him with her.'

'Horse shit!' Castlemaine senior spat, his features twisted in derision. 'She's been leading you by the dick. It's the woman you were after. You'll have other sons, why make such a big deal over this one?'

The anger lay cold in the pit of Greg's stomach. It sharpened his mind and brought him out of the stupor of weariness. 'He's my son. He belongs to me. How can you expect me to turn my back on him?'

'Because you are a Castlemaine!' The old man thumped the

arm of the chair, feverish spots of colour livid on his ashen cheeks, his torso racked with the effort.

'Nicholas is a Castlemaine. Doesn't he have rights?' Greg was aware that he shouted at the old man – something unthinkable in the past – but he was beyond reason.

'Not when his mother endangers everything we've worked for.' The rasp became a cough and the anger a fight for breath.

Greg hurried to hold the glass of water to the old man's mouth. He regretted his outburst, for he hadn't realised how far his health had deteriorated. The flesh under the lightweight jacket had little substance, the framework of bones seemed brittle, and the once proud tilt to the old man's head and shoulders was weighed down by the pain he must be suffering.

'I'm sorry, Dad,' he said softly, the regret genuine. 'But my son's important to me.'

'Stop fussing over me, boy.' He was waved away and the room fell into a silence broken only by the rasping wheeze in the old man's lungs.

Greg watched him. Dad was an ageing eagle, bereft of all his strength and bright plumage. Even so, the old man still had the power to overawe him. He'd never managed to conquer that fear, merely harnessed it and used it to fuel his ambition. It had made him strong, but did he love this sick old man?

Not really, he admitted silently. I admire him, respect him, yet he was never the kind of father who taught his sons with love and kindness. Perhaps you and I are cast from the same ambitious mould, and we have used one another to forge our futures. Greg mentally shrugged. Whatever the reason, the old man had been good to him, and taught him a lot. Perhaps that was what love was really about – a meeting of minds and ambition – a recognition of strengths and weaknesses within the other – working together for the common goal.

'What's eating you, boy? Come on. Spit it out.'

The voice was weaker now, almost querulous, and Greg

realised his father was close to exhaustion. 'I was remembering all the things we've achieved together, Dad. We've come a long way, and if things turn out right in three weeks' time, then ultimately the decision about what to do with Nick, will be yours.'

The old man looked at Greg with a gleam in his eyes. It was a familiar gleam – one of cunning. 'So, for the moment, you're willing to sacrifice your son and forget about the English girl in return for the glory and prestige? Interesting. But what will happen to your noble intentions when I die?'

Greg had the urgent desire to shift in his chair and avert his gaze, but his father's scrutiny held him there. 'They won't change.'

'Bullshit! You'll never let go. I know you too well, boy.' He coughed, but his scrutiny never faltered. 'And what about your brother? Gonna turn your back on him too?'

Greg shrugged. 'Vic's a bum. He made me look stupid and balled the whole thing up. He had to be taught a lesson.'

'That's what this is really all about, isn't it? Your goddam pride. Just remember, boy, you had a hand in losing your wife – you're using Vic as an excuse.'

'Vic's a liability, Dad – you know that as well as I. I'll make sure he doesn't starve to death, but it's time he took charge of his own life. He should thank me for letting him go. He'll be much happier doing his own thing.'

Castlemaine senior nodded thoughtfully. 'Maybe. But don't make an enemy of your brother. Vic has the power to hurt you and hurt you badly.'

'He's not my enemy, Dad.' Greg was startled, but the warning echoed his own persistent doubts about his brother.

'He could be. Sometimes it's wise to look at those nearest us to find the roots of betrayal. They know more about us than perhaps we do ourselves.'

Greg was shocked into silence. Surely Dad was mistaken? Vic wouldn't betray him, just as he hadn't the stomach for killing him when he had the chance.

The old man's voice interrupted the troubled thoughts.

'It's easy to make enemies when you're rich and powerful. You'll have to show more strength of character if you want to remain president of the company.'

A shaft of fear speared through Greg.

Gregory Castlemaine senior chuckled and his chest rattled with the effort. 'Don't fret, boy. I'm not about to call a board meeting – merely giving you fair warning. Your behaviour, and that of your wife and brother will be the topic over many a dinner table, but it can do no harm to the reputation you already hold within the business community.' He leaned forward. 'Why did you leave her in California when you knew something was wrong?'

How the hell did he know about that? Vic's mouth's been flapping again. Dad's right. He'll have to be watched.

'My pride allowed her to run,' he replied with more honesty than he cared to admit. 'I couldn't believe she would do it.'

'Goddam fool. I told you she was the wrong woman for you, but you young men are so impatient, so hot when it comes to a bit of skirt.' He regarded Greg from beneath his eyebrows. 'Why didn't you stick it to her and leave it at that? There are plenty of rich American women to marry – women whose families can open doors and increase our influence in high places. OK, so some of them look like the rear end of a mule, but you could have had your affairs, lived your own life without the fear of scandal.'

Greg clenched his fists, tightly reining in his temper. 'I loved Gabriella. I didn't want an arranged marriage like Vic's.'

'Huh! Leave love to the poor. Look how your Mom supports me. Love has nothing to do with it. I married her because we were both ambitious. She had the class and the connections, I had the money and the business brain.' He glared at Greg, then sighed. 'Get Bruno. He's in the kitchen.'

Greg was relieved the interview was over. It had done nothing to clear the air, nor resolved the problem of what to do about his wife and son.

'I'll expect you in three weeks' time. My place, eight p.m. sharp. The senator has been dealt with and we should have no problems there, but that was a damn fool thing to do, Greg. By killing Leo you've opened up a whole can of worms. See to it that nothing like this happens again. We have people who are well paid to take care of the dirty laundry – let them deal with it next time.'

He looked up from the wheelchair and smiled, but it was a weary, weak effort. 'Never mind, boy. You're strong and intelligent, you'll have other kids.'

Greg shook his hand. There was a smell of death on his flesh, a dryness, a decay, but patrician pride shone from those feral eyes. 'So long, Dad.'

The old man gripped his hand and Greg was surprised by the strength in those bony fingers. Then with a gesture to the silent Bruno, Gregory Castlemaine senior, was wheeled towards the bank of elevators.

Greg began to unknot his tie. I'll miss the old bastard when he's gone, he thought. Miss his wisdom and strength, his perception and cunning. I'm about as close as I'll ever be to loving him.

At the door to the lift, the old man turned to Greg, his expression grim. 'If you want your son, then go and get him. But wait until I'm gone. It won't be long now. Just be careful of Victor. You've hurt his pride and a wounded animal becomes a dangerous enemy.'

PART TWO

12

Tyler stepped into the shower and let the hot water revive him. He felt good. The early morning work-out had made him realise that despite his age, he could still lift weights with the best of them down at the gym. His knee might make him limp, but the muscles in his chest and arms were pumped up and as strong as ever. Even the girl in the pink leotard had given him the eye and she couldn't have been more than twenty-five.

He began to whistle as he dried himself. He enjoyed women's company, but he would never be tied down again. He was not the marrying kind. Marion had taught him that.

Wrapping the towel around his waist, he shaved and rubbed his close cropped hair dry. He liked to keep it short, less bother. Breakfast was orange juice, strong sweet tea and scrambled eggs which he ate in the kitchen. It was going to be a fine day, the sky looked clear and the sun already shone brightly through the window.

Dressed in a white shirt, clean denims and a comfortable tweed jacket, he pulled on the highly polished Doc Martens and tied the laces. After years of wearing army boots, these were like slipping into well worn slippers. They were the only sensible thing punks had adopted. Glancing at his watch, he realised there was plenty of time to get to the office. The habit of rising early and the morning work-outs were a routine to set him up for the day. After the strict regime in the army he needed the gym to keep his body tuned. Too many hours sitting in the car on surveillance made him feel sluggish.

That was why he didn't like domestics, but it was work and the bills needed paying. He could have taken the post offered by Nottingham University to teach Middle-Eastern languages, but the thought of sitting in musty class rooms and teaching spotty youths was too much. He needed space, fresh air and the freedom to come and go as he pleased. It would have been worse than marriage. There was the civil service of course, a lot of the other guys had taken that route, but he'd had enough of orders and pen pushers to last him a life time.

Thinking about the office and the day's appointments brought him back to Smith. It had been three weeks since his initial call, and Smith had been on the blower nearly every day. Tyler's curiosity had been whetted. 'I'll soon find out what he wants – if he turns up today,' he muttered as he climbed into the ancient Escort he used for work.

The car purred into life and eased through the early morning commuter traffic. It might look battered and nondescript, but under the bonnet was a finely tuned, powerful piece of engineering. Tyler had stripped her, tuned her, oiled and cherished her. Like Jezebel, she would never let him down.

The office was on the ground floor of a three-storey Victorian terrace. It had a cellar which they used to store files, security systems, protective clothing and a hundred and one other things they might need on a job. Above them was a theatrical agency and on the top floor was a young graphic designer. Tyler parked the car round the back. A line of garages served the terrace and he had keys for four of them. He locked the car, pocketed the keys and went through the back door into the office.

On his right was a kitchen and toilet, to his left were two rooms furnished to conduct interviews in privacy. Down the long passageway he pushed open the door into the main room and smiled at Dot who, as usual, had arrived before him.

'Morning, Mr T.' she said brightly as she marked her place in the Agatha Christie novel. 'Coffee's made and here are your letters.' She handed him a sheaf of brown envelopes which he took reluctantly.

Dot was in her late sixties and shouldn't really be working at all. A spritely widow, with a shock of silver hair that never seemed to look untidy, she was dressed in a lilac cardigan and sprigged cotton dress. Her one vice was reading crime novels – she never went anywhere without one. She had been the first person to answer their ad for a receptionist. Bored with housework, Dot didn't like knitting or coach trips and needed something to do that would stop her from going round the bend.

Tyler and Bill had taken to her immediately and now they wouldn't know how they would cope if she left them. She was efficient, never minded working odd hours, and often had to go without wages when times were tough. As he'd remarked to Bill last week, Dot was a diamond.

Tyler sipped his coffee and dropped the letters back on his desk. They could wait.

'Have you eaten this morning? I brought some croissants,' Dot said hopefully.

'I'm fine, thanks. We'll have them mid morning.' Dot still tried to mother him, but after the night he'd taken her back to the flat and cooked her a dinner of Persian rice and lamb stew, followed by his favourite baklava, she knew he could take care of himself. That was another thing they both liked about her. She didn't try to take over.

Tyler put down his coffee and reluctantly looked through the post. It was as he thought, bills. Damn this recession. The bloody fools in Westminster didn't know what they were doing. The high streets were a testimony to that. Half the shops boarded up, the other half hanging on by their finger nails.

'Bill told you about Mr Smith, then?' asked Dot, peering at him over her half-moon spectacles.

She reminded him of his old headmistress when she did that and it made him grin. 'Yeah. Surprised he made contact after our last meeting.'

Dot sniffed and folded her arms under her corseted bosom.

'Nasty, vulgar little man. Far too much jewellery if you ask me. Never trust a man with rings on all his fingers, is what I say.'

'You could be right, Dot,' he said thoughtfully.

'I didn't think you'd want to meet him outside the office, so I made an appointment for him to come here at midday.' Dot smiled with satisfaction. 'He didn't like it, but I said here or you wouldn't see him at all.'

'That's fine. What else is happening?'

'Bill's fitting the security system at the sheik's, so he won't be in today, but he's got his pager if you need him. And I've arranged for you to escort Crown Prince Ali Hassan to Saudi next week. At least we can pay a couple of bills when that's done. The King always pays promptly. And in cash.'

Tyler nodded. It was, as Sniffy would have said, a nice little earner.

The morning progressed with telephone calls and the answering of letters. They went over the books and managed to pay the electricity, the rent and the VAT, but the others would have to wait until the end of the month.

At one minute to twelve Tyler heard footsteps on the concrete stairway leading to the front door and looked up. There was a sleek BMW parked on the double yellow lines outside. It had to be Sniffy.

'Make yourself scarce, Dot,' he said quietly as he cleared his desk.

The flight into Paris had been uneventful, and after resting at a small hotel just outside the city, Gabriella had hired a car the next day and driven north into Normandy. It was a part of France she knew and loved, having been a favourite haunt during family camping trips in the school holidays.

The three weeks at the campsite in Les Andelys had given her the chance to relax and take stock of her situation. The caravans and tents were nestled between chalk cliffs and the river Seine, their position guarded by Château Gaillard, Richard the Lionheart's 'saucy' castle which perched majestically above them on the cliffs. Gabriella's caravan stood beneath the trees at the far end of the site, and the only person she had spoken to during her stay was the man who came each morning to deliver bread.

It was very early morning and the mist still lay on the river and shrouded the trees. Dew glinted in the grass and no one stirred in the surrounding caravans as Gabriella hurried back from the showers. She shivered at the unaccustomed chill around her neck and quickly let herself into the caravan.

The bob she'd styled back in Alberquerque was gone, now her hair was close cropped, layered and spiky, the black dye luridly streaked with red. She towelled it dry and grinned ruefully at her reflection in the window as she remembered the night she'd hacked at it with the blunt scissors. Streaking it had been messy and time consuming, but as a disguise, the results were satisfying. 'You'll never make a hairdresser, though, Gabby. God, what a mess.'

Nick was awake now, and after feeding him and making him comfortable, she cleaned the caravan and checked her luggage. The Louis Vuitton hold-all had been replaced by a rucksack, the handbag by a leather tote she'd bought for a few francs in the local market, but they served as window dressing for her latest makeover.

Her clothes too, had become a part of that change. Gone was the silk shift dress and the Chanel trousers and blouse – and as she pulled on the long, fringed skirt and tie-dyed t-shirt, she gave a wry smile. '*Plus ça change, plus c'est la même chose*,' she muttered. 'But if it gets me home, what the hell?'

The new Doc Martens had been deliberately scuffed with a Brillo pad and Vim, but they were comfortable over the thick socks. A long black cardigan, cheap jewellery and heavy eye make-up finished off the look.

Gabriella eyed her reflection thoughtfully, then turned away and began loading the car. It would take an hour or so to get to the coast – if she missed the commuter traffic and stuck to the motorways and didn't get lost – the car would have to be dropped off at the Hertz office, and the ferry times checked. It was going to be a busy day – but there was something she had to do before she left France.

The port of Le Havre was busy with the summer tourists, and after leaving the car, Gabriella hitched the rucksack into a more comfortable position, checked the straps on Nick's sling and swung the tote bag over her shoulder.

'I feel like a pack mule,' she muttered as she made her way towards the pay phone, but the ferry was leaving in half an hour, there was no time to waste on moaning.

'Hello, Edith. Gabriella. Could I speak to Mum please?'

'Gabby! At last! We've been trying to get hold of you, but Jake said you and Greg had gone away for a few weeks and couldn't be reached. You sound as though you're just around the corner. When are you coming home to show us the baby? Your mother and I were thrilled to get the photographs. We can't wait to see him.'

Gabriella smiled as Edith Maybury put down the receiver with a clatter without waiting for a reply. Her mother's housekeeper had been with her for years, and although she was almost seventy, she still hadn't learned to take things slowly.

'Gabriella? How are you darling? Where have you been?' Helen Whitmore's voice sounded fogged with sleep, but then it was very early morning.

Gabriella felt the tears threaten and had to swallow. I can't give in now, she thought. Can't allow myself to fall apart after having achieved so much. But I'm so very pleased to hear mum's voice.

'I'm fine, Mummy.'

'It's been a long time since you called me that, Gabby.' The voice at the other end was suddenly alert. 'Something's wrong. What's the matter?'

Gabriella leaned against the dirty window of the telephone box. 'Nothing I can't handle.' I shouldn't have called her, she thought. She'll only worry – but oh, how much I need to hear her voice. She cleared her throat. 'I have the baby with me. We're both OK.' The last word was a sob, quickly extinguished. Hang on, Gabby, she admonished silently.

'Where are you? At the airport? I'll send a taxi.' Helen Whitmore's tone was firm and no-nonsense.

The sound of that practical, reassuring voice almost broke her resolve, yet she held on. There must be no risk to the two elderly women, no chance that a tapped line and probing ears could bring danger to that small cottage in Norfolk. But the sound of that lovely, familiar voice made her feel like a child again, and she longed for the comfort of a soft lap and sheltering embrace.

'It doesn't matter where I am. I just wanted you to know I'm all right, and that the baby's safe.'

'What the devil's happened between you and that – that MAN?' Helen Whitmore had never approved of Greg, and was not afraid to make her feelings known.

'I've left him.'

'About time. I wondered when you'd see sense. Come home, Gabriella.'

'I can't, Mum. I can't explain, either. Please don't ask me any more questions.'

'Stuff and nonsense. Tell me where you are and I'll arrange for you to get home. We'll see this thing through together. I'm not scared of that social climbing upstart.'

Gabriella inhaled sharply at her mother's careless words. 'Please don't talk like that. You don't know these people like I do. They'll come looking for me and the baby, and I just wanted to make sure you understand how important it is to be careful. It's better you know nothing.'

'If your father was alive, you wouldn't have got into this mess. Gabby, I'm worried about you and the baby. I want to help. Tell me how I can help.'

'Just talking to you helps, Mum, but there is something you could do for me.'

'Name it.'

'Do you still have my old building society book? The one I kept to pay my car insurance and things?'

'It's around somewhere, but what on earth . . .?'

'Could you please find it? There should still be some money in there and I need the pin and account number. They'll still be valid, won't they?'

'I suppose so, darling, but why all the mystery? I could telephone through and get you a ticket home. Pay on the old plastic. Just tell me where you are and I'll arrange it this end.'

'I can't let you do that, Mum. Please find the book and I'll ring back in a few minutes.'

The pips went and Gabriella replaced the receiver, cutting off her mother's frantic voice.

Leaning back, she realised how much that call had affected her. The sound of her mother's voice had made her long for home and familiar surroundings. Yet that was one place she could never return to, she would have to find somewhere else to live until Nick was old enough to take care of himself – and that was many years ahead. As he grew older he would ask questions about his absent father, and then what? Should I lie to him, cover up the truth and pretend he was dead? Or should I tell him everything and hope he'll accept that I've done the right thing?

She clucked impatiently and checked her watch. It was time to ring back, the ferry was already loading, and thinking like that served no purpose.

'I found it, but there's only a hundred and fifty pounds in the account, so I'm sending Edith into town later to put in some more.'

'Thanks, Mum. What's the account number?'

Helen Whitmore sighed and recited the numbers. 'I want you to promise to ring me again, Gabby. I'm almost frantic with worry.'

'It's too risky, Mum. Please try not to worry. We're both fine, but I want you to promise not to contact the Castlemaines. They're dangerous and I don't want you at risk.' There was a hitch in her voice as the pips went. 'I love you Mum. Love you.'

Gabriella heard the last coin drop into the box and the line go dead. She was alone. More alone than she had ever been – and nothing would be the same again.

Sniffy hadn't changed much since their last meeting. His suit was now designer, rather than Savile Row, his shoes handmade, his belly more rotund. There was no hair at all on that pink dome and the beady eyes were still sharp and mean as they swivelled between the folds of porcine flesh.

Smith stood in the door way and lit a cigar, the rings on his fingers glittering in the sunlight. But Tyler's attention was on the man behind him. A human gorilla with muscles and nothing between the ears.

Tyler touched the khukri knife sheathed and prominent on the desk. He noticed Sniffy's eyes follow the movement, saw the nervous flick of the man's tongue over his full, red lips. Good. Sniffy had got the message.

'Hello Tyler. See you 'aven't changed. Nice office.'

'The gorilla stays outside, or we don't talk.' Tyler saw the man glower and ignored it.

Smith flicked a glance at the bodyguard and nodded. The man shut the door behind him, but Tyler could see the dark shadow through the glass and knew he was listening. Let him. He had nothing to hide.

Smith loosened his jacket and took a seat, his cigar held between thumb and forefinger, his eyes watchful, his smile uncertain.

Tyler waited.

Smith cleared his throat and brushed his trouser leg. 'I asked for this meeting because I'm in a tight spot and you were the only man I could think of with the know-how to solve the problem.'

Tyler remained aloof, but he could see the beads of sweat on the other man's top lip. Whatever Sniffy wanted, it had to be serious. He'd never seen him so nervous.

'You ain't making this easy, Tyler, me old mate,' said Smith through his cigar as he tapped his rings on the metal arm of the chair.

Tyler kept his silence, his expression deliberately stony.

Smith cleared his throat. 'I have a friend who needs to find someone. He's willing to pay very well for your services, Tyler. In fact, 'e asked for you specifically.'

Tyler leaned on the desk and laced his fingers, but his gaze never left Smith's face. 'Then why didn't he come to me direct? I'm in the yellow pages, the *Police Review* and the *Telegraph*.'

Smith tried to cross his legs, gave up and crossed his ankles. 'He don't want a scandal, Tyler. He has very high connections and insisted I acted as go-between. You see, if the newspapers got hold of this, it could turn messy.'

Tyler was intrigued. Sniffy was lying.

'I could have met him somewhere private. Discretion is part of the service.'

'These people are paranoid about publicity. That's why I 'ad to come 'ere today.'

Tyler watched a drop of perspiration roll down the flushed cheek and drip onto the silk shirt. There was a ring of truth in what he was saying, but it still didn't smell right.

'I'll need to know more than that, Smith. But if this has anything to do with drugs, you can get out now.'

Smith puffed on his cigar, seemed to find it distasteful suddenly and mashed it in the ashtray where it lay smouldering in a stinking heap. 'I swear on my mother's life. It has nothing to do with drugs. I wouldn't have come to you, knowing 'ow you feel.'

Tyler felt the short hairs on his scalp prickle. Smith's mother had died years back.

'How come you never get put away, Smith? You're in every dirty deal in the East End, but here you sit, larger than life and twice as ugly.'

Smith leaned back and hooked his thumbs in his straining waistcoat. 'I pay my shooters enough to take the rap. What's a few years in stir, when you can come out to a couple a hundred grand? It's like I say, Tyler, me old cocker. Money talks. Where there's shit, there are always flies.'

Tyler grunted. 'Delicately put as always, Smith. Why are you here?'

Smith looked at Tyler, then sighed and rested his chubby hands on his chunky knees. 'I'll be straight with you.'

That's a first, thought Tyler.

'I promised these people I'd get you for the job. It's my neck on the line if things don't go to plan.'

'So your shooters won't take the rap for this one, eh? Must be serious.'

Smith ignored the gibe and carried on. 'There's a girl missing. They think she may have got into bad company.'

'She certainly has if "they" move in your circles.'

'I don't need to take this shit.' Smith's face was suffused with anger, his piggy eyes blinking rapidly. 'This is serious stuff I'm offering.'

Tyler leaned back. He was enjoying Smith's discomfort. 'Do carry on. I'm fascinated,' he said dryly.

Smith swallowed and fumbled to light another cigar. 'There's a kid involved too. They've both disappeared and the family's desperate to find them.' He paused for a moment and reached into his inside coat pocket. Pulling out a large brown envelope, he laid it on the desk. 'Here are the details.'

Tyler touched the envelope. He could feel Smith's bodyheat on the paper and it wasn't pleasant. 'Why can't you do the job? You have the men, the contacts.'

'No one with your qualifications, Tyler. My men are muscle.

Without my business brain, they would be nothing.' The tongue darted over the lips and Tyler could see the gleam of hope in the other man's eyes.

'If these people are so highly placed, then why come to a lowlife like you? How do you fit into all this, Smith?'

The man on the other side of the desk visibly bristled at the insult, but struggled to maintain his composure. 'We do business. All legit. Nothing to do with drugs,' Smith added hastily.

Tyler hadn't missed the inner struggle to remain calm, and heard the desperation in the man's voice, but he kept his hand on the envelope, his gaze pinned to the fat, dewy face.

'What kind of business?' He asked smoothly.

'I'm the front man for a couple of gaming houses they own in the City. All kosher, all above board. It's just they don't want everyone knowing their business.'

Tyler didn't believe a word of it. The larger casinos were owned by the aristocracy, Arab princes or American millionaires. None of which would have had anything to do with a worm like Smith. It didn't matter anyway. He was intrigued and if he decided to do the job he'd soon get to the bottom of things.

He opened the envelope and spilled out the contents. There was a picture of a young woman, a snapshot of the same woman cradling a baby, and a computer print-out of their details. The biopic gave her name and age and place of birth. He digested the few salient points about her family. There was no mention of a husband.

'Is Whitmore her name now, or her maiden name?'

'It's 'er maiden name, she wouldn't be using 'er married one.' Smith sat forward, his face eager. 'So you'll take the job then?'

'Who is this girl, Smith? And why does her husband's family want to find her so badly? What's she done?'

Smith looked uncomfortable and refused to meet Tyler's gaze. 'I never said it was the husband what was looking for 'er. She's nobody special. Just a mixed up kid who's run away and got herself into trouble.'

Tyler slammed his hand over the photographs. 'Don't bullshit me, Smith. Little old ladies living in Norfolk don't own casinos in the City. Where's the husband? Who is he?'

'He's abroad,' Smith muttered sullenly.

'Where, abroad?'

'Um, America.' Smith looked shifty. 'But we know she's on her way to England.'

Tyler looked at Smith and realised he would never learn the truth from him. He studied the photograph again, and admitted silently that his curiosity was roused. There was a lot more here than a simple runaway.

'You going to do it, or not?' Smith's patience had obviously run out.

Tyler gathered up the contents of the envelope. 'I'll think about it, but if I decide to take the job, around the clock surveillance and the greasing of palms in the right places, doesn't come cheap.' He paused. 'Ten thousand a week.'

The amount he'd quoted was almost three times more than he usually charged, and he expected Smith to argue the toss, or at the very least to barter. But he needed to know just how much hold his 'client' had over him, and how badly they needed to find this girl. It could give him an insight into just what he was getting involved in.

Smith gaped, then clamped his mouth shut and simmered. Tyler could almost see his mind working behind that smooth, pink forehead.

'Done. Here's the first week's money. My client doesn't want to waste time.' He took out ten bundles of new notes from his briefcase and slapped them on the desk.

Tyler froze. He'd seen at least another ten similar packages in the briefcase before Smith slammed it shut. Whoever it was behind Smith meant business and they had the payroll to back it up. That kind of money didn't come easy. It had to be either as Smith said, highly placed inherited money, or something far more sinister.

The short hairs on the nape of his neck prickled. It was always a sign of impending danger. He flicked through the bundles, threw them into a drawer, locked it and pocketed the key. That would take care of the bills, and then some.

'I'll keep hold of that while I consult my partner – don't reckon on the deal being done until I get back to you.'

Smith was about to explode, but Tyler slammed his hand on the desk and silenced him. 'No promises, Smith. I need to know much more before I agree to this latest scam of yours – and it has to be a scam – it's the only thing you deal in.'

The silence stretched between them and Tyler watched the inner struggle to remain calm on Smith's face.

'When did this girl leave America, and how did she travel?'

'Flew out three weeks ago from Dallas.' Smith bit his lip and tried to cover his gaffe by relighting his cigar. 'At least, that's what I was told.'

Tyler nodded as the adrenalin began to pump. This was going to be a job he would enjoy. Not the run-of-the-mill surveillance it had seemed to begin with. 'What's the name of your client, Smith?'

Smith hauled himself out of the chair, obviously eager to leave. 'Let me give you a bit of advice, Tyler. Don't stick your nose where it's not wanted. Just find the girl and the kid. She has to contact her mother at some point. The old girl's on her last legs apparently, and there's no one else.'

Tyler moved away from the desk and followed Smith to the door.

Smith turned suddenly and looked up at him. 'Let me know within the next twenty-four hours if you're taking the deal, Tyler. My client's in a hurry, and there could be a bonus in it if you get yer skates on.' He thrust a heavily embossed business card into Tyler's jacket pocket and opened the door. The gorilla was leaning against the wall exploring his nasal cavities and snapped to attention as Smith walked past him.

Tyler watched them drive away. Going back to his desk, he picked up the telephone and paged Bill. Within minutes his partner called back.

'Bill, we need to talk,' he said grimly. 'My place, eight o'clock tonight.'

Greg was about to leave his apartment when the telephone rang. It was Smith. He listened to what he had to say then disconnected.

Smith had remarked that Tyler Reed knew he was dealing with a professional, and had therefore asked few questions, but that wasn't the adjective Greg would have chosen to describe Smith. They'd never met, but his intermediary had given Greg a vivid resume of Smith's character. He had a sharp mind, but, like Vic, the stench of the slums hung over him – a sweatiness in the fawning, subservient way he'd dealt with his man that Greg could not admire. Yet he knew Smith wouldn't let him down, there was too much money at stake, too many powerful people who wouldn't take kindly to the Cockney screwing things up.

Greg's smile was sardonic. Smith would behave himself, and see to it that Reed followed suit.

He smoothed back his hair, straightened his tie, buttoned his jacket and forgot about the repugnant little man in London. It was time for the meeting at Dad's. With a curt nod to the waiting bodyguards, he led them down to the car where Jake was ready behind the wheel.

The limousine was followed by a black Mercedes through the traffic, the bodyguards keeping up a relentless exchange of observations with the guard who sat beside Jake. They were ready to move in swiftly at the first hint of trouble, even though his father's apartment was only a short drive away.

As a Castlemaine, Greg was used to protection, but now the billion dollar deal had been set with the South

American cartel, he would have an even tighter circle of guards around him.

He thought back to the days when he and Vic were boys. To the days when security was at a minimum and they'd been free to run barefoot in the family orange groves of Southern California. How long ago that seemed, how different everything had become once the monolith of the family empire took over their lives and engulfed them. He remembered the taste of the sun-warmed oranges they'd picked from the trees, and the mellow light of the setting sun on the sepia stone of the villa. Now the only fruit he ate had been waxed and irradiated of flavour.

Greg stared out of the window – but he no longer saw the tower blocks and sidewalks of New York, his mind's eye was on the past.

It had been a very different world in the days when his grandfather had sown the seeds of the dynasty. It had been a world of prohibition and gun-running – of mobster rule. Yet Gregory Castlemaine had played the game with astute cunning and an iron will, and when the laws changed and the mobs were dispersed and in prison, his business was legitimate, his wealth assured – untouchable in the eyes of the law, yet bankrolled from the profits of the underworld.

Greg twisted the diamond in his earlobe. On the face of it, things had changed since those earlier days, but the violence was still there, the mistrust and disloyalty just as quickly and cruelly stamped out – but now it was time to play the diplomat, to move within the right circles, know who could be bought, and who couldn't. Ultimately, it made little difference – every man had a price.

He pulled his thoughts into order and stared out of the window at the New York streets, and towering office blocks. The pride swelled within him. It's because of me and my knowledge of the stock markets that the Castlemaines either own or hold a majority share in a high proportion of the businesses in this city. They may be fronted by men that are acceptable in all echelons of society, but behind that respectable façade beats the true heart of the Castlemaine empire.

As the limousines pulled up in front of the tower block apartment, and he was escorted into the building, the thought of his responsibilities to that long, bloody history made the adrenalin pump.

13

'Where you heading, then?' The girl's face was elfin beneath the heavy eye make-up and mop of purple and red hair.

'Dublin,' Gabriella replied as she lifted her face to the sun and wished her stomach wouldn't roll quite so much. They were seated on the leeward side of the ferry, and the crossing from France to Ireland was much rougher than she'd expected.

'Give ya a lift if yer want. Me and Grant's goin' that way. There's a festival on.'

'Yeah? That'd be great.' She smiled at the girl dressed in rags, who was far too thin, and who couldn't have been much more than fifteen, but from whose eyes gleamed a lifetime of experience. 'My name's Ellie, by the way. And this is Nick.'

'Scarlet.' A slender hand emerged from the frayed cuff of an ancient leather jacket and stroked Nick's head. 'Kids are all right ain't they?'

'When they're asleep, dry and fed,' Gabby laughed in return. 'The sleepless nights aren't so much fun.'

'Where's your bloke then?' Scarlet's attention was on rolling a cigarette.

'Gone,' replied Gabriella shortly.

Scarlet swiftly twisted the end of her smoke and lit it. A pungeant fragrance drifted around them. 'Fancy a toke?' The reefer was offered and Gabriella shook her head. Scarlet shrugged and stared into the distance, her eyes almost closed.

'Blokes ain't much use. Most of 'em only want one thing,

then when they get it, they're off. Grant's all right though, we been travelling with the others for a while now, but I still wouldn't trust 'im completely, if you know what I mean. A bloke's a bloke – there ain't no changin' them.'

Gabriella buried her face in Nick's hair and smiled. Such wisdom from one so young. If only she'd been half as wise. She was tempted to ask why she'd chosen to live like a gypsy, to ask how old she was and why had she left home. Yet questions led to questions and she didn't want to lie to the kid. From the look of her, she'd heard and seen it all before.

'Won't Grant mind if I tag along?'

'Nah. There's a load of us – one more won't make much difference, and there's plenty of room in the bus.'

Scarlet finished her smoke and Gabriella fought the sea-sickness. Nick slept through the whole journey as if he was a seasoned traveller. It was an hour later that Cork was sighted and they made their way down into the hold.

The bus was an ancient charabanc. Daubed with fluorescent paint and slogans, it reminded Gabriella of something straight out of the sixties, but she felt strangely at home with the group of travellers who accepted her with no questions and no curiosity. And as she climbed aboard, she realised why. She looked like them, acted like them, and with Nick and the rucksack she had become one of them. A traveller – a modern nomad within a tribe of nomads.

Tyler opened the door to the flat. 'You're early.'

Bill Reynolds preened his red handlebar moustache and grinned. 'Nice to see you too,' he retorted as he made for the kitchen. Popping the tab on a can of beer, he drained it in one and reached for the next. 'Needed that. Bloody dusty in that cellar.'

Tyler playfully punched Bill's expanding gut. 'No wonder you're putting on weight. Why don't you come down to the gym? Could take years off you.'

Bill finished the second beer, and reached for a third.

'You can race about on that infernal machine and lift heavy things if you want. Real men don't need to impress the girlies with testosterone-inflated muscle,' he said, his hazel eyes twinkling.

'I suppose you think that toffee-nosed accent and dashing moustache can do it all for you,' taunted Tyler as he opened a beer for himself. 'Bloody private school oik. You're all the same, got your brains in your balls.' It was said with affection and taken as such.

Bill ran his hand through the unruly swirl of red hair that topped a face liberally sprinkled with freckles. 'You've either got it, or you haven't. The ladies prefer a man with taste. It's amazing what a bit of Gilbert and Sullivan can arouse.'

'You want to see what a Harley does, me old mucker.'

Bill put a brotherly arm over his partner's shoulder. 'Tyler, Tyler. Old son. Class always tells. My father and his father before him were high ranking commissioned officers in the Brigade of Guards. It's in the genes.'

'Bollocks.' Bill would never change. He was a gifted linguist, speaking French, Russian and Arabic like a native. It was this talent which had interested the Special Air Services. He was a man who liked to laugh, a man who appeared at ease with himself and those around him. Theirs was a friendship of understanding, trust and ease. When men had to live and work together in tight, dangerous situations; where their lives depended on the man next to him to move at a glance, go in at a sign, watch his back, it had to be a marriage of sorts. Each man one part of a whole   bonded in thought, word and deed to the other.

Yet Tyler had seen another side to Bill. The dark side. They were all aware of their darker half, and in the SAS that part of their personalities was honed to absorb the horrors they encountered and the things they were ordered to do. Bill had allowed the demon to obliterate reason on just one occasion, yet it had been enough to make them both re-evaluate what they were doing with their lives.

They had been under deep cover in Iraq for three months. Bill almost unrecognisable without his precious moustache, his hair dyed black, his skin darkened. There was a plot to kill Sadam Hussein, nothing unusual in that, but this time an Englishman was involved and they had been sent to get him out. The man had been caught up in something he had no control over – something which would have been against all he believed in had he known the true identity of his new confidantes, yet he'd been seen with the wrong people, in the wrong places and for that Hussein wanted him dead.

Jack Ripley had lived most of his adult life amongst the Marsh Arabs of Southern Iraq, south of Basra, close to the Iranian border. He was a peace-loving man who taught the children how to read and write. A God-fearing man, who had never taken on the mantle of Sunni or Shi'ite Muslim, but who lived with the desperately poor, fiercely proud Marsh people in peace. He was honoured and respected by them, and that was frowned on in Baghdad. The Marsh Arabs were a nuisance, vermin to be hunted and annihilated, not educated.

Tyler and Bill had eventually found Ripley, but they were too late. His decapitation had been noted in a thick book – his body buried in a communal grave outside the prison walls. Although it was against their orders, they decided to go back to warn the Marsh Arab elders of the reprisals that would surely follow.

What they found in the huddle of cane and daub shelters and poisoned rivers had turned their stomachs. Women and children lay where they had fallen, their limbs splayed, their faces ghastly in death. Old men still sat at their fishing nets, but their eyes were sightless as they stared into the bleak horizon, their blistered faces gaunt in the agony of death. Livestock lay dead, vegetables and fruit were piled in sweet decay and flies buzzed and flitted in black swarms. The village had been untouched by mortar or bullet, but the mosque, a poor thing compared to the one in Baghdad, had become a charnel house when the mustard gas came at prayer time. At least they had made their peace with Allah before they'd been wiped out.

Yet it was the sight of a mother and her dead infant, gassed at the moment of birth, that had finally turned Bill into a vengeful, raging man. Tyler couldn't find it in himself to disagree when Bill vowed to avenge their deaths, and so, breaking every rule of the SAS code, they had returned once more to Baghdad.

It had been easy to track down those who had carried out the atrocities – they had boasted about it in the coffee houses and bazaars – were hailed as heroes by their fellow army officers. One by one Bill Reynolds and Tyler Reed had coldly, clinically and without conscience, eliminated them. Yet Bill had taken things further than Tyler would have liked. He'd cut off their balls first and stuffed them in their mouths to stop them screaming as he slit their throats. It was the coldest revenge he could think of and Tyler recognised the need for Bill to purge the hatred, even though it sickened him.

Bill seemed to have survived that one long moment of vengeful hatred. Now he was outwardly content, Iraq a long way off. Yet both men had suffered the aftermath of their actions and Tyler knew Elaine's ultimatum had come because of the nightmares Bill had experienced – knew Bill had taken the only way out for someone who had crossed the line and become unstable. For him, retirement was necessary to his sanity.

Tyler knew that deep down, Bill would always hate Hussein. He'd watched his tight, angry face when the British pilots had been displayed on television during the Gulf War, and heard the anger as Bill paced the floor and outlined his ideas of how he would rid the world of such evil. Yet he was coping with it. Every day he could see the man coming to terms with his life, coming to accept the things he'd done, put them behind him and look to the future. They never talked about it, but both men knew the other was there if needed. It was a good partnership.

Bill strolled into the living room. His suit fitted well and his tie was old school. He grimaced at the sound of Elvis crooning from the stereo. 'Don't you have anything more uplifting? A slice of Verdi, or "Madame Butterfly" for instance? Look at this lot.' He waved a hand over the vast collection of fifties' records which Tyler had inherited from his father and added to over the intervening years. 'No wonder you still have the urge to be an ageing rocker, Ty. You don't give your senses the opportunity to mature and appreciate the finer things in life.'

Tyler didn't take offence. He was used to Bill's weird taste in music and could ignore his pontificating. He leaned against the door jamb, then after a long swig of beer, went and sat down. 'I've as good as agreed to take Sniffy's case.'

Bill looked at him from beneath fiery eyebrows, his moustache twitching in amusement. 'I thought we were going to discuss it first. What made you change your mind?'

Tyler twisted in his chair and casually studied the overladen shelves of books that covered the wall. 'Ten thousand notes a week.'

Bill's eyebrows shot up and he nearly spilled his beer. 'We don't need the money that badly, old son. Hell, it has to be bent for that kind of dosh!'

'That's what I thought, but there's a girl out there with all the answers. Until I find her, I won't know the truth. That's why I've decided to take the job.'

'Curiosity killed the proverbial cat, old son. Watch your back.'

'I mean to, but for now we can pay the bills, the rest of the money will have to be banked. If the case leads to drugs, then Sniffy can have the balance back. Someone is payrolling him, and I mean to find out who.'

'That's all very well, Tyler, but if we get in too deep, what's to say Sniffy or his backer won't let go? I think you'd better tell me everything that went on this morning.'

Tyler handed over the brown envelope and drank his beer while Bill read the contents. If his partner refused to have anything more to do with it, then he would let it go, but he would be sorry if that happened. It would leave him wondering.

Bill placed the envelope back on the table and Tyler gave a verbatim account of his conversation with Smith. When he finished there was a long silence, which Bill finally shattered. 'You're right, Tyler. There is more to this than meets the eye. I don't like the smell of it at all.'

Their gaze met and held.

'What do you want me to do?' Bill said in weary acquiescence.

Tyler breathed more easily. He'd seen the doubts flit over his partner's face and had been sure he would reject it.

'I want you to get hold of Tom Wyman. He is out of prison, isn't he?'

Bill nodded. 'Got out about six weeks ago, but I don't know if he'll want to get involved again. He doesn't like it in gaol, no computers.'

Tyler nodded, Bill had a point, but he needed Tom's special skills. Tom Wyman was a genius with computers. A short spell in the army had honed his skills to razor sharpness and earned him a dishonourable discharge. He had infiltrated the vast computer network of a leading bank and after a court martial and several months in prison, had approached Bill and Tyler for work. That had been three years ago. Now, at twenty-nine, he had just finished another eight-month stretch in the Scrubs.

'If the silly little sod just kept his nose clean, he could make a good living. I've tried talking to him, but it goes in one ear and out the other.'

'Greedy, that's his problem,' said Bill, grimly. 'Got caught hacking into a bookmaker's this time.'

'Tell him we'll pay well. We need him to find her bank or building society accounts and her National Insurance number along with her NHS number. Track down her passport, driving licence, credit cards. Easy for a man like Tom.'

Bill made a note in the little book he kept in his top pocket. 'What else?'

'Get a copy of her birth certificate and find out who her parents are. Dig deeper, it could lead us to distant relatives, places we wouldn't otherwise think of looking for. I'm going to check out the mother, then see if I can find her friends. She had to go to school somewhere, spend holidays somewhere, visit the same places time after time. Someone must know where she is. No one disappears completely. Especially not with a baby.'

Tyler paused as his mind went over all the possibilities. 'There's a whole subculture out there. Shoals of homeless sleeping rough. I don't think she'll be amongst them, but you never know. Could be in a squat a few streets away – London's a magnet for runaways. Once we've got her credentials we can start with the DHSS.' He rubbed the beer can against his forehead. It was still cold and it helped ease the frown lines he knew were etched on his face.

'We'll need to contact the Sally Army and the Samaritans. I'll also put the word out at the Met. and call in favours from a couple of Masonic friends.'

Bill lit his pipe and filled the room with clouds of smoke. 'Could take months,' he said once it was burning to his satisfaction. 'If she doesn't want to be found, then it's nigh on impossible.'

'Yeah. We'll just have to hope she gets careless, or decides to stop running. If she is sleeping rough, then there's a good chance the police will pull her in – but I suspect I'm clutching at straws.'

Bill chewed his moustache and stared into space. They'd had jobs like this before and the failure rate was too high to be optimistic.

'I'll need you to run things this end, Bill. You'll have to do the prince's escort and the security chauffeuring for the Saudi oil minister next week. The anti-hijack driving lessons can go on as usual, bring Lester Grant in to help you. He could probably do with a bit extra on top of what the Met. pays.'

Bill nodded and carried on scribbling.

'I'll report in every evening, get Tom to do the same. She'll have to sign on with a doctor, because of the kid. See if you can get anything through the Catholic Society. It's probable she'll turn to them as it says in the dossier that she was brought up a Catholic and they have a good system for finding runaways.'

'What will you do if you find her?' Bill's voice was low, his gaze steady.

Tyler crushed the beer can and threw it in the waste paper basket. 'We'll cross that bridge when we come to it. Depends what's hidden under the dung heap, and until I dig deeper, I can't make that decision.'

'Best of luck old man. Wish I was coming with you.'

Tyler laughed. 'No you don't you old coot. Swap a nice warm bed with Elaine for a solitary billet in the middle of nowhere? Do me a favour.'

Bill was suddenly quiet. Then he too crushed his can and threw it into the basket. 'I miss the excitement, Tyler. Still can't get used to the easy life.'

Tyler understood. Yet he also knew Bill preferred tinkering with security systems and driving at speed with some oil sheik in the back seat to sitting in a damp, cold huddle in a faraway bivouac. He wouldn't feel comfortable away from the stability of home any more, regardless of his wishful thinking – so he said nothing and they shared another beer before Bill left the apartment.

The long summer day had dwindled into dusk as the convoy of buses and motorbikes pulled off the road into a field. They were five miles outside Dublin and would resume their journey in the morning.

Makeshift tents were hastily erected and firewood collected. Gabriella left Nick asleep in the bus and helped prepare an evening meal of sausages, burgers and beans which was consumed with great energy. Cans of beer and bottles of wine littered the ground around them as they talked and smoked and listened to the strum of someone's guitar.

Gabriella fed Nick and wrapped him up warmly, though the night was mild and the sky clear, and joined the others around the fire. The guitar player was a youth of about eighteen, with hair down to his waist, terrible acne, and a goatee beard, but he knew what he was doing, and soon they were all singing along with him.

Gabriella smiled and clapped and sang the words of the old favourites. This was a time warp, a moment when the rest of the world didn't exist and all the troubles were little ones. She'd never felt so contented, or so in harmony, but knew it couldn't last – travelling was no life for a baby, and she would soon grow tired of washing in cold water, never getting things dry properly and living hand to mouth. But for the moment it was a respite in the turmoil, a breathing space before she set foot in England again and resumed her new life.

Morning broke and the camp slept. The bus was cold, the condensation iced on the windows. The pervasive odour of unwashed bodies and musty clothing filled the enclosed space and the lingering reminder of last night's reefers and cheap wine permeated the blanket and sleeping bag Gabriella had borrowed.

She fed Nick and changed his clothes and nappy quickly. Her own clothes felt grubby and she yearned for a bath or shower, but as there was no running water, no kettle, she had to make do with a baby-wipe. Ready for the day, she gathered her things together and strapped Nick in the harness. The others slept on, mutters, grunts and snores coming from all sides of the bus.

Scarlet was huddled next to Grant in a grubby sleeping bag, and opened one bleary eye as Gabriella picked her way through the bodies.

'Not staying? Should be a good gig in Dublin. Great bands. The Swamp Rats are playing.'

'I've got a ferry to catch, Scarlet. I can't stay. But thanks for letting me crash here for the night.'

'No probs. See y'round maybe,' Scarlet replied sleepily before snuggling closer to Grant.

Gabriella smiled as she watched them sleep. Babies, the pair of them. *I wonder where her parents are, and what happened to make her live like this.* She sighed and headed for the door. *At least they're free.*

She left the bus and tramped through the long grass past the smouldering bonfire and out into the road. She'd noticed a bus stop the night before, and when she'd left the others to check out the timetable, she'd realised that the Dublin bus passed right by the field.

Waiting at the side of the road, the Dublin to Holyhead ferry ticket in her pocket, she ran over her plans. It would take time and money, but with luck and the cash from the building society account, she should be in Berkshire within the next forty-eight hours.

14

The long gravel drive hadn't been raked, the undulating lawns that breasted it needed cutting, and there was a definite air of neglect hanging over the once beautiful Berkshire mansion. Mellow stone walls were somnolent in the early morning sun, the peaceful, rural scene marred by the presence of very modern scaffolding and sheets of black plastic covering a large section of the roof.

Gabriella climbed out of the taxi and looked up at the ancient portico with its Ffynnes family crest of Lion rampant, and the words 'Sola Bona Quae Honesta' carved in stone beneath. Judging by the state of the place, Charlotte Ffynnes-Newbold was suffering the same fate that most of the landed gentry had to face these days. Inheritance tax.

With Nick firmly strapped in his sling, she tugged the wrought-iron bell pull. There was a time, she remembered as she waited, when the door would have been opened by a butler at the sound of an approaching car, and her bags would have been whisked away and unpacked before she'd finished a welcoming drink in the drawing room.

The scrabble of dog claws on a stone floor and the impatient, sharp commands to 'shut up', was followed swiftly by the rattle of bolts before the door flew open and Gabriella was surrounded by a leaping, yapping pack of Jack Russells.

'Can I help you?'

Gabriella grinned in delight at the obvious confusion of her childhood friend. 'It's me. Gabriella. Can you call off the hounds of the Baskervilles? They're frightening the baby.'

Charlotte peered more closely – she never wore her glasses despite her myopia, and happily admitted to the vanity that was the reason for this omission. 'Good Lord! What on earth have you done to yourself? You look absolutely ghastly.'

'Thanks,' retorted Gabriella dryly. Charlotte didn't look too hot either. The corduroy trousers and gunboots were topped off with a man's sweater that had seen better days, and the face that had always been carefully made-up was now bare and rather weather-beaten. 'The dogs?'

'Sorry. Bloody animals. They're totally out of control and if I'd had my way the whole damn pack of them would be shipped off to outer Mongolia. But you know how Jonathan is.' Charlotte clutched Gabriella's arm and pulled her into the hall before firmly slamming the door on the pack.

Gabriella became a little unnerved by Charlotte's prolonged scrutiny. 'It's a long story, Charlie. I'll explain later.'

'I need a drink. Come on.' Charlotte led the way, although Gabriella was very familiar with the house. The echoes of their childhood were in every corner.

Moments later, settled with a large gin and tonic on a dilapidated couch, Gabriella took Nick out of the sling and bolstered him beside her in a pile of cushions. Despite the warmth outside, there was the customary roaring log fire. The central heating was as ancient as the house and had never been efficient, and the high ceilings and stone floors were chilly even on the warmest of days. Yet, to Gabriella, it was the closest thing to home. The place she'd come to in school holidays, and half terms when her parents were posted abroad, the place where she had always felt free.

Charlotte eyed the baby. 'What is it?' She'd always preferred horses to children and had sworn, at the age of ten, never to have any of her own.

'HIS name is Nicholas.'

Charlotte nodded, her short-cropped hair swinging round

the black velvet alice band that had become her trademark since boarding school. 'I think you'd better spill the beans, Gabby. What on earth are you up to – and why the ghastly dye job on your hair?'

Gabriella had rehearsed her answer in the taxi ride from the station, and although she hated the idea of lying to her friend, she had to think of the consequences if she didn't.

'I've left Greg. The marriage was a ghastly mistake and the hair cut and dye were just a spur of the moment thing.' She attempted a carefree grin, but her face muscles were tight and the last three weeks of living out of a hold-all were beginning to tell. 'You know, Charlie. Change your man, change your hair style.'

'Bit drastic, old thing. And if you don't mind my saying – you could do with a bath. You'll never pull another stunner like Greg looking like that.' She cocked her head. 'Perhaps you should set your sights on an Englishman next time. They may be boring and absolutely useless in bed, but they're far too inhibited to mess about with other women or throw tantrums. These rich American playboys are all very well for a bit of fun, but one should never marry them.'

Gabriella chuckled. Charlotte had, unknowingly, just given a graphic description of the state of her marriage to the plodding, unimaginative Jonathan. 'Another man is the last thing I want at the moment, Charlie. But I would be grateful for a few days here. We've been on the move for three weeks and I'm at the end of my tether.'

A frown creased the tanned brow as Charlotte took a moment too long to answer. 'Of course you can stay. After all, this place is almost your second home . . .'

Gabriella heard the hesitance and her spirits plunged. Charlotte had been her one hope of sanctuary. Greg had never met her, she'd been unable to attend the wedding, and since their marriage, there had been no opportunity for her to visit. He would never think of looking for her here in Berkshire, and she needed time to gather her strength and plan for the future before moving on again. 'If it's inconvenient, then . . .'

'Good Lord, no! My goodness, what you must think of me. It's just that since my father died, we've had to open the place up to paying guests. Ghastly Americans, darling. Daddy must be swivelling in his grave. They come here for house parties and the hunting and shooting. Money's good, but honestly, Gabby, it's frightfully wearing having to listen to their pretentious gabble. There's a party due in about three hours, actually. But if you think you can bear it, you're very welcome to stay, and it might be fun to have someone I like at the dinner table for a change.'

Gabriella felt trapped and ill at ease. This was something that had never occurred to her. Americans in the Ffynnes ancestral home – her place of safety was suddenly open to all kinds of danger. The kind of wealthy Americans who would patronise such an enterprise were just the same Americans Greg and his father had in their pockets.

'I won't take part in the socialising, Charlotte. I'm far too tired and wouldn't be very good company, so if you don't mind, I'll just move into the nursery wing and stay there. I can look after myself and the baby – you won't even know I'm here.'

Charlotte finished her drink and put down the glass with a thump on the side table. Her blue eyes never wavered.

'That's most unlike you, Gabby. Why do I get the feeling that there's far more behind that haircut and grotty outfit than you've let on? You might as well tell me the truth – you know I always could get you to spill the beans in the end, regardless of how much you resist.'

Gabriella grasped Charlotte's hand and held on tight. 'Please, Charlie, not this time. I want you to promise not to tell anyone I'm here. I'm very serious about this. No one. Understand?'

Charlotte bit her lip. 'I'll have to tell Jonathan. But you

make it all sound so . . . dangerous. You really are in trouble, aren't you?'

'Not if you keep my visit secret, Charlotte.'

Vic slammed his way out of the Chicago apartment, the crash of the door blotting out the sound of his wife's shrill voice. As he headed for the subway, his feet pounded out his frustration. Another night in the hated restaurant, where he was watched and pointed at. Another round of arguments with a chef who had no respect. His staff had been chosen by Greg, his life was not his own. He was still ruled by his family, and yet was no longer a part of it.

His anger with his brother had turned into a dark thing that festered and squirmed deep within him. Dad deferred to Greg, confided in him and made it obvious he preferred his company. Even his mother worshipped Greg, refusing to see what a bastard he really was. And that was what hurt. He'd tried to be a good son, a loyal brother, a worthy member of the family, yet Mom still had that look of admiration in her eyes when Greg was around. The look that had never come his way, however hard he'd tried.

Vic knew his parents tolerated him, maybe even loved him, but not with the pride and passion they bestowed on Greg. It had always been the same, and now, because of his brother, he was an outcast. He'd heard the whispers, seen the overt looks and sly smiles as he went to the restaurant every day. How quickly his fall from grace had been monitored and talked about. How soon his status as Greg's brother had disappeared. His wife nagged, his sons looked at him with scorn. Nothing he could say could convince them their father was still a man to be reckoned with.

Maybe it's because I've lost my pride, my sense of worth, he thought. Not so long ago I would have been delighted to be free from the family's shadow. Delighted to come and go as I pleased, to do my own thing and not have Dad looking scornfully over my shoulder. I too had dreams, but after all this time they've come to nothing and now it's too late. The restaurant does good business, and the bank deposit from Greg is welcome – but what does it all add up to?

'I'm surviving on hand-outs,' he spat, as he glared at the dark tunnel entrance to the subway. 'A frigging sweetener to keep me quiet and out of the way.' He bunched his fists in his pockets. 'Well, I've had enough,' he muttered darkly into the hollow silence. 'It's time to get my own back. To put the cat amongst the pigeons and whilst they're all busy fighting, I'll step in and take over. I can do it – I know I can. After all, I'm a Castlemaine.'

He grimaced as the through train battered the wind against him and swirled litter round his feet. Then he smiled. I still have friends who listen to my grievances, and sympathise with me. They still tell me the secrets of the inner circle that have their noses up my brother's ass. He thought of the secret meetings he'd attended with the powerful men who didn't like the way Greg was handling the South American cartel. Too many old and trusted men had been brushed aside to make way for Greg's new generation of wise-ass kids and 'get rich quick' manipulators. Reputations had been destroyed, pride damaged – making them vengeful alies.

Vic cupped his hands around the lighted match and drew smoke into his lungs as he waited for his train. The kid was Greg's Achilles heel, and if the information was correct, then it would only be a matter of time before Tyler Reed found him.

That's when I'll strike, he thought, the adrenalin boosting his morale. With Nick in my grasp, I'll have the lever to oust Greg – then I'll take my rightful place in the family business.

The nursery Gabriella remembered so well had changed. Gone were the rows of dolls, the teddy bears and tiny tea sets. A damp patch in the corner had peeled the wallpaper, leaving it to hang forlornly over the nursery-rhyme frieze. Dust motes danced in the pale sunbeams that squeezed through the shutters and the comfortable chairs were covered in sheets. The rocking horse stood abandoned in the centre of the room, echoes of his grandeur still visible in the remains of his mane and tail and flaking paint.

Gabriella stroked his nose, remembering the races she'd won on his back, and as the rockers creaked against the bare floor, she felt the emotions rise to the surface. In that one moment of weakness, she felt as abandoned as the horse, and she was tempted to wallow in self-pity – it was easier than being strong. If only Nick could have the stability of a home such as this to grow up in – if only he had the chance, as she had done, to know the pleasures of nursery teas and picnics, of smelling the sweet aroma of fresh straw in a stable, and the touch of a velvet nose of his very own pony – but that kind of life existed only in her memory: sunny, warm days when it never seemed to rain, and life held no cares for the little girl she had been then.

With an impatient snort, she crossed the room and threw back the shutters. They crashed against the wall, echoing through the room as dust settled on the bare floor. She lifted her face to the last warmth of the day. I will survive this. I will find the strength to begin again.

'Changed a bit since our day. Are you sure you'll be OK up here. There's always the Empire Suite. It's a bit mouldy, but I can get a fire going and change the bedding.'

Gabriella hadn't heard Charlotte come into the room, and the sound of her voice brought her sharply from her reverie. 'We'll be fine up here, Charlie. A bit of cleaning won't kill me, and there's everything we need.'

'I brought these. Nanny's bed must be damp, hasn't been used for yonks.' Charlotte was dressed in long black velvet, a choker of pearls at her throat and discreet pearl studs in her earlobes. In her arms she carried a pile of bed linen and an electric blanket. 'I'd offer to help, but the Yanks have arrived and I have to do my lady-of-the-manor bit.'

Gabriella laughed. 'It's a part you can play to perfection. Don't daunt them too much, Charlie, they may not come back.'

Charlotte giggled roguishly, reminding Gabriella of the girl who'd shared a dormitory, and told outrageous stories all through the night, risking expulsion so many times that it had become a battle of wits between the headmistress and Charlotte's very wealthy father. The school had prospered over the years of Charlotte's education, and she had finally ended her career there as head girl.

'The haughtier I get, the better they like it.' A frown wrinkled the carefully made-up brow. 'Extraordinary.'

Gabriella took the sheets, but Charlotte's hand stalled her. 'Are you sure you don't want to tell me what all this is about, Gabby? I know something's very wrong, and I want to help.'

Gabriella pecked her on the cheek and pulled away. 'I know you do, Charlie, but giving us shelter for a few days is more help than you could ever imagine. Trust me on this. You don't want to know any more. Now, go and entertain your Americans.'

She watched her friend leave the room, saw the backwards glance before she closed the door, and knew Charlotte would not let it rest until she knew everything. Gabriella sighed as she crossed the nursery and headed for Nanny's old bedroom. Her stay at Broderick Place could only be temporary – how temporary, depended on Charlotte's curiosity.

Tyler gave the Harley one last polish and threw the tarpaulin over her. He didn't know how long it would be before he saw her again, but he had to make sure the damp and dust didn't get to her intricate mechanics. It would have been nice to travel to Norfolk on her, but the drawback with a Harley, was its capacity to attract attention. He armed the security system and locked the garage, then climbed into the Escort and drove off. It would take about an hour and a half to reach Norfolk.

*　　*　　*

The village was one of a string which crossed the flat lowlands. The sort of place a motorist could drive through without really noticing. Fields of sugar beet sprawled across the almost featureless landscape, the dark green foliage bright against the rich, black earth. Trees, arthritic with the wind, gave little shelter to the crops with their spidery branches and weather-beaten leaves. Houses were scattered behind hedgerows and clustered along the side of the road, their thatched roofs sweeping low over diamond-paned windows and Suffolk-pink walls. Here and there was a modern house, looking out of place and from a different world, but the character of the village was too strong for them to spoil it.

The inn was sixteenth-century. Settled into the earth and sprawling, it looked peaceful behind the vast, spreading oak that grew in the centre of the village green. The long, thatched roof huddled over the crooked windows, black beams threaded their way over the walls and a collection of flower tubs and hanging baskets added colour. Benches and tables had been arranged on the shingle outside the front door and there was a children's play area with swings and slides at the back.

Tyler parked the car and sat for a moment drinking in the peace and tranquillity. This place re-enforced his decision to make his home in England. It was so quiet, so green and lush after the squalor of the Middle East. Here, a man could breathe, take his time and tune into the sound of his own heartbeat.

The day promised to be fine, the sun clear in the almost cloudless sky, the dew sparkling on the grass and glinting in the trees. He grinned at the sound of a cockerel in the distance. Silly bugger was a bit late, it was past nine o'clock.

He locked the car and wandered through the village.

Briar Cottage was in the lane behind the pub. Set back from the road with a narrow, flower-filled garden, it might have come from the pages of a children's story book. Painted the inevitable pink, it had a thatched roof, oak beams and leaded windows – there was even a rose clinging to the walls and trailing over the front door. It reminded him of the witch's house in *Hansel and Gretel*, but there was no evil here, merely comfortable old age.

The curtains were open, but with the sun behind the house, he couldn't see into the rooms, and there were no signs of the occupants. Further investigation revealed a dairy pasture further down the road, but after tramping across it, he realised Briar Cottage was surrounded by other gardens. The only way he could keep an eye on the place was to rent a room in the pub.

The landlord of the Royal Oak was a man in his early forties, tall, balding and jovial. His accent was southern, his handshake firm and friendly, his gut a testament to his affection for his trade.

'Mind your head,' he warned as Tyler was about to collide with a low beam. 'I have to walk with a permanent stoop in this place, but I wouldn't change it for the world.'

'Yeah, these old places have got character, haven't they?' replied Tyler with a grimace as he dodged yet another beam. He would have hated to live here. With the low ceilings and tiny windows, the place was claustrophobic.

The bedroom smelled of polish and old timber. The ceiling sloped abruptly over the bed and the floor undulated beneath the heavy furniture. Although small, it was ideal, as Tyler could see Briar Cottage through the low, paned window.

'How long you planning to stay?'

Tyler shrugged and pointed to his bag. 'Depends how long it takes to do the translation. I have this theological text to decipher. It's in ancient Aramaic, so it could take quite a while.'

The landlord looked nonplussed as Tyler hoped he would. Not many people were interested in ancient religious texts, so they wouldn't be a point of discussion like a novel.

'You won't be disturbed, only me and the wife live here. We don't get many people staying, it's out of the way, but

214

it can get rowdy in the evenings. It's the only place for miles where the locals can get a bit of entertainment.'

Tyler smiled. 'It's fine. Thanks.'

When the man had left, Tyler pulled his bag onto the double bed and opened the window. The cool breeze was full of the scent of the late roses which clung to the eaves and drooped down the walls. At the end of the pub's garden and across the hedgerow lane, Briar Cottage slumbered in the morning sunshine. He had a clear view of the front door, any visitors could be easily monitored.

Tyler unpacked the typewriter and put it on the table under the window, then spread out sheaves of texts to one side and lined up a ream of virgin paper on the other. A tape recorder, arabic dictionary, thesaurus and Koran completed his preparations. If anyone came into the room they would see what they expected – the tools of a writer's trade.

Returning to the bag, he took out the powerful binoculars, and sat in front of the window. He adjusted the sights and began a slow sweep over the cottage.

He could see the sitting room clearly – with low beams and chintz furnishings, it looked comfortable and cheerful. The kitchen also faced the lane and he could just make out a stack of cookery books and a row of oak cabinets.

The woman's face loomed back at him from an upstairs window, and for a heart-stopping instant, he wondered if she'd seen him, then realising she was deep in thought, he studied her, noticing at once, the likeness to the Gabriella in the photograph.

'So this is the mother,' he muttered, as he adjusted the lenses.

She was a delicate creature, slender and pale, with the aura of an invalid. Her eyes were a faded blue beneath hooded lids, her hair more silver than gold, but still thick and long if the bun at the nape of her neck was anything to go by. Her chin was resting in the palm of her hand, and Tyler could see the swollen knuckles and misshapen fingers, the pale skin and threads of blue where the veins pushed at the thin flesh. Old age and arthritis could be cruel, he mused – once upon a time this woman had been a beauty.

Tyler guessed she was in her late sixties, but there was a fragility about her which almost made her ageless – a softness in the smooth face and graceful neck. She must have been a dancer, or a model when she was young, he decided, for she reminded him of a ballerina he'd once dated, with eyes like a startled fawn and limbs so slender he'd been afraid of breaking them.

He grinned at the memory. Chloe might have looked fragile, but she'd possessed an amazing strength and had had the stamina of a horse. She could make love for hours, then go on to a gruelling rehearsal, followed by the evening performance. He'd been exhausted, sated and bewildered by her, but she'd had ambitions and left him for the dance director of a prestigious ballet company. Perhaps this woman, too, had the steel core behind the gossamer façade? He'd been around long enough to know appearances deceived.

Tyler watched her as she sat in thought. There was something familiar about her that nagged in the back of his mind – but he dismissed the idea as fanciful. The memory of Chloe had put the idea in his head, that was all.

Panning across the cottage, he tried to see into the other room, but the window was tiny, the panes too close together to see much, so he returned to the mother. A woman of roughly the same age was talking to her, her hands fluttering, her eyes starling bright and intelligent in her round, friendly face.

She wasn't very tall, Tyler guessed, because she stood only inches above the seated Mrs Whitmore, but there was a lot of energy in that little body. Her curves made her motherly, her dress was sprigged cotton beneath the white cardigan and her tinted blue hair was swept back from her face in thick waves. An attractive woman, one who still enjoyed life, by the look of her.

Tyler watched them for a few moments and felt a stab of

pity as Mrs Whitmore struggled to her feet. Her spine was curved, her progress slow as she leaned heavily on walking sticks and left the room. The housekeeper was no whim of a wealthy widow, but a necessity, and Tyler was disconcerted. He hadn't been prepared for Mrs Whitmore's age or disability.

'I can't just go marching up to the front door and ask for Gabriella,' he muttered as he put down the binoculars. 'If the old girls don't know anything, it will worry them. I'm just going to have to find another way.'

'This is delicious, Brian,' mumbled Tyler through the crusty pastry and tender steak. 'I don't often get the chance of a home-cooked lunch.'

'Yeah, the wife does a good pie. Want some more?'

'Great.' He hesitated for a moment as he munched. 'I don't suppose you know where I could find a Mrs Whitmore? Friend of mine asked me to look her up. Distant aunt, I think.'

Brian Staines wiped the froth from his lip and put down his beer glass. 'Mrs Whitmore? Of course. Briar Cottage. Can't miss it – it's in the lane behind the pub.'

'Really? That is a help,' said Tyler. 'I don't suppose you know anything about her do you? I can't very well just go and knock on the door without knowing what to expect. My friend just said she was an ancient relative who'd appreciate a visitor.'

Brian laughed and laced his fingers over his belly. 'She's not dotty. Not that old, either. We don't see much of her because of the rheumatoid arthritis, but Edith Maybury, her houskeeper, comes in now and again with the Ladies' Guild for a sweet sherry.'

Brian looked set on talking and Tyler finished his pie in silence, but he didn't learn much more than he already knew.

'My friend said something about a daughter.'

'Won't do you no good, mate. Got married about a year back. Lives in the States.'

'That's a shame. I was hoping to meet her.'

Brian shook his head. 'Hasn't been back. Mrs Whitmore did go out for the wedding, though. Edith was full of it, even brought the wedding snaps to show the wife.'

'What happened to Mr Whitmore?'

Brian's expression was suddenly wary. 'You seem to want to know a lot about the Whitmores.'

'Writer's curiosity. Once we get started, we don't know when to stop.'

'Want another?' Brian gathered up the glasses, poured two more beers and came back. He seemed to have accepted Tyler's explanation, for he was only too willing to carry on where he'd left off.

'It was before our time,' Brian said as he settled down. 'The old boy must have died about five, six years ago. He was something in the army according to Edith. After he came out, he bought the stud farm in the next village.'

Tyler decided he'd asked enough questions. 'How about a game of dominos before it gets busy, Brian?'

'Prepared for a thrashing, are you? Right, lead on.'

Gabriella had spent a restless night. After the heat of America, the silence and damp of Berkshire settled uneasily around her. Huddled beneath the blankets, she gave up on sleep and shivered. She'd forgotten just how cold these old houses were, forgotten how they creaked and moaned, how the pipes complained every time someone flushed the lavatory or turned on a tap. Yet Nick had slept through the night, seemingly undisturbed by the adventures of the past three weeks, and now he lay in the cot beside her, oblivious to his surroundings.

Her thoughts returned to their hasty flight, and she nestled further into the blankets as she wistfully conjured up the sun-drenched balcony overlooking the Californian beach. The past three weeks had blurred into a dreamlike haze. Another state, another disguise. Then the final change before catching the ferry to Ireland, the baby merely adding to the illusion of modern traveller.

Nick was waking, his soft whining becoming more restless as his hunger took over.

Gabriella changed his nappy, then wrapped him warmly in a blanket before putting him to her breast. The long day stretched before her. There were decisions to be made, favours to be asked, a plan to be put in action. But it would all depend on Jonathan and Charlotte.

The stud farm was fifteen miles away, but the new owners could shed no light on the previous occupants. The place had been sold by Mrs Whitmore through agents and none of the original staff had been kept on. The local police had no one on their books listed as missing, but the village bobby liked the sound of his own voice and Tyler let him ramble on.

'Whitmore, you say? Brigadier in the army by all accounts. Rum sort.' PC Small chewed on a toffee, his gaze misted in thought. 'There was talk he'd been in the Specials, if you know what I mean.' A conspiratorial wink accompanied this announcement.

Tyler felt a rush of adrenalin sharpen his concentration. 'Do you mean the SAS?'

PC Small chewed his toffee and rocked on his heels. 'Mrs Maybury's hubby was in the same regiment. But it was all very hush, hush, so I suppose we'll never know for sure.'

'Men like that are sworn to secrecy. Surely Edith Maybury's just romancing?'

'Romancing or not, Whitmore could ride and shoot better than any man I know. And round here, that's quite a feat.' He regarded Tyler for a moment, then his tone sharpened. 'There isn't anything wrong with the Brigadier's widow is there?'

Tyler shook his head. PC Small was too much of a gossip to say more. 'Just making enquiries about a missing girl.'

He climbed back into the car and headed for the pub. He must talk to Bill.

* * *

It was early evening before she could do much, Jonathan had taken his usual commuter train to London, and Charlotte had been occupied with entertaining her visitors. Now, in the lull between afternoon tea and dinner, Gabriella made her way to their apartments in the south wing. In the tote bag were the final pieces of her haul from the California house. If Jonathan was willing to buy the figurines, he could make a good profit when he sold them on. He had the contacts in the antiques trade, and would find it easy to lay a false trail through the auction houses and dealers.

Gabriella noted the damp patches on the walls, the pockmarked panelling, the threadbare carpets and shoddy furniture. Desperate times called for desperate measures, and although she didn't like using her friends in this way, it was obvious they had fallen on hard times and they could be doing each other a favour.

The door to the south wing was ajar, and as Gabriella lifted her hand to knock, she was stilled by the sound of Charlotte's angry voice. Shocked by the implications of the ensuing argument, she had no compunction about listening in.

'What on earth were you thinking of, Jonathan? How dare you put me in such a ghastly position. Whatever am I going to say to Gabby?'

'Don't say anything. Really, Charlotte – this was never any of our business in the first place – the ruddy woman should think twice before haring off.'

Gabriella leaned closer to the door as Charlotte's voice dropped several decibels.

'Did you stop to wonder why she went "haring off", as you call it? Did it even occur to you that it's frightfully odd for two strange men to turn up at your office and offer you money for information about her?' She gave an exasperated snort. 'Really, Jonathan, you can be very dense at times.'

'I did think it odd, but when they explained about her

nervous breakdown, and her disappearance from the nursing home, I thought it best to be honest. Her poor husband is at his wits' end – especially as she's gone off with the baby and everything.'

Charlotte uttered a derisive snort. 'Gabriella might appear a tad flaky at the moment, with all that ghastly hair and tatty clothing, but I've known her since we were still in nappies, and she's one of the sanest people around. She ran away for a reason, and knowing Gabby, it was a very good one. Did it occur to you to find out if these men were telling the truth? Just who were they, and what questions did they ask?'

Gabriella's pulse was racing as she waited for Jonathan's delayed reply. Just how much had he given away?

'They had identification, which I checked. They were very respectable, came from one of the oldest law firms in the City,' he said pompously in an effort to bluster his way out of the tight corner Charlotte had obviously pressed him into. 'They even gave me the number of the nursing home in New York, which I rang. Spoke to the psychiatrist, who was most concerned for her and the baby's welfare, especially after I told him she looked like some down and out hippy.'

'Don't believe a word of it,' she retorted sharply. 'How many pieces of silver does betrayal cost these days, Jonathan?'

'Enough to pay the workmen and catch up on a few bills for the new central heating system,' replied her husband defensively.

'Disloyalty to one's friends is bad enough – to be paid off like some cheap turncoat is just too ghastly. You seem to have forgotten my family motto – "Only the best things are the honest ones" – Daddy must be swivelling in his grave.' Charlotte paused, then added decisively, 'I must warn Gabby.'

'Bit late for that, old thing. They're due here in less than an hour. Wanted to come back with me, but I managed to stall them. Didn't want you to be in the dark. I . . .'

Gabriella didn't stay to hear the rest. She was on the move, the shadows of the old house closing in on her, the darkness of the night through the windows holding a menace that seemed to reach out and touch her.

Up the stairs two, three at a time, then along the corridor and into the nursery. It took only minutes to grab her belongings and strap Nick into the sling. Yet those minutes seemed to stretch into eternity, each beat of her pulse, each tick of the nursery clock bringing Greg's men closer.

As she raced down the back stairs, the rucksack thumping against her spine, she collided with Charlotte, whose eyes were wide in her flushed, guilty face.

'I didn't . . .'

'I know. Just give me time to find somewhere to hide. Please, Charlie.'

Charlotte nodded. 'Here. Thought you'd need this. It's all I have . . .'

Gabriella planted a hasty kiss on her friend's cheek as she clutched the wad of notes. 'I shan't forget this. Thanks.'

'Go through the stables and out towards the lake. There's an old mini parked behind the boathouse.' A key was thrust into Gabriella's hand. 'Good luck.'

Gabriella turned and ran for the kitchens. Her footsteps echoed on the flagstone floor as the front door bell jangled in the panel above the butler's dresser.

They were here. Time had run out.

15

G reg's mood was dirty, his patience stretched to breaking point as he shouldered past the woman and walked into the office of the East Side casino. This was something he had no business doing, but because of his agent's incompetence and the absence of his intermediary, as well as his brother – he'd been forced into it.

Jake closed the door behind him and waited.

'Mr Castlemaine, this is an honour. We don't get to see you often. You should have told me you were coming. I would have arranged an entertainment for you.'

Greg eyed her balefully. Lila was the only person in the casino who knew his identity, and although she'd obviously been caught unawares and was shocked at seeing him, her voice remained husky, as her dark hands nervously plucked the silk evening gown.

'I could call a couple of the girls. Or have the side room prepared if you wanted to shoot craps.'

'You seem on edge, Lila. Is there something bothering you?' Greg studied her from the tips of her painted toe nails to the sweep of the auburn wig that enhanced her mulatto skin. She might be a whore, but she was very beautiful.

'Everything's fine, Mr Castlemaine.' The soft Louisiana accent was a turn on. 'Business has never been better.'

Greg lit a cigarette and watched her through the smoke. He liked these games of cat and mouse, and Lila was a predatory cat with sharp claws, and an even sharper mind. He would need all his wits about him.

'That's what I like to hear. Perhaps you'd show me the books.' He paused. 'Or is that inconvenient?'

'Not at all,' she said quietly, but he noted the way her glance slid away from him, and her reluctance to open the safe.

He made himself comfortable in the leather chair as she spread the books on the desk. Her anxiety was tangible, and he made no move to look at the books before him, merely watched her walk away and busy herself at the bar in the corner. Surprise visits were always profitable enterprises – they cleared smoke screens and allowed him to view the situations as they really were; sorted out the cheating from the honest, the loyal from the conniving.

'If business is so good, how can you explain the drop in takings, Lila?' He had still made no move to open the ledgers, and his tone was casual.

The vodka bottle rattled against cut glass as she poured her drink. 'We've had expenses, Mr Castlemaine. New girls, a coupla lucky punters.'

Greg watched silently as the vodka was downed in one. The whore's hand was shaking.

'The new girls cost nothing compared to their earning potential. The casino hasn't paid out more than usual. Perhaps you haven't had time to bring the ledgers up to date?'

Lila approached the desk from the other side of the room, glass in hand, eyes wide and guileless. 'I keep the books in good order, Mr Castlemaine. They are up to date.'

Greg opened one, his index finger jabbing at the profit and loss columns. 'Then perhaps you can explain your manner of accounting, Lila. You see, the figures don't add up.'

'The money has been coming in, yes. But I've had expenses which are down in this ledger here.' She grasped the red leather folder and riffled through the pages.

Greg made a show of examining the figures, then looked

up at her and smiled. It was deliberately cold, that smile, and he saw how it chilled her composure.

'You've been dipping your sticky paws in my money. What have you done with it?'

'Running this place and keeping thirty whores don't come cheap.' Her voice was suddenly shrill, her stance defensive as her gaze swivelled towards the two bodyguards at the door, then back to Greg.

'Ten thousand dollars is missing, Lila. Whores don't cost that much.'

He jerked his head towards Jake and the man crossed the room to the bar. The hidden compartment was behind the optics. Greg regarded Lila as she watched Jake take out the second set of account books.

'We had a coupla lucky punters downstairs. There was a fight during the convention and we had to clean up and the contractors cost more than we expected to get the work done on time,' she said quickly – too quickly. 'I tol' the man all this! What shit he tryin' ta lay on me?' Her Louisiana accent had slipped to the cotton fields where she'd come from, her demeanour that of the street where she'd begun her trade.

He'd suddenly had enough. In one stride he was beside her, his fingers gripping her wrist until the glass fell to the floor.

'Don't bull-shit me, Lila. Admit it. You got greedy, then you got careless. Did you really think I didn't know about the second set of books?'

Lila tore away, her expression surly. 'Like I tol' d'man – I got expenses. That second set ain't nothing to do with de business.'

Greg hit her – hard. She fell against the table sending bottles and glasses smashing to the floor. 'You've got no manners, Lila.'

Lila put her hand to her face, all belligerence gone, fear sharp in her eyes. 'I don' mean no disrespect, sir. The money goes to Roberto every day. He d'man. He de one responsible if there's a shortfall.'

Greg hit her again, and for an instant it was Gabriella's face in front of him. It was good to feel flesh against flesh. To feel the heat on his palm, the sting in his fingers. He raised his arm to strike harder.

Lila screamed as his ring caught her lip and drew blood. 'I'll pay you back! Please, don't hit me again!'

Greg mashed the cigarette into an ashtray and grasped her throat. Looking into her frightened eyes, he could feel her heat, smell her fear – it was a strange, exotic fragrance, sharp, yet heavy with musk, that brought with it the darkness of the ghetto, the pulse of the voodoo drums and the erotic spell of the forbidden. 'Leave us,' he ordered the bodyguard.

As the door closed behind Jake, he turned his attention back to Lila. 'How you gonna make up for cheating me, Lila? What you gonna do to make amends?' His voice was thick with arousal, his body ready.

Hope flared in her dark eyes and he felt her relax. The electricity between them was highly charged.

'I ain't cheated on you, Mr Castlemaine. But I got savings, almost six thousand dollars. Take it. Take all of it.'

She tried to break free, but his grip was steel. His free hand reached for her dress. With one tug it fell to the floor. She was naked beneath the silk and he caught his breath at her voluptuous promise.

Their gaze met and held. This was something the whore understood.

Greg ran his fingers across the delicate collarbones, then felt the weight of her generous breasts as he brushed the dark nipples into tight, thrusting arousal with his thumb. Then, with luxurious, orgasmic pleasure, his hand moved slowly down the sweep of her waist and over her flat belly to the coarse hair between her legs. She was wet and he was impatient.

'I make you happy, baby,' Lila murmured, moving against his hand and freeing his erect cock. 'Let Lila love you, like you ain't never been loved before.'

'Shut your mouth,' he rasped as he grasped her buttocks, lifted her from the floor and slid into her.

She brought up her knees and wrapped her long legs around his waist.

With every stroke he rammed her against the wall. He wanted to hurt her, wanted to enforce his control – needed to make her pay for what she and Gabriella had done to him. Lila disappeared, and in his imagination this was his cheating wife. His pace quickened, his anger increased, his fingers gouging the soft flesh of her backside making her cry out and squirm. The sound of her spurred him on. He wanted to hear her pain – hear her beg – feel her terror.

All too soon it was over, the fast, furious need dissipated. Yet the anger was still there – still burning.

He pushed her away and adjusted his clothing. Lila was nothing. He would only quench the fury when he had Gabriella at his mercy.

Lila slumped to the floor and with clinical detachment he watched her cower at his feet. 'Get up.'

She pulled the tattered dress over her nakedness and edged up the wall to face him. The wariness was back in her eyes.

The blade of the flick-knife glittered in the electric light and he smiled as the raw, pink flesh gaped in the tawny brown of her cheek.

Lila screamed and tried to hold the lips of the wound together, but the blood streamed through her fingers as she stumbled across the room to the mirror.

'Go back to the streets, Lila. It's all you're good for. That,' he said, pointing to her face, 'is a reminder never to cross me.'

'How long you think I'll survive out there?' she yelled, all control gone. 'Who wants a whore with a face like this? Please – you have to give me another chance.' Her tears mingled with the blood and she sank to her knees before him.

Greg looked down at her – he felt nothing.

'You have one hour to get out. Then I never want to see

227

you or hear from you again. Should you decide to sing to the cops, you'll be one very dead whore.'

It was when he'd returned to the apartment in Manhattan and was standing beneath the hot jet of the shower, that he realised he was close to the edge. Tonight, when he should have remained cool and detached, he'd almost lost it.

Gabriella had found a way to destroy that carefully constructed façade of controlled calm behind which he'd carved out his rise in the family business. The episode at the gaming house merely enhanced the outrage he'd held back for so long – it wasn't the whore's fault – even though she was just as devious as his wife – but Greg recognised his own lack of control over the situation and vowed he would never let it happen again.

I should have left it to Jake, he thought as he turned off the shower and wrapped a towel around his waist. Yet the memory of the whore's body forced him to admit he'd found the episode more satisfying than he should have. Old habits died hard, he'd lost his virginity to a black whore, his father had paid for her for his thirteenth birthday – and even now the smell and touch of a black skin had felt good.

He was lost in pleasant reverie as he prepared for bed, and the sound of the telephone startled him. After listening to Smith at the other end he smiled and cut the connection. Remembering Charlotte had been a stroke of genius, and it had taken little effort to track her down. Now Gabriella was within his grasp. In the next few hours he would have her.

Gabriella heard the click of the latch as the kitchen door closed behind her. After the brightness of the house, the night seemed to close in, bringing a menace to every shadow, every sighing tree and creaking branch. As she paused to adjust the blanket around Nick, she felt the sharp nip of winter in the air, summer was only a memory, and the moon was playing hide and seek behind turbulent, racing clouds.

The gravel crunched under foot as she ran for cover behind the hedge of Hydrangeas. It seemed that the noise she was making must be heard in the house, but as she crouched in the shadows, she realised it was only her fear that enhanced every sound.

Keeping low, she followed the hedge until she came to the edge of the woods, then scurrying across the strip of grassland, she thrust her way through the brambles and fallen trees until she came to the old oak she'd played in as a child. The hollow in the trunk was still there, the soft, leafy floor that smelled of earthy secrets could still give her shelter for the few moments she would need to catch her breath.

She crawled inside and held the baby close. Nick began to squirm, his tiny fist pummelling his face as he sought the comfort of his thumb. She held him tighter, kissing his face, easing his thumb into his mouth, breathing into his hair, whispering words that made little sense, but might just encourage him into contented silence. One cry and someone might hear them, one sound and they would be lost.

Inching away from her hiding place, she darted between the trees and headed for the lake. Giving the geese pens a wide berth, she knew it would add several minutes to her flight, but she didn't dare rouse the sleeping birds, they were better than any alarm system.

Despite her care in holding him close, Nick's restlessness grew. His mewling turned to grumbles and it would only be a matter of time before he gave full vent to his discomfort.

'Shhh, darling. Shhh. Not long now. Please, my love, don't cry. Please don't cry,' she whispered desperately as she stumbled over fallen branches and treacherous roots.

Each snapping twig, every rustle of leaves made her pulse race, and when the shriek of a vixen tore through the night her blood seemed to freeze. It was the sound of chilling, bloodcurdling intensity – too similar to that of a tortured baby for her to ignore it.

She stopped, rested her cheek on Nick's downy head and

fought the panic. The sound of a vixen on heat was nothing new, the forest surroundings familiar, her imagination must be brought under control – and quickly. They were too vulnerable out here.

The lake glittered in the momentary gleam of moonlight, its surface gently ruffled by the autumnal breeze. The tree cover was thinner here, the trunks slender, the undergrowth cut back to make a wide path around the lake. Dinghies lay upturned on the man-made shingle beach, and the boathouse was just a ghostly outline against the water.

Nick began to cry. It rose into a crescendo of wails that rang across the lake and lifted into the trees. Birds rustled at the disturbance, and something fairly large crashed through the debris of the forest floor to burrow out of sight.

Gabriella clasped Nick's head and began to run in earnest. The sound of the shingle beneath her feet no longer mattered, she had to find the car before the gamekeeper alerted the people at the house.

The Mini was parked in the lee of the boathouse just as Charlotte had promised. Fumbling with the key, Gabriella finally managed to unlock it. Not waiting to release the baby from the sling, and turning a deaf ear to his screams, she jammed the key into the ignition and started the engine. It roared into life and she slammed the door and hit the accelerator.

The little car bounced over the rough path, the steering wheel almost ripped from her grasp as they hit a particularly deep rut. Gabriella tightened her grip on the wheel and put her foot further to the floor. The headlights swung crazed arcs through the trees, putting up birds, making rabbits scurry.

Nick screamed and writhed against her, but nothing could break her concentration as she fought the sliding, spinning tyres and jolting terrain. In and out of the trees, left then right, up hillocks and down into deep hollows, the engine roaring, the chassis creaking alarmingly.

Time had no boundaries – it seemed to stretch endlessly

as the minutes ticked away and there was still no sign of the bitumen road that would lead to the keeper's cottage and Courtenay village.

A badger, caught in the glare of the headlights, trundled ponderously across her path.

Gabriella gritted her teeth, rammed the Mini into third and swerved. The little car slewed sideways, rocked violently, caught the rear bumper on the bole of a tree, then shot forward with a grinding, tearing rip of metal as she found fourth again and jammed her foot to the floor. The tyres found the bitumen, held, then with a screech of rubber propelled the car towards the lodge gates.

They were closed.

Gabriella swore, and was about to brake when she noticed the running man. It was Arthur, the estate manager. He was opening the gates – and waving her through.

For the second time that night, she had Charlotte to thank for her loyalty and quick thinking.

16

Tyler pulled on his jacket as the night closed in. It was time to telephone Bill.

Nothing moved on the road and the village itself was dark and almost silent. It was as the landlord had said – isolated and without much nightlife. He would have to be careful. A stranger here would cause comment.

The night had brought with it a sharp damp which clung to the grass and dripped from the trees, but it was the sort of night Tyler relished, and he tramped vigorously over fields until he was some distance from the village.

His knee felt stiff at first, but as he walked, it eased. He liked to stretch himself, to pit his strength against the elements and feel the wind on his face, after the K's he'd tabbed in the army, this was small beer, but at least he was mobile.

After an hour, he rested against the bole of a tree, massaged his knee, then took out his portable phone.

Bill answered almost immediately. 'I got hold of Wyman and he'll start tomorrow. The bad news is he picked up a nasty habit during his stay at Her Majesty's pleasure – coke – so he needs the money.'

Tyler expelled a sharp breath. 'Stupid sod. With a brain like his, he could have really made something of himself.'

'Ours is not to reason why, me old son. How's it going up there?'

'Comfortable. Heard anything from the Sally Army yet?'

'Bit early. They're going through their records, and

I've arranged to meet someone from the Catholic Society tomorrow.'

Tyler told him what he'd found out about Gabriella's father.

'Well, I'll be darned. Old Wily Whitmore, eh? I never made the connection, but now you mention it, I seem to remember someone saying he'd bought a spread in Norfolk when he retired. Hell, Tyler, you must remember him, he took us on that survival course when we were doing basic special training. Tough bastard. Reminded me of my grandfather.'

Tyler shook his head. 'I was down in Portsmouth then, my course was later, with Swinburn.'

Bill went on to fill in more of Whitmore's background and Tyler stared out at the landscape, his mind sifting through the information, trying to make sense of it all.

'Did he have any other specialities, apart from survival? Anything to do with narcotics or South America, for instance?' Tyler was trying to link his thoughts and ideas into a pattern, but wasn't having much success.

'Never let on if he did. His line of country was Singapore and the Far East – spoke Malay like a native. He was stationed in India for a while, but stayed in England for the latter part of his career. Explosives and subliminal infiltration were his bag.'

Bill took a breath and Tyler waited. It was intriguing to put a background to the photograph of the girl. This was no ordinary runaway.

'His other passion was horses and he kept a hunter back in Hereford. Bastard of an animal. The old man was the only one that could get near it.'

Tyler grinned. Bill's aversion to horseflesh was well known, ever since he'd been bitten on the rump by a particularly sour tempered Arab stallion in Dubai. According to Bill, he still carried the scar, but Tyler had declined the offer to inspect the evidence.

'What's all this got to do with the daughter?' Bill's tone was overcasual, as though he knew what Tyler was thinking and had to steer the conversation back to a safer topic.

'Maybe nothing. Just trying to find out more before I talk to the old lady. If Smith's involved, there's trouble somewhere. I just want to be forewarned, that's all.'

'I'll speak to you tomorrow then. What are you going to do?'

'I've got to make sure no one else is watching the house. Should only take a couple of days to get used the old girl's routine, but I don't want to go blundering in and frightening the life out of them if they've already had a visit from Sniffy or his cronies. At least, with the service background it'll give me some point of reference when I speak to her.'

Bill laughed. 'Just show her your credentials, Tyler. I'm sure she'll be impressed.'

'Sod off,' he hissed, and cut the connection. Silly bugger, he thought as he lit his cigarette.

Gabriella had driven through the night, stopping only for petrol and to feed and change Nick, now she was leaving the M23 and approaching Brighton.

The town had changed beyond all recognition, it was more a city than a seaside resort, the traffic crawling, the parking nonexistent, the population swarming along the pavements, and for a while she found it difficult to get her bearings. Then she was out of the one-way chaos of the town centre and on the seafront. Heading west, towards Hove, she looked for a parking space and stopped.

Why she had come here, was the question that nagged her as she sat on the seafront and watched the gulls wheel and glide in the wind. Brighton had been a favourite day trip resort when she was young, with the long beach and the two piers, and the funny little lanes and antique shops where mum loved to browse, but apart from that it held no significant importance.

Perhaps it's because I have such fond memories of the place, she thought. We'll be as safe here as anywhere. I have to stop running sometime.

She looked around at the graceful buildings that proudly faced the promenade, admired the gracious curve of the Edwardian terraces and the newly painted façades of the seafront apartment blocks. There would be plenty of guest houses in the side roads where she could lose herself for a while until she found something more permanent.

She eyed her reflection in the mirror, and gave a derisive snort. 'Time you got out of these rags and did something about your hair, my girl. No self-respecting landlady will give you houseroom as you are.'

Gabriella turned the key in the ignition. It was time to change the disguise again. Greg had already attacked from an unexpected position – the game of chess was still in progress.

The sound of the recorded typewriting was a necessary distraction and one that Tyler soon managed to ignore as he watched the women over the next four days.

They spent most of their time in the sitting room, or at least Mrs Whitmore did. Her chair had been placed near the window where she could watch the comings and goings on the street, but she wasn't idle. Her arthritic fingers struggled with knitting needles and wool and when tired, she read or watched television. The only visitors were the tradesmen and postman. The two women were living their lives in the same way they had probably done for years – as friends and companions in genteel retirement.

It was soon obvious that he was the only watcher, and when he used the long distance listening device and caught snatches of their conversation, it had become clear that the two women were undisturbed by outside events, and there was nothing to suggest any anxiety or tension.

Yet it worried him. To all outward appearances, Mrs Whitmore had no idea that her daughter was missing – and where was the loving, concerned husband who was willing to pay over the odds to find her?

'Curiouser and curiouser,' he muttered.

The feeling of being watched was very strong. So strong, that Gabriella looked over her shoulder and scanned the street behind her. Don't be so paranoid, she scolded silently. You're letting your imagination get the better of you.

Yet the feeling persisted, and grew to overwhelming certainty and she clutched the baby and quickened her pace. Was it only her overtaxed imagination – or were the streets strangely deserted, giving the shuttered houses a menacing glower in the dim street lights. Even the muted throb of disco music echoed her heartbeat – enhancing the vulnerability – the isolation she suddenly felt. She hurried along the pavement, her sneakers muffling her progress.

The huddled shapes of parked cars lined the side street, their windows opaque, staring back like blind men's eyes. Was someone behind that dark glass? Watching, waiting?

A cat shot out of the gloom and with a hiss of resentment disappeared down the steps of a basement. Gabriella bit down on the fright, but the tension remained in her throat, in the set of her spine and the grip on the baby.

She could feel the eyes, smell the danger, taste the fear. A shudder ran over her. It had been careless to go out without the car so late when she could have eaten in the guest house, but the room was claustrophobic and she'd needed fresh air. Yet she hadn't realised how jumpy she still was, hadn't thought of the dangers on the streets. This was Brighton – not LA.

'Give us a quid, lady.' The voice boomed from the shadows of a shop doorway.

Gabriella spun round as a hand clutched her arm.

'I ain't eaten today. Go on – give us enough for a cuppa tea.'

She snatched away from his grasp, her pulse racing. 'I don't . . .'

The derelict spat at her feet, his eyes wild beneath the matted hair and woollen cap. 'Yes you do. Now hand it over!'

His breath was rancid, his clothes filthy, and he was not alone. Other shadows were moving in the darkness, and a large, unkempt dog was sniffing her leg.

Gabriella scrabbled in her pockets and found a few pennies which she threw to the pavement. As she backed away and began to run, she heard them curse after her.

The guest house was still brightly lit, and as she raced up the stairs and locked the door behind her, she vowed never to do such a stupid thing again.

Vic belched softly behind the napkin, then wiped the spaghetti sauce from his mouth. The one good thing about the restaurant was the food. He could have as much as he liked, when he liked, away from the prying eyes of his wife, who constantly complained about his spreading girth, and tried to feed him lettuce leaves. He patted the mound which stretched his waistcoat then took a sip of wine. He was feeling satisfied, both in appetite and ambition.

The meeting had gone well this afternoon, but it wasn't yet time to move. Dad was stubbornly clinging to life and Greg wouldn't do anything about Gabriella and the kid until the old man was out of the way. When he did, Victor planned to be ready to make his move, he already had people looking for her.

The waitress approached the table and began to clear the dishes. She was about nineteen, with short blonde hair and a complexion as smooth as a peach. Her figure was nicely rounded, just the way he liked it and she wasn't afraid to show it off.

He watched her breasts jiggle beneath the tight t-shirt and realised she wasn't wearing a bra. His erection was sweet torture as she bent over the table. Her ass was tightly sheathed in a very short, black skirt and he could imagine very clearly what it would be like to slide his hand up those long thighs and slip his fingers into her pussy.

He was tempted to try. Maybe she didn't wear panties, either. His need grew as he thought of the dampness he would find there, the soft, clinging muscles that could suck at his dick and make him come. His wife always had a headache.

She moved away and he sighed. Francine wouldn't even consider giving him a quickie, she was already doing that for the chef. He'd heard them once in the storeroom when they'd thought he'd left for the night and had jacked off as he watched through a crack in the door. He'd used one of the street girls later and had been amazed at his stamina. Never before had he been able to screw so many times, in so many different positions. It had made him feel young and virile again. Reminded him of his rutting youth.

I paid the price, he thought ruefully. A dose of the clap which drove me nuts for weeks. It had been the one time he'd been glad his wife wasn't interested in sex. He could never have come up with a reasonable explanation. His erection shrivelled at the memory and he was brought out of his musing by the head waiter.

'Your brother's on the line, Mr Castlemaine,' he said as he plugged in the telephone and left it on the table.

Victor hid his surprise and waited for the man to leave. Greg couldn't know about his plans, could he? Had someone talked?

'Hi, Greg. How's it hangin'?'

'Fine, Vic. Just fine. Look, I know it's late, but we need to talk. Meet me at Murphy's place.'

Vic swallowed. He could feel perspiration gather in his armpits, and suddenly his stomach was too full, the spaghetti sauce too rich. He felt a flicker of pain in his chest. Murphy's place? It was a dive. What the fuck was Greg doing in Chicago?

He cleared his throat before answering. 'OK, bro. But what's so urgent it can't wait until tomorrow?'

'We'll talk later. There's a car on its way.'

The call was abruptly terminated and Vic looked stupidly at the receiver before putting it back. 'Shit! What the hell does he want?'

He pushed the table away and struggled to get out of the deep leather banquette. There was spaghetti sauce on his tie and his suit was crumpled, yet there was no time to go home and change. Greg's car was already waiting outside.

The driver was silent as they swept through downtown Chicago, and Vic stared out of the window at the hookers. At this moment he would have preferred a dose of the clap rather than face his brother.

The car pulled up outside the amusement arcade and pool hall and Vic looked up at the spluttering neon sign with a shudder of unease. Something didn't smell right – this was not Greg's usual territory – and if it had been possible, he would have run, but the driver was beside him – opening the door and waiting for him to move. He would have to go in.

Murphy's Pool Hall was a vast, dingy expanse of green baize tables and low, shaded lights behind the bustling arcade. The odour of stale tobacco, sweat and spilled beer had permeated the walls and stained the carpet over the years and now it hung over the almost deserted room like a pall. Victor was very familiar with the place, it had once been his domain, his responsibility to oversee the management and keep the accounts in order for Greg.

'Mr Castlemaine says to wait,' muttered the bodyguard and indicated for Vic to sit at the bar.

He watched him move away and join the group of men on the far side of the hall, and as he reached for his cigarettes, he found his hands shook so badly, he had difficulty in lighting up.

Greg didn't acknowledge him, he had eyes only for the man standing in the centre of the group.

Vic watched him smooth his tie and lift his chin. He knew the signs, understood their meaning. There was going to be trouble and he didn't want any part of it. He turned to the barman and was handed a bourbon. Downing it in one, he asked for another, but as he reached for it, Greg's voice cut through the silence.

'Call yourself an accountant? You fucked up, Michael!'

'How was I to know the IRS was gonna do a raid?'

Greg picked up the billiard cue and the circle of men fanned out. 'I pay you to take care of the IRS. You have no excuse.'

Victor gulped the second bourbon, but he couldn't look away.

The billiard cue hit Michael across the nose and there was an audible crack and an explosion of blood. It struck again and opened the man's eyebrow.

'I didn't tell them nothing, I swear! Don't do this Greg – Mr Castlemaine – please – I have a family.'

'I'm your family, Michael. You should have remembered that when you squealed to the IRS.' The cue was rammed into his gut, then brought up fast and smashed into his jaw.

Michael fell like a rag doll over the pool table, his jagged breath loud in the echoing hall. 'They didn't get to see the private books, Mr Castlemaine,' he sputtered through broken teeth. 'All they saw were the accounts for the legit businesses.'

Victor watched Greg hit Michael again, and the unease grew. For the first time in his life, his brother was out of control – gone was the impassive façade and the ice-cool sadism – the man was eaten alive with a rage that was overwhelming, and coupled with his newly acquired status – Greg Castlemaine was more dangerous than ever.

Greg crashed the cue against Michael's kidneys, putting his weight behind the beating, then he lifted the cue and split the man's skull. As Michael slid to the floor, Greg dropped the cue. 'See to him,' he rapped, as his chest heaved with the effort he'd expended.

Victor watched two men struggle to carry the hapless Michael out of the back door. The man was screaming, filling the echoing hall with his agony. A tremor of fear fleeced his shoulders. Brutality had never bothered him before, but he had no liking for it when it involved his own physical pain, and his conscience was troubling him. Just what did his brother have in mind for him, tonight?

Greg turned to face him, his breathing under control, the sweat mopped from his face.

Vic watched him. Everything about his brother was sharp, clean, perfect, and he hated him for it – was afraid of the chameleon qualities that could change so rapidly. He gulped down the last of the whisky and stood up. Was it his turn next?

Greg put his hands on Victor's shoulders and held him at arms' length for a moment as he looked into his face.

'The restaurant business doesn't appear to be doing your health, or your figure much good, Vic. We must do something about that.' He clicked his fingers and two drinks were placed on the bar. 'Some music, Freddy. Then get out.'

Vic found it took all his willpower not to flinch from his brother's touch, and was relieved when Greg moved away and he could sit down. 'La Traviata' was playing on the stereo and the soprano's voice was giving him a headache. He felt the pain in his chest again – and wanted out.

'Cheers.'

Vic lifted his glass in reply and drained it. He needed something to quell the nausea, for this was a different Greg, a man who excuded a menacing power, and he didn't know how to deal with him. Yet he was all too aware of his brother's scrutiny.

'You're very quiet, Vic. Something wrong? Did that little scene bother you?'

Vic shook his head. He didn't dare speak, the sound of his voice would give him away. Just how much did Greg know about the meeting this afternoon? He was giving nothing away, in fact he was being charming – but then he always was just before he struck.

'I called this meeting because I think it's time we talked. Brothers shouldn't fall out over a woman – and I miss you. Look what happens when you aren't around. Things fall apart and I have to deal with them myself.'

Vic's mind was working fast. Greg knew nothing of the plot against him. It was only Gabriella again. The relief made him weak, but he was careful not to show it.

'I agree. No woman's worth fighting over.' He attempted a smile, but it felt wrong and he abandoned the effort.

'I need you to come back, Vic. I'm a busy man, and I shouldn't have to jeopardise my position by coming to places like this and dealing with the dross. I need someone to oversee my other business, someone whom I can trust.' Greg's gaze was steady, his thoughts masked by his inscrutable expression.

Yet Vic thought he saw a fleeting glimpse of something dangerous in those eyes. 'What about the restaurant? It's only been a matter of weeks and the profits are way up. Some of my ideas have really taken off.'

Greg waved his hand dismissively. 'Nickels and dimes compared to the money you could earn working with me, Vic. I'm sure your wife would appreciate your return to the fold. I hear she's given up her social engagements.' He fell silent, his eyes penetrating, his hand steady as it held the glass of barely touched bourbon.

Victor swallowed the bitterness. That was typical of Greg – scorning his achievements, pouring cold water on any enthusiasm he might have had for the business he'd been forced to run.

'Why the change of heart, Greg? Why now, when you have everything you want?' Greg was up to something. He never did anything without a reason. Never made a move unless it was for his own advancement.

'As the president of the corporation and the head of the cartel, I have to surround myself with those I really trust. You are my only brother. We shouldn't be at war, we should be fighting on the same side. This is a chance for both of us to make more money than we ever dreamed of. Are you willing to take it? Do you have the balls to risk everything and go for broke?'

Victor didn't like what he was hearing. Greg was drawing him back into his web. But why? What was the truth behind those softly spoken words? He drew on his cigarette and stared at the carpet. I really have no choice, he thought in desperation. Greg's not a man to take no for an answer.

'Do you need so long to make up your mind, Vic? I thought that as my brother, you would be eager to return to the fold.'

Vic resisted the urge to run his finger round his collar as his mind raced. It would be easier for him to watch Greg from the inside, he argued silently. Easier for him to know his every move. Going back would place him in a better position for when the time came to take over. As his brother, his right-hand man, he would be above suspicion. His heart thudded and a thrill of excitement tingled in his crotch. Greg was offering him more than he could have hoped for. His own victory was assured and very close.

He struggled to keep his voice low and sincere as he looked back at his brother. 'I'll come back if you promise never to undermine my decisions or doubt me again. I might not be as ambitious, or as powerful, I might not be so cool headed and ruthless, but I am family – and that's got to count for something.'

Greg hugged him and slapped him on the back. 'I have enough power and ambition for both of us, Vic. Just be my eyes and ears and watch my back. That's all I ask.'

I'll watch your back, all right, Vic thought coldly as he looked over his brother's shoulder. And when the time's right, I'll stick a knife in it. I'll show you who's stronger, and prove beyond doubt, that Victor Castlemaine will never remain in your shadow again.

*   *   *

'Strewth! My bloody feet are killing me,' groaned Jackie Dawson, as she kicked off the high heeled shoes and massaged her instep. 'Fancy nipping into the kitchen and making us a cuppa, luv? I'll watch the sprog.'

Gabriella grinned. She had been in the guest house for a week, but already it felt like home. Jackie was Australian. A woman who would never see the right side of forty again, but with the disposition and vitality of her native sunshine. Her figure was voluptuous, but in proportion, and her hair an abundance of sandy curls which swept around a heart-shaped face that was liberally dusted with freckles.

Having made the tea, they sat in companionable silence and watched Nick gurgling in the watery sunshine that glimmered on the carpet.

Jackie lit a cigarette, put her stockinged feet up on the coffee table and blew a stream of smoke to the ceiling. 'Only three in for dinner tonight,' she sighed. 'This season's been patchy, the busy times're getting fewer every year. Won't be worth opening at all soon.'

Gabriella made sympathetic noises, but her mind was turning over the plans she would have to make for her own future.

'Why did you come to Brighton, Ellie Castle? You're not really on holiday, are you?'

Gabriella tensed. She still felt uncomfortable with her shortened name, and as her past was necessarily secret, she didn't know how to answer such a direct question.

Jackie loosened the belt on her skirt. 'That's better, bloody thing's cutting me in half.' She regarded Gabriella with cool blue eyes, then shook her head. 'In this business luv, I get to see them all. Blokes cheating on their wives, wives cheating on husbands, kids out for a bit of naughty, the moaners and bludgers. But I never had one like you.'

'I didn't realise I was supposed to fit into a particular catagory of holiday-maker,' Gabriella retorted a little sharply. 'I just wanted a break by the sea.'

'Huh. That what you call it?' She peered through a haze of smoke, but there was no malice in her tone. 'I know it's none of my business, but I've been watching you and I get the feeling you're in some sort of trouble. You never let the sprog out of your sight, or go out in the evenings, or mix with the other guests. No one's phoned since you arrived, and you've had no visitors or mail.'

She dropped her feet from the table and leaned forward, her expression concerned. 'You look like someone who's been through the mill. What's the story, Ellie?'

Gabriella shrugged and looked away.

Jackie sighed. 'You have too much class.' She shrugged as she searched for the right adjective. 'Too much . . . polish. Despite the hair and the clothes, you talk like a real Pom – with a plum in your mouth. A girl like you doesn't come to a place like this unless she's running away from something.'

The silence stretched between them. Gabriella maintained a cool dignity against the onslaught, but the urge to speak, to unburden the things she'd seen and done, was almost unbearable.

'I've come to see you as a friend, Ellie Castle. Who is it you're so afraid of?'

The tea cup rattled in the saucer. 'Just drop it Jackie.'

Jackie eyed her curiously, then settled back to smoke her cigarette and watch Nick. When she spoke again, her voice had softened and there was sadness etched in her face.

'At least you've got Charlie. When my old man went walkabout, he left me nothing but debts, bruises and this white elephant.' She stubbed out her smoke. 'We couldn't have kids. Good thing really, he'd probably have knocked them about too.'

'Sounds as if you're better off without him. You seem cheerful enough.'

'Got to be in this business, but it's the nights that get me down. The empty bed, no one to talk to when I can't sleep, no cuddles or intimacy. The little things.' She sighed. 'The world's made up of couples. Other women see a single female as a threat to their carefully constructed marriages. I've had my share of blokes, but one nighters aren't really for me, and sometimes it can get bloody lonely.'

Gabriella knew how she felt. 'I agree. The nights can be lonely, but at least they're safe.'

'Beat you up, did he? Charlie's dad?'

'No. But it was only a matter of time.'

'Wise girl. Wish I'd had your sense. Trouble is, it's the bastards that are the most attractive.' She fell silent for a moment. 'I loved Bob, despite his temper. Should have left him years ago. But I was scared to go, scared to stay. He did me a favour by leaving, gave me no option but to carry on without him, and it hasn't been as bad as I'd feared.'

'I felt just the same, but the baby had to be safe, and I knew his father would never leave without him.'

'Why don't you tell me about it, Ellie? You look like you need a mate, and I know when to keep my trap shut.'

Gabriella shivered, and the need to talk became more pressing. She looked at Nick, then back at Jackie. Perhaps she could talk a little, just enough to satisfy the other woman's curiosity and get rid of some of the burden she was carrying.

'I met Charlie's father two years ago in America. I was teaching aerobics and saving to buy my own place. I had such dreams, Jackie. I was going to build an empire, have premises in the best part of London, with a gym, a dance studio and beauty parlour to cater for all the rich women who wanted to be pampered.'

'Sounds like heaven,' murmured Jackie as she lit another cigarette.

Gabriella nodded. 'Then I met Gr . . . his father and everything changed. He swept me off my feet, and before I had time to think about it properly, I was married and pregnant.'

'Must have been one hell of a man.'

She nodded as she conjured up an image of Gregory

Castlemaine. 'He was tall, handsome, very wealthy, dark eyed and sexy. I was hopelessly in love with him – thought I'd got it made.'

'Sounds scrummy. So what went wrong?'

Gabriella thought before she answered. The chessboard images were strong, the dark figures of Greg and Victor etched against the white walls of the Californian mansion.

'I saw something I shouldn't have. It was something that made me realise I'd put my son in danger. So I ran,' she said finally.

In the ensuing silence, Gabriella relived the awful night she'd seen Greg's true colours, then the riot in LA, and the instant of recognition that had nearly meant her downfall in Albuquerque. She shuddered at the memory of brown eyes capturing green. Of fear being a spidery thing that crawled deep inside and remained there.

'They nearly caught me twice. If it hadn't been for a kindly Texan and a bottle of hair dye, I wouldn't be in Brighton now.'

'Sounds interesting. Tell me more,' Jackie said with a playful leer.

Gabriella giggled, and ran her fingers through her short, dark crop. It was so good to be able to laugh about it now. At the time she'd been afraid of her own shadow.

'He was over six feet in height and width, with an enormous stetson. I was afraid he would draw attention to us with his size and loud voice, but Texas seems to grow their men big. There were plenty like him.' She paused – her mind skipping to the mundane. 'I'll have to do something with my hair. The roots are beginning to show.'

Jackie stabbed out her cigarette. 'Did a bit of hairdressing back in Sydney. I'll sort it out for you – made a bit of a hash of it, if you don't mind me saying.'

'You're not the first to make that comment,' she answered wryly, thinking of Charlotte.

'So, all this happened in Texas, then?'

Gabriella bit her lip. She'd said too much already, and Jackie was too sharp – too inquisitive.

'You also said "they" – who else were you running from?' Her face was still, her gaze clear and steady.

'My husband's a powerful man. When someone breaks the rules, there are plenty of others he can call on to do his dirty work.'

'So what happened next? God, this is better than a film.'

Gabriella fell silent, then shrugged. Jackie wouldn't let it drop until she was satisfied she knew it all – but that wasn't possible. 'There's not much more to tell. I flew to Paris, then after a few weeks, I came into England from Ireland. The rest, as they say, is history.'

'Strewth, that must have taken some bottle, Ellie.'

She shrugged. 'I had Charlie to think about and all the time he was in danger I never worried about how much courage it would take.' She became aware of Jackie's arm around her as the tears finally came. It was as though a great weight had been lifted from her shoulders.

'What about your family? Is there no one who can help you?'

Gabriella pulled back sharply. 'No one. What I told you is between us. I want you to promise.'

Jackie hugged her. 'I promise. Come on. We deserve a gin and tonic.'

Once the drinks had been poured and Gabriella had dried her tears, things looked a little better. Even the sun had come out from behind the rain clouds.

'What made you choose the Costa Geriatrica? Brighton's not half as glamorous as it was – hardly Southfork, Texas.'

Gabriella shrugged. 'Came here a few times for the day out. Memories of childhood are always sunny, don't you think? I suppose I was looking for the security I took for granted in those days.'

'And have you found it?'

'Not really. I still look over my shoulder – watching for a

face in the crowd – someone following me. But I suppose it'll get easier. Why do you stay if you're not happy?'

Jackie made a derisive noise in her throat. 'Who wants to buy a guest house in the middle of a recession?' She shook her head. 'I could have gone back to Sydney, but it's been too long. I don't have family there any more and all my mates have married or moved away.'

She regarded Gabriella solemnly. 'What are you going to do next? I bet you haven't much money, and my seventy-five quid a week must be eating into your savings.'

Gabriella got out of the chair and picked up the baby. She held him close and looked out of the window. The sea reflected the grey sky and rain spattered against the glass.

'Brighton's our start of a new life. If I could only find a job, then I could plan, but there's nothing around that pays enough for me to work full time and have a minder for Charlie.'

'I wish I could help, but I don't need anyone. Thought about the social? You must be eligible for something.'

'Can't. Too risky. He could trace us.'

'Fair go. I'll ask around, maybe I can find you something in the bigger guest houses. Pay won't be brilliant, cash in hand mostly, but it'll be a start. If you could get two or three cleaning jobs, I'll gladly look after Charlie. He's a ripper little bloke.'

Gabriella felt the emotions well up for this stranger who'd become a friend. 'Thanks,' was all she could say without disgracing herself by crying again.

'We girls have got to stick together. Don't let the bastards grind you down, is what I say.'

Greg sat in front of the window of his hotel suite and looked out at the Chicago skyline. Millions of lights twinkled in the darkness, the tall, black towers of steel and concrete mere shadows against the backdrop of the heavens. The sweet, heart-turning voice of the soprano drifted from the stereo and filled the room. Opera was a passion he'd been introduced to by his father, now, as he listened, he felt the tension in his shoulders ease.

The hand-on violence had given him an adrenalin rush, and worked off the frustration at having Gabriella slip from his grasp yet again. To have come so close – and then to have lost her because a snivelling, weak-kneed English aristocrat didn't have the guts to keep his trap shut and control his wife – was the final humiliation that broke through his icy reserve.

He hated to admit it, but perhaps there was more of the ghetto inside him than he cared to acknowledge – for the scene at the pool hall had not really been necessary. Michael was a fool, but not disloyal – he just hadn't been in the right place at the right time or had the glib tongue to forestall the IRS as Vic would have done.

Yet, once started, Greg had found he couldn't stop. There was a great deal of excitement in hearing a man beg, in seeing flesh split and hearing bones crack. A good deal of satisfaction in burning off the frustration and anger he wanted to expend on Gabriella. Michael had just been an excuse.

He closed his eyes, the scene running through his mind. Michael's hospital bills would be paid, his wife silenced with a fat cheque – he would have to look for another accountant for the Chicago gambling franchises.

Lighting a cigarette he put his mind to the meeting with Victor. It had gone well, much better than he'd thought, and Dad had been proved right – his brother would definitely have to be watched.

How much better to do it where he could see him. As his second-in-command he couldn't make a move without him knowing. But he won't have access to the real heart of the business, Greg decided. Victor's no entrepreneur. He must merely be made to think he is important.

Greg stabbed his cigarette out. If what his spy had told him was true, Victor was a danger. A danger to him and the delicate balance of power within the cartel. Betrayal from within carried a death sentence and he, Gregory Castlemaine, would be the executioner if his brother was found guilty.

17

It was still raining in Brighton, the cars sending a gossamer spray over the pedestrians as they scurried along the pavements. Nick, or Charlie as he was now called, was snug in his second hand pushchair, dressed in three cardigans and a terry jumpsuit, but the rain was soaking them both and she resented having to spend more of her precious money to buy an umbrella, a raincoat and sweater.

The trans-world flights had cost more than she'd bargained for, Charlotte's mini was parked up because she couldn't afford to run it, and the cost of the guest house had depleted her cache of money. To compound her misery, she'd discovered that in her haste to escape from Charlotte's she'd left the miniatures and figurines behind. They would have been no use anyway, she'd realised, causing comment if she tried to sell them on the open market, and there was the risk of Greg tracing her through them. Now she had enough money for a down payment on a bedsit, and little else. She would have to find work – and quickly.

The woman in the job centre had been encouraging, but not much help. There were few jobs going, but nothing in the way of teaching. Gabriella felt the frustration build. She didn't have the time to hang about spending more money. As a last resort, she'd turned to the social services, but they needed to know too much and she'd left empty handed.

Now she was back at the job centre for yet another interview. Her hair was blonde again, trimmed into a neat petal cut, thanks to Jackie, and although her clothes were second-hand they were clean and neat, yet her usual optimism was wearing thin.

'There's something here, came in today. Not teaching, I'm afraid, but it may help as a stop-gap. The Royal Hotel need a chambermaid for the rest of the season.'

Gabriella felt a surge of hope. 'I'll do it. Can I go for an interview today?'

The woman smiled, made a telephone call and handed Gabriella an appointment slip. 'Let me know how you get on.'

'You're looking cheerful, Ellie.' Jackie gave her the once over. 'Where're you off to?'

'A job interview.' Gabriella told Jackie about it and felt as proud as she had the day she received her degree. Silly really, she scolded herself. She would only be making beds. 'Would you look after Charlie for me? I shouldn't be long.'

'No worries. We'll get along just fine without you, won't we Charlie boy?' Jackie nuzzled his hair and the baby laughed in delight.

Gabriella felt a twinge of jealousy. Since that mad flight from California, Nick had never been out of her sight and it felt odd to see him in another woman's arms.

'Christ, I nearly forgot. Mrs Wells at the Beau Regarde needs a cleaner. Here's the address. She's a bit of a dragon, but it'll be cash in hand and could fit in well with the chambermaiding.'

Gabriella laughed and hugged her. 'I feel as strong as Lancelot today. What's one dragon, when I have a friend like you?'

'Get outa here,' Jackie said with a laugh. 'And good luck!' she called as Gabriella closed the front door behind her.

The Royal faced the promenade and pier. A long glassed-in balcony covered the ground floor frontage and she could see a collection of elderly people sipping afternoon tea. It all looked so English, so calm and genteel. Surely nothing bad could happen here?

The door of the Beau Regarde closed behind her and she ran down the steps. Like her, or loathe her, Mrs Wells had given her the job – albeit at a slave wage, for it was cash in hand. Chambermaiding at the Royal started tomorrow, Nick could be with her at both places, and the minor matter of her P45 could be dealt with later, even though it did mean she was on emergency tax. It was early days yet and who knew what the future would bring, but things were looking up at last. This was turning out to be a very happy Friday.

Now for a bed-sit.

The best of a bad lot was in a terrace of run-down Victorian villas that fronted a steep hill behind the station. The owner was a woman who was in a hurry and barely gave Gabriella a glance as she showed her round.

'There are to be no men visitors, no alcohol or drugs,' she mumbled through a cigarette. 'If you break the rules then you're out.' She looked Gabriella up and down. 'I don't take DSS,' she said sharply.

'I have work,' said Gabriella quietly.

'That's something I suppose.'

'When can I move in?'

The woman shifted the cigarette from one side of her mouth to the other. 'Room's empty. Move in today. Fifty quid deposit and a month in advance. Rent due every Friday.'

Her hand came out of the folds of her raincoat and snatched the notes from Gabriella. Heading for the stairs, she stopped and turned. 'Bathroom and lav are down the end of the hall. The kitchenette is next to your room. Keep it clean.'

Gabriella stood in the doorway and regarded the room she would call home until something better turned up. It was a soulless place, a narrow rectangle furnished with a single bed, a chest of drawers and a wash basin. Hooks on the wall served as a wardrobe and the faded wallpaper was peeling in the corner where the damp had seeped through. The carpet was grey, stained and thin and the curtains hung dismally over grimy windows.

She threw open the window to get rid of the smell of stale tobacco, cheap wine and damp, but the view outside was as dismal as the room. A row of windows in a grey brick wall stared back and down below was a concrete yard with a line of dustbins forming ranks on both sides. The smell of overboiled cabbage and frying onion drifted up from the rooms below. Slamming the window shut, Gabriella decided she almost preferred the smell of cigarettes.

Jackie insisted on inspecting it. Now she stood in the doorway, hands on hips and shook her head. 'Strewth, Ellie, this place's a dump. Come back with me, luv. I can't let you stay here.'

Gabriella hugged Nick. It was time for them to be independent. 'Thanks, Jackie, but you're full up next week and it's not fair to expect you to house me. We'll be OK once I've cleaned it up a bit.'

Jackie stared hard. 'OK, but I won't let you stay here until I've done something about it.'

Striding out of the room, she lead the way to a row of second-hand shops around the corner. Ignoring Gabriella's persistent refusal to take anything, Jackie soon rounded up clean blankets, pillows and sheets. A rather battered cot and mattress was unearthed from a pile of junk, and a gaudy lampshade with moth-eaten fringing was added to the collection. Then she raided her own cupboards and presented her with polish, bleach, carpet cleaner and air freshener. When this was piled in a box, she added a pair of curtains and a worn eiderdown.

'No time like the present,' she said, then laughed. 'Come on Miss Stubborn Independence. Let's polish and scrub and make that hovel a palace. Then we'll crack open a bottle of wine and toast the place.'

Gabriella gave her a hug. She didn't have the best jobs in

the world, or the most pleasant of surroundings, but she had a friend, work and shelter. Best of all – she was free.

Tyler stood in the covered porch and waited. He could make out a shadowy figure behind the bevelled glass and knew he was being scrutinised.

'What do you want?' The querulous voice told him Mrs Whitmore was nervous about opening the door.

'My name is Tyler Reed, Mrs Whitmore. I was in your husband's regiment.' Not strictly true, but he would explain later. If he got the chance.

'Do you have any identification?'

Tyler had expected this and slipped his old army pass through the letter box. He should have handed it in when he left the services, but it had been overlooked and he'd found it useful. Hopefully it would open the door.

'What's your number and rank, soldier?' The voice was now sharp and business like.

Tyler grinned. There were no flies on this old duck.

'Major Tyler, William Reed. Royal Engineers. 77935.'

The chain was pulled back and the door opened a fraction. The pale eyes regarded him for a moment, then Mrs Whitmore handed back his pass. 'How can I help you Major?'

'I've come to pay my respects, ma'am. I understand the Brigadier passed away.'

Mrs Whitmore put her head to one side and stared. 'You're a little late, Major. He's been dead for nearly five years,' she snapped. 'What do you really want?'

Tyler felt a stab of admiration. Mrs Whitmore might look frail, but he hadn't been mistaken about the inner core of steel.

'My business partner, William Reynolds remembers the Brigadier very well, Mrs Whitmore. They were together in Hereford for a while, and he asked me to call in and give his regards.'

The door opened a little wider. 'Captain Bill?'

Tyler nodded and grinned. 'Once seen, never forgotten, ma'am. Red hair and a handlebar moustache.'

Mrs Whitmore's face lit up. 'And a temper to match.' She chuckled. 'He helped start my car, once. My ears still burn when I think about the rollicking he gave the mechanics for not servicing it properly.'

'I can imagine. He hasn't changed.'

'Please come in. I don't for a minute believe you've come all this way to talk to an old lady about Hereford, but whatever it is, it must be important, and nothing much interesting happens in my life any more.'

Tyler stepped into the narrow passage and she indicated for him to go into the sitting room. When she was comfortably seated, he perched on the edge of an overstuffed couch and looked around him. The room was cluttered with small tables, footstools and easy chairs. A collection of porcelain figurines was displayed in a glass case and there was a gas fire in the hearth. Heavy furniture made the room appear smaller and despite the morning sunshine, it was gloomy.

'I can offer you tea, Major. But you will have to make it yourself. My housekeeper is out.'

Tyler made his way to the kitchen. It was neat and clean and it took seconds to plant the bug under the sink – it was far more efficient than the long distance gadget. As he waited for the kettle to boil, he wondered how he could place another in the sitting room.

The tea was poured, the silence broken only by the hiss of the gas fire and the tick of the grandmother clock.

'We need to talk, Mrs Whitmore. It's about your daughter.' He watched for a reaction, but Mrs Whitmore was either a very good actress, or she suspected nothing.

'Are you still in the army, Major Reed? I thought you said Captain Bill was your business partner.' She looked at him over her tea cup, her expression guileless.

'I was invalided out almost ten years ago. Bill signed his

papers a year earlier. We run a detective and security agency in London.'

'That must be very interesting,' she said as she regarded him steadily. 'But what has this to do with my daughter?'

'Have you heard from her in the last few weeks, Mrs Whitmore? Do you know where she is?'

'I don't see that it is any business of yours, Mr Reed. My daughter left home over two years ago. She's an adult. She can come and go as she pleases.'

'Mrs Whitmore,' Tyler said quietly. 'I have reason to believe Gabriella is in trouble. Because of the respect we all had for the Brigadier, I want to help. But I can't do that without your co-operation.'

Their gazes locked.

'My daughter is in America.' Her chin had come up, but there was a wariness in her eyes.

'Are you certain, Mrs Whitmore? I have information to the contrary.'

'Then your information is wrong, Mr Reed. Now, if that is all, I must ask you to leave.'

Tyler looked around the room in exasperation. There had to be some way of convincing her to tell the truth. She knew something – he could see it in her eyes – but she was afraid. Had someone else been here asking questions? Or had Gabriella been in touch and warned her?

His gaze fell on the collection of citations and medals – a history of bravery shown in battles by the Brigadier and his father over the past fifty years.

'Who Dares, Wins, Mrs Whitmore. I have the same citation for bravery behind enemy lines as your husband. He earned his in the Far East, mine was awarded for something that happened in the Middle East. Your husband was a hero, someone we all wanted to emulate. He was a hard taskmaster, but his expertise in jungle warfare and survival was second to none.'

He turned to the old lady, the silver-framed citation in his hand.

Her gaze dropped to her lap. 'The army was his life and when he had to retire, it was as if a light had gone out in him.'

Tyler put down the citation and picked up a photograph. 'His only daughter. What would he have done if she was in trouble?'

'If he was alive today, Gabriella would never have had to . . .' Her voice tailed off as she realised the implication of what she'd been about to say.

'Never have to what, Mrs Whitmore? Run away?'

'I never said that,' she retorted. 'What I meant was, she would never have married such an unsavoury character. My husband would have given him short shift, I can assure you.'

Tyler put back the photograph that must have been taken when Gabriella was seven or eight. There were several others, making a resumé of Gabriella's life.

Here she was in her school uniform, hair plaited, two front teeth missing. Another, grainier picture of her astride a plump pony, one of her digging in the sand, a fourth in her cap and gown for her graduation. Yet it was the last one that held his attention. She stood under a bower of white roses in a gossamer dress. Her face was lifted towards her new husband and the radiance in that look was undeniable.

He studied the bridegroom. He was handsome, but there was a haughtiness in the tilt of his chin and a cruelty in the mouth and hooded eyes that spoke of hidden menace. He was dark haired and tanned, but undoubtedly American – maybe even had the touch of Latin about him. It was hard to tell.

He picked it up and turned to face Mrs Whitmore who was watching his every move. 'What happened? Why did Gabriella run away from a man she was so obviously in love with? They had only been married a year.'

Her hands fluttered on her lap. She was distressed, and he didn't like what he was doing, but he had to get to the truth.

'Who is he, Mrs Whitmore? Who's the man your husband would have seen off?'

The fight seemed to go out of her and she sagged against the cushions. 'How do I know I can trust you? For all I know he could be paying you to find my little girl.'

Tyler ignored the stab of guilt and sat down opposite her, the photograph still in his hands.

'I don't know this man, but I get the feeling he knows me.' Without mentioning names, he told her about Smith's visit to his office.

'So, you're doing his dirty work? I thought you were an officer, a gentleman.' Her tone was sneering.

'That's how it started, Mrs Whitmore, but as soon as I realised who Gabriella was, I knew she had to be in trouble.' He took a deep breath. 'The kind of trouble she will never get out of without help. The man who came to me has connections with the lowest, most violent criminals. A girl like her does not belong in his world.'

She took the photograph and brushed her fingers over Gabriella's image. Then she sighed. 'His name is Gregory Castlemaine. They were married on July 14th, 1991. In New Jersey.' She looked up from the photograph, her pale eyes troubled. 'I didn't want her to marry him, but she wouldn't listen. He was handsome, rich, could give her everything. But I could see what kind of man he was – I just didn't have the evidence to prove it to her.'

Tyler held his breath. Castlemaine – a pseudonym for something European perhaps – an anglicised version of an Italian name? It was a short step from Italian to Sicilian. From Sicilian to Cosa Nostra and the underworld of Sniffy Smith. He pushed the thought aside. He was letting his imagination get the better of him. Just because Sniffy was involved, didn't necessarily mean he was a part of the so-called Men of Honour. He was, after all, only an East End mobster.

Mrs Whitmore's voice broke into his thoughts. 'In a strange way, he reminded me of Gabriella's father. Very masculine. Liked being in control. But there the resemblance ended. My husband was never cruel; he killed, yes – but only in battle –

but I could see the sadism in that man's eyes, the coldness of someone who had lost their soul a long time ago.'

'Is that why she ran away? His violence? Did he slap her around, or was there another reason? Something more sinister.'

Mrs Whitmore shook her head, but her gaze shifted away. 'If he did, she never said. She always sounded happy on the telephone, and her letters were full of him. She was high on life and love and being young and all the things a bride should be. I don't know what happened.'

'So you knew she'd run away. How did she contact you?'

'Oh, dear. I'm not very good at all this cloak and dagger stuff. But I suppose I've already said too much.' She sighed, seemed to make up her mind and looked him in the eye.

'I got a phone call several weeks ago, but she wouldn't tell me anything. I'm afraid I know as little as you.'

'Have you told anyone about this? Has anyone come to the house asking questions?'

She looked down at her gnarled, swollen hands. 'Once. Just after Gabriella phoned. A fat, common little man with a Cockney accent and far too much jewellery. I didn't let him into the house and gave him very short shrift.'

She lifted her gaze and Tyler saw the glimmer of unshed tears before she knuckled them away and stared back at him in defiance. This was some tough old broad. The Brigadier would have been proud of her.

'Gabriella warned me to be careful. She said someone would try to find her and the less I knew, the better. That's why I was so cagey when you turned up.'

Tyler was lost in thought. 'Do you have any more photographs, Mrs Whitmore? Wedding pictures of the bride and groom and their guests, for instance?'

'How will they help find my daughter?'

'I don't know. But we have to start somewhere.'

'Over there, on the bookcase. It's the white album.'

Tyler got up and crossed the room. The shelves groaned

under stacks of magazines and knitting patterns. A vast collection of paperbacks, mostly crime fiction, filled every available inch of space. Dot would have had a field day, he thought wryly.

The album was with three others on the bottom shelf.

She turned the pages, her crippled fingers fumbling over them until she found what she wanted. 'That's the only one with all the family. The only names I remember are Victor's and Gregory's. The man in the wheelchair is the father, and the elegant, thin woman with the face-lift and dyed hair beside him is the mother.'

'Could I keep this, Mrs Whitmore? There's someone I'd like to show it to.'

'If it will help Gabriella.' Her stare was direct, her eyes sharp with intelligence. 'I'm an old woman, Mr Reed, and crippled with arthritis. It doesn't matter what happens to me. But Gabriella and Nicholas have their whole lives ahead of them. If the wrong people find them, I fear for their safety.'

'Do you have any idea of where she could be hiding, Mrs Whitmore? Is there a special place she always went? A friend she knew she could rely on?'

'When you're in the army, you don't make many friends off base. Gabriella had childhood friends, but they are scattered all over the world now, and her best friend, her oldest friend, Charlotte hasn't seen her since the engagement. I know, because I took the risk and phoned her. Of her university chums, I know little. I don't think she would risk going to them, but if you wait a moment, I'll put a list together.'

Tyler watched as she struggled with the pen and paper and labouriously wrote down names and addresses. Her skin was almost translucent in the gloom, she was very tired.

'She has simply disappeared, Major Reed. At least I know she's not dead, otherwise, why did they employ you to find her?'

'What is it you're not telling me Mrs Whitmore?'

She cut him off with a wave of her hand. 'I've said enough.

Edith will be back in a minute and she knows nothing of this. I would like to keep it that way.' She handed Tyler the list and the photograph and slammed the book shut. 'Please put this back, then drop the latch on your way out.'

Tyler tucked the photograph in his pocket and replaced the album. As he did so, he dropped a tiny bugging device behind the pile of magazines. If anyone else came to the house, he would know.

Mrs Whitmore's voice startled him.

'She's working. She phoned and asked for her P45. Find her, Mr Reed. But be very careful.'

Tyler held his breath. 'Where did you send it?' he said carefully.

'A mailing address in London. Here it is. Now go.'

'I've got photographs of the husband now and a name. Castlemainc. Mean anything to you?' It was late afternoon and Tyler had only just managed to get hold of Bill.

'No, nothing.'

'I'll need you to cover for me for a couple of days, Bill. We can afford to contract out some of the work in hand. I need to see Chuck. Being in the CIA he may be able to shed light on the husband.'

'That's a bit of a bummer. I saw his mate Brett the other day and he's on leave until the end of next week. But that works out fine, because I have the Prince to escort before then and you know the Sheik won't agree to a contractor.'

Tyler sighed, it was only Sunday night. 'Monday week, then. Heard from Tom?'

'Yeah, not much so far. He managed to track down her National Insurance number but no sign of her having applied for work yet. He's keeping an eye open.'

'She is working. Tell him to get onto it. And fast.'

'The only thing he did come up with was a deposit of five hundred pounds into her building society account six weeks ago. It was paid in, in Norwich and taken out the next day from one of those hole in the wall jobs at Holyhead.'

Mrs Whitmore hadn't said anything about putting money into the account in Norwich and it could only have been her.

'So, she came in from Ireland. Anything else?'

'Simmons from the Met. is keeping his ear to the ground, but he's come up with nothing. The priest has put the word out, but it looks like a long haul.'

Tyler sighed. They were getting nowhere.

'Keep on trucking, or whatever you rockers do in your spare time. I'll see you on Monday. By the way, Smith's been round asking about progress. I told him we'd let him know if there was anything to report.'

'For Christ's sake, what does he expect? Miracles?' Tyler exploded. 'Some people go missing for years.'

'Countryside getting on your tits?'

Bill laughed and Tyler chuckled. How well his partner knew him.

Gabriella tossed a pebble into the sea and leaned back on her elbows. She and Jackie had fallen into the habit of meeting for lunch and as it was fine, they had come to the beach.

'I've been working for over a week, but my feet are still killing me and my back aches constantly.' Gabriella sat up and grimaced. 'I'd forgotten how exhausting it is to make a couple of dozen beds every day.'

'Tell me about it,' mumbled Jackie through the inevitable cigarette. 'I've been in the business over fifteen years and my feet still give me grief.'

'I must be getting old. When I was a student I used to sail through the work. Now, I feel about ninety.'

'You don't look bad on it,' said Jackie with a grin. 'Glad we managed to do something about your hair, though. Looks better natural, and that style really suits you.'

Gabriella squinted into the sun. California seemed a lifetime away, yet she wouldn't have changed anything. The freedom she had was limited by Nick and the hours she had to work, but he was safe. She ran her fingers through her short cropped hair and sighed.

'I just hope a teaching post comes up before too long. I'd forgotten how petty people can be in a hotel.'

'You mean dear Sheila Wells? How you getting on with the old bat?'

'She tells me what to do. I do it. She complains. I do it again.' Gabriella felt the giggles bubbling. 'Her name should be Sheila Shylock. She stands over me and keeps an eye on her watch and if I leave one minute before my time, she docks my wages.'

'Cow,' gasped Jackie and they both collapsed in laughter. Nick woke in his pushchair and stared at them in disgust and it set them off again.

'I won't have to put up with the Mrs Wells of this life for ever. Something will turn up. At least we have a future now,' said Gabriella once she'd regained her composure.

'Good on ya. How you coping with the bed-sit? I'm surprised you haven't both gone down with something.'

Gabriella shrugged. 'Charlie's been a bit chesty, but a trip to the doctor sorted that out. The nights are difficult though. I feel isolated from the others where I work, and it's the same in the bed-sit. A cut-glass accent is a hindrance, even though I've tried toning it down. The others seem so young, so carefree – yet we are all about the same age. Most of them are Irish and they have so much fun, that sometimes I wish I could be a part of it.'

She fell silent and thought about those long nights when she couldn't sleep. How the darkness closed in and made the room seem smaller – how isolated she felt when she heard the chattering of the other lodgers as they went out for the evening.

Yes, she acknowledged, it was the nights that brought back the loneliness. The nights that made her secret a burden. Yet in the sunlight she felt differently. It was another day of freedom, and although that freedom was frail, she clung to it. She had a roof over her head and money in her pocket, the Castlemaines were on the other side of the Atlantic and all was right with her world.

'I'm surprised you get any sleep at all, then. The Irish hotel workers are notorious for their drinking and wild parties. I could tell you stories that would make your hair curl.'

Gabriella laughed. 'I think I'll pass. My hair's been through enough.'

'I think you have as well, Ellie.'

Gabriella looked at Jackie and shook her head. 'Don't Jackie. Leave it.'

Her friend's face was concerned, her blue eyes suddenly serious. 'You never talk about your family, Ellie. Are your parents still alive? Can't they help you?'

Gabriella sighed. Jackie would never let go, but at least this was safe ground, it couldn't hurt to talk a little.

'Dad died before I graduated. I write to my mother, but I never post the letters. The less she knows, the better.'

'You really are in trouble, aren't you? Why won't you trust me, Ellie?'

Gabriella scooped up a handful of pebbles and watched them trickle through her fingers. 'I do, but it's better if I say nothing. Those letters to mum, and the trips to the church, are my way of dealing with it – my release.'

Jackie lit another cigarette. 'Church never did anything for me, except tie me to a man I grew to hate. Bunch of bloody hypocrites, if you ask me.'

'I used to think like that, but I've found that church has helped me restore my faith in the future. I miss Mum though. Miss the sound of her voice, and not being able to confide in her. With Daddy being so impossible, Mum was the only one I could turn to – the only one who listened to my problems.'

She tucked the blanket more firmly over Nick's legs. The wind was whipping from the sea, tossing the waves up onto the pebbles with thunderous applause, and although they were in the lee of a breakwater, it was still cold.

'He was army, wasn't he?'

Gabriella chuckled. 'He issued orders every morning as though Mum and I were lowly conscripts. He liked to run the place like a military barracks. I don't know how Mum put up with him all those years.'

She picked up a smooth, round pebble, felt the weight of it and tossed it into the sea. Fate could be manipulated, circumstances changed. To dwell in the past, to allow it to rule the future, would serve no useful purpose.

'Mum was already in her forties when she had me. I wasn't an afterthought, merely one hell of a shock.'

'I bet that upset his routine,' remarked Jackie, dryly.

Gabriella's mood lightened. 'You could say that. Not only was he burdened with a baby when he should have been thinking about retirement, but horror of horrors – I was a girl!' She laughed. 'Poor old Dad. He never did quite get over it.'

Her vision misted as she thought of those times. 'My teenage years were tough on all of us. Dad tried to come to terms with the fact that his "little soldier" was almost a woman. Mum insisted I wore frilly dresses and went to regimental dances to meet the "right" kind of young man. I was stuck in the middle, trying to find my own identity.'

Jackie nodded. 'My parents were a bit like that. I married Bob to get away. Worst thing I could have done.'

'I didn't go that far, but I did feel trapped by Dad's domineering rule and Mum's equal determination to turn me into a young lady.' Gabriella grinned. 'I was a bit of a tomboy, back then.'

'You don't say,' grinned Jackie as she surveyed Gabriella's jeans, sloppy sweater and Doc Martens. 'You do surprise me.'

Gabriella leaned back onto a salt-bleached groyne and watched the racing clouds and wheeling, screeching gulls.

It was a day when everything was in motion, when nature displayed her impish humour by tangling hair, snatching hats and whipping salt from the sea. A good day – one that refreshed and cleaned away the cobwebs.

'It wasn't all bad. I have happy memories and I'm fit and healthy because of it. I can shoot and ride as well as any man, can survive in the open for days. Being on that army base also taught me a lot about men and survival. I soon learned how their minds worked, how their false flattery was a means to an end.'

She watched the sun disappear behind a cloud. The lessons learned in Hereford had been eclipsed, like the sun, by Greg's brooding good looks, his aura of power and his persuasive talk. He was a man made of the same mould as her father – tough, energetic, confident and domineering – and she'd believed all of it – had returned to her childhood role model and become once again, a malleable victim.

'It'll do you no good remembering the mistakes, Ellie. The future's all that matters now. Come on, it's getting cold, and I could do with a cuppa.'

The two women hauled the pushchair up the steep bank of pebbles, then with a final tug, they managed to get it onto the promenade.

'What are you going to do with the rest of your day off? Want to come back for dinner? I've got plenty.'

'I'm off to the job centre. Maybe they've got something in the teaching line today. Dinner sounds fun, I'll bring a bottle of plonk.'

'You're on. See you about six.'

As Gabriella walked up the main shopping street into the precinct, she barely gave the bright windows a glance. She needed to find something more permanent, because the end of the season was drawing close, and soon the hotel and guest house wouldn't need her. Not only would she lose her job, but she would lose her bed-sit if she didn't have money coming in, and she didn't relish the prospect of being homeless in the winter.

The job centre was busy as usual and as she steered the pushchair between the notice boards, she felt her spirits tumble. Then on the last board she saw something that gave her a glimmer of hope. The post was for a resident, assistant matron in a private school along the coast, and interviews were being held next month. Yet, when she had collected the application form, she saw that most of the questions could pose major problems.

I can't go on being Ellie Castle, she decided. I've already faced Mrs James at the Royal with my P45 and given her an explanation, it wasn't easy, but I managed it and she was very understanding. I'll fill in this darn form, tell the truth and to hell with it. My university tutor should give me a reference, and if I'm lucky enough to get an interview, I'll just have to explain my circumstances without going into too much detail, and hope they'll understand.

With the first real surge of optimism she'd felt for a long time, she filled in the form and handed it back before she could change her mind. Things could only get better.

Tyler was bored. There was nothing more tedious than spending over a week listening in to the chatter of two elderly ladies. Their sole interests seemed to be local gossip and the start of the rugby season. The time hadn't been totally wasted though, Mrs Whitmore's list had been gone through and telephone calls made, the only information he got was from Charlotte, and that had been subliminal. She knew something, he could hear it in her voice, and in the things she didn't say. That one deserved a visit – and fast.

To Tyler's relief, Bill arrived early on the following Monday afternoon, his hair and smile as bright as the sunshine. He shook hands with Brian Staines and was introduced as Tyler's co-translator. When the two men were alone upstairs, Tyler explained his set-up.

'I stay in here while she cleans and makes up the bed, but the tape recorder keeps track of what's going on in the cottage. The other recorder is for the sound of typing. It'll drive you nuts, but it's necessary. No one's been to the cottage and there have been no telephone calls. It's as quiet as a grave over there.'

'Right oh. I checked with Chuck's office, he came back this morning, so I arranged for him to meet you at Lacey's. Now off you go and leave me to the two old ducks.'

'Thanks. I'll let you know how things work out.'

Gabriella smoothed the duvet cover and plumped up the pillows. One more room and she'd be finished for the day. It couldn't come too soon, Nick had grizzled all night and now she had a thumping headache.

'Ellie? You in there?' Sharon poked her head round the door. 'You seen Wayne? Little bugger's gone off again.'

'Probably hiding in the linen closet,' replied Gabriella as she took a final look around the room. 'It seems to be his favourite place.'

'I'll be glad when he starts playschool.' Sharon was nineteen, a single mum and a cheerful influence amongst the other chambermaids. She turned away, then stopped. 'By the way, you've got a secret admirer.'

Gabriella almost dropped the dirty laundry. 'What do you mean?'

'Some bloke was hanging about downstairs when I came in this morning. You were just ahead of me and he asked me what your name was.'

Gabriella dumped the laundry in the wagon and closed her eyes. Her head was thudding, her heart was marching time with it. 'What did he look like?'

'Tallish, fairish, quite good looking, but not really my type. I like the dark haired, blue eyed ones. But he seemed very taken with you.'

Gabriella's thoughts whirled. It wasn't Greg or Victor, but it could have been someone they'd sent. She spun round, grasped Sharon's arms and looked into her startled brown eyes.

'What did you say to him?'

'Oy! Watch it.' Sharon pulled free and fluffed up her blonde perm. 'What's got into you? I thought you'd be flattered.' Her normally bright face was suddenly sharp and belligerent. 'I was only being friendly.'

Gabriella rubbed her brow and tried to clear her head. They couldn't have found her so soon. Could they? 'Sorry,' she said distractedly. 'But this is important. What exactly did he say?'

Sharon folded her arms and tightened her lips. 'It was just a bloke. Blimey, anyone would think you had something to hide.'

You don't know how right you are, she thought. She took a deep breath to still her impatience. 'Don't be daft,' she said as lightly as she could. 'Go on. Tell me about my secret admirer. What did he want?'

Sharon seemed pacified and reached into her apron pocket for a stick of gum. 'Well,' she mumbled as she chewed. 'He was quite nice looking, as I said. Bit on the thin side, I like them with muscles, but clean, if you know what I mean. Sharp suit, nice tie. He was a Londoner, full of the usual old chat. Easy to talk to.'

'What did he say?' Gabriella wanted to shake the information out of the silly little air-head, but she smothered the temptation.

'He said he was working down here with his mate on the new Debenhams, and had seen you about, but didn't have the nerve to chat you up, because he thought you were married.' Sharon winked. 'I put him straight on that one. No point in making the path of true love tougher than it needs to be.'

Gabriella gave a sickly smile. Her world was caving in and this idiot girl was prattling on about love. 'What else did you tell him?'

'He wanted to know your name, and Charlie's name, and

how old you both were. He asked how long you'd been working here and when you'd be getting off duty and had your day off.' She popped her gum and swirled it round her mouth. 'He also asked if you lived in. I said no, but as I don't know your address, I couldn't help.'

The relief was overwhelming. 'Is that it?'

Sharon grinned. 'I said we'd consider letting them take us out on a double date. He seemed really interested.'

'I bet he was,' muttered Gabriella, feeling sick. It was no longer safe in Brighton. Genuine or not, the man was a threat. She would have to move on.

Tyler was still trying to take in what Chuck Myers had told him about the Castlemaine family. The noise in the bar seemed a world away.

'She could be a vital witness for us, Tyler. If we could get her to talk, we might come closer to nailing these bastards once and for all.'

Tyler shook his head. 'Just because she was married to one of them, doesn't mean she knows anything.'

Chuck looked doubtful. 'My guess is she began to have her doubts. She's her father's daughter. Something happened to threaten her or the child, and I wouldn't mind betting it had something to do with Leo Spinoza.'

'Who's that?'

Chuck waved a dismissive hand. 'Just a bit of scum. Coke was his bag, got too greedy and began to dip into the cartel purse. He went missing, but his body turned up three days ago at the city dump. His eye had been shot out. I only mentioned him, because he was Gabriella's driver.'

Tyler could see the excitement in the other man's face, a glow in the eyes, a quickening of speech, and it began to ring warning bells.

Chuck must have read the doubt on Tyler's face, because his next words came in a confidential, persuasive rush. 'I bet she knows more than she realises. She could give us names, dates, contacts.'

Tyler knew he had to stop his friend. Gabriella had enough to worry about without the CIA on her back. 'I doubt she'd be of much use, Chuck. She's very young and they weren't married long. Greg wouldn't have exposed her to more than was neccessary.'

Chuck changed tack. 'How's the investigation going?'

Tyler saw the alertness in Chuck's face as he waited for the answer to the almost casual question, and was careful in his reply. 'Not good. She seems to have vanished. I've tried everything, but so far have come up with a big fat zero.'

'Well, when you do find her, keep me in mind. She might not be a big fish, but it's the little things, that added together, could make it possible to blow the lid off the whole shebang.'

'So, you're not looking for her then?' Tyler tried to read the devious mind behind that handsome veneer.

Chuck shook his head and finished his beer. 'Like I said, she's a very small fish in a very large pond. It would take too many man hours to track her down. But we would certainly like to talk to her if you find her. She could be useful in nailing a certain Governor we've had our eye on.'

'With a husband like that on her tail, I doubt she'll surface for a long time. I may never find her.'

Chuck laughed, all solemnity vanished. 'Oh, you will, Tyler. You will. Now you got the bit between your teeth, you ain't never gonna let go.'

When Tyler returned to the Norfolk pub, he found Bill with his feet on the table, his nose buried in a martial arts catalogue.

'I suppose your share of the wages this month is going on another Samurai sword?'

'Maybe,' Bill replied, tossing the magazine onto the table and dropping his feet to the floor. He was a black belt in karate and a fanatical collector of Japanese fighting weapons. Elaine nagged about them cluttering up the place, but Bill ignored her and often spent hours polishing the intricate sword handles.

'So, how did the meeting go?'

Tyler sat on the bed and poured himself a cup of coffee from the thermos. 'The Castlemaines are as dirty as it gets, Bill. The CIA have been itching to prosecute them for years.' He filled Bill in with the details. When he'd finished, they both sat in silence, each with their own thoughts.

Bill broke the silence. 'And I thought we were just dealing with the local hoods and Sniffy Smith.' He gave a long, low whistle. 'Oh, boy – are we in deep shit. Do you think the mother knew about her son-in-law's underworld career?'

'She suspected, I'm sure.'

'It could explain the letter that came second post.'

'What letter?'

'Edith was very excited and told Mrs Whitmore it was from Gabriella. But the old lady merely looked at it and slipped it under a book. She said the writing was similar, but it was from a friend. Edith didn't sound too convinced. It was only after Edith had left the room, that Mrs Whitmore took out the letter, read it quickly, then put it under her knitting. It hasn't been mentioned since.'

'Where's the letter now?' Tyler's voice was sharp.

'Torn into little pieces and buried in the rubbish.' He must have seen Tyler's excited expression, because he added quickly. 'The bin men came late this afternoon. There was absolutely nothing I could do about it. It's gone.'

'Shit!'

The only sound in the room was the tap, tap, tapping of the typewriter tape. It was no longer a nuisance, merely a background noise which they could both ignore.

'You know, Bill. If we do find Gabriella, we could lead Castlemaine straight to her and we mustn't do that. Yet, if we don't find her, she could spend the rest of her life having to look over her shoulder.'

'Mmmm. What if we find her and she doesn't want to play

ball with the CIA? I don't fancy getting caught up in a cartel vendetta.'

'What are you trying to say, Bill? Do you think we should just give Smith his money back and tell him to get stuffed?'

Tyler shook his head. 'It won't work, mate. They'll just find someone else. At least we know we have Gabriella's welfare at heart. Someone else may not be quite so curious as to where the money's coming from. They would just do what they're being paid for and move on to the next job.'

'I don't like it,' sighed Bill. 'I wish we'd never got involved with Sniffy. That bloke always brings trouble.'

18

The cemetery was on a hill in New York State. Fifty acres of manicured lawns and white marble stretched before them, giving a panoramic view of the suburbs. The coffin was draped in flowers and the summer breeze wafted the cloying scent of lilies and hot-house roses over the mourners.

Greg clasped his gloved hands and watched as the coffin was lowered into the ground. Despite the warmth of the sun and the thickness of his black coat, he felt chilled. It was all so final – so inevitable – and his mind refused to accommodate the thought that one day, he too would occupy a place on this hill.

He looked around at the grim faced mourners. Everyone who mattered was there, from the glitterati of the entertainment world, to the suits from the financial and political society that his father had manipulated during his life. Old money was represented, as was new, and overseeing it all were the paparazzi, the hacks of Hollywood, rubbing shoulders with the journalists from the *Financial Times* and *Washington Post*. In death, as in life, his father was a man who commanded attention.

'Come, Mother. It's over,' he murmured as he cupped her Dior-clad elbow and led her from the graveside.

Mariah Castlemaine's stilettoes sank into the grass, but she kept her head erect, and her shoulders square. The neat black hat was perched on the side of her head, the gossamer veil enhancing her high cheekbones and pale skin. The grey eyes beneath the veil remained dry, but she dabbed them with a scrap of cotton – always mindful of her mascara.

'I'll miss him, Greg. He was an arrogant bastard, but the house is going to seem awful quiet without him.'

Greg ducked his head and smiled. Mom was rarely home anyway, there was always some fund-raising committee to sit on, or a charity dinner to attend, then there were her lovers to entertain. She had always been discreet, but widowhood would suit her – now she could have the fun without the restrictions of marriage.

'I'm sure you'll cope, Mom. Besides, you'll always have me and Vic to call on if you need company.' It was an easy offer to make. Mariah would never be short of company – not now she was worth millions. But it wouldn't hurt to check on some of her friends – gold-diggers would definitely have to be weeded out.

'You're a good son, Greg. Your Dad was very proud of you and so am I. Thanks for helping to arrange things today – I couldn't have done it without you.'

Greg took in the elegant figure and aristocratic face, the determined tilt to the chin and the iron in the eyes. A surge of pride swept through him. Why the hell couldn't he have married someone like her? Dad had been right – he should have stuck to his own kind.

He pushed away the thought as the other mourners approached to offer their condolences. It was two months since Gabriella's betrayal, but it still hurt to think about her.

He turned to Victor. 'Take care of Mom. See she gets back to the apartment safely and wait there for us.'

Vic nodded and reached out to put an arm around his mother's shoulder. It was shrugged off.

'I'm quite capable of seeing myself home, Vic. Besides, Sir Arnold Braithwaite has already offered me a lift in his Rolls, and is waiting.'

'Way to go, Mom,' Greg breathed, before turning back to deal with the reporters.

*   *   *

278

Gabriella tried to appear relaxed, but it wasn't easy when a bunch of sharp keys dug into her palm. They were her only weapon, but could be very effective if jabbed in an attacker's face.

The car had been parked outside the house all night, the man inside the Cortina the same one who'd been outside the hotel the day before. The same one who'd been asking questions. If he made a move to abduct Nick, then she was ready.

She kept her eyes on the pushchair and walked purposefully on. If she could just get to the hotel, she had a plan – whether it worked or not depended on the watcher – but as he hadn't made a move yet, it seemed likely he'd been ordered to watch and report. If that was the case, she had a chance.

As she turned the corner and headed up the seafront, she heard him start his car. As she pushed the pram towards the staff entrance, she saw the Cortina's approaching reflection in a shop window. Her pulse jumped and her grip tightened on the pushchair and keys as she kept away from the kerb. The game of chess had begun again – would she be as lucky this time around?

Pushing open the heavy door, she dragged the pram inside and took a glance out into the street. He'd parked and was now opening a newspaper. There was not a minute to lose.

The pushchair was heavy now she'd put her rucksack underneath it and slung her bag over the handle, but everything she possessed as in those bags. She hurriedly wheeled it through the long corridors and lugged it up and down flights of stairs until she reached reception. One look into the street confirmed the presence of the taxi she'd called earlier from the house.

Five minutes later she was on her way. But she didn't dare hope she was out of trouble. Not yet. Not until she was well away from Brighton.

*   *   *

Vic looked at the five men who sat around the table and felt a glow of satisfaction. These men would help him repay Greg for all the insults he'd had to bear over the years. His mother would finally look at him with pride, his wife would shut her fat mouth and his sons would respect him. His time had come and he didn't mean to waste another minute.

The secret meeting place was a grubby attic room at the top of a rooming house in the Bronx. The paper was peeling, there was a stink of boiled cabbage and stale urine in the air, and the light bulb was broken. Yet in the flicker of the candles there was a warmth of clandestine companionship. They had eaten well from food brought in earlier, and now the table was littered with the remains, chairs pushed back and cigars lighted.

Reiina was the first to break that companionable silence. 'You want one of my men to finish him off? I know plenty who would and the funeral has opened up an opportunity. That's why we could all meet like this today.'

His voice was harsh from years of cigar smoke, his hair iron grey and thinning over the vast dome of his head. His belly was rotund beneath the expensive waistcoat and watch chain, and although he wasn't a tall man, there was a sense of controlled violence behind that generous girth. An electricity in his blue eyes that was magnified by the thick lenses of his steel-rimmed spectacles. He was known as the Fox in Las Vegas, and with good reason. Reiina had connections with the Cosa Nostra, and was not a man to cross.

Victor shook his head as he puffed on the Havana cigar.

'No. He's mine.' The smoke trickled from his mouth and ringed his head like an obscene halo. 'But I'm pleased to hear your offer, Don Reiina.'

'How can we be certain everyone here can be trusted?'

Vic turned at the sound of the lazy drawl of the South American. 'Because you all have a reason to see Greg wiped out,' he said firmly.

There was silence in the room as Vic regarded each of them. The stony-faced Assad Suliman glared back. His eyes were winter cold, his short, square body encased in a suit of grey. He was a grey man, from the tip of his iron hair, to the toes of his granite-coloured shoes. His loyalty had never been questioned. His hatred of Greg was consuming.

'So, what's your plan, Victor?' The speaker was Hal Courtney, a young man of thirty-five who headed a small, but outwardly respectable shipping company.

Vic knew that Hal's company had done business with his father for many years and he'd been assured of Greg's continued support, only to see it given to a rival company. Now his share price on the stock exchange had fallen and the business was in deep trouble.

Vic looked at the young man with the Fifth Avenue suit and friendly face. He might appear harmless, he thought, but behind that all-American openness, lies a viper. No wonder Greg wanted nothing to do with him – they were too alike.

'My plan concerns his wife and son.' He paused for effect. 'My brother will be at his most vulnerable when he finds them – which he will do very soon, for I have, this morning, received news of their whereabouts. One of my men is keeping watch until I give the order to move in and take them. Gabriella and Nicholas are our bait. He won't be able to resist – and when I have all three . . .' He let their imaginations work out the rest.

'Ellie! Where the hell are you? Are you OK? What happened?' Jackie's voice was sharp with concern at the other end of the line.

'I'm fine. We're in Hastings.'

'Where in Hastings? I'm coming over to make sure you're all right.'

'No, Jackie. It's best this way. I'm sorry I had to leave without telling you, but things have changed.'

Gabriella looked out of the window at yet another row upon shabby row of Victorian villas. Hastings was run down, showing her age, and it was ideal for her purpose. The population was transitory, the majority on the dole and living in bed-sits. It would be easy to remain anonymous – no one asked questions here – poverty had its own form of social rules. Yet how long would it be before they caught up with her again?

'What are you doing about money? I had the dragon on the phone, breathing fire for being dropped in it with no cleaner. And the hotel aren't too happy either.'

'I start in the kitchen of a local bistro tomorrow. Money's lousy, but I'll get by.' She paused for a moment. 'The car's parked outside the bed-sit. I've left a phone number in the glove compartment. Ask for Charlotte and don't speak to anyone else. She'll tell you what to do with the Mini.'

'You're frightening me, Ellie. What the hell's going on?'

'Has anyone been around asking questions?'

'No one here, but the dragon lady said a bloke turned up this morning asking for a Gabriella Castlemaine. She told him to push off, and luckily kept her trap shut about me, but from his description, we both got the impression it was you he was after. What's going on?'

'Drop it, Jackie.' Gabriella was aware that her tone was sharp, but it was too late for regrets. 'Just forget you ever knew me. Goodbye, and thanks for being such a good friend.'

Tears welled as she cut off Jackie's anxious voice, and she ached for the solace of friendship – but this was the only way to survive – the only way to ensure Nick's safety.

Vic felt a surge of triumph as he dismissed the meeting.

'We'll not meet again until it's time to move in. Even then, a password will be the only communication. When you hear the word, *mezzanotte* – midnight – you will know to begin.'

The men nodded, then silently left the rooming house, their hats pulled over their eyes, their collars lifted to their chins against the blustering, chill wind of the Bronx.

Victor sat in the light of the guttering candles and began to laugh. It grew from a chuckle to a full-bellied roar that bounced off the peeling walls and cracked ceiling. Once Greg knew Gabriella was in Brighton, he would follow as surely as night followed day. He would travel without his posse of minders – with only his trusted brother at his side.

The brother he'd scorned – the brother he'd banished from the inner circle – the brother who hated him.

19

The interview at St Michael's Preparatory School for boys had gone well, and Gabriella followed the senior house master along the covered path on a tour of the ancient building which was almost lost in a fold of the West Sussex Downs. Thick columns of stone supported the cloisters, and through them she caught glimpses of a playing field, the chapel and the spreading oak that was such a feature of the place.

'In the early seventeenth century, St Michael's was a monastery. The evidence of its past can still be seen in the arched windows, the heavy doors and fine stonework.' Simon Brooks' voice held the awe of a historian as he stopped to point out a carving in the stone.

Gabriella watched his face as he talked. He was younger than she'd expected, about thirty-five, with thick brown hair, horn-rimmed glasses that slipped down his nose and an air of bewilderment, worn like a cloak against the modern world.

His hair needed cutting and the cuffs of his tweed jacket were frayed, which made her wonder if he was married. He didn't look as if he was, no wife would have let him wear those dreadful green corduroy trousers. Yet it didn't seem to matter. Simon Brooks suited his clothes as he suited his surroundings, he was at home within these silent stone walls and peaceful grounds, at ease with the smell of books and blackboard chalk.

She followed him into the chapel and breathed in the centuries' old fragrance of incense and flowers. Someone had decorated the altar with freesias and their perfume mingled with the must of old prayer books and damp stone. There was nothing to compare with the atmosphere of a much loved and well-used church, and she could imagine the children in here, filling the place with sound, adding energy to the atmosphere left by those who'd gone before.

'You seem lost in thought, Mrs Whitmore. They say that if you listen very carefully you can hear the monks at prayer.' Simon Brooks pushed his glasses up his nose.

She looked up at him. He was very tall, a little too thin, with bony hands and an angular face, but his eyes were brown and filled with humour behind those horn rims and his mouth was generous and sensual. He was very different to Gregory Castlemaine.

'I can believe that,' she said. 'It's very peaceful.'

Simon laughed and led her out of the chapel. 'Not after the children arrive, it won't be. You'll hardly recognise the place.'

Gabriella stopped walking. 'Does that mean I've got the job?'

His dark eyes studied her and she wondered if he could read the desperate plea in her face.

'I think you'll be good for us. In an old place like this, where we masters moulder into old age, it's important to have youth and vitality in the staff room. You and your baby will be very welcome and we'll do our best to make sure your privacy is respected. What you told me today will go no further than the Head.'

Gabriella grinned, feeling ridiculously pleased. 'Thank you,' was all she could say and it felt inadequate.

'With your qualifications, I'm sorry I can't offer you a teaching post.' Simon Brooks shook her hand. His clasp was firm and warm – so was his smile. 'I'll see you on the fifth of January. It will give you time to settle in before the children arrive on the tenth. If there's anything you need, just come to me or Matron. I hope you'll be happy here.'

Later, as she pushed the pram out of the station and up the long hill to her digs, she realised that the world looked different. Where there had been grey clouds, there was sunshine – where there had been uncertainty, was now hope. Even the peeling paint of the bed-sitter didn't look so bad. In another eight weeks she would be gone.

The house was silent as she wheeled the pram along the hall. It was a silence that felt ominous and her scalp crawled in apprehension. A hasty look over her shoulder reassured her no one was lurking in a doorway, but she still felt uneasy.

'Ridiculous,' she muttered. 'I've been up here alone before, felt the silence before. Why should it be different now?'

She gripped the handle and dragged the pram, bumping and jolting up the three flights of stairs to her room. 'It's my one day off,' she hissed as she struggled to manoeuvre the pram around a tight corner. 'It's a day to celebrate, and I won't let my mind play tricks on me to spoil it.'

Pausing for breath before negotiating the final flight, she felt the silence closing in around her, so she began to sing a particularly filthy rugby song she'd learned from a fellow student at university. She'd become tired of looking over her shoulder, too accustomed to searching faces in a crowd, too aware of every sound in the night. It was time to relax a little and enjoy her good fortune.

Yet, for all her bravado, she couldn't quite shake off the feeling of unease.

It was three o'clock in the morning and Bulldog and Marley parked the car and crossed the wasteland that fronted the Angel House Estate. Their progress was stealthy as they moved through the shadows and on past the graffiti-stained walls and boarded up windows. The moon was lost behind scudding clouds and most of the street lights on the Brixton estate had long since been vandalised. Bulldog, overweight and sweating, aimed a kick at a cat that hissed at them as they climbed the stairs to the sixth-floor flat.

Marley's tread was light and athletic up those foul smelling concrete steps, and he paused momentarily to wait for Bulldog, and to tuck his Rastafarian coils into the oversized beret. He grinned, white teeth gleaming against his dark skin. 'Move yer arse, Bulldog, man. We ain't got all night.'

'You wanna stop grinning like that, you black bastard, someone'll see ya.' Bulldog was gasping, the sweat dewy on his flushed face.

'You're the one that's gleamin' mate. A ruddy beacon in the night. At least I got me own camouflage.' He chuckled, and without waiting for Bulldog, raced up the final three flights.

Bulldog tramped his way up the stairs and hauled himself onto the sixth floor landing. Marley was leaning against the balcony railings, his long legs stretched across the narrow walkway as he waited.

'You ready?'

'I been waitin' for you, man. Let's go.'

Bulldog wiped away the sweat with his t-shirt, and caught his breath. He nodded to Marley, who took the wallet of keys from his pocket and carefully inserted one of them into the lock of flat 684.

As the door swung open, they eyed one another and moved stealthily into the narrow hall. Bulldog closed the door behind them and followed Marley into the bedroom.

The man was asleep, and snoring, the duvet pulled over his head. On the table beside the bed was a flickering candle, and the evidence of a coke addict's habit. The fine white powder still dusted the table-top and the razor blade winked in the candlelight.

Marley dabbed his finger into the traces of powder and smeared it on his gums. 'Good shit,' he whispered. 'Didn't get this from me.'

'Shut the fuck up, Marley,' Bulldog hissed.

'Why? He's out of it. He don't know shit.'

Bulldog pulled back the duvet and hauled the sleeping man

upright. 'Wake up, dickhead. This is a nightmare!' Bulldog giggled as he shook him.

'Wha . . .? Who . . .?'

'It's the boogey man come to get ya.' Marley loomed over him, his face inches from the bleary eyes and gaping mouth as he gave a war whoop.

Bulldog repeatedly slapped the man's face, rocking his head on his shoulders. 'Wake up, arsehole and get yer brain in gear before y'lose yer balls. I wanna talk to ya.'

The eyes focused and fear shadowed the face. 'What do you want? I've got nothing worth nicking.'

'Hey man. No need to worry. You tell us what we want to know, then you can go back to beddy-byes.'

'Yeah. You wouldn't like me to lose my temper. I ain't pretty when I do that. Now you tell Bulldog where you been hidin' Mr Smith's property. 'Cos he wants it back.'

The face was sharp with alarm, the eyes restless, as though seeking a way out. 'I haven't got anything that belongs to Smith. I don't know what you're talking about.'

Bulldog's punch was fast and hard – and the man bent double as the air exploded from his lungs.

'Where is it?'

'I haven't . . .' He retched, and bile dribbled down the front of his nightshirt and onto his bare knees.

His feet thundered on the bare floorboards and he screamed as a series of blows blackened his eyes, cut his lip and opened up an old wound on his eyebrow. Marley's fingers were snared in his hair, stretching his neck and keeping his head still so Bulldog's aim was true.

'There isn't anything of Smith's here,' he gasped. 'I don't know what you're talking about.'

A karate chop across the nose was instantly followed by a stream of blood, and the man screamed again.

'Let's 'ave a butcher's then. Come on.'

Bulldog plucked the beaten, cringing man from the bed as

though he was a featherweight. Marley's flick knife gleamed in the candlelight.

'No. No. Don't cut me. I've got nothing. Look. Look around. There's nothing of Smith's here.'

'Cool it man. I only wanna see what yer hidin' in here.'

Marley slit the mattress and pulled out the stuffing. This was followed by the pillow, the duvet and the sheets. He pulled down the curtains, ran his hand along the pelmet and ransacked the drawers of the cheap dressing table. The clothes on the hanging rail were searched, the linings ripped, the pockets turned inside out. Shoes were parted from their soles and heels and photographs ripped from their frames. Marley was thorough – it was the reason Smith had hired him.

Bulldog dragged the man into the sitting room. 'Where is it?' he growled.

The man shook his head as he tried to maintain his balance.

Marley crossed the room to the bank of computers. They were neatly set out on a long table, the filing cabinets and computer discs labelled alphabetically. He picked up one of the computers – held it aloft – then crashed it to the floor. The screen exploded, blue smoke siphoned from the innards and a lick of bright flame quivered and died beneath Marley's boot.

'Not my computers. Please. You can't do this.'

Bulldog's fist rammed into his kidneys. 'Marley likes breaking things, so if you don't hurry up and tell us where Smith's property is, he'll just have to break some more.'

Marley picked up another computer. It crashed to the floor and the man sank to his knees. 'All right,' he shouted. 'I'll tell you. Please don't damage anything else.'

Marley's hand lay nonchalantly on the top of the final computer. It was the most expensive.

'I put it somewhere safe – but not here.'

'Then you'd better get dressed and show us. 'Cos we ain't leavin' without it.' He nodded at Marley who trashed the final computer and began to riffle through the computer discs.

'Don't. Please don't. It's taken me years to . . .'

'Hey man. I'm just havin' a little fun while you go and get dressed. The quicker you move your arse, the less fun I have.' Marley grinned, tossed the disks into a hold-all and trashed the printer.

The man hobbled to his room and fumbled into his clothes. He was hurt, bad. He could hardly breathe through his nose, or see through his eyes. A couple of teeth were missing, and something sharp in his side knifed pain through his chest.

The sound of the flat being ransacked came to him through the half-closed door. He eyed the door for a moment, his pulse racing. He was trapped and there was nothing he could do about it – but if he could fob them off with the less revealing and edited copy, there was still a chance the original would find its way into the right hands.

Of his own fate, he felt less sure. When Smith played rough, very few survived to tell the tale.

It was after midnight, New York time, when Greg switched off his portable telephone and climbed back into the car. It was cold outside and the stink of diesel fuel and sewage was strong in the oily waters of New York Harbour. He'd been inspecting the warehouse security for a shipment that was due the next day and the call had come as he was leaving.

Jake looked over his shoulder, one eyebrow raised in query.

'The apartment, and put the heater on.'

The sleek Mercedes roared away from the towering cranes and dark, silent warehouses and headed for the lights and movement of Manhattan.

The warm air took the chill off Greg's flesh, but it couldn't disperse the coldness around his heart. Ben's terse message had been all too clear.

He looked at his watch, then stared out of the car window.

The passing cavalcade of neon signs as a blur, the jostling pedestrians mere shadows against the glitter of the shop windows. His mind was working; sifting, discarding and plotting his next move. Victor had chosen powerful allies, but the young Ben had proved his worth as a spy. He hadn't been sure they would accept him, but he was a good actor, with just the right touch of innocence to mask the razor-sharp mind. His reward was a screen test with one of the most powerful men in Hollywood. After that, if he survived tonight, it was up to him.

Greg lit a Gauloise and drew the smoke deep into his lungs. Every man had a price. 'Forget the apartment, Jake. Go straight to Luigi's.'

As the Mercedes and its escort turned off the main road and headed for the restaurant in Little Italy, Greg began to make his telephone calls. There were ways of dealing with turncoats, but some things he couldn't do alone.

The three cars pulled up outside the restaurant and the body-guards waited on the sidewalk as Greg made his last calls.

The first call he made was to Sam Weinberg, the father of Ben, and close friend of the departed Gregory Castlemaine senior. The other was to Cecil Trant who was in town for Dad's funeral, and whom Greg had known and trusted for years. They were of the same age and had shared lodgings at Harvard. He was closer than his own brother. At the thought of Vic, he swiftly climbed out of the car. This night would be one he would find memorable – but not for long.

Luigi's restaurant was on three floors. The basement had been turned into a coffee house where the sweet pastries and pastrami sandwiches catered for the day-time passing trade. The ground floor was the main restaurant, decorated in green and white, with piped Italian music and chequered cloths on the tables. Greg and his entourage swept through the restaurant and headed for the stairs.

The top floor was private, used only by the Castlemaine family who owned the building and those on either side. The only rooms up here were a large dining room with shuttered windows and discreet lighting, heavy velvet curtains dividing it off from a comfortable seating area where there were deep chairs and a well stocked bar.

Luigi was a short, fat little man related by marriage to Vic's sister-in-law. As he trotted up the stairs behind him, Greg was once again reminded of an eager, undisciplined puppy.

The wonderful aroma of garlic and hot crusty bread made his mouth water and he realised he hadn't eaten since the light meal after the funeral. He walked through the dining room and into the seating area which smelled strongly of leather, fine wine and Havana cigars. He'd always liked this room, it reminded him of his club in London.

His coat was lifted from his shoulders and hung reverently on a hanger by Luigi, who was obviously doing his best not to appear flustered at the late and unexpected arrival of his guest.

Greg loosened his jacket, sat in a deep, winged chair and accepted a Martini. After he'd sipped and given his approval, he dismissed everyone but Luigi and Jake. 'I'll be here all night, Luigi. See that dinner is served immediately.'

'How many are dining, Mr Castlemaine?' Luigi hovered nervously.

'I eat alone, and I want you to bring all the courses together. I'll begin with the Mediterranean Prawns, then have the fettuccine with garlic bread and green salad. Champagne with the prawns, red wine with the fettuccine and brandy with coffee. No dessert. See that my men are fed downstairs. On no account am I to be disturbed.'

He hooked a finger into the little man's shirt front. 'Forget what you see, Luigi. Remember only that I ate alone and stayed all night. Now go.'

Greg spoke quietly to Jake for a moment, then watched him follow Luigi. Satisfied his plan would work, he sipped the very dry Martini and smoked a cigarette as the waiters laid the table with white linen, crystal and silver.

The buzz of his portable phone interrupted his thoughts and he picked it up. The adrenalin was beginning to pump.

'Everyone's in place.' The voice at the other end was muffled and Greg could hear a juke box playing in the background.

'You know what to do?'

'We begin with the Fox.'

Greg almost smiled. The man had been a thorn in his side for too many years. He was too influential – too old – too cunning. It would be a pleasure to have him gone.

Greg wiped his lips with the linen napkin. The prawns were delicious, and so was the champagne.

The telephone burred.

'It is done.'

Greg sipped the Champagne. It was a good vintage. Reiina would have appreciated it. Now for Sanchez.

The prawns finished, he drew the plate of fettuccine towards him. It was superb, Luigi had excelled as usual. Four minutes later the telephone rang, and after he'd listened, he replaced the receiver and took another forkful of the pasta. The taste seemed to be enhanced by the news that Sanchez was no more.

'Now for that Arab bastard Suliman. I should have dispensed with him a long time ago,' he murmured. 'He's been dangerous ever since the fiasco in Iran – the little turd never gave up on his vendetta.'

Greg lifted the glass of wine to the light. It gleamed blood red and tasted of Italian sunshine. His thoughts were interrupted once more by the ringing of the telephone. He listened and smiled and took a sip of wine, savouring it on his tongue. The Arab was no longer a problem.

He pushed the fettuccine to one side and poured a snifter of brandy. He was sated. All in all, it had been a most satisfactory day. There was just the young upstart to deal with – and it would be perfect.

*　　*　　*

'Lady luck just ran out,' said the muffled voice at the other end of the line.

Greg sipped coffee. He was content. Hal Courtney should have known that gambling with loaded dice was dangerous. He rolled the Havana between thumb and forefinger, sniffed it and cut the end. He took his time to light it, then watched the smoke curl to the ceiling. *Now for my brother. But this time I'll do the job properly, not allow sentiment to cloud my judgement.*

The telephone interrupted his thoughts and he snatched it up impatiently. 'Castlemaine.'

'Smith, from London.'

Greg felt a surge of excitement. 'What is it?'

'Wyman's come up with something.'

'It's late, Smith. Get on with it.' Greg's patience was fast running out for the Cockney.

'She's in Sussex, but someone's already ahead of us – Wyman took longer than we expected to crack.'

'Reed must have found her.'

'Nah. He's running in circles getting nowhere fast. Turns out it was one of your lot – well, your brother's.'

Greg rammed his fist into the arm of the chair. The rage, and the hatred for his brother was searing. 'How long has he known about my wife and son's whereabouts?'

'Five days at least.'

'Is the boy with her?'

'Never lets 'im out of her sight.'

'Does Reed have this information yet?' Greg was thinking fast. It would take almost a day before he could reach the south coast of England and he didn't want Reed, or anyone else getting there first.

'It's only a matter of time. Reed's been pushing Wyman to come up with something, and 'e's bound to smell a rat when Wyman doesn't show at the office. What you want me to do this end?'

'Get rid of Wyman. Then leave it for twenty-four hours

before contacting Reed. Pay him off. Tell him we've found her and she's safe. If he asks too many questions, offer him another five grand – that should keep him quiet. If not . . . well, I don't have to spell it out, do I?'

'My boys've already dealt with Wyman – he ain't goin' nowhere. Reed ain't daft, 'e won't cause no problems.'

'See he doesn't. Don't do anything else until I get there. I'll catch Concorde's next flight. Meet me at Heathrow.'

Greg lit another cigarette and watched the smoke curl to the ceiling as a flutter of excitement made his heart thud.

It was all coming together.

Tyler rolled over, the sound of ringing had been mixed with his dream, and as he grabbed the telephone, he tried to focus on his watch. It was seven o'clock in the morning.

He groaned. The last three weeks had been spent on the road contacting Gabriella's old classmates, and after visiting the haughty, diamond-hard Charlotte the night before, he'd finally hit the sack at about four this morning – still none the wiser as to Gabriella's whereabouts.

'Reed,' he barked.

'You still asleep?'

The amused accusation at the other end didn't help make him feel better. 'Dot,' he mumbled as he massaged his head. 'What can I do for you?' He stifled a yawn.

'Tom didn't call in last night and when I tried to ring him, I got the engaged signal. After an hour of that, I called BT but they said the phone's off the hook.'

'Probably sleeping off a hit. Shouldn't worry about it.' Tyler was peeved at being disturbed by something so trivial – but he was soon brought to jolting awareness.

'I thought that, so I went round there. He's gone, Tyler. The flat's been wrecked, his computers smashed. Neighbours say they heard a lot of noise earlier this morning, but put it down to a drugs party. Then one of them said he thought he saw Tom being bundled into a car. According to the neighbour,

Tom looked pretty badly beaten, but when I asked questions, the man clammed up. You know what they're like on the Angel.'

'Where are you now?' Tyler had the phone jammed between shoulder and ear as he clambered into jeans and wrestled with shirt buttons.

'In a phone box outside the Wellington Arms. Do you think I should call the police?'

'Not yet. I doubt anyone else thought to do it and I've a fair idea who's behind this. I'll be with you as soon as possible.'

'Want me to do a search?' Dot's voice was tremulous with excitement.

'No,' he said firmly. 'You're to promise you'll stay out of there. Angel House Estate is no place for you, and I don't want you involved.' Tyler's voice was stern in his urgency to get the message across. 'Stay in the car and keep out of sight. Keep an eye on the flat if you can, and make a note of anyone who goes in or out. Car registrations, descriptions, everything.' He thought of something else. 'And Dot, for heaven's sake don't follow anyone.'

'Right you are.'

The line was disconnected and Tyler had a moment of unease. At the very least, Dot pictured herself as Miss Marple – that's what came of reading too many murder mysteries – and it could put the silly old bat in danger.

'Just hope to God she listens to me for a change,' he muttered, as he dragged on socks, stuffed his feet into trainers and grabbed a jacket.

Slamming the door shut behind him, he raced down the steps to the car. The mobile phone was held to his ear by his shoulder.

'Whashamata?'

'Bill, for God's sake wake up,' he bellowed as his partner sleepily answered the call. Tyler quickly related his conversation with Dot.

'Get back up to Norfolk and talk to those two old ladies.

Make them tell you where that bloody letter came from. I think Tom's disappearance has something to do with our missing girl.'

Greg looked at his watch as the limousine raced through New York city and headed for Victor's apartment. Concorde would be leaving for London in less than two hours. There was no time to waste.

Vic jabbed out his cigarette and took a swallow of bourbon. There was a sour taste in his mouth and his head felt at odds with the rest of him, light, and stuffed with smothering clouds of cotton candy. There was also a nagging pain in his left arm and his chest felt tight and uncomfortable, yet nothing he did could dispel the malaise and he had finally given up on the idea of sleep.

He stared morosely at the television set and let the drone of the news reporter wash over him. The apartment was silent without his wife and sons, but for once that silence was ominous, and he tried to concentrate on the flickering screen.

'There's news coming in of a series of bizarre murders in and around New York State. Our reporter is standing by with this news flash.'

Vic wearily rubbed his face and attempted to erase the strangeness he was experiencing. It was as if he was watching himself from somewhere near the ceiling and he wanted nothing more than to return to normality – to be able to lie down, close his eyes and sleep. But the pain in his arm was like a band of steel, and his chest seemed tighter than ever.

'The killings began at one thirty am New York time in the Ambassador Suite of this hotel on Fifth Aveue. By two o'clock this morning the lives of four men had been wiped out.'

He looked through his fingers at the screen and froze. Reinna was staying in that hotel. Coincidence? He had the awful feeling it wasn't.

'There seems little doubt that the deaths are some form

of execution. Each one bears the hallmarks of gangland retribution.'

Vic's heart thudded and the cordon of pain began to circle his chest, but his gaze was riveted to the screen as he fought the waves of nausea.

'Mob killings on such a scale were thought to have come to an end after the massacres of the nineteen fifties and sixties. But in New York this morning, there are four men lying in the morgue. Four men who appear to have nothing in common, but who had come to this city for the funeral of Gregory Castlemaine the Second. They are thought to be Don Reiina, Hal Courtney, Assad Suliman and Emilio Sanchez.'

The pain held him in a grip of steel and a bloody haze filled his eyes as he realised he was having a heart attack. The sweat gathered in cold droplets on his forehead and he wrapped his arms around himself and rocked back and forth for comfort.

'Jesus, oh, sweet Jesus,' he groaned. 'What am I going to do? Who can I turn to, and how long before Greg finds me?'

He staggered to his feet and went to the window. Down there somewhere was his brother – waiting for him – planning some diabolical end to his life. 'I need a drink,' he muttered

Tossing back the Bourbon he found his vision clearing and self preservation kick in. With the others gone there was only one thing he could do – only one place he could go. His life was worth nothing if he stayed here. He would have to ignore the pain and get out – now.

The journey across London seemed to take for ever. Stop, start, traffic lights, road works and dawdling motorists. Tyler fretted behind the wheel, took risks he wouldn't normally consider and came close to losing his temper which was unusual, but the tower blocks of the Brixton council estate finally came into view and he pulled the car up behind Dot's pink-and-white Mini. Damn thing looked like a fairy cake. All it needed was a cherry on top.

Before he had time to climb out of the car, she was beside him, her face flushed with excitement, her hand clutching her notebook.

'Two men came in an orange Cortina. Here's the licence number. Nasty looking pair, black Rastafarian thin and mean, the other was white, fat, with lots of tattoos and long greasy hair.'

She shuddered, but didn't quite manage to look as horrified as she pretended to be. 'They went in as if they knew Tom wouldn't be there.' She leaned close to him and added conspiratorially, 'I bet they were looking for something.'

'Are they still in there?' Tyler looked up at the sixth floor flat, but there was no one moving around up there except for a woman hanging out some washing.

Dot shook her head. 'They were in there for about an hour, then they drove off. I would have followed, but I thought it wiser to stay put.'

Tyler put his arm around her shoulders. 'You've done well, Dot. Take the rest of the day off.'

She stepped back, indignation writ large in her eyes and her expression. 'I'll do no such thing, Mr T. I'll keep guard here and sound the horn if those two thugs come back. I would never forgive myself if they hurt you.'

Tyler gave an exasperated sigh. This was getting ridiculous – he was a big boy now, and what earthly use Dot would be in a ruck – God only knew. He eyed her for a moment, then realising he was beaten, he gave up. There was no way Dot would leave now, she'd got the bit between her teeth and short of knocking her out and carrying her home, she was here to stay.

'All right, but you stay in the car.'

Dot nodded reluctantly, climbed into her Mini and shut the door.

'Lock it.'

She obeyed and glared back at him.

Tyler took one last look at her, then strode across the

quadrangle of bare concrete and climbed the stairs to the sixth floor. The lift was, as usual, out of order.

The pale blue door to number 486 had been kicked in. It said something about the neighbours that the cops hadn't been called – hear no evil, see no evil – the law of the urban jungle – it could be them next time.

Tyler pushed open the door. It was dark inside the one-bedroom flat, and only silence greeted him. He turned on the light and eyed the destruction.

Tom had been extraordinarily tidy, with his books neatly indexed and his computers and files neatly positioned. Now they lay in a jumble of jagged metal and ripped pages. Wires lay coiled like snakes across the bare floorboards and Tom's computer discs had all been taken. The chairs had been split, their stuffing billowing from the fabric covers. The curtains were closed and there was a suspicious dark stain that had dried on the wall.

Tyler picked his way across the debris to examine it. It was blood. Black scuff marks of heavy boots streaked across the polished wooden floor, and the claw of desperate fingers scratched the door jamb. This was not the result of a drugs party – this was the scene of a systematic beating and search.

But had he jumped the gun? Did all this have any link with Gabriella and Gregory Castlemaine?

He looked around the rest of the flat. The bedroom cupboards had been emptied, the mattress slashed and pulled to pieces. Drawers were thrown haphazardly onto the piles of clothes and books which littered the floor. The kitchen was the same. Every drawer and cupboard ripped away, tins and packets emptied and thrown to the floor with jars of jam and sauce. The flies had already begun their work on the pork chops which lay trampled under the table. How Tom would have hated it.

'Where are you, Tom?' he murmured into the silent room. 'Who the hell did you upset and what were they looking for?'

Tyler moved through the flat, his mind working fast. Tom had dubious friends. He'd spent time in prison and was now addicted to smack. Perhaps he'd kept a stash and had run out on his supplier, or knew too much and had to be silenced. Whatever it was, he'd taken his secret with him.

Or had he? Tom liked to keep records – had a fanatical obssession for data. This had to have something to do with his work as a computer hack. He would have known how dangerous it was, and kept a record of everything he'd been doing over the past few weeks. But the files and the discs were missing – or so they appeared.

Inch by inch he began searching the flat – moving broken furniture, lifting smashed computers, feeling for loose floorboards. There were no secret recesses in the walls, no false skirting board, or hidden safe. The bathroom had been virtually demolished. The bath panel had been ripped away, the air vent torn from its niche, the cistern lid dropped and broken to the floor. There was only the kitchen left. Kicking the debris of Tom's household shopping aside, Tyler searched the floor. The linoleum had been scored and pulled from its moorings, the doors of the cupboards ripped away. His optimism took a dive. There was nowhere else to look.

A fly buzzed, settled on the pork chops, then rose quickly and dived bombed him. He waved it away and idly watched it circle and return to the meat. Then he sighed and left the room.

Pulling the door closed, he hesitated. Opening it again, he twisted the handle. It didn't budge, and instead of a sliding locking mechanism, there was a rotating ball of plastic that slipped into a niche on the opposite door frame. Moving swiftly to the other doors he checked them. All of them had cheap brass handles, all of them could be locked in the conventional way. So why was the kitchen one different?

He returned to the kitchen door and eyed it thoughtfully. Like all the others in the council flat, it was made of plywood, and was hollow, but as he tapped his way over it, he realised there was something behind the door handle.

302

Searching amongst the debris of the sitting room, Tyler found a small screwdriver Tom must have used on his computers. It was too small to grasp easily in his big hands, and it kept sliding away from him, but it wasn't too long before he'd loosened the four screws in the metal plate.

Behind that plate was a thin cigarette case, wedged in the gap between the two sheets of plywood and taped firmly to them. He eased it out and opened it. There, in a plastic sleeve, was a computer disc.

Greg stepped out of the elevator and looked at the deserted hallway and open apartment door.

'Looks like he's gone, Jake. Check the apartment anyway.' His voice didn't betray the anger and frustration he felt, but his hand shook as he lit a cigarette. With Vic on the loose and sweating, anything could happen.

'Nothing here, Mr Castlemaine. But he left in a hurry. The TV's still on and the ice hasn't melted in his drink. What do you want me to do?'

'Find the bastard and kill him. I'm leaving you in charge while I'm away.'

'You're not planning to travel alone, sir?'

Greg saw the surprise in the other man's face and drew on his cigarette to give himself time to collect his thoughts.

'Please, sir. Let me come with you. The others can find Vic. It's too dangerous for you to be out there without protection.'

'Jake, how long have we known each other? Ten, twenty years?'

The other man nodded.

'Thank you for your concern and for your loyalty, but I have to do this alone. Besides, with all the killing tonight, it's better I disappear. They won't expect me to travel unguarded.' He smiled grimly at his own humour and pressed the elevator button for the ground floor.

'Then at least let me drive you to the heliport.'

Greg acquiesced, but his thoughts were with his treacherous wife and the baby she had with her in Sussex. The game was almost over, the pawns captured and dismissed. Now there was only Gabriella – and she had been manoeuvred into a corner.

20

G reg saw Smith as soon as he'd cleared Customs. He was smoking one of his fat cigars, and his grotesque figure was poured into an expensive suit.

'Mr Castlemaine? It's a pleasure to meet you at last. Did you have a good flight, sir?' Smith's voice was gravelled as he chewed on his cigar and offered a sweaty palm.

Greg ignored the hand and fixed him with a glare – it had not been a good flight, because his mind had been occupied, not only with his wife, but with the problem of Victor. He was a loose cannon in a minefield – had nowhere to turn, nowhere to hide – but was perfectly placed to detonate an explosion beneath the structure of the Castlemaine empire – it was the only weapon he had left in his arsenal, and Greg had no doubts that his brother would use it.

'Wyman?' he asked tersely.

Smith inspected his chewed cigar. 'Propping up a motorway.'

'Reed?'

'He don't know nothing yet. I thought it best to contact him after you'd left the country.' Smith reached into his breast pocket. 'By the way, there was a fax come in for you about an hour ago.'

Greg regarded Smith coolly as he took the slip of paper. There was something behind that eager, darting glance he didn't trust. The man was holding out on him, but if Wyman

305

had been silenced and Reed was in the dark, what else could there possibly be?

He drew on his flagging energy and put the doubts aside. Whatever it was, he would find out soon enough and deal with it – there were far more important things to do than wonder about Smith.

Lighting a cigarette, he looked at his watch. It was three o'clock in the afternoon, but his body clock was still on New York time. It had been a long twenty-four hours, and lack of sleep was beginning to take its toll.

He skimmed the fax and screwed it angrily into a ball and tossed it away. Vic had been sighted, but had given Jake the slip, and was still unaccounted for.

'Where is she exactly?

'I got the details here, and a road map.'

Greg snatched them from Smith's hand and studied them. 'Where's the car? We're wasting time.'

'In the short-term car park, Mr Castlemaine.'

Greg followed Smith out of the airport, the biting wind tearing at his clothes and searing his face. He suddenly no longer felt tired and the adrenalin began to flow. How surprised Gabriella will be to see me, he thought. I wonder how long it will take before that high-class, arrogant composure crumbles into a snivelling whine. The thought of it made his stride longer, his pace quicken. He was looking forward to seeing his wife again.

As he hurried towards the bank of lifts, he felt in his pocket for the gift he'd brought her. It wouldn't take the place of Nick, but it would be a reminder – if she survived long enough.

That's up to her, he thought grimly. I've come all this way for one reason – and I won't be leaving without him.

Smith signalled to the human lump of lard behind the wheel and opened the back door of the BMW. 'My boy will drive us, Mr Castlemaine. He knows the way and we may need 'im at the other end.'

Greg stood back and surveyed the car, the driver and Smith.

'That won't be necessary. I'll drive myself.' He opened the driver's door and jerked his head.

The bodyguard looked from one man to the other, decided who was in charge and climbed out.

'But Mr Castlemaine. Greg. You can't. It's dangerous out there. What if something happened to you while you're on my turf?' Smith was shuffling from one foot to the other in his agitation, a dew of sweat glistening on his bald head. 'I can't let you do this.'

Greg glared at him, his finger jabbing Smith's chest with every syllable. 'Don't dare give me orders. If I say crawl, you crawl. If I tell you to jump, you jump. Now get out of my way – you're wasting my time.' He climbed into the car.

'But Mr Castlemaine, how am I supposed to get back to London? I thought . . .' His self-importance had shrivelled into angry consternation.

'Get a cab.' Greg slammed the door on Smith's protest and activated the central locking. He could see the bodyguard's hesitant approach and threw him a look which stilled him.

Smith was shouting, his face puce, his hands banging against the glass and pulling at the door handles.

Greg pointed his index finger at the angry face and mimed the shooting of a pistol. Smith stepped back and Greg switched on the engine. Without another glance at either man, he headed out of the car park.

The roads south were wide and well-marked, familiar territory for a man who'd spent a great deal of time in England as a youth. He knew exactly where he was heading, and Hastings was only about two hours away.

Tyler slammed his way into the office and headed straight for Bill's computer. 'Get onto Blake in traffic and run a trace on that car registration. I wouldn't mind betting it belongs to Smith or one of his cronies.'

'Right you are Mr T.'

Tyler grinned at Dot and waited for the computer to boot

up. 'Let's hope it's not all in code. Never understood Tom's mania for secrecy, but thank God for it. I just hope this sheds some light on our missing girl and her baby.'

The computer buzzed for a moment, the screen cleared, then two words stared back at him. 'Shit!'

Dot looked up from her telephone call and frowned.

'Sorry. The bloody thing's got a password.'

'He hid it for a reason, Mr T, so it has to be important. It either has something to do with drugs, or what he was working on at the time of his disappearance. I read a book where the detective found a disc, and the code to break into the information had a link to the case the victim was prosecuting in court. Try it – you never know.'

Tyler grinned. 'Miss Marple to the rescue, eh?' He stared in bewilderment at the screen. Why the hell didn't I think of that? Probably too wound up, he decided, too over eager to get on with things and have a result.

With the awkwardness of the unfamiliar, he began to type. It took some time with one finger, but all too soon he had run out of the pseudonyms for street drugs.

'Access Denied.'

Tyler thought a moment, then tried the names of the drug dealers who worked Wyman's patch.

'Access Denied.'

His patience was being stretched. God, I hate machines. If this was a man – I'd have hit him by now – and got the information I want. He glared at the screen, had another idea and typed in 'Gabriella Whitmore.' Getting no response, he tried 'Castlemaine.' Then his own name, followed by Smith and everyone associated with him.

Still nothing.

'Now what?' He was exasperated. 'Computers aren't my thing, Dot, and that damn cursor's still blinking at me.'

Dot made a sympathetic noise in her throat, and carried on with her telephone calls.

Tyler knew that computers were a complete mystery to her

as well, and accepted the fact that she could be of no help. He glared at the 'Access Denied – Enter Password,' his pulse beating the same tattoo as that little white cursor – but he was left uninspired. The message calmly stared back – unmoved by his impatience.

With a snort of frustration he got up, poured himself a cup of coffee, then grimaced as the sour, stale taste hit his throat. Dot must have forgotten to change the pot from last night, but he couldn't blame her – it was turning into a rough day.

He stared moodily out of the window to the street. Out there – somewhere – was the answer. But what the hell was it? His gaze travelled randomly over the room, although he barely took in what he was seeing. The pattern in the carpet was a blur of faded colour, the damp patch on the ceiling something he'd been meaning to see to for ages, the regimental pictures on the wall a collection of faces and names from the past – most of whom would never grow old.

Regimental pictures. His eyes moved back to them, and lingered. What if . . .?

Tyler slammed down the coffee cup, spilling the contents in his haste to get back to the computer. Tom had served in the Royal Engineers, it was the one thing they both had in common. With a rising sense of optimism he began to type in the names of the regiments and the countries he and Tom had served in.

'Access Denied. Enter Password.'

Undaunted, he went on to type in the names of the commanding officers, the ranking listings, the names of the barracks.

'Access Denied. Enter Password.'

The disappointment was sharp. The failure bitter.

'I don't know what else to do, Dot. I've tried everything. Wish Bill was here, he likes playing with these damn things.'

Dot had finished her telephone calls and was sitting, arms folded, watching him. 'You can't just give up, Mr T. Remember your old army motto. Who Dares Wins. That disc may have cost Tom his life, and . . .'

'Dot! You're a genius,' shouted Tyler as he rattled off the SAS motto on the computer keys.

The screen cleared dramatically and there, in an almost endless list, was what Tom had taken such pains to hide.

'Would you look at this,' he muttered in amazement to Dot who was now leaning over his shoulder. He gave a long, low whistle as the damning catalogue of information filled page after rolling page.

There were names and addresses of drug runners, dealers, users and refiners – of safe houses which took in the human carriers who swallowed the stuff in condoms and waited for nature to take its course – addresses of importers, shipping companies and private airlines used to smuggle the stuff in from Europe, South America and the Far East – lists of sharcholders, backers and front men of companies owned by the Castlemaines in London – of bank transfers to tax havens, which had been tracked labouriously through a massive network of double dealing, laundering and investment – of men whose money funded some of the largest companies in the world, but who remained shadowy figures lost in a plethora of red tape and ownership transfers.

Tyler sat back and watched the roll call of corruption, his composure so shaken, he could hardly take in what he was seeing. Yet the links between Smith, the Castlemaines and the world's drug cartels were clearly defined. Sniffy Smith was playing with much bigger boys than he'd ever imagined.

'No wonder Tom hid this disc. It's dynamite. He must have hacked into Smith's personal computer, then, finding the South American connection, somehow found a way to get into Castlemaine's system and raided that.'

He leaned forward, his face grim as the information kept coming. 'Jeezus! Even the fucking IRA are involved. Sorry Dot. But look . . . Arms shipments – money coming in from America, transferred to Libya, brought back through the

Middle East and Russia in the form of arms. All cartel-backed
– all brought in in the guise of charity. Tom must have been
mad to mess with all this once he realised what it was.'

'It explains why the flat was wrecked and Tom's missing.
God alone knows what they've done to him.'

Tyler looked up at Dot's worried face. His private opinion
was that Tom was probably dead – he just hoped he was so
high on smack when he was abducted that he wouldn't have
felt much, because the men he'd cheated wouldn't have given
him an easy death.

'Tom knew the risks, Dot. Silly young fool. But none of
this helps us to find Gabriella Whitmore,' he said grimly. 'If
we don't find her – and soon – Smith or Castlemaine could
get there before us – and I don't fancy her chances of coming
out of this alive. I was so sure this disc would lead us to her,
but I never suspected all this.'

The screen went blank.

'That's it, then,' said Tyler as he reached to switch off the
computer.

'Wait, look!'

There was another message. 'For Tyler. Channel View,
Updyke Road, Hastings. You know what to do with this
disc. Tom.'

Tyler's heart was banging against his ribs – Tom hadn't
let him down after all. Then a thought darkened his elation
and he slumped in the chair. Tom must have been playing
both sides, using this information to blackmail Smith – and
ultimately the South Americans and the IRA! Christ, what a
mess – what an absolutely bloody fool. Yet it explained the
lad's reluctance to reveal Gabriella's hiding place – he must
have been using it as a lever to pressure Smith.

'Do you think he told them about Gabriella, Mr T?'

'I hope not, for her sake, but if he did, then Castlemaine
is probably already on his way to Hastings.'

Tyler fumbled for the disc, his haste making him clumsy.
He put it in an envelope. 'Get hold of Bill and tell him to come

back immediately. Say nothing about this over the telephone, Dot. This information could get you killed, and so far, neither Smith, nor Castlemaine know we have it. I'd like to keep it that way.'

He waited for her to acknowledge and accept his order. 'When Bill gets here, ask him to wipe off the last message, then send this anonymously to Tim Parker in CID. He'll know what to do with it.'

'I hope you get to Hastings in time, Lord knows what they'll do to that poor girl. And poor Tom . . . What about poor Tom?'

Tyler squeezed her shoulder and made comforting noises, but his mind was working fast. Tom was beyond help, he was no longer a part of the equation. It would take about an hour and a half to get to Hastings – he just hoped the others hadn't already got there.

Dot began to tidy the desk, her back turned to him, her voice unsteady. 'You were right about the car. It's owned by a Jason Claybourne, a known associate of Smith, wanted for GBH, ABH and several charges of aggravated burglary. I told the police about Tom and his flat, and they're looking into it. I hope I did the right thing, only no one else on that estate seemed to care.' She had turned away from her tidying and stood with her hands on her hips, defiance clear on her face.

Tyler gently put his arm around her shoulder, gave her a hug and smiled.

'Yeah, you did the right thing, Dot. Now, I'm going home for the Harley, she's faster through traffic than the car.'

He took the Beretta from the gun cupboard, loaded it and strapped on the shoulder holster. If he had to face Castlemaine, then he wanted to be prepared. Damn Tom for playing both sides. Why the hell couldn't he have been straight for once?

Greg followed the winding, twisting hill down into Hastings. The sea glittered metallic grey in the distance and the promenade and pier were almost deserted. A light rain spattered the windscreen and a few solitary gulls wheeled and cursed in the bleak afternoon glower.

The map was detailed, the street easy to find. He drew up outside the villas and eyed the broken railings and crumbling steps. The house, like all the others was unkempt and from another era – the last refuge of the dregs of humanity. An ignominious end for the woman who could have shared a wealth beyond her dreams.

He sat in the car for a moment, running over his plan of action, when he realised he was not the only person watching the house. A man was sitting in a small white van on the other side of the road, and after he'd telephoned Smith to confirm it was one of his, he saw him answer his mobile, then drive away.

Satisfied he was alone, Greg left the engine running and stepped out into the drizzle. As he climbed the steps to the front door, he watched for signs of life – but the curtains remained closed, and no one challenged him.

The door was ajar and he pushed it open to reveal a long narrow hallway and winding staircase. The house was on four floors – and according to Smith, Gabriella's room was at the top.

Greg stood at the bottom of the stairs and listened. The pervasive odour of damp and old carpets, and Indian take-outs came back to him – but all was quiet – nothing moved.

He climbed the stairs swiftly and silently, and as he reached the top floor landing, he heard the sound of a key turning in a lock. Gabriella was about to leave her room.

Greg melted into the shadows of the communal kitchen – and waited.

Gabriella stepped out of the shower and quickly dried herself. She'd spent longer in the bathroom than she'd planned, weariness had caught up with her and she must have dozed off. Dressing rapidly in jeans, shirt and sneakers, she thought of Nick alone in the room and hurried up the short flight of stairs to the attic bed-sit.

Her footsteps faltered and she looked over her shoulder. The feeling of being watched was so strong that her skin prickled and the hairs on the nape of her neck bristled. Could there be someone hiding in the long, twisting hallway of the old Victorian villa – someone who was waiting for her – someone who stood between her and the baby?

The lights on the timer switch went out and the hall was plunged into shadow. The house closed in as time stood still and the tension became palpable.

Gabriella shivered and her pulse raced as she stumbled up the last few stairs. Every corner was shadowed, every doorway hid an intruder – every twist in the hall was a hiding place. Her breath hissed as her gaze flickered back and forth. The house was unusually deserted and silent, too old – too labyrinthine – its high ceilings seeming to loom down, the heavy pillars advancing as shadows ran inky fingers over the landing.

'The baby,' she breathed. 'I must get to the baby.'

She edged forward into the darkness, every nerve wired with dreaded anticipation – ready to defend herself, and the child.

The door to her room appeared to be ajar, but that couldn't be, she'd locked it, pulled it behind her and tested the catch – the key was in her hand, poised between her fingers to jab and gouge. Yet as she reached the threshold, she knew it was no flight of imagination, no shifting of shadows or trick of light.

Her pulse drummed in her ears, and filled her head – the dread almost suffocating as she brushed the door with her fingertips – afraid to look – afraid not to.

The door creaked on rusty hinges, and the stench of French cigarettes hit her immediately. The sob of fear and desperation was muffled as she bit down on it and pushed the door further. It was all too familiar that smell – and there was only one person she knew who smoked them.

She steeled herself for the inevitable – honed her courage to razor sharpness to face the reality of Nick gone – of Greg waiting for her.

The baby slept innocently in his cot, his cheeks rosy with warmth, his mouth moving as though at the breast.

Relief was overwhelming – but short lived – the nightmare just begun.

Small and black, it lay on the pillow beside her baby. Cold and imperious, it stared back at her from sightless eyes carved into the ebony. Gregory Castlemaine had left her the black king.

Almost transfixed by those eyes – to the emblem of Greg's wrath, she moved like a sleepwalker to the cot. She couldn't scream, couldn't cry out – her emotions had been frozen, her thought process caught in a morass of confusion and conflicting emotions. Terror and despair had silenced her.

The creak of a floorboard snapped her out of the trance. But it was a heartbeat too late for her to turn and attack – an instant before she felt the crushing blow to her head and the whiplash in her neck as he struck.

She crashed against the wall, the air punched from her lungs as he brought up his knee. The death knell of his blows rang in her ears and her mouth opened to scream as the silken noose tightened about her throat.

The scream was ripped away – the breath stifled as she clawed at the ever tightening throttle. Silk tore beneath her fingers, slipped from her grasp, cut into the softness of her throat. Darkness closed in – shooting stars and bright, white lights dazzled and flashed as her lungs fought for air and her blood drummed.

The last thing she saw was Greg's smiling face as she sank to the floor and unwelcoming darkness – the last thing she heard was his soft, caressing voice.

'Check and mate, Gabriella.'

21

Gabriella knew that the present danger her son was in was far more ominous than anything that had gone before – so she fought her way out of the darkness and towards the light.

She felt the noose slither against her throat, and gulping in the musty air of the carpet, she heaved with the effort to fill her lungs again as she opened her eyes, ready to attack. Greg was here, beside her, prolonging the agony – playing with her like a cat with a bird.

And all the while there was someone hammering at the door.

She opened her mouth ready to scream, to give vent to her fear, to let the demons of her despair escape – but a hand smothered that scream, and her breath was stifled as she was lifted from the floor and held fast.

She could smell him. Feel the coldness of his steely fingers, the hardness of his body as he held her in an iron embrace. Black clouds filled her head again, threatening to suffocate her in that claustrophobic embrace from which there seemed no escape.

I mustn't black out again, she thought wildly. I can't let go of reality. If Greg's still here – then Nick must be close by. I have to fight for him. Oblivion's a luxury I daren't afford.

The thought gave her strength and she lashed out with her nails, raking over the smothering hand, kicking with heels

317

against the rock-steady pillars of his legs – using her elbows to dig into ribs.

The hands increased their grip, lifting her higher, pinning her to his chest, squeezing the air from her lungs.

She felt his breath on her cheek, the coldness of his lips on her ear and renewed her attack.

'Stop struggling, Gabriella.'

The sound of the voice, so different to what she'd expected, made her hesitate.

· 'I'm not your husband. I'm here to help.'

She didn't believe him. It was a trick – another of Greg's games. She twisted in the man's embrace, raking at his hands, clawing for the face she could not see.

Fingers pinched her nose, the hand filled her mouth cutting off the air.

She bit hard and tasted blood. The pressure from the arm around her waist merely increased.

'Stop it. Think. Castlemaine's gone. Nicholas's gone. We're wasting time. You have to trust me. I'm here to help Goddam it!' The voice was close to her ear, and a stubbled chin rasped her cheek.

She fought to breathe, reflected on her options and stopped struggling. If he thought she'd yielded, he would release her, then she could run. Greg and the baby couldn't have got far.

The hand released its pressure over her mouth and nose, but hovered menacingly, and the grip around her waist was as strong as ever.

Gabriella gasped, swallowed and filled her bursting lungs. She still couldn't see her attacker.

'My name is Tyler Reed,' said the deep voice in her ear. 'I'm here to help. You won't achieve anything if you make a fuss and start screaming. I need you clear headed and as calm as possible. I'm not going to hurt you. I promise.'

Gabriella heard the authority in the man's voice and felt

the grip around her waist slacken. She tore away from him and whirled round.

He backed away, his body pressing against the door, deadening the frantic knocking as he nursed his bitten hand. He was tall and broad, with close cropped brown hair and brown eyes. The crescent-shaped scar on his chin showed white through dark stubble. Blood from his hand spattered his shirt and leather jacket.

'Get out of my way. I have to find my son,' she snarled as she charged at him, fingernails clawed to attack.

He held her off as though she was a bothersome fly, his gaze steady, his body blocking her only escape.

'How the hell do you think you're going to catch up with him? Do you have a car, a bike?'

'Don't get clever with me, you bastard. He's got my baby and you're in the way!' She aimed a kick where it would hurt.

He caught her ankle, unbalanced her for a second, then, as she swayed, he grasped her hands and pulled her back to his chest.

'Don't start that again you silly bitch. Now shut up, keep still and listen.' He shook her – hard. 'Are you listening?'

There was something in the intensity of his glare that made her stop fighting. Something in the way his voice conveyed the urgency she herself felt. Perhaps he really was here to help.

'There's nothing you can do on your own. If you call the police, they'll make you fill in forms and lose precious time. I'm all you've got.'

She looked up into his steady brown eyes and saw he understood her bewilderment, her reluctance to believe; but most of all she recognised the same stamp of authority her father had possessed and knew she would have to trust him.

'Army, right?'

The man nodded. 'Hereford. Your father was one of our instructors.'

Her spirits lifted. Hereford could mean only one thing.

'Every minute we stay here gives him more of a lead. We have to go.'

'Go where?'

He released his grip on her wrists and she massaged them as her thoughts whirled. 'He'll be heading for the States. He wants Nick with his family.'

'Right. Come on.' Tyler grabbed her jacket, threw it at her, then opened the door.

They ran straight into a crowded landing. A babel of noise greeted them and they almost knocked over the student who had been hammering on the door.

'You all right, Ellie? What's going on?' The student who lived in the next room pushed his way through the crowd and grabbed Gabriella's arm. His face was bloody, his left eye almost closed beneath the cut and bruising. 'Who's this? What's he want?'

'Did you see a man with the baby?' Gabriella shrieked at him as she clutched him and looked at the others who were jostling to see what was going on.

The boy stepped back, his brow wrinkled. 'Yeah. About fifteen minutes ago. I tried to stop him, and he nearly broke my jaw. Luckily, the others heard the noise and came running or. . . .'

Gabriella burned with frustration. 'Did you see which way he went?'

The student touched his swollen chin and shook his head. 'But he's driving a BMW. I noticed it parked outside with the engine running. I rang the cops – they're on their way.'

'I saw him go.' The girl from room five piped up. 'He went east up the seafront. Won't get far, though. I've just come from there and there's been an accident and the traffic's piled up for about two miles.'

'That's a start. Let's get out of here.' Tyler pulled Gabriella past the others and down the hallway.

They negotiated the last turn in the stairs and headed for the front door.

'What are you? A mercenary? Why were you looking for me? Who are you working for?' she gasped, as she raced to keep up with him. Her lungs felt bruised and she needed answers before she went hurtling off into the unknown. He might have been army once, but now . . .?

'It's a long story, I'll tell you later,' he said shortly as he pushed through the door into the street. 'I hope you aren't scared of motorbikes. Here, put this on and do up that jacket.'

Gabriella caught the helmet and stared down at the Harley Davidson XLCR. She was an evil-looking tart – sleek and black, with a seat like an armchair, a tank like a whale and enough chrome to put a gypsy caravan to shame – but to give her her due, she was magnificent.

'Nothing scares me,' she said defiantly as she strapped on the helmet.

Tyler looked at her, the ghost of a smile twitching his mouth. 'I did,' he said as he swung his leg over the Harley.

'That was different. You took me by surprise. Can we get on with it. We're wasting time.'

She climbed on behind him. Compared to her father's old bike, it looked dangerous, and despite her bravado, she wasn't at all sure if she had the bottle to ride such a monster.

Tyler brought the engine roaring to life and conversation became impossible.

Gabriella rested her hands at his waist and waited. She was sick with apprehension for Nick's safety, and it pushed her own welfare into second place. She knew then, that she had the courage to face anything – even this stranger and his demonic machine.

'You'll have to hold on tighter than that.' He looked over his shoulder, then pulled her hands around his waist until she was pressed against the smoothness of his worn leather jacket. 'Just keep your eyes closed and lean with the bike. Otherwise, we'll be thrown. Ready?'

'Get on with it,' she snapped. Greg was getting away

while this macho mercenary waffled on as if she was a half-wit.

Tyler tweaked the throttle and the bike pulled away from the kerb.

Gabriella clutched a handful of leather jacket as she was almost thrown by the bike's acceleration. She pressed tightly to his back, her spine rigid, her eyes shut. Something hidden beneath his jacket dug into her stomach and she guessed it was a gun.

Dear God, what's going on? Who is this man? Why does he want to help? And where's the baby? So many questions. So few answers. The situation was out of control and there was nothing she could do but hang on for the ride.

She pressed closer to the broad back and opened her eyes. The road flew – too close for comfort – beneath the wheels, as they weaved through the traffic. Her hands tightened around his waist and she froze.

'Lean woman! Lean with the bike! You'll have us in the bloody ditch!'

Gabriella heard and tried to relax. She remembered her father's words on that first day he'd taken her pillion on the Norton. She'd been eleven and terrified. His voice came back to her, calm and authorative. 'Relax. Become one with the bike, until it's an extension of yourself, then you will be in charge.'

Her hands loosed their clutch, her body melted against his, and she moved as one with him. Today was different, she had not learned to trust fully the man in front of her – yet she could bear anything – put up with any insult or danger, and find the necessary courage to deal with whatever happened next. For Nick needed her and this was the only person who could help.

I have to trust him, have to believe he can bring Nick safely back. I just hope he knows what he's doing.

'I'm on my way. Should take about three hours once I get out of this traffic.'

'Right'o. Everything's set here. I'll meet you at twenty-one hundred hours. There's a message by the way, Mr Castlemaine. From Jake.'

'Go ahead, but careful what you say on this open line.'

'He said to tell you the bird was singing but his heart wasn't in it. Silence is golden.' The man paused. 'That make any sense to you?'

Greg felt a momentary sadness, but it was all the mourning he would do for his snivelling brother. If his heart hadn't given out, Jake would have silenced him.

'Understood,' he replied gruffly, and switched off the car phone.

He glared at the woman in the car next to him. He was stuck in a traffic jam and Nicholas was attracting attention by screaming up a storm in the back seat.

'Nosy broad,' he muttered as he turned up the radio to drown out his son.

Puccini's 'Madame Butterfly' soared into the confined space, but the combined noise did nothing to salve his frayed nerves. He wanted out of Hastings – the further the better. Gabriella's body could already have been found if that interfering young punk had come to.

I should have finished him off, he thought bitterly. The whole episode had been rushed, and uncivilised, leaving a certain dissatisfaction that he found unsettling. I wish I could have taken time with Gabriella, too. Should have killed her slowly and painfully – didn't realise she'd put up such a fight, or have so much stamina and strength.

'Will you shut the fuck up! You're giving me a goddam headache, Nicholas.' He snatched a glance over his shoulder. The kid looked safe enough strapped into the carrycot on the back seat, the seatbelts holding it firm, and there were blankets to keep him warm. Jeez, what a racket – it's driving me nuts.

The traffic began to move through the road block and filter past the accident. He lit a cigarette. Once they were on the motorway, Nick would probably fall asleep. Surely he couldn't keep up that noise for much longer?

As the traffic finally eased and his foot pressed on the accelerator, he began to experience the elation of success. Getting to Gabriella had been far easier than he'd envisaged. The locked door had been child's play to force once Gabriella was safely out of the way in the bathroom. Then it had only been a matter of watching and waiting, until he had her.

The boy from the other room had been a complication, an interference that had made her killing a hurried affair, but the swift upper cut should have knocked him out long enough. I don't think he'll recognise me again, and by the time the cops are on the case, I'll be long gone – Gabriella in the past, dead and buried. Nick back where he belongs.

Greg increased his speed as he filtered onto the east-bound motorway. With Vic and the others dead, and the Feds floundering, the sky's the limit. Now, I'm less than twenty-four hours from home.

He smiled and beat a tattoo on the steering wheel. 'I'm a lucky man – I have it all.'

Tyler crouched over the handlebars and gave the Harley full throttle as they followed the BMW onto the motorway. The 1470cc engine growled and the bike leapt forward, eating up the miles, making the wind bite his face and numb his fingers. The only blemish on the perfection of the ride was the nagging doubt. He'd promised the girl who clung to him that he would rescue her baby – but what if he couldn't? How would he face her if he failed? He banished the doubts. There was no room on the agenda for failure – never had been.

I have to trust my instincts on this one, he thought grimly, as he kept the BMW in his sights.

Tracking down the car had been easy, thanks to the kids back at the rooming house. It was, as they had said, stuck in a traffic jam and as he'd threaded the Harley through the idling cars, he'd seen it. As he edged closer for a better look, he'd recognised it as Smith's car by the custom paint job. Yet the driver wasn't Sniffy – and he would have to wait until they were clear of traffic before he could risk getting any closer for another look.

His thoughts were gloomy. There was no guarantee the baby was in the car. Gregory Castlemaine was a devious bastard – Sniffy could have Nicholas and be driving in the opposite direction. He frowned. The girl sitting so quietly behind him had gone through enough, it was best to keep his thoughts to himself.

The wind whipped at his jacket and stung his bare hands. It was getting colder and the sun was beginning to disappear behind storm clouds. As the shadows lengthened he switched on the powerful headlight. The traffic had dwindled to a trickle, now the BMW was the only car in the fast lane. He held a steady course, closing in, until the Harley's headlight illuminated the driver.

The BMW was moving fast as it swerved into the middle lane.

Tyler edged closer, his mouth dry in anticipation. He tweaked the throttle and she obeyed instantly, taking him into the fast lane and holding steady. Now he had clear sight of the driver.

The long nose and high forehead were all too familiar, the dark hair and diamond stud instantly recognisable. Castlemaine had chosen to do his own dirty work – and he was alone.

Tyler dropped revs. In the staccato flashes of the overhead lights he saw what he was looking for. The baby's mouth was open, legs and fists angrily pummelling the air as he lay strapped in a carry cot on the back seat.

Gabriella shifted behind Tyler. Nick! She let go of the leather jacket and reached out. He was so close she could hear him crying, could see the tears glisten on his face, and feel his anger.

The Harley swerved and the back wheel skidded beneath her. She grabbed a handful of leather jacket as they dropped back, but she saw only the racing car which was pulling away from them.

'That was Nick!' she screamed in Tyler's ear. 'Why didn't you do something? He's getting away!'

He didn't answer as he fought to keep the Harley upright.

Her grip tightened on his jacket and she pressed her mouth to his ear. 'Please, Tyler. Please,' she sobbed as she saw the BMW pull further away. 'Do something.'

'What d'you want? To run him off the road with the baby in the car? Are you mad?' He yelled back.

The anger burned and she longed to grab the handlebars and press the throttle. *I could make this Harley go faster, could make her catch up with Greg. Why the hell isn't he doing anything?*

'He'll get away,' she yelled. 'You've got to stop him.'

'For God's sake stop screeching in my ear and sit still! I know what I'm doing.'

Tyler felt the grip on his jacket loosen, then her arms slide once more around his waist. *Poor kid must be frantic, she'd even forgotten her fear.* She might have an answer for everything and think she was tough, but her tension was being transmitted through his back by the clenching of her fists against his belly and the stiffness of her body as she pressed close.

But that was the least of his worries. Despite his reassurance just now, he actually had no idea of what to do next. *The car was built like a tank and if Castlemaine tried to run us off the road, we wouldn't stand a chance.* He hoped the crash helmets had given them anonymity. Castlemaine had left Gabriella for dead, so he wouldn't expect to see her again.

Tyler steadied the bike and they stayed back from the car. *All I can do is tail him and wait. With the baby on board I don't dare take chances.* He looked at the petrol gauge. The tank was two thirds full which meant they had a lot of miles to go before refuelling. Best to get help though, just in case I lose the bastard. Tyler reached into his jacket for the portable phone, but the Harley was too heavy to steer with one hand and it swerved dangerously close to the kerb.

'What are you doing?' Gabriella's voice was high pitched with fear as she clung to him.

'Sorry. Hang on.' He thought of asking her to make the call, but realised in the same moment that she could never do it. They were on their own.

It was quite dark now, the sky black above the orange sulphur lights. The car's tail lights shone brightly up ahead and Tyler kept his distance. He didn't want to spook Castlemaine, didn't fancy giving chase with Gabriella riding pillion – she was jumpy enough and could become a hazard if she panicked.

He relaxed his concentration on the car as he thought about his passenger. She was the first female he'd taken on Jezebel, although there had been plenty of others who'd wanted to ride pillion. In a strange way it had become something of a taboo, which was ridiculous really, for Gabriella and Jezebel seemed to be getting along just fine. It was just that the Harley meant more to him than a collection of nuts and bolts, and he guarded that affection jealously.

Castlemaine took the exit south east and headed for Kent. The motorway petered out and they were on a dual carriageway. Twenty miles later Tyler reduced his speed as Castlemaine turned off onto a country lane.

'Where the hell's he going?'

'Dover?' Gabriella was looking over his shoulder.

Tyler shook his head. 'He'd have stayed on the motorway.'

The hedgerow brushed his leg as he kept the Harley in its shadows. Oast houses loomed out of the night, rabbits skittered and swerved to avoid his wheels as an owl shrieked in a fluster of feathers close to his shoulder, then disappeared into the darkness.

Castlemaine would soon realise he was being followed – it was time to make a move.

Tyler gripped the handlebars and opened up the throttle.

The Harley leapt forward, the front wheel almost leaving the ground in its eagerness to catch the car. Closer and closer until he saw the orbs of red against the dark bulk – Castlemaine's tail lights.

The man glanced in his mirror as the Harley's headlight blinded him.

Tyler rode on – drawing closer – now level – their speed suicidal in the narrow, twisting lane. He locked eyes with the driver – his intention clear.

Castlemaine's face glowed white in the gloom, his lips drawn back in a snarl as he jerked the steering wheel.

Tyler was ready, and took evasive action, but the BMW edged closer – pushing the Harley towards the ditch – thrusting them into the thorny hedgerow. His knee touched the driver's door as the metal foot rest scratched the paintwork. He felt Gabriella tense.

'Hold on girl!'

Castlemaine pulled away, picked up more speed and edged back in for the kill. The XLCR was trapped. The hedges flashed past, the trees shadowed the moon – then were gone. Oast houses loomed, farm buildings huddled, the lane writhed beneath them and fields appeared – and disappeared.

A hairpin bend – a deep ditch beside them, yawning, waiting for Tyler to miscalculate. The hedgerows closed in and tree branches clawed his helmet as he battled to keep the Harley upright and out of trouble – but the Land Rover was approaching fast and on the wrong side of the road – its lights blinding – they were cornered – with no room to manoeuvre.

He braked hard, feet down to find purchase on the tufted weeds at the lip of the ditch, injured knee on fire with pain as the effort wrenched and tore at the old wound.

The XLCR's tyres screamed and smoked as it tried to find a grip on the worn tarmac and muddy grass. She almost lost it – found a hold – and stayed on course.

The Land Rover disappeared round the corner, its horn blaring, its rusted bodywork scraping his leg, as the down draught pulled them towards it.

The BMW swerved in a screech of rubber, the body rocking on the chassis, the engine roaring, gears grinding. With the force of a pile driver it made matchwood of a farm gate, slew sideways in the mud and finally came to rest broadside in a juddering slam against a tree.

Gabriella was frozen in horror to the bike. The car headlights pointed at the sky, its engine throbbing like a great cat. The sound of opera filled the night and the flashing yellow of the indicators showed the surrounding tree trunks as a macabre, waxen audience.

Nick's screams tore through her paralysis. She was off the bike, legs shaking, heart hammering, deaf to Tyler's shout of warning as she stumbled over the rough, muddy ground. She was oblivious to everything but the need to reach the baby, and as his cries drew her on, she began to pray.

The door was cool to the touch and as she tried to wrench it open she looked through the window. There was no sight of him, but she could hear him – he had to be in the shadows, out of reach.

'You'll never have him, bitch.' Greg's voice roared out of the darkness, drowning the music and the sound of Nick's cries.

Gabriella jolted as the bullet scored a hit and burned fire through her arm. Yet the growl of the car engine and the spinning of the wheels spurred her on. She grasped the door handle and clung to it as the car slewed in the mud and pulled away from the tree.

'So long, Gabby!'

'Give him back!' she screamed as she felt her grip on the handle being torn away by the speed of the car.

She ran alongside, her feet sliding in the mud as she hammered on the door. 'Give him back! Bastard! You're a bastard!'

The snub nose of a pistol was thrust out of the driver's window and a shot rang out – to be followed by another.

The tyres gripped, splashing her with cold, clinging mud and the rear bumper caught her a numbing blow on the thigh as the car slewed crazily forward.

Gabriella was still running as the BMW headed for the gate. But her steps faltered as the headlights picked out the fallen man beside the motorbike.

Gregory Castlemaine stopped the car and leaned out of the window. 'See you in hell.' He fired another shot.

Gabriella hit the ground in the same instant the bullet struck the tree behind her.

Greg crowed victorious laughter. Then the car was out of the field and roaring away.

Gabriella scrambled up and ran to Tyler. The fear for her child was raw – the nausea bitter. 'How bad is it?' She fell to her knees in the mud.

'Only a graze. It's my knee that's the problem. What about you?'

'I'm fine.' Gabriella was aware she'd been hit, but couldn't feel anything but desperation.

'Come on. We have to get going. If you'd done as I'd said, I could have got a clear shot,' said Tyler.

Gabriella studied his face and the way he was keeping his weight off his leg. He looked very pale and blood stained his face and dripped onto his jacket from the bullet wound in his cheek.

'I'll drive,' she said, heading for the bike. Greg was getting away – there was no more time to lose.

'You'll have a job. That's one of the heaviest bikes made – not built for a woman.'

Gabriella glared at him. 'I'm not some half-baked bimbo. I've driven bikes before. You look as if a gust of wind would blow you over and I haven't got time to stand here arguing.'

She grasped the handlebars and threw her leg over the seat.

Her arm was almost pulled out of its socket as she was yanked away.

'Leave the heroics. Get on the back and do as you're told. No one drives this Harley, but me.'

Gabriella saw him wince as he moved his injured leg onto the footrest, but felt little sympathy. The Harley was a monster and it was ridiculous for a grown man to make such a fuss about a bit of old machinery. Besides, she thought grimly as she climbed up behind him, he's a male chauvinist pig – he deserves everything he gets.

Tyler turned the key and pressed the ignition button. Nothing happened.

'Don't let me down you bitch. Not now,' she muttered into Tyler's back. 'Get your great metal backside into gear and get us out of here.'

Regret for her previous, uncharitable thoughts made her keep her voice down. She didn't need the sharp side of his tongue again – even if he was her knight in black leather.

The engine coughed twice and she held her breath, urging it to hold. It coughed again, growled, then roared into life. With a deep sigh of relief, she leaned against Tyler and with a screech of tyres the Harley leapt forward.

She looked over his shoulder. There was no sign of Greg, no gleam of the car's tail lights. Yet he couldn't be too far away.

The night closed in and all that existed was the throb of the Harley's engine and the beam of headlight on the snaking lane. It no longer mattered that his knee was agony, or that the wind had frozen the bullet gouge in his face – his concentration was fixed only on the way ahead.

Then he saw them – twin orbs glowing red in the darkness. It was the BMW.

He slowed and held back to avoid being detected – the ploy to run them off the road hadn't worked last time, but the odds on a second attempt being successful were in Castlemaine's favour.

He decided to stay back and wait. Castlemaine was heading for somewhere specific, and wherever that was, it meant he would have to stop – and that's when he would make a move. He refused to allow himself to think of all the things that could go wrong – there were too many of them. Especially if Castlemaine used the gun again. That had been an unwelcome surprise.

Tyler hugged the corners and stayed close to the hedges as the road was eaten beneath the Harley's wheels. Tendrils of briar clawed at his clothes and tore his jeans – cracks and potholes jarred the bike's delicate balance and jolted his injured knee – but he hung on grimly and could feel Gabriella do the same.

The road dipped, then snaked up a steep incline. Tyler watched the car headlights sweep towards the sky, then turn sharply away and disappear. The night seemed blacker than ever – the road was deserted. It was as if the BMW had never existed.

Tyler eased off the throttle and let the engine idle as he reached the top of the hill and looked around. It was too deserted – too still – and the short hairs bristled on his neck.

Greg rammed the car through the wooden gate and winced as the chain and padlock thudded against the bodywork, but his attention was focussed elsewhere. The field was empty and dark – and it was not supposed to be.

He looked swiftly over his shoulder. The motorbike couldn't be far behind, he'd noticed the headlights in the distance as he'd reached the brow of the last hill.

He began to sweat. The plane should be here by now – where the fuck was it?

Switching off the stereo, he made a circuit of the airfield. Perhaps the pilot had put down on the other side. It would be logical, considering the job he had to do tonight.

Greg's hands clutched the steering wheel as the headlights

revealed emptiness. His frustration burned and he chewed his lip. It was all going wrong. Gabriella's appearance had shocked him – she should have been dead – and who the fuck was the idiot on the bike? Now the plane was missing and he was stuck in the middle of Kent with nowhere to hide. Something must have happened to the pilot, but if that was so, why hadn't the man radioed in and told him?

'Fucking asshole! Where the fuck are you?' he yelled at the empty skies.

He switched off the engine and climbed out of the car slamming the door with such force, it rocked the BMW on its chassis. Nicholas was still screaming, but at least it was muffled by the blanket he'd thrown over him.

The moments ticked away as he scanned the sky, watching the scudding clouds, looking for the gleam of white, listening for the drone of the engines. But the sky remained empty, and the only sound he could hear was the wind in the grass and the muffled sobs of the baby.

He looked around him, then back to the road. Headlights were approaching fast and now he could hear the roar of a bike. The sweat was cold on his brow. It was time to get out of sight. Time to make the last stand and finish this once and for all.

Gabriella could feel the tension in him and she leaned close to whisper in his ear. 'What's the matter?'

'That is,' Tyler replied, nodding towards a turn-off.

Gabriella looked over his shoulder and felt her skin crawl with icy premonition. The wide expanse of concrete led to a small airfield, but it was like no other she'd seen. The tall tower that stood beside the runway was in darkness and the hangars were shut and barricaded with rolls of barbed wire. A broken chain lay abandoned across the road, the padlock clanking against an iron post in the wind. A weathered sign forbade trespassers.

The Harley's headlight showed up the runway and the clutches of weeds that thrust their way through the broken concrete. Ivy and Russian vine ran haywire over the tumble of deserted shacks. The aura of abandonment, of neglect and decay hung over the place like a caul. Of the car and Greg, there was no sign.

'Do you hear what I hear?' murmured Tyler.

Gabriella drew in a sharp breath. 'A Cessna! Quick. We have to get to Nick before it lands!'

Tyler edged the bike closer to the gate and Gabriella crouched behind him.

I don't like the look of it, she thought. There's no sign of Greg or his car, yet I know he's there. We could be heading straight into a trap.

'Get off and hide.' Tyler murmured as he stopped the bike. 'I'm going to see if I can flush him out.'

Gabriella shook her head. He wasn't getting away with that. 'If you go, I go. It's my baby out there.' She buried her fingers in his jacket and took a firmer hold, her heart hammering in time with the throb of the Harley's engine as Tyler digested her decision.

He capitulated and they began to move forward.

Greg watched the glimmer of white from the shadows. As the hum of the Cessna engine became a steady drone, he looked back towards the broken gate and the place where he knew the motorbike waited. His hands trembled in anticipation on the steering wheel, and his mouth set in an angry line. He eased his foot down on the accelerator, his hand poised over the automatic gear stick.

The plane was coming at last, but there was unfinished business to take care of before he left.

The car roared as it shot from behind the watchtower and headed straight for the bike. Greg switched on the lights, cleaving the darkness with shards of painful brilliance that he knew would blind and disorientate them. He aimed the pistol and fired. Then gave a grunt of satisfaction as he heard the bullets thud into the bike.

They had nowhere to turn – nowhere to hide. The game was almost over.

'Jump!'

Tyler took evasive action, but as he yanked on the Harley's handlebars and gave her full throttle, the car collided with her front wheel and he was catapulted into the air.

The world around him was filled with the scream of tortured metal, the shatter of glass and the hiss of escaping steam. Tyres screeched and he thought he heard his own howl of pain above the crack of bone. Sky and earth became one as they spun in and out of his vision. Tumbling, jumbled chrome and spinning wheels floated round him. He hit the ground and the air was punched from his lungs.

The last sound he heard was the cry of a baby.

Gabriella opened her eyes, but she could see nothing. It was as if the lights of the car had burned her retinas – great beams of white, searing brightness that would not diminish – her head was full of them.

Heaving oxygen into deflated lungs she struggled to make sense of her surroundings. She'd seen what was about to happen, had jumped a heartbeat before Tyler shouted. Now she was lost and there was something wrong with her shoulder.

She tried to sit up but pain sliced up her arm and into her chest. Sinking back into the grass, she fought to regain her sight and senses. Greg was out there somewhere, watching from the darkness. Or had he assumed they were dead and boarded the plane?

The abandoned airfield stretched before her, hidden by the darkness and the lights in her head. It was as though the spirits of the long dead airmen were closing in as the night filled with the sound of ticking engines and hissing steam.

Somewhere in the distance she heard the insect buzz of a

circling Cessna engine. Her spirits tumbled in a spiral of pain and anguish. She'd lost.

Then the one sound she hadn't dared hope for brought her to her knees. It was Nick – and he was close.

She struggled to pull off her shirt and with her teeth gritted against the pain in her arm and chest, she made it into a rough sling. She would have to move fast – ignore the pain – forget everything in the urgent haste to find the baby. Greg waited out there somewhere – and as there was no sign of Tyler – she was on her own.

Her vision was slowly clearing, the dazzling white light fading to mere pinpricks, but as full sight returned, she shivered with horror.

Tyler was lying several feet away under a gorse hedge. He wasn't moving. The Harley's fairing was wrapped beneath the wheel arch of the BMW and the bike lay in a crumpled heap of twisted metal.

She began to crawl towards him. If Tyler could be roused, then she stood a chance.

He was very still and his leg jutted at a strange angle to his thigh. A dark bruise of blood stained his jeans. She put her hand on his neck. There was a pulse, but it was thready, and he felt cold to the touch. She put her good arm beneath him and cradled his head. The shock of the fall and the pain in her shoulder were nothing compared to the desperation of her plight.

'Tyler. Tyler, wake up. You've got to help me,' she whispered urgently.

His eyelids fluttered, his mouth opened, then his head slumped against her chest and she knew she was alone to face her husband.

Nick's cries and the approaching sound of the Cessna drew her back from the crevasse of despair. *My baby needs me – I'm wasting time. Tyler will have to fend for himself.*

She laid him on his side in case he choked, then as she pulled his jacket round him, she remembered the gun he'd used earlier. With a weapon she wouldn't be quite so vulnerable.

'Good grief,' she muttered as she pulled the kukhri knife free from his belt. It was heavy and curved with a blade that broadened at the tip. 'I hope I don't get near enough to have to use this. But what good will it do against a gun?' she murmured as she struggled to put it through her own belt.

The handgun was sheathed in a shoulder holster that had become entwined in his sweatshirt and was now pinned between Tyler and the ground. He was a dead weight, and no amount of pushing and shoving could move him. She would have to leave it.

As an afterthought, she pulled the mobile phone from his pocket, but as she switched it on, she heard Nick's cries drift across the field. That wasn't the lusty cry she'd heard before – he must be hurt.

Leaving the phone within Tyler's reach, she crawled away. There was just a chance he would regain consciousness, then he could call for help.

Keeping to the shadows, her breath as ragged as her pulse, she listened to the approaching plane and remembered the lessons taught to her so many years ago by her father. Slowly, slowly, she approached the car. There was still no sign of Greg, but there was a chance he too had been injured, perhaps even dead.

I have to take that risk, she thought. As long as I can get Nick out of that car, I can make it out of here.

Her sneakers made hardly a sound on the broken tarmac, but every whisper of grass, every breath she took seemed to echo into the night. She crawled the last few metres up to the door and leaned her burning forehead against the cold metal. Her ribs ached and her heart thudded, but she was close – so close, she could hear Nick's trembling hiccups. Inch by inch she rose from her crouch to peer through the window.

The driver's seat was empty – Greg nowhere in sight – the plane was touching down on the far side of the field.

With a swiftness born of fear she wrenched open the door and reached in. Tearing frantically at the harness, her fingers slipping, sliding, jabbing at the stubborn catches, she was almost sobbing with frustration as Nick's squirming body and drumming legs made the task more difficult.

The last buckle fell loose and she picked him up, held him, drank in the smell and the feel of him. It felt so good, so wonderful to have his weight in her arms again. She held him close and smothered him with kisses as she stroked back his hair, touched his face, his hands, his toes. She had to familiarise herself with him again, to reassure herself that he was safe and that apart from being hot, frightened and rigid with anger, he was unharmed.

'Thank God,' she breathed into his hair as the tears rolled down her face. 'Now help us get out of here.'

She turned from the car, her attention focused on the baby – and walked into a wall – a yielding wall – one made of flesh and bone and tailored clothes.

Her grip on Nick tightened as fear engulfed her and she backed against the car.

'We have already said goodbye, Gabriella. Give me back my son.'

Gabriella shook her head, her arms enfolding the baby, holding him close, feeling his heartbeat close to hers. She was trapped against the car – but the strength to do battle had not diminished. 'You'll have to kill me first.'

'Don't think I won't,' he snapped. 'Now hand him over.'

'No.' Gabriella spun round and dumped the baby back in the car.

Greg took a step, the gun steady in his hand.

Gabriella gripped the top of the car door. The pain in her shoulder made her head swim, and she knew she was losing touch with reality – but she was the only thing between Greg and the baby – she had to stop him.

The best form of defence being attack, she drew on every

ounce of strength and rammed the door into his chest as he pulled the trigger.

The hollow click was testament to the empty chamber and the force of the door spun the gun out of his hand and into the darkness.

Greg stumbled back with a curse, and Gabriella sprung forward with such force that he fell to the ground. Her nails raked, her feet kicked, her teeth sank into the hands that reached for her neck. Hatred spurred her on – fear for her child gave her courage and she forgot her injuries.

The plane was taxiing towards them, its lights casting eerie shadows over the airfield.

Greg was too strong – too angry – and she was punched away.

She rolled with the punch, felt the blade of Tyler's knife scrape her spine, and crawled towards the car.

A hand caught her ankle, held, then slipped as she kicked out. She felt the smooth, cool bodywork under her fingers, heard the baby cry – so close – yet so far away as a grip of steel ringed her ankle and dragged her back. She clawed the earth to find a hold, but the ground was slippery, the clumps of weed fragile.

'It's over, Gabriella.'

Greg flipped her on to her back, knelt astride her and pinned her to the ground. His face was a waxen mask of hatred, the wake of her claw marks dark against his pallor as he reached for her throat. 'One twist and I break your neck.'

'Never,' she gasped as she fought to escape. If only she could reach behind her for Tyler's knife. . . .

'How are you going stop me?' he sneered, his grip increasing on her throat. 'Your boyfriend's dead. There's no one else to help you. Nick's mine.'

Gabriella's fingertips skimmed the knife handle, but Greg's weight pressed her into the ground, making movement in her injured shoulder almost too painful to bear.

Greg smiled, but it was lupine, cold and snarling. 'You

disappoint me, Gabriella. You've played a fine game until now. But you of all people should know when you've reached an impasse.'

Gabriella struggled, but his grip was intense. His face swam before her and she knew what pleasure he was taking in killing her. She could see it in his eyes, in the tilt of his head, in the sadistic curve of his mouth. She made one final desperate attempt to reach the knife, but it slipped away from her.

The baby's cries echoed in her head and she knew she could no longer help him. It was over.

Blue lights and the roar of many engines filled the darkness behind her eyes and in her head. The Cessna raced along the runway and took off within feet of her and Greg, the downdraught tearing at their hair and clothes, churning grit and debris into spirals of stinging projectiles.

Adrenalin coursed as Greg loosened his grip and raised a shout to the disappearing plane. She reached for the knife, grasped it, and pulled it free.

Greg twisted to face the invasion that swarmed over the field towards them, his face white with fury.

Gabriella thought she must be hallucinating and took a firmer grip on the knife and kept it behind her back. Yet the police cars were real enough – the sound of their sirens loud enough – Tyler's stumbling figure all too familiar.

Greg spun towards her and pulled her to her feet. His face was close – so close, she could feel the warmth of his breath, the hammer of his heart.

'You can't win, Gabriella. I'm too powerful, too much respected by the people who run this country. No court will ever find me guilty.'

His eyes glittered with malice as he snaked an arm around her shoulder, and caressed the back of her neck. 'And even if they dared press charges, I'll never let Nick go. I'll always be there – watching and waiting for the moment to kill you. You don't get rid of me that easily.'

Gabriella winced as his fingers twisted in her hair and forced her head back until she was staring into those crazed eyes. Now she could see the madness in him, and knew it had not been an idle threat. If Greg lived, there would be no escape for Nick. He would live under the shadow of his mother's death sentence.

Her grip tightened on the knife.

'No,' she yelled into his astonished face as she thrust the blade into his throat.

Gregory Castlemaine the Third sank to his knees, his hands desperately trying to staunch the fountain of blood. Then he crumpled to the ground and lay still.

Gabriella looked down at him. She felt nothing.